The God of Make Believe

Book One of His Unfinished Kingdoms

Henry Hines

First Edition

Book Design by Natalia Junqueira
Map Design by Linda Heinrich

ISBN 9798861996075

Henry-hines.com

DEDICATION

To my family, friends, and students.
They fill my life with stories worth telling.

POA
AT THE TIME OF FINLEY'S LANDING

Tile of the Colossus

Tile of the Herald

Tile of the Shepherd

The Godstrom

Finley led them to the hole where Huck would now stay. The headstone would be ready in a week or so. The name "Hutchinson Kerrick" would decorate its face, along with a depressingly short span of years.

And even though the headstone was unfinished, and the flowers were already fading on the wet earth, none of this mattered to Finley. In his mind, you didn't need monuments and performances to remember a friend. All you needed were memories.

The creature that lurked beside Huck in the coffin agreed with him.

As the sun set and the shadows lengthened in the graveyard, the creature settled in for a listen, making itself comfortable in the little box they had buried Huck in.

Finley faced the group, tears collecting in his eyes, even as he fought to keep his voice level.

"Should I go first?" All eyes were focused on the pile of dirt. "Okay. I met Huck when I was about five years old. It was kindergarten, and we were both terrible at naptime, so the teacher would always put us in the corner, far away from the kids actually sleeping, and we would just play games. It started with rock paper scissors, and we played it so much we started to get bored with so few options. So we made it rock-paper-scissors-tank-banana-blender-pencil sharpener, and on and on.

"Soon we lost all track of the game's rules, but we never really stopped playing. We'd see each other in the halls and throw each other a new move like 'bazooka' or 'fish attack' and see what the other one would come up with. I think people started to think we were in some sort of weird cult, always flashing messages at each other." He chuckled, but as the sound escaped him his eyes fell on the pile of dirt were his friend lay.

"We played it all through high school, and I thought we would carry it on to college too. And to the rest of our lives. Huck, why did you have to—" Finley choked, letting the words stay lodged in his throat. He looked up at his friends, but none would meet his eye. "Does anyone want to go next?"

Finley retreated and Yosef stepped forward.

And so it went, each of the young people sharing a memory they had of dear dead Huck. Some were funny, most were not, but it did not matter to the creature in the coffin.

The stories just made it hungry.

Huck never gave the thing a proper name, though he tried to give it everything else, but it was only in death that he finally gave the creature what it needed.

Now it was free, and ready to bring the curtains down on the story it had first crafted centuries ago.

All it needed to do was devour the tasty looking tear-soaked children above it.

The creature ripped its way out of Huck, bursting into the coffin they had buried him in. It clawed its way through the wood and dove into the earth, and no one heard it as it burrowed through the mud like a swarm of worms.

It waited there for a moment, inches from the surface. And to its surprise it discovered it was an empathetic creature, because the children above it seemed so lost.

But it knew just the solution.

It surged up to its wonderful meal, and they heard it at last as it erupted from the dirt, its talons flashing in the light of the moon.

But the boy in the box had one final card to play, and as the talons came down, he spoke those first and final words.

Once Upon a Time…

The five children vanished, inches from the claws of the killer. The monster roared in rage, scything at the air, desperate for the blood of the five who had come to bury their friend.

But they were gone.

Gone.

They were on Poa. And a new story had begun.

Chapter 1: The Detective's Landing

The first thing you must understand is that this world does not make sense. The second thing you must understand is that you can force it to.
(Letter 1, Paragraph 1, Lines 1-2)

"You look a little lively to be a corpse, you sure you're in the right place?" were the first words that Finley heard.

He opened his eyes and found a man leaning on a shovel looking down on him. The man's eyes were gray, his hair was gray, even the skin of his face seemed to have been bleached of all color until it matched the smoky clouds that hung overhead. And he had the nerve to look at Finley like he was the oddest thing in the world.

"Of course, I'm not a corpse," Finley replied, his voice rough from disuse. The dreary light that managed to work its way through the clouds stabbed into his eyes like knives.

"Could have played me for a fool then. You seem to be in the proper spot for one."

Finley looked around, raising his hand to block the dull sun. He lurched upwards and found that he and the gray man were surrounded by graves. There were columns of jades and slabs of white marble. He saw pillars of black basalt and granite graves etched into strange shapes he could not recognize.

With a lurch of shock, he discovered he had been asleep on top of the stone lid of a coffin.

"Crap. Must have passed out here last night. Closest thing to a bed I could find I guess," Finley said, pulling himself to the side of the coffin. "Sorry."

"No trouble. That man's been in the ground for almost five hundred years. I'm sure he didn't begrudge the company."

"He was an excellent sleeping companion. Not a snorer at least."

"Are you sure you aren't dead yourself? You have the look of a corpse."

"Not dead, unfortunately. Just awake," Finley said, and mustered enough energy to lean forward so that he could massage his temples. His mouth tasted like sand, and every breath roiled the acid storm in his stomach. But that was typical of his wakeups lately.

"I'm talking about how you're dressed, boy."

"What's wrong with how I'm dressed?"

"Looks like something only the dead would be caught in."

Finley looked down at his clothes. "What's your problem? It's a new suit. A little crumpled, sure, but still dashing overall," Finley said, turning to face the gravedigger, and for the first time he looked at what the man was wearing. While the man's skin and hair were the gray of rain clouds, his clothes were as vivid and multi-hued as a rainbow. It was an assault of color, a riot of shades and tints so bright that he looked like he was made of stained glass.

"You look like a fool, boy, that's all I'm saying. Foolish to dress in such drabs, even more foolish to fall asleep here. Especially today." The gravedigger nodded to a spot behind Finley.

He turned and saw what he was interrupting. They were burying someone at the edge of the graveyard. A crowd of mourners stood around the hole in the ground, they too dressed in the gaudy and dizzying colors of the gravedigger. A woman was conducting a service, and she alone was dressed in a robe of a single color, a deep red.

He could not see the body, but he could see the scandalized looks that the crowd sent his way. The overwhelming strength of his own jackassery overpowered his stupor for a moment, and with a burst of speed he slipped off the tomb and hid behind the gravedigger to avoid the hateful glares.

"You couldn't have said anything sooner?"

"I've always avoided confronting madmen if I can help it."

"I'm not mad."

"Yet your behavior and your dress say otherwise," the gravedigger mused. "Did you caper here after a show or something, jester boy? Or did the voices in your head lure you here?"

"Don't be a jerk. I'll have you know I was here last night for a funeral—not my own!" Finley added when he saw the look of triumph in the other man's eyes. "A funeral for a friend. We all came back afterwards, but the rest of the night is a blur."

"That friend another one of your band of clowns?"

"If I was a clown I would find you funny. Have you seen anyone else lying around here?"

"Just the dead. No one else has been foolish enough to fall asleep here during the funeral of a warden."

"What's a warden?"

"You leave your brains on the tomb?"

"I wish I had. Who's the person being buried over there?" Finley said, emerging from behind the gravedigger to stand beside him. The funeral across from them had continued, with only the occasional hateful glare thrown at the intruder.

"Just who I said. One of the city wardens. Got crushed during that bolthead riot a few weeks back. They're giving her a hero's funeral. I'm sure they won't mind you intruding though, the wardens are such a forgiving lot."

Finley only understood about half of the words, but the recognized the sarcasm in the gravedigger's voice.

Finley sucked in a breath to demand an explanation for the strange words, but the gravedigger spoke again before Finley could.

"It's starting," he said, looking up into the sky.

Finley's head tilted up and his stomach sank to his shoes as he saw the stars fall to earth.

They were delicate pinpricks of light at first, hot balls of fire a very safe hundred lightyears away. Then they exploded in size, growing larger and larger until it seemed the sky was choked with stars rushing to join the funeral of the warden. A blinding flash of light ripped through the early morning fog as Finley ducked behind the tombstone.

He waited, expecting to hear the thunder of impact, but nothing happened. He peeked over the stone and saw a field of dancing stars among the graves.

And they looked like flowers.

Finley's eyes began to adjust to their glow and saw that what he first took for massive falling stars were in fact only the size of light bulbs. They had large white petals that glowed with brilliant light, and within the center of the petals there was darkness where the light did not shine. Veins of delicate black threaded the petals like spiderwebs.

"What the hell?"

"Poor choice of words," the grave digger replied.

The glowing flowers drifted along, ducking underneath the legs or passing beside the arms of the mourners, until they stopped amongst their silent ranks as if they too were part of the service. But it seemed the mourners could not touch them. Finley watched as a small child reached out a grubby fist for one of the glowing flowers. As her hand grasped at the flower, it vanished from view. The others remained, still glowing, but solemn.

"Maybe I really did leave my brain on that tombstone," Finley whispered.

"You never been to a funeral before?"

"Not one of these. What are those things?"

"Ghostlights. You only really see them at funerals. They're just little watchers. Some think they're a kind of Guardian for the other side, or that they ferry the souls of the dead, but I think that's all bunk. Ghostlights seem more like death voyeurs to me. They'll be gone in a moment. They never hang around for long after the burial."

"Why are you acting like falling stars are normal? Where the hell are we?" Finley said, gripping the man by the shoulders and spinning him around to face him. "Where have you taken me?"

The gravedigger met his eyes, not a trace of concern on his face. "You're in Oshroar, city of Ghostlights and Guardians. And I haven't taken you anywhere. You woke up on my graves, remember?"

"Where is Huck's grave then, huh? That's where I was last night."

"I just dig them, son. I don't worry about their names."

"We buried him last night!"

"Only one I've dug in days is for the warden back there. And her name wasn't Huck. You sure you know where you are, boy?"

Finley dropped him, stung by the man's words. He looked beyond the boundaries of the graveyard. There was no rumble of cars stuck in traffic, no screech of tires or honking horns. There were no roads at all in fact, nor were there telephone poles and planes flying overhead. The three rivers of his home were gone, and all the boats that swam on them. It was all gone, and it was all different.

Beyond the graveyard he could see a city made of stone with towers that choked the sky. Each building seemed to have a glittering spire upon it, as if they were competing to be the first to touch the clouds. The buildings had crowns that glowed with copper and brass, or shone with silver and gold, each shimmering in the sky. The stones of the towers were deep green and decorated with large whorls and eddies, and as the sun rose behind Finley, the city began to look like a wave about to crest, only seconds away from crashing down upon him.

This city slept in the shadow of an unknown mountain, a vast and jagged thing that loomed over the city's spires. But when his eyes focused on the ancient lines of the mountain, he lost his breath.

It was not a mountain, but a monument: a massive stone carving of a man who rested on the mountain like a jagged throne. He towered alone above the city, his arms encircling a place that was unmistakably his.

Behind this immense figure and the city it held in its arms, the horizon was in motion.

The world could not seem to make up its mind on what belonged at the edge of the plains. For a moment it was a mountain range, and then a desert moved in to replace it as the mountain range slid away, and then the desert retreated as an ocean took its place. It changed again and again, but the city and statue stood still as the world moved around it.

Finley's mouth began to tremble, and his hands went cold. He thought of a child playing with his toys in front of a flickering television screen, and, without meaning to, he began to laugh.

The laugh ripped through his body like a shiver, leaving him gasping for air. The gravedigger reeled away from him, finally an expression of surprise replacing his look of condescension, but Finley could not stop laughing. Even as the crowd turned from the burial to see the madman who had intruded upon their service, he could not stop his wild cries.

The crowd was muttering now, the faces shifting from mourning to anger. But it seemed the Ghostlights did not share that feeling. They rushed to his side, twirling around him like fireflies. And Finley felt his laughter leak away, entranced by the strange floating flowers. As they spun they started to fade away. The lights inside their petals dimmed and dimmed until the Ghostlights vanished from view and Finley stood once more alone.

He looked up and saw the advancing crowd. There was a man leading it with the unmistakable look of power to him. He swaggered forward, his jaw jumping with anger, his hands reaching for a weapon that was not there, removed for the funeral.

"Oh, wardens are cops, aren't they? That figures." Finley felt strangely uncaring about the approaching pissed off wardens. He chalked that up to shock. After all, he had had a very eventful morning. He straightened his suit as they approached. "Hold my tombstone for me, sir. I hope to be back asleep on it soon."

"Aye. Whatever you want," the gravedigger said, his face slack with surprise as he pointed a quivering finger at Finley's chest. "You seem to have picked up a passenger, by the way."

Finley looked down. One of the Ghostlights had not vanished with the others. This one gave off much less light than its fellows. The dark veins inside its glowing petals were larger and more widespread, like a negative copy of the flowers that had disappeared.

It sat, perched on Finley's lapel, like a carnation in his buttonhole. It nuzzled into his chest, making itself comfortable before stilling in place. Its light dimmed, until it was as low as the light of a guttering candle. Its petals rose and fell, rose and fell.

It had fallen asleep on his chest.

Finley looked up to face the gravedigger. He could see the wardens over the man's shoulder, growing closer and closer, arms already reaching for Finley. "I thought you said they don't touch people?"

"They don't."

"And that they don't stick around?"

"They don't do that either."

"I guess I'm special then," Finley said, his voice light and airy even as his mind swirled with shock at his strange morning.

Then they arrested him, and the flower too.

Chapter 2: The Detective's New Partner

I pray that you have not joined me in this place, but I fear you might have. I worry that, like me, you have found yourself in a land of chaos and miracles. A world that seems to have been designed by a child.
(Letter 1, Paragraph 1, Lines 3-5)

Finley stroked the flower's gently snoring petal and it nuzzled further into his chest as if seeking warmth. "So do you have to feed this thing or something?" Finley asked the wardens closing in on him.

Several of the wardens stepped forward, anger flashing over their faces. But they stopped at the raised hand of the man who seemed to be in charge. The rising sun shone off his bald head, but it did nothing to dispel the shadows that lingered in his deep eye sockets.

"Pay no attention to him. Go back to the service, I'll take in our newest loon. He seems quite interesting," the man said, his eyes on the flower on Finley's chest. The priestess who had conducted the service peeled off from the rest of the group to stop in front of Finley's confronter.

"What's he doing here?" she asked, her voice slow and strained, weary from her homily.

"No idea. He's playing tough and stupid at the moment, nothing that a night in a cell won't fix. You'll have an answer soon."

"Thank you, Orsos," she said, and she clutched his arm. He bowed.

"Just doing my job, Sister Sinoh."

The Sister turned to gaze upon Finley. Her eyes scanned his face, and then shifted to the Ghostlight on his lapel. Her eyes widened, her mouth opening in shock, before shaking her head and walking away.

"You're gonna put me in a cell? What for? Getting lost?"

"You have a profound gift for understatement Mister...?"

"Marsh. Finley Marsh."

"Mr. Marsh. You did much more than get lost. You slept on a grave like it was bed, you mocked the death of one of this city's heroes with your laughter, and now you play with a Ghostlight as if it were an errant butterfly and have the temerity to feign innocence. That is the behavior of a madman. Yes, I think a hole in the ground will improve your behavior."

"Wow, how noble. You're quite a guardian angel."

"No, I am not that," Orsos said, anger flashing across his face before once more settling into stonelike stillness. He pointed Finley forward and out of the graveyard.

Finley set off, but he tried to keep his stride smooth to not jostle the Ghostlight sleeping on his lapel. He turned and waved to the gravedigger as they walked out.

"Sorry for interrupting the service. I didn't mean to cause a fuss. Thanks for all the help though."

The gravedigger gave a half-hearted wave back, before picking up his shovel again.

Finley, with his new walking companion treading only a few steps behind, made his way out of the graveyard and toward the city proper. The city's immense bulk loomed ahead, trapped behind gates of stone. The massive statue of the man loomed still higher. The horizon seemed to have stilled, and the plains beyond the city stretched to the horizon without interruption.

"The horizon was moving earlier, wasn't it? I could swear that there was an ocean behind the city for a second."

"Why did you interrupt the service?" Orsos asked behind him, ignoring his question.

"I didn't mean to. I just woke up there."

"You woke up in the graveyard? Why would you fall asleep there?"

"I didn't. At least, I didn't fall asleep in that one. I seemed to have moved during the night."

"Ah yes, of course," Orsos said, his voice thick with disdain. "And the Ghostlight on your chest? Was that with you when you slept?"

"Oh no, it's a new friend. I'm lucky I made one so fast in this place. Although I feel that you and I, Orsos, are growing too closely too quickly. You can go back to the service if you want. I should be fine from here," Finley said, flashing as big a smile as he could, trying to seem harmless.

"I think not. I have more questions for you to answer now that your own hysteria has passed."

"I'm afraid my hysteria comes and goes. I might not be much help."

"Did you come just to mock the funeral?"

"I wouldn't laugh at something like a funeral."

"And yet you did."

"And yet I did," Finley admitted. "Or at least I laughed near one. But I wasn't laughing because I found your service funny. It's just all I could think to do when I met my new friend here, and when I saw that fellow over there," Finley said, indicating the statue that loomed over the city.

It was a gargantuan thing, and Finley felt like less than an ant trapped under its gaze. The figure's face was roughhewn and cragged: an immense brow with an uneven nose, a cut that might once have been a mouth. Clouds formed about its head and neck, and snow graced its shoulders.

"The Shepherd. You act as if you have never seen or heard of such a thing."

"I couldn't even have imagined it."

"Are you from one of the wild tiles? How did you come to this one?"

"What's a tile?"

"You're even more unbalanced than I originally thought, Mr. Marsh."

Finley felt the glowing flower stir upon his chest as he stared at the monstrous Shepherd. "Yeah, that would explain a few things," Finley said and ignored the snort of derision from behind him.

They journeyed still closer to the city, the gates opening before them. They were vast stone things, as thick as a man with his arms outspread. But they swung easily, gliding across the ground at an unnatural, even pace.

People walked the streets beyond the gates, and though the towering Shepherd loomed over them, they seemed as normal as any people Finley had ever seen. They had a horrible sense of fashion though. They were wearing only slightly fewer clashing colors than those who Finley had met at the burial.

They marched into the square. The gates began to shut behind them and Finley turned to spy the means of how they opened and closed the massive doors. Two huge statues flanked the doors, both half the size of the wall. They were made of crude stone and were jagged at the edges. Their faces had a harsh, unfinished quality, yet they had eyes of a deep and shining green.

And they moved.

The statues' legs plodded forward as they pushed on the stone doors. They changed their grip on the edges as they pushed it back into frame. When the doors slammed shut, the figures froze in the same instant, the glow in their eyes dimming to a low spark.

A hand pushed at Finley's shoulder, spinning him around. Finley's eyes broke from the sight before him to see Orsos, a grim smile playing about the man's face.

"Welcome to Oshroar, Mr. Marsh, the land of the Shepherd and its Guardians," he said, indicating the statue that towered over the city, and the much smaller statues carved in its image. "Your cell is this way." He spun Finley back around and pushed him forward.

Finley lurched into motion, his mouth agape. Orsos remained behind him, prodding him forward and back, left and right, directing him to his imprisonment. Finley's mind wandered and spun as he moved like a sleepwalker.

He saw men and women walking the streets, going about their normal lives. Children played games in the alleys, tagging each other or throwing a crimson ball, which seemed to float in the air for far too long before falling again. And all around were walking statues that no one paid a glance to.

Families walked beside a hulking figure of stone carrying planks of wood. A child played with a slow-moving stone statue only slightly taller than himself. An old woman and her young companion were carried in a basket by a Guardian made of bricks. The statues walked the streets, carrying out daily tasks or standing at attention in the alleys. They helped people cross the street or carry heavy burdens. They labored at building tall towers or digging holes.

The Shepherd loomed over Finley, blotting out the sun, and all around him marched creatures of moving stone. He couldn't tear his eyes away from the goliath, terrified it would leap into motion just like its much smaller brethren.

Orsos led the stunned Finley into a low building in the middle of the city. They passed officers in black and white. The officers took Finley's hand and pressed it into ink and then onto stone, leaving a dark imprint. They placed him in a cell with a small window. Inside there was a hole, a chair, a bucket, and a bed.

Finley had never seen something so beautiful.

He collapsed onto the bed, desperate to fall asleep and out of this madness. But then he saw the light dancing against the prison walls. Finley sat up to look at the Ghostlight dancing in the shadows of the room.

"Hey," Finley said. The flower shrank back at his words, hiding behind the chair in the corner of the room.

"Wait, wait, it's okay," Finley assured the little specter. "I'm not gonna hurt you. In fact, I could really use some help! My name is Finley. What's your name?"

The flower poked out from behind the chair. Its pool of light fell onto Finley, and he gave the flower what he hoped was a harmless smile and tried not to move a muscle otherwise.

"I really do mean you no harm. I'm not sure what you are, but I bet you're really friendly, almost as friendly as I am. And I hate to impose on a new friend so soon, but I could really use some answers as to what the hell is going on!" Finley babbled.

The flower did not respond with movement or sound, but its light did shift. The dull yellow glow coming from its petals shone just a bit more, banishing the shadows of the cell just a bit further.

"So far, you're the only person since I woke up who hasn't arrested me or made fun of me. I'm not sure what you are, but you seem kinda magical? Can you unlock a cell door or magic me away? Can you at least make some part of this make sense?" The flower's petals stood up a little as it got closer to Finley.

And then an image flashed into his mind like the strobe light of a camera. It was of a young man with tight black curls sitting on a prison bed. He had a gray suit on and looked disheveled.

And he had a familiar stupid look on his face.

The image vanished, melting back into the recesses of his mind. Finley was left staring at the flower that was still floating in front of him.

"Was that me?" Finley asked, feeling silly even as the question came out of his mouth. "Did you just show me myself?"

The flower gave a little twirl in the air, its yellow light shifting into a deeper orange.

"Okay. Was there a reason why?"

The flower still did not reply.

"You didn't...you didn't mate with me just now, did you?"

The flower gave off a flash of light that Finley desperately hoped meant 'no.' He was much too young to be a father.

"Can't you help me at all?" Finley begged, his voice ragged and desperate.

The flower stilled. All at once the light faded from the cell, and the white petals of the flower became the black of the void. It spun in the air just like the horizon had not so long ago, forming a wall of darkness around Finley.

A new scene appeared in his head. He was wearing his brand-new suit and lying on a bed. The bed was too small for him, its frames pressed on his sides and his head and his feet, boxing him in. There were flowers at the end of the bed, fresh pale lilies in huge bundles.

He couldn't smell them.

He couldn't feel anything at all.

There was someone standing over him, whispering in his ear. It was so faint he couldn't catch all the words, but he could hear the tears in the other person's voice, choking their throat and clogging their nose.

The voice pulled away, and Finley could finally see the speaker's face.

And it was him!

His own face stared back at him, and it was a picture of perfect agony.

"Stop it!" Finley roared. He stumbled backwards until his back hit the cell wall. The Ghostlight zoomed away, suddenly alight again. It shook itself, and when it saw Finley still cowering in the corner it flew to his side. It twirled around him, nosing at him like a concerned puppy.

"What did you just show me?"

The light gave no answer. It just poked at him some more, checking him for damage, trying to figure out why he had shouted. Amused despite himself, Finley started to calm down as the Ghostlight scanned him from top to toe.

"I'm okay, buddy. I'm alright. See?" Finley waved his arms to show that everything still worked.

The Ghostlight flew a little loop the loop, flashing bright yellow in relief.

Finley eased himself to the edge of the bed again. "So you can put pictures in people's minds. Sometimes real and sometimes not. That could be useful. Little creepy that they're all of me, but I guess I should be flattered. Any updates on that unlocking thing though?" Finley asked, but the flower did not respond, still looping about the room.

Finley cradled his head in his hands and tried not to panic. He had a terrible, impossible thought that would not let go of his mind. He wanted nothing more than to lie back down and sleep until this nightmare ended. Yet that curiosity remained, that thing that had gotten him into trouble before.

Finley rose and picked up the bucket he guessed was meant to be his food trough or water source. He knew what the hole was for. He raised the bucket to head height and then dropped it, watching it fall. He picked it up and dropped it again. And again. And again.

The flower flew over to investigate the noise, and as the bucket rose and fell, it soon joined in on the flight, rising with the pail, falling with the pail. It twirled and glowed in what Finley thought might be joy or even laughter. He did not share in the emotion. After a while he gave up on the bucket, sat on the bed, closed his eyes, and when Orsos came to question him, Finley was ready.

The sun set beyond the horizon, and the city on the other side of Finley's window fell into an eerie green light as the eyes of the Guardians illuminated their unceasing work. Finley fell in and out of sleep but didn't move from the bed.

He heard footsteps echoing down the hall. His cell door opened, and Orsos stepped into the room. He had changed in the hours since Finley had seen him. Orsos had cast aside his colorful robes and had put on a tunic of black and white with bronze buttons. He marched into the room, carrying a chair with him. He placed it before Finley with slow, precise movements. Orsos sat across from his captor, the lines of his uniform straight and pressed.

"Are you ready to answer my questions?" Orsos asked, with a tired voice.

"Yes." Finley got up from the bed and sat in the other chair.

"How old are you?"

"Almost eighteen. I should really be in your juvenile section."

"Where are you from?"

"Pittsburgh, Pennsylvania."

"Where is that?"

"The United States of America. You've never heard of that place either have you?"

"No. Did you make it up?"

"I lack the imagination. May I ask you a question, Warden?"

Orsos tilted his head, and the straight lines of his body fell out of order. He stared at Finley as if the boy was a slide on a microscope.

"You're different than you were before, Mr. Marsh. I was not aware that my cell had magical powers, but here you are polite and under control. What changed?"

"I had a realization. This isn't Earth, is it?"

"What's Earth?"

Finley's stomach sank through the floor, but for all his dread he could not suppress a flicker of triumph. He had figured it out.

"Earth is the planet that I'm from. It's where Pittsburgh is. You see, I wasn't sure at first. I thought I might be going crazy just like you seem to think. The flower didn't help much with that, but you see them too, don't you?

"The ball of light, the city, even the Guardians I could have brushed off. Maybe I had a stroke, or I was in a coma. Hell, maybe I was dead. But it's always the little things that give it away." Finley stood up, and once more he picked up the bucket, and dropped it from eye level. It fell to the floor with a crash.

Neither one flinched.

"The gravity is different here. It's just a little less than on my planet. The bucket falls too slowly. It took me a while to notice, but I got there in the end. No, I'm not crazy, this is just another world. And a weird one, if I say so myself." Finley returned to his seat. Orsos's expression of interest had not changed.

"But you look like a human being, everyone here looks like a human being. So you're not aliens, I guess. You didn't abduct me, did you?"

"No, Mr. Marsh. I arrested you."

"Same difference. Let me answer your next few questions. I don't know how I got here, I don't know where here is, I don't know why

I'm here, and I have no idea why the flower is following me," Finley said, the words flying out of his mouth, but as he finished, he felt himself deflate.

Orsos watched him. The warden had a strange half smile on his face.

"You don't believe me, do you?"

"I believe that you believe it. But do I think you are a being from another world, an alien that I was just unlucky enough to stumble upon? Of course not. But you are an interesting man, Mr. Marsh, and perhaps I can make use of you," Orsos leaned forward as he spoke, and now his eyes burned with determination rather than amusement.

"As I have said before, Mr. Marsh, this is the city of Oshroar. A city of one and a half million souls, and I am its warden. I protect it, guide it, and try to keep it from killing itself every other day." Orsos got up and walked to the window, gesturing grandly at the streets below. His eyes glowed with affection, but the sneer never left his mouth.

"As you are new to this 'planet' allow me to give you some directions. The planet is called Poa. You are on the Shepherd's Tile, and if you ever want to leave this cell again you are going to help me."

"How could I possibly help you? I nearly collapsed when I saw the city for the first time."

"You can help me because of the thing floating over your left shoulder."

The flower had ceased turning cartwheels and had instead begun to twirl in place, its petals shaking as it did so. However, as Finley and Orsos gazed at it the Ghostlight froze. Orsos's gaze burned into the flower, which retreated in fear behind Finley's head, hiding from the warden's eyes.

"What? The little guy? I don't even know what it is. Just a glowing flower," Finley said, and the flower spun out from behind his head to rest in front of his face. Its upper petals rose like hackles, and it seemed to be glaring at him.

"You really don't know anything do you? That is a Ghostlight. A fascinating feature of our city, but a useless one. Any attempt to interact with a Ghostlight in any way always ends in failure. But this one seems to have a strange fascination with you, one that I plan to make use of." The Ghostlight turned once again to face Orsos, seemed to remember its fear, and slunk back behind Finley's head.

"For what?"

"To solve a murder."

Finley shuddered, his mind flashing back to the grave of his friend. "How?"

"The key is in the name Mr. Marsh. Some, only some, believe that the Ghostlights are the shepherds of our dearly departed, taking them to the next world. It is an old legend, very few even know it. Most believe that the Ghostlights are just a strange natural phenomenon, but one no more special than lightning or thunder."

"What do you believe?"

"I believe that I am out of options, Mr. Marsh, and out of time. So why not find out if the folktales have any truth to them? If that Ghostlight gives us some sort of insight into the life and death of the victim, then I'll let you go, and you can hop on back to Pittsburgh, wherever the hell that is," Orsos said, his eyes never leaving Finley's face.

Finley looked back and saw it all. The redness of the eyes, the black bags beneath his gaze, the slope of his shoulders, the tightness of his grip. This was a man on the edge of exhaustion, and one desperate enough to trust a mad alien.

Finley could work with that. But that word, murder. It set his heart racing and robbed the breath from his lungs. Yet it was the only way out.

"I'm in!" Finley said, a grin stretching across his face.

"You're...in? Just like that?"

"Just like that. I desperately want to leave this cell, Warden, and I'd love to help you." Finley jumped to his feet and gathered the Ghostlight into his hands to place it on his shoulder.

Orsos did not move. "You're much less insane than when we first met."

"Maybe I just needed to be properly motivated. I care deeply about justice," Finley lied, easy as breathing.

"Of course," Orsos said, his voice laden with sarcasm as he opened the door, and held it open for his two new helpers. Finley stepped into the hall, and felt a lightness return to his step.

He let Orsos walk in front of him as he began his real mission. His eyes roamed the hall, looking for windows to leap out of, halls to duck down, anything he could use to run away. He tried his best to remember the city and its streets, but it was hard to see through the fog of horror that had gripped him then.

He remembered one street though, one empty construction site that seemed abandoned. He could disappear there if he needed to hide.

His thoughts of escape derailed as the flower shook upon his shoulder, burrowing into the warmth of the crook of his neck. He gave it a little pat as they followed Orsos down the hall.

"I wonder if I should give you a name, pal. I had no idea that I was traveling with a ghost this whole time, and such an important one at that. Still, I feel bad calling you 'flower' or 'ghostlight.' So what kind of name should it be?" Finley could see the muscles in Orsos's back clench as he talked.

"Any evidence that you can provide that you are not a crazed maniac would do wonders for my peace of mind, Mr. Marsh," Orsos said, his tone whip sharp as he led Finley up a flight of stairs and into the central passage for the building.

Finley let the comment slide. He thought he was handling this whole 'on another planet with a ghost for company' thing rather well. Meanwhile, his eyes roamed the hall, searching for anything that might be of use.

Finley had never been to prison before, but he did not imagine they often looked like this. The hallway he walked down now was lush and opulent. He walked on polished wood floors, and paintings adorned the walls. Men and women in black and white worked in these offices, laboring at mountains of paperwork. Bureaucracy seemed to be a universal constant.

Stone creatures moved throughout the building, carrying boxes of documents or patrolling the halls. Unlike most of the Guardians that Finley had seen, however, these were dressed for combat. The rough stone of these Guardians was carved into the shapes of armor and helmets. They had scales of stone, but no weapons. They stood on guard throughout the halls, and their eyes of glowing gems seemed to track Finley as he walked. He quickened his pace, nearly bumping into Orsos as the warden turned right and descended another staircase.

Finley followed and felt the temperature plummet. The air grew cold as the windows disappeared. The light took on a sickly bluish quality as they journeyed down. Orsos opened a door at the end of the hall, and Finley hurried in.

Low stone tables littered the room. Shelves of instruments and equipment hugged the walls. And the temperature dropped even further, so that Finley felt like he had ice underneath his skin. The Ghostlight burrowed deeper into his neck, slipping underneath his shirt in its attempts to escape the chill. Orsos seemed unaffected.

A slab dominated the room. It was ten feet to a side, and an immense blanket covered the figure atop the slab. Orsos gripped the edge of the cloth and with a jerk ripped it from the body.

"You neglected to mention that part," Finley said.

A broken Guardian lay on the table. It was made of a rough dull red stone, the same color as bricks. It was larger than Finley, but shorter than some of the other Guardians he had seen, only six feet tall, but it was quite wide. It was spread out on the table, and whatever had given it life had clearly left it. One of its arms had fallen from its shoulder, as well as one of its knees. The sockets of its eyes were empty.

As one, Orsos and Finley began to circle the Guardian.

"Did it have a name?" Finley asked, his horror at being in a morgue replaced with curiosity.

"It had an official designation. You can find it on the bottom of its left heel."

"What makes you think I'll be able to read your language?" Finley asked, but he circled around anyway to study the creature's foot. To his surprise he found normal numbers and letters on the bottom of its heel.

"Wait, wait. I can read this. 'M. Guyot.' What kind of name is that? Does it mean anything?"

Come to think of it, he could read the tombstones as well. Why was everything in English on an alien planet? And they even spoke English?

Questions for later.

"Why would it? It's just a laborer, they all have strange names like that."

"What happened?"

26

"We found Guyot here in a back alley by the main gate in a little pile. The person who found it had never seen a broken Guardian before, so it went straight to me."

Orsos circled around the slab, his hands clasped behind his back and a look of calm appraisal on his face as if he were examining a car, or a hole in the road.

Finley felt odd. Huck's funeral had been open casket, so he had seen a dead body before. But what was he supposed to feel here? He could imagine the story of a dead person, but he struggled to do so for this stone creature. Did it have friends? Could it?

"Did it have a family?" Finley asked.

"Are you joking?" Orsos said, a sneer on his face.

"Every death affects somebody," Finley said, ice gripping his heart.

"It's a thing, Mr. Marsh. Are you going to ask me if your shoes have a family next?"

"Jerk," Finley muttered. "What's so remarkable about Guyot? Why do you need me?"

"Guardians don't stop, Mr. Marsh. They have worked unceasingly for three thousand years. They'd grind down to dust before they ever stopped. This one didn't. This one laid down and died, along with the three others before it." Orsos threw aside the curtains that had obscured half the chamber.

Three other lumps of rock and stone lay on slabs. Each were varying hues of brown rock, and each looked like a shattered puppet upon the ground.

"Two other laborers, and a builder. All within the last month. That's more broken Guardians in thirty days than in the thirty centuries before it. And people are starting to notice."

Finley walked down the line, examining the heels of each one of the creatures. The names M. Toba, M. Ararat, and M. Tabor were carved into the base of the statues. While they varied in size and in color, the three statues had little apparent differences. Each had broken limbs, and empty eyes, but no signs of deliberate damage or attack.

"How do they break? What causes them to turn off?" Finley asked.

"I don't know."

"Why not?"

"Because they've never broken before."

"What makes you think that they were murdered?"

"Because these things are eternal, Mr. Marsh. The Shepherd himself is supposed to crumble and fall before his creatures ever do. Yet here these four are, lifeless, and all in month. Someone must have murdered them, although I don't know why or how yet." Orsos eyes seemed to glow just like a living Guardian's as he looked at the broken creatures with terrible anger.

"You have a suspect?"

"Oh, yes." But Orsos did not elaborate further.

"It's not me, is it?"

Orsos's lips quirked up for a single instant. "No, Mr. Marsh. It's not you, not for now."

"Awesome, I'm not sure my system could handle another shock. What do you want me to do here, Warden? I'm a kid, not a detective. And I don't know a thing about these Guardians."

His breath fogged in the icy air of the room, but he didn't feel the cold. His heart was beating as it had never done before, and his blood felt like rocket fuel as it pumped through his veins. He felt lighter than air, as if every step would send him dancing, or fleeing.

"Four dead eternal beings. I believe this qualifies as something strange and unexpected. I thought I should get my own unexpected alien on the subject, and his Ghostlight," Orsos said, his voice dripping with contempt, but his hand was pointed at the bundle on Finley's shoulder.

The glowing flower shivered beneath Finley's lapel, and it resisted as he pulled it into the freezing air. Its light was dull, and the black veins that spider-webbed across it face seemed to have grown. Finley pushed it forward, encouraging it to float, but it remained rooted to his hand. Finley looked at Orsos, appealing for help, but the man didn't lift a finger.

Finley flushed, glaring at the flower. He ran its light down the surface of the first Guardian, M. Guyot. The shining flower's faint beams played across the broken Guardian. Finley held his breath, and Orsos leaned forward.

Yet nothing happened.

Orsos shook his head, muttering faintly to himself as Finley worked. Finley ran the flower down the legs and up the chest of the statue,

28

circling around it. He held it over the figure's head, desperate for some reaction.

The flower shivered more and more in his hands, rattling against the insides of his fingers like they were the bars of a cage. Finley's breath fogged in front of him, and his heart continued to race.

Every breath felt like he was breathing poisoned gas. The alien smells scorched his nostrils, the unnatural light from a sun not his own set his teeth on edge. His ears ached for a familiar sound. The lift of a voice he knew, the call of a friend.

But he was alone.

Where were Theo and Gwen and Mel and all the others? What had brought him to this strange world? Did it bring them too, or were they stretched out on slabs like these?

Was this what it felt like for Huck's mom when they took her to see the rest of her boy?

When she called Finley, her voice quivering with misery, he hadn't asked how Huck had died.

Why hadn't he done that? Had he been afraid of the answer? Had he been terrified that she would tell him that Huck had done the unthinkable?

Impossible! Huck was the bravest of them all.

Why was Finley the weak one?

Why was he such a coward?

Why wouldn't this flower work right!?

"WHY WON'T YOU DO SOMETHING?" Finley yelled at the flower, and then his voice died in his throat.

He looked into depths of the shining light, past the petals and the black veins, and though it had no eyes he could have sworn that it looked back at him.

He opened his hands, and his heart sank down, down below his stomach and into his shoes. It was not shivering from the cold. It was afraid.

Finley felt the faint touch of shivering petals against his hands. He felt a hot pain behind his eyes and nose, and knew he was about to cry.

"I'm sorry. I didn't realize. I didn't know that you were afraid of whatever this is," Finley said to the flower still shaking on his palm. It shied away from him.

29

"This is all new for me, buddy. I mean, a new planet, a murder, and now I'm talking to some sort of ghost flower! I don't know what's going on or how I got here. But that's no excuse." And now a few tears did fall from his eyes. "I shouldn't have asked you to do something that scares you so badly."

The flower quivered, its light still low.

"I'm sorry to say it, but you're the only friend I have in the world. I guess it makes sense you already hate me. Honestly, you're better off for it. Being my friend seems to be bad for people's health. Lethal even."

The tears finally escaped, and he could feel them dropping down off his face to freeze on the floor. "Oh Huck. Why'd you have to do a thing like that?"

The flower stilled, its light dimming until they were black as the void between stars. It floated into the air so that it was level with his eyes, and another image popped into Finley's head.

He was driving a car.

It was a Toyota Highlander 2011. The seats were patched with duct tape, the radio didn't work right, and he loved this car almost more than anything.

And there was someone else's hand on his, forcing him to jerk the steering wheel.

The car fell out of his control. It leapt off the road, into the fence, over the embankment, and he was flying now!

He saw the road vanish in his rearview mirror. And the eyes staring back at him were blue.

Blue eyes?

He didn't have blue eyes.

But Huck did!

Finley stumbled back, his chest shaking with gasping breaths. He could still feel that hand on his. But it wasn't his hand, was it? It was Huck's. And someone had grabbed it. Someone had forced Huck to crash!

The flower still floated in front of him, waiting for him to make the connection. "What was that? What did you just show me?"

The Ghostlight did not move.

"Was he murdered? Did someone murder Huck?"

The Ghostlight's light brightened, regaining some of its color. It shook itself like it was coming out of a trance.

"Tell me!" Finley begged, reaching for the flower again, but the Ghostlight zoomed away from him until it floated over the body of the Guardian. There it waited, flashing a dull blue.

"The Guardian? What does that have to do with Huck?"

The image appeared again in front of his eyes. That hand in Huck's car, grabbing hold of the steering wheel, sending his friend's car off the road and Huck out of his life.

The image vanished, and all Finley could see was the broken Guardian, and the flickering Ghostlight.

"Okay, okay. So there's some sort of connection…some sort of clue."

The Ghostlight twirled, sending flickers of sparkling blue throughout the room.

"And you want me to find it? You want me to solve this murder?"

The Ghostlight flashed blue again.

"And if I do, you'll show me what happened to Huck?"

One more flash. They gazed at each other, the alien detective and the ghost flower, and Finley felt that he and the Ghostlight were beginning to understand each other.

"Okay, partner. You have yourself a deal," Finley said, a smile on his face as the game began. "But I'm gonna need your help if we want to solve this mess."

The light burst from the flower, banishing the cold fog that had haunted the room. The temperature rose as the flower floated above the broken Guardians, and Finley relished the look of surprise that graced Orsos's face as he and his partner set to work.

Finley moved from one body to another, searching for clues in the soft light his partner was casting. The flower continued to circle the bodies, acting as a searchlight.

"Can they hurt each other?"

"You want to explain what all that was about, Mr. Marsh? Who in Shepherd's name is Huck?"

"No questions, only investigations!" Finley said, almost manic as he circled the body. "Can they hurt each other?"

"They don't."

31

"Yes, but can they?"

"A hammer doesn't pick itself up and hurt another hammer! It's a tool, not a person, Mr. Marsh," Orsos said, growing frustrated.

"If it can be murdered, then it seems pretty damn like a person to me." The soft glow of his partner's light bathed the Guardian, but he could see nothing new on their corpses. Just piles of stone in the shape of people.

He came back to M. Guyot, Orsos still standing by the side of the dead creature. The man's posture remained locked and rigid, but Finley could feel waves of cold disappointment coming from the man. Finley turned to him, ready to argue that he should not be returned to his cell, when a thought occurred to him.

"I've been doing this all wrong," Finley said, turning away from the dead Guardian and to the Ghostlight. "I should have just asked you. Sorry, still new at this. Partner, you just showed me an image. You projected something right into my head. I don't know where you get those images from, but do think you can do it again?"

The flower stopped, its glow shifting through the color spectrum until it was a soft green. It seemed to cock its head, all its petals titling to the side.

"Is there anything you can show me that has to do with this Guardian? Can you show me what killed it?" Finley asked.

The flower's light shifted blue, and it zoomed from its lofty position down to the Guardian's body. The Ghostlight landed on top of its head, settling its petals against the Guardian's stone skin. The flower stilled. Orsos stepped forward, opening his mouth to speak, but Finley's outthrust arm stopped him cold. Finley raised a finger to his mouth to indicate they needed silence.

Another minute passed, and the flower's position did not change. Orsos could be quiet no longer. "This is ridiculous, for flock's sake what is that thing—" And the flower erupted in light. Finley raised his hand to block the glare, a grin dancing upon his lips. His new partner had exquisite timing.

The blinding light faded, and as Finley's vision cleared, he no longer saw the morgue. He saw a dirty and desolate street. It was caked with brick dust, but there were gaps where massive footsteps had walked.

There was blinding pain in his head. It was worse than anything he had ever felt.

In fact, it was the first thing he had ever felt in centuries.

The street disappeared, and Finley stumbled onto the table behind him as he lurched back into his own head. He heard a rumble of anger beside him and turned to see Orsos steadying himself against the wall. He looked green with nausea.

Finley paid him no mind, but instead lurched into motion to stand at the top of Guyot's corpse. "Partner, I need light!" Finley said, stirring the Ghostlight back into motion.

"What was that?" Orsos growled.

"That was what you wanted. That was a clue. I think my partner just put us inside Guyot's head for a moment, and that head was in pain."

The Ghostlight shot up, spreading beams of light onto the skull of the dead creature. Finley leaned in and saw it. A slight gouge just by the corner of the Guardian's temple. Here the light did not shine, rather it seemed to absorb the light to become a deeper sort of darkness. Finley spread his fingers around the skull of the dead Guardian, and felt more and more of the scratches, at equal intervals around the head.

He moved to the next Guardian down the line, and the next, and the next, and found the same mark on each one of the skulls of the dead creatures.

"Are these supposed to be here, Warden?" Finley asked.

"No, no they are not. Shutter the ghost," Orsos said, and Finley gestured to the flower to zoom back into his closed hands. The light vanished, and so too did the markings on the Guardians. Finley had the ghost come back, and the markings returned as soon as the light did.

"I knew it would work," Orsos said. "I knew it."

"You were right after all then. My partner can show us things from the other side. They can show us memories. Something attacked this Guardian and went right for its head. That must have been what killed it. Do you have any idea what those marks are, or what they could be from?"

"No, but it's a start. Guard!" Orsos shouted.

"Er, I thought we had a deal?"

"It's not for you," Orsos said, as the thunder of the warrior Guardian's heavy footsteps echoed down the stairway. The door shot open, and a massive figure filled the doorway of the morgue. Its stone fists were clenched, scales of rock covered its shoulders and sides, and its pale green eyes burned across the room. Orsos waved his hand, and the Guardian came closer. At another gesture it dropped to its knees as Orsos's fingers swept about its head.

"No markings," Orsos said.

"No shadows," Finley replied.

"We could check the rest of the Guardians in the city, and I bet we wouldn't find any more of these markings. Only the dead ones have them," Orsos said, studying M. Guyot once more. "They look familiar. I don't know how. They look almost like—"

"A crown," Finley finished. "The markings of a crown."

"And maybe our murder weapon. Mr. Marsh, you and your…partner, have been of great aid. The city thanks you for your service."

"Is that all? I get to go free right?"

"Not at all. I'm hiring you. Welcome to the wardens, Mr. Marsh. You start right now," Orsos strode from the room, forcing Finley and his partner to race after him. Finley heard hard footsteps behind him as they walked up the stairs. The Guardian below was following them.

Orsos led the mismatched group up into the light, past the warrior Guardians and the office drones back into the main lobby where Finley had stumbled in just the day before. Orsos right hand swooped out and seemed to pluck a young officer from thin air. She too fell into step with the odd band as they marched outside the headquarters and into the glaring sunshine. Orsos turned back, and while his expression remained sharp and grim, Finley could feel energy and purpose radiating from the man.

"Mr. Marsh, I am placing you and your partner on this case. I need you to question people, track down clues, and solve a murder. Are you up to the task?"

A murder mystery on an alien planet? It sounded like one of Huck's stories, the kind he would weave into their D&D games. Was that the connection to his death? Was that what the Ghostlight wanted him to do? Play a game?

34

Finley could do that. He had always loved those sorts of puzzles, and he couldn't deny how fast his heart was beating at the idea of leaping into one again.

His friend was dead. His friend would always be dead. But maybe, just maybe, it wasn't Finley's fault. And if it took the rest of his life, Finley would catch the person who really took Huck away.

Finley's eyes went to the ball of light floating by his shoulder. "What do you think, partner? Are we game?" The Ghostlight flashed a bright glow and gave a twirl. "Yeah, I believe we can do that."

"Somehow, I thought you would say yes. I want you to go to the temple district and question the clerics there, the Crooken. They oversee maintaining the Guardians, but they have been extremely unhelpful thus far."

"Why should they listen to me? Do I get a badge by the way?"

"Because you'll be bringing your partner with you. Priests tend to be a bit more cooperative when you bring the thing they worship with you. I want you to find me some answers, and I want them today. And if they refuse, show them visions from the hereafter."

"Will you be coming too?"

"Someone else will have to keep you sane, Mr. Marsh. I have other matters to attend to. Deputy Moro will be your watcher now. Keep him from hurting anyone, Deputy." The deputy snapped a sharp salute.

"She'll take you where you need to go and kick down any doors in between. Treat her as you treat me. I'll keep your cell open for you in case you get out of line," Orsos said, but Finley was hardly listening. The blood was pounding in his head, and he felt that if he took one single step he might never stop running. The questions that haunted him flew to the back of his mind. Instead, excitement and energy infused him, and as his heart quickened so too did the flashes of his partner.

"Keep the ghost out of sight until you need it, Mr. Marsh," Orsos said, and as Moro watched with wide eyes, Finley gave a gesture and the Ghostlight zoomed into his sleeve and out of sight. She noticed Finley looking at her and forced her features to be expressionless once again. She snapped one more salute and began to walk off. She got a few yards before she turned and gestured at Finley, indicating he should follow. Finley moved to obey but felt a hand on his shoulder. He turned and saw Orsos's eyes glaring into him, with the Guardian adding its own burning eyes to the glare.

"Oh, and Mr. Marsh. Please don't try to run. I'd hate to lose my useful little alien before he helps me solve the case. Hawksbill here is going to keep an eye on you." Orsos gestured at the Guardian looming over his shoulder.

"He's a slow mover, Mr. Marsh, but he never stops. Nor should you. Good hunting."

Finley turned away, a cold fire burning in his chest as he thought of the answers the Ghostlight could reveal.

Behind him, he heard slow and steady steps.

Chapter 3: The Scholar's Panic

I hope that you will find these letters. I have attempted to capture all I know of this place within their pages. My wish is that they will serve as a guide to this strange land. Perhaps you might add to them with your own discoveries. I want to know you are all okay.

(Letter 2, Paragraph 1, Lines 1-4)

Theo woke up where the sky ended and space began.

He hovered for a moment, and the world spun beneath him. A sphere of perfect blue with spans of green forests, yellow deserts, belching volcanoes, towering statues, flowing rivers, giant shells, toxic smokestacks and more and more. And each of these places was in motion, ducking around and between each other as if in the middle of a magnificent dance.

A patchwork planet, twirling about.

For a moment Theo thought he was dreaming. Then he started to fall, and realized it was a nightmare.

The wind pulled at his face, dragging his muscles to the back of his neck. His heart fell out of his chest and vanished somewhere in the bottom of his stomach. A scream built at the base of his throat, but it could not escape his mouth.

He was falling.

Down.

Down.

Where was he?

How did he get here?

Sometimes in these dreams he could fly, if only he thought about it hard enough. He tried to focus, to think past the pain as the wind battered him through the air like a broken leaf. He thought of a bumblebee hovering above a flower. A butterfly alighting on a branch. A bird taking wing.

But nothing happened. Instead he just kept falling, like a bowling ball tossed out of a skyscraper.

Theo craned his head downwards, trying to see where he would make his tiny little crater, and found himself looking at a swirling tumor of darkness in the heart of the world.

It was a storm, the mother of all storms. It stretched from horizon to horizon, a rolling sea of blackness lit with bruised purple lightning. It gazed at him like the malignant eye of a giant, and Theo tried desperately to look away.

But he was only falling faster now.

Thunder cracked, and even from miles above it, the sound hit Theo like a physical wave of agony.

He rolled, desperate for something to stop his fall into the abyss, and to his surprise he found something else floating in the sky.

A castle, with sweeping battlements and tall towers, only upside down, clinging to the underside of a boulder floating through the sky like a wandering leaf.

And he was already falling past it.

Faster now, so fast that he could feel the blood leaving his head. And darkness was creeping in, blessed unconsciousness.

At least he wouldn't have to be awake when he fell into that unending storm.

In the final moments before his brain turned off all the lights, he thought he saw a shadow on the clouds. The outline of a boy, flying through the sky like an angel. His arms were outstretched, a smile on his face.

And Theo knew no more.

He jolted awake, but this time his back was on smooth stone. A blue sky was overhead, and he heard the hum of people's voices in the other room. There was the clatter of pots and pans, and the scent of food burning.

Theo smiled. Just a dream, everything was fine.

And then the thunder cracked so loud beneath him that he thought his spine had broken.

Theo yelped, curling into a ball.

The thunder roared again, and Theo could feel it starting. That numbness at the tip of his tongue and the edges of his fingers. His stomach was a ball of acid, eating through his skin. His heartbeat grew louder and louder until it overwhelmed the thunder.

Tears spilled from Theo's eyes as he tried to get ahold of himself. But he was on the ride now, and there was no getting off.

His limbs shook, a constant shiver rattling his bones and sending his teeth clattering. His thoughts were out of control, racing faster and faster.

He was dead. He should be dead.

Falling, always falling, with nothing but darkness under his feet.

Where was he? How did he get here?

Where was everyone?

They left him. Of course they left him!

Useless Theo. Pathetic Theo!

There was a voice whispering next to Theo's head, but he couldn't make out any words. It was calm though, as steady as a rock. Theo tried to grab hold of that voice in his mind, tried to anchor his rampaging thoughts to that solid point.

And as his limbs shook and his heart bounded, Theo focused on the one thing he could control.

He breathed in, slowly, counting second by second. He breathed until it felt like his chest was a balloon and he was about to lift off the floor.

Then he let it out, even slower. He had all the time in the world, he didn't need to rush. He did another breath.

He worked his way through the routine, as familiar to him as his own face. His heart slowed. His limbs stopped shaking. The tears started to dry on his eyes.

And he could understand the voice now. "Good weather today, pressure's low, only a bit of cross breeze. Smells like autumn on the air, don't you think? Don't know why, we're hundreds of miles from any trees, but it just smells like fall to me, for some reason."

"I smell it too," Theo said, his voice ragged and broken.

"Right? Maybe they're cooking up something with pumpkin and cinnamon in the kitchen. Or maybe Tanner's doing something new with those candles he's always yammering on about."

"Could be."

"Could be," the voice said, before venturing slowly, "are you feeling better now?"

"Yeah." Theo dragged himself into a sitting position. He stared at his dress shoes while he dried his eyes. "Where am I?"

"Why don't you look and see?" the other boy said. He gestured with his gloved hand to the wall.

Theo steeled himself, wary of another panic attack. He crept to the edge of the wall and found a gargoyle hanging upside down beneath him, glaring back up at him.

He was in a castle, but it was upside down.

He looked out. There was a curtain wall, but it clung to the immense rock ceiling far above. There was a tall tower, but it stabbed down into the abyss below rather than the sky. There were stone walkways, but now they were decorations on the roof, and narrow bridges of wood and rope connected the towers.

Below, far below this upside-down castle, there was a storm without end. It hung below like a vast tapestry of venomous black and poison purple. Lighting stitched it, and with every flash the storm seemed to pulse with rage.

"Am I awake?" Theo asked.

"I should hope so. You're talking and what not."

"What is this place?"

"Ah, difficult question. We haven't had a guest in decades, and we like our privacy, so let's just say this is a school."

"A school?"

"Oh yes, one of the last ones, and the best."

"I just graduated high school."

"Probably not a school as high as this one, right?" the other boy said, giggling at his pun.

But Theo was still too numb to join in. "No, probably not."

"You've made quite an impression by tumbling through our air space. But you seem human, Falling Boy, so I'm not too bothered."

"Human?" Theo croaked. "What else am I supposed to be? And who are you?"

"Elwyn Burke, Lancer First Class," the other boy said, sketching a bow. He tripped as he tilted forward, and his feet twisted together as he tried to catch himself. His arms swung as he attempted to find his balance, but he overcorrected and toppled face first into the curtain wall.

"Oh, okay. Well that makes perfect sense. Call me Theo Lambert, then. Confused First Class."

40

"Ow," Elwyn said, clambering carefully to his feet. "Damn. Pay that no mind. It always takes me a few days to get my land legs back after I've been flying."

He rubbed his head and glared accusingly at the wall. He was blond as a dandelion and apparently just as graceful. He wore a battered leather jacket with brass buttons and fur poking out of the collar. His pants were creased khaki, like something out of an old war film, and his boots were high and brown. A strange helmet and apparatus hung from his shoulders, connected to a device of twisting gears he wore like a backpack.

He was cute, Theo decided, and then immediately shushed the thought. He just had an abysmal panic attack in front of this boy, and this was probably all a dream anyways. Or, he thought as he looked at the storm below, a nightmare.

"Alright, Falling Boy, uninvited guests are a bit above my paygrade, and I was on my way to help out with the flying lesson anyways, so why don't you tag along. I'll let the professor interrogate you." Elwyn spun on his heel and walked back into the castle's depths.

Theo, having no idea what else to do, followed but was careful to walk well back from Elwyn in case the boy bumped into something that might fall.

As he walked, he tried to make sense of this odd place. The castle did not stand on solid ground, with blocks of stone laid each on the other to form high walls and parapets. It didn't stand at all, in fact. It hung like a gigantic bat above the abyss, but the rock it clung to was even stranger.

Theo craned his neck, trying to find what the castle was attached to, but as he followed the roof of rock far overhead it kept ending in open space.

He thought at first it must an outcropping, something clinging to an impossibly tall mountain. But he could not find that immense structure, try as he might.

He spun until he thought his neck would break. But there wasn't a speck of solid ground in sight. His breath became ragged, and he forced himself to count it as he reached the only possible conclusion. The rock the castle clung to was not attached to anything.

This castle, this rock, it floated above the void, tethered to nothing at all.

The hallway they walked through had new wood floors, but an old stone ceiling with footsteps worn into it. They entered a great hall and stepped lightly around chandeliers that rested on the floor rather than chained up above. They hustled past a grand staircase, but its steps started a dozen feet over Theo's head, and they went up into the roof rather than down to the floor.

Nausea gripped Theo's stomach like an iron vice, and he seemed to sway with every step.

Had this once been a normal castle? How could it possibly end up in the sky, and upside-down at that?

What a funny dream he was having. Usually his sleeping thoughts were filled with all the things that could go wrong in his normal world. Missed classes, bad grades, stupid words. Normal fodder for an anxious boy's nightmares. But flying castles and endless storms? This sounded more like something Huck would dream up.

Elwyn paid it all no mind however, and walked through at all as if it were perfectly normal to wander through a topsy turvy fortress above an endless storm.

He led Theo further into the castle, through still more rooms where the ceiling had become the floor until they arrived at a courtyard next to the great tower.

One side of the room opened into the sky like the mouth of a cave. Pairs of fighters, of all ages, dueled with swords or spears and shields. Some wrestled in groups, others stretched themselves into contortions so complex it made Theo's muscles ache.

The wind invaded the room in billowing gusts that sent Theo back on his heels. But the fighters barely flinched. Some even seemed to ride every swell, as graceful as dancers.

In the corner stood an old woman in the same sort of flight suit that Elwyn wore, although hers bore the marks of years of service. She looked out the vast opening into the bright blue sky, the wind swaying her iron gray hair.

"So, this is the boy who fell past my castle," she said, without turning around. Her voice was low, but her syllables were clipped, measured, and unwelcoming.

"Guilty as charged, Strafer," Elwyn said.

"Knock off the chipper, Elwyn. It's professor Litvak when we're on the ground." Litvak turned around. For all the woman's scorn, her face was smooth and unlined, only her clenched jaw showed her irritation. Her eyes scanned Theo from top to bottom, and then hardened like cold flint.

"What brought you here, falling boy?"

Theo swallowed past the anxiety and forced out "I don't know."

"That is the answer of a child."

"It's the truth. I just woke up, and I was in the sky."

"Sounds like a born flyer to me, professor," Elwyn said, grinning widely as Litvak became still sterner. "I figured I would take him straight to class."

"Amusing. You wish me to teach this intruder?"

"Visitor, professor."

"Whatever you wish to call him it is clear this fellow has never seen the sky before," she said, now pacing around Theo. "You should know that I'm the one that sent Elwyn winging after your falling hide. You flew about as well as a dog caught in a hurricane. How Elwyn expects you to soar is beyond me, especially considering how poorly you lie."

"Lie?"

"Do you honestly expect me to believe you just 'woke up' above the endless eye of the Godstrom?"

"It's not a lie!" Theo said, anger flaring.

"Well it must be a miracle then. But I have trouble believing in such things. Elwyn may think you are an amusing curiosity, Falling Boy, but I find myself unimpressed. However, you should be happy to know that I no longer think you are a stormkrow. At least they can fly." She turned back to the window, dismissing Theo with a wave of her hand.

"No, I think not, Elwyn. His form is flabby and weak. He's afraid of me and he's afraid of the sky. And worst of all, he's a wretched liar. Take him back. This boy wouldn't last two seconds in the Godstrom, and I've watched too many of my students tumble past me and into the black."

"Hold it, professor. You're being unfair. I saw Theo above the storm. I'm the one that flew out there, and trust me, he was only moments away from flying himself."

Theo faced the boy, blush ripping across his face, but he didn't know how to contradict Elwyn in a way that didn't have Litvak throwing him off the castle.

Him fly? Impossible.

But Elywn was still talking. "He looked right into the storm's eye and didn't scream. He deserves a chance."

"You're a precious fool, Elwyn, and too quick to think the best of someone."

"Maybe he's sign, professor. One even this fool can see."

She flinched at his words. "I'm not taking chances."

"I thought this castle was a place of faith, of impossible things." She swiveled to face him; her face clouded. "Am I wrong?"

Her hands clutched at her neck, tightening around a pendent beneath her clothes.

"You wish to test him, then? Follow me."

She led them across the room to the center of a ring that lay in the middle of the place of arms. A wooden circle as wide as a wagon wheel lay inside the ring. Litvak directed Theo to stand atop the circle as she moved to a series of levers in front of him. Elwyn stood to the side, arms crossed, but the smile had returned to his face. He gave Theo a thumbs up.

"Flight is an art form, and while the bird and bee instinctively know how to do it, we must study it. Some scholars study for years without ever achieving more than a glide. This castle is littered with those that feel they were denied a gift that the lucky received." Litvak gestured at Elwyn and herself. Her voice had slipped out of its steady and clipped pace. Now it rose and fell with passion as she continued to lecture.

"But there is no gift, there is only determination. Flight requires an effort of supreme will, of total self-mastery. We shall see if you are capable of such a thing." Theo shuffled his feet and heard a dull tap as he did so. He tapped his shoe, and heard it again, and with dawning horror he looked into Litvak's eyes.

"Before you can fly, we must first study how you fall. Begin." Litvak pulled the first lever.

The ground dropped out from Theo's feet as the trap door opened. He tumbled down into space, desperately trying to grab onto the sides of the hole, until wind shot up that sent him flying upwards.

The wind struck him like a thunderclap, nearly spinning him onto his back. He spread his arms and legs as far as he could and managed to prevent the turn. He hovered in space, caught in an unceasing fall, before the eyes of Litvak and Elwyn who watched him flounder with a professional eye.

Theo tried to adjust his form. Images of eagles and flying squirrels tumbled through his mind. He cupped his hands, tucked his head forward, and flexed his arms hoping to fall close enough to the edge that he could grab onto it.

The wind raced up his newly positioned arm and along his back, sending the sweat on his neck shooting down his spine. He floated a few inches forward, until he was almost within reach of solid ground.

Litvak spun a new dial, and the wind changed. It pummeled him up so that he soared above Elywn and Litvak's heads.

Theo's stomach surged upward, his pulse began to race, and he knew what was coming. He shut his eyes and tried to breathe, to control his flailing muscles, but the wind kept battering him, shaking him like a bent leaf. He could not count his breaths, he could not find his heartbeat, and his brain was spinning faster and faster out of control.

He could feel a scream building inside his throat and mind that threatened to consume him.

The wind shut off.

Instead of yards, he fell inches. His head hit the stone floor with a dull thud but did not split open. Litvak had lowered him during his panic attack. They stood over him now, observing.

He felt their gaze bore into his back, that same judgmental stare he had felt all his life. He forced himself to count. Heartbeats and deep breaths ticked by as his body began to relax.

Two panic attacks in front of the same cute boy. He had the worst luck in the world.

He pulled himself into a sitting position, his hands steady again. Theo did not know how much time had passed. Elwyn sat beside him, but Theo would not meet his eye. He looked into his lap and at his own clenched hands. He made sure that they did not shake. Litvak stepped into the corner of his sight.

"It is over. I have seen what I needed to see."

Elwyn's hand tried to rest on Theo's shoulder, but he shook it off. Theo forced his head to lift and saw Litvak staring back at him.

"You were in the air for three minutes, but I only needed one. You have control of your hands and your form. You never tumbled or broke your wings. You even managed to glide for a bit, that's more than most can manage during their first fall. But there is a separation I cannot tolerate, a split I'm still trying to figure out."

She crouched down in front of him, and her face seemed to fill Theo's world. She prodded his head with the point of her finger.

"Here." Her finger dropped and poked his chest, "and here. There is a disconnect. A break between your mind and your body. You're afraid of something. Something that the body already knows. But you're not afraid of me, or of Elwyn. You're not even afraid of falling, are you?" Litvak said, as her head turned to the side. "No, I can see it in your eyes. You've been falling a long time, haven't you? You're not afraid of it anymore."

A shiver shot through Theo's heart.

"Professor..." Elwyn said, his face filled with apprehension.

"What are you afraid of, Theo?" Litvak said.

"That this is real," Theo whispered. "That this isn't a dream."

"You think you're dreaming?" Litvak asked.

"I AM dreaming."

"No, you are not. This is real," the professor said, and her arms rose and spread to encompass the rest of the room, the rest of the floating castle, the rest of the endless void it floated in.

"It can't be real! Floating castles, a sky without end. It's impossible! I'm in a dream, I'm in a dream, I'm in a dream. If this is real, then where are my friends? Explain that."

"This is real, child. I cannot speak for your friends. Perhaps they are gone, perhaps they are missing. This is real, and until you accept it you cannot and will not fly."

"It's impossible."

"Yes, and that is precisely what we accomplish in this funny little castle of ours." There was a soft brush of air, and Theo opened his eyes.

Elwyn floated above them both, his feet inches off the floor. There was not a trace of strain upon his face as he flew in front of them like a visiting angel. It was as if they were the dull ones who had simply forgotten how to fly.

"Seems like falling is a bad habit of yours, Theo," Elwyn said, floating before them without a care in the world. "Why don't we fix that?"

Theo lost his breath. It was just like before, when Elwyn had pulled him from the sky. A boy flying through the sky as easy as if he were going for a walk.

In his dreams, Theo flew far above his fears. Why couldn't he make that real?

"I want to fly," Theo said, and his voice was as steady as his hands.

"Are you ready to try again?" Litvak asked.

"I am," he said, and he moved to the circle as Litvak returned to her instruments.

He thought of his friends, so different from him; brave where he was scared, strong where he was weak. They were lost just like him, but he would find them in this dreamlike world, even if he had to do the impossible.

Litvak threw the switch, the ground dropped out from Theo's feet, and he tried to fly.

Chapter 4: The Scholar's Flight

As near as I can tell, this world has only a few rules. Every tile is different, and every tile spins and twists just like the rest. My own tile turns once every three months, and the people here seem devoted to keeping time with various clocks, hourglasses, sundials, and other strange devices. It's pretty boring. I hope you all have landed on similar tiles.

(Letter 2, Paragraph 3, Lines 2-5)

The sun rose and fell on a floating castle and Theo argued with himself. Which was worse, falling from a great height, or fearing to fall from a great height? Theo worried he would never arrive on a definitive answer, as, in his mind, they both sucked.

The air zoomed from Theo's lungs as he fell back onto the hot stones of the castle's place of arms. Theo felt the aches and the pains of a hundred falls as he gathered himself on the floor. He waited for his heart to pound, for his pulse to race out of control, to panic. It never came. With a grin, he rose to face Litvak.

"What are you grinning about, Falling Boy?"

"Nothing, ma'am," he said, trying to shutter his grin.

"Exactly, your form is still dreadful. We're done for the day. If the bruising is too bad, please see the doctor. I feel I have invested far too much time and effort in you for it to be beaten out of you already."

"Yes, ma'am," he said, though he still held a trace of a smile. Her words were harsh, yes, but even he could tell that he was improving. He had been in the air for over fifteen minutes this time. He had even managed to glide.

"Professor, where can I find Elwyn? I haven't seen him all day. He said he was going to help me with 'not being the clumsiest boy in the sky,' which is pretty rich coming from him."

Litvak turned back to face him, her face as unreadable as the stones of the castle. "He's on assignment, Theo. He won't return for several more days."

"Assignment? What's that mean?"

"He's away."

"Off the castle? Where would he go? Did another island float up without me seeing it?" Theo asked, smiling softly at the thought of the other boy flying from castle to castle. But then he saw Litvak's face.

Her eyebrows had come down on her forehead like thunderheads, and suddenly Theo realized where his friend had flown off to.

"Into the storm? What in god's name would cause him to do that?"

"Careful, Theo. You know not of what you speak," Litvak said, but though her face was still, and her voice calm, her feet had floated off the floor, and little swirls of wind whipped about in her shadow.

"Why can't I know? Is it dangerous or something?"

"Far more than you realize."

Theo's heart shuddered into overdrive, and he tasted acid on his tongue. He smelt the scent of lilies on the air, the same flowers that had decorated Huck's casket.

"He is? Where is he? Did I do something? What can I do to help?"

"Attend to your lessons, boy. That is all you can do."

"Wait, professor. I've been here for weeks. I'm breaking myself to pieces trying to learn to fly, and you've been a wonderful teacher, but maybe if I knew what was going on I could help. This place, it doesn't make sense.

"Why is the castle upside down? It clearly wasn't meant to be that way. Elwyn disappears and never tells me why. People all over the castle have worse scars on them than I've ever seen. I see flashes at night below the castle. You're working on something! And I bet it's something important, something worth doing."

Litvak shot forward, looming over him like a towering storm cloud. "Just because I've agreed to train you doesn't me I trust you, Theo Lambert. You appear above my castle without explanation and expect us to throw you all of our secrets? No.

"You have to earn that sort of trust."

She settled back on the ground, now much shorter than him. She turned away from him and walked into the central tower, the tower that Theo was forbidden to enter, the tower that was guarded at all times by armed men and women.

"I just want to help my friend. Please."

"You are not yet ready, Theo. We are not yet ready." She disappeared into the darkness.

Hot disappointment rose in his chest. He looked at the trap door beneath his feet. He wished someone would come along and drop him into the sky.

Theo let his feet take him where they would. He found himself walking from the place of arms and out into the castle grounds. New bridges of stone connected the towers to each other, joining the strange upside-down worlds of the castle's inside,

He walked across the bridge, skimming his hands across the rough stones. From this spot he could look down and see the east and west towers stabbing down into the blue void below. The tiles on their roofs had gradually fallen away, the nails having never been intended to hold against gravity's pull.

He forced himself to walk farther out than he had ever been, beyond the safe confines and enclosures of the castle proper. At last he found himself within sight of the curtain wall. It clung to the great roof of rock above Theo's head, some hundred yards in front of him. In between the castle's core and this far off wall was the yawning mouth of open sky, and a span of rock no wider than two feet.

His heart started to pound as he saw the narrow bridge, which seemed delicate as a ribbon in the wind. A single slip from that would send him tumbling into the open sky, back into the maw of the storm.

The wind roared so loud that Theo could not hear himself counting in his head, could not hear the rhythm of his racing heart. But he heard voices on the gusts.

"Coward."

"Friendless."

"Useless," the wind whispered, and each voice sounded like his own.

That familiar helpless feeling crashed through his chest, and he longed so desperately to be free of it that before he knew it he had stepped onto that bridge above infinity.

The wind rattled his sides and shook his bones, and Theo took three steps before he could stop himself. He kept his eyes locked on his feet and the ribbon of stone they walked upon. He tried to ignore the blue to either side.

Litvak's instructions filled his head, and he moved his arms and angled his chest, and now the wind rushed along him instead of battering him.

He rode the gusts until his feet seemed to just graze the rock beneath, and he danced in between the lashings of solid wind.

Is this what Elwyn felt when he flew? Why would you ever touch the ground again?

And even though the wind pulled at his cheeks and stabbed at his eyes, Theo grinned, until he looked up and found rock ahead of him. He had reached the safety of the curtain wall.

"Woohoo!" he roared. "Take that, you stupid storm."

He was still giggling as he began to explore the gateway carved in the solid stone of the curtain wall. Inside, the wall was as hollow as a drum.

Dust and grime coated the floor, and it was clear no one had been here in some time. Theo passed through a broken door and into what was once a barracks. There was a massive hole broke the solid wall of stone. Beds, tables, and chairs cluttered the walls, having been blown back by the terrible wind.

And he was not alone.

A strange thing sat on the edge of the broken room. It had coarse gray skin with large cracks that splintered its hulking body as if it were made of dry broken earth. High black wings flowed from its shoulders and were folded underneath its arms. Its mouth, filled with rows and rows of dull yellow teeth, sucked the air. It had eyes of swirling silver, like smoke trapped beneath glass. It studied him, its eyes roaming across his body and face with a dull, brutal intelligence.

The thing rose off its haunches and lumbered towards Theo, its stocky legs flexing beneath its weight, its talons scraping the floor.

Theo stumbled away. His back hit hard stone, and he realized that he had retreated in the wrong direction, the door was several feet to his left.

The shambling thing bore down upon him, and Theo saw that its arms ended in cruel claws the color of stone. Its eyes locked with Theo's as its clawed hand reached out and shut the door.

"Theo." Its voice was so unlike its appearance. It was smooth and kind, the voice of a friend.

Theo backed further away, his flailing arms searching for something, anything to defend himself with.

"Theo," it called in its siren voice. It lumbered toward him, claws outstretched, the scent of ozone leaking from its mouth.

Theo's searching hands found a beam of wood from the broken bed, and with a whirl Theo brought it over the creature's head, once, twice, and then a third time.

The beam cracked in his hand, sending splinters shooting into Theo's palm.

The creature's head spun around, but as Theo watched it turned back to him, its silvery eyes flashing with light. Its claws slashed at Theo.

He lurched back just in time but fell onto the broken wood beneath him. The creature lunged forward, the wood cracking beneath its feet as Theo crawled away.

Theo threw planks and boards and other debris at the creature, but its claws slashed them away as its wide mouth sucked and groaned that same word over and over: "Theo. Theo."

It wrapped one of its claws onto his leg, its talons ripping into his skin. Theo cried out, just as his hands found the handle of something made of heavy steel.

Theo lunged forward with the knife of a long dead soldier and plunged it into the creature's stomach even as its right claw lanced at his legs. Over and over, he tore into the creature's middle, and it gave a howl of fury and threw him to the side.

Theo thudded to the hard stone, stunned. He climbed to his feet and tried to stumble to the door.

His leg gave out, hot fire pulsing through it.

The creature stood over him, leering at his pain. Its eyes flashed like crooked lightning and its mouth loomed wide as it leaned over him.

Something flashed at the edge of Theo's eye, and he blinked.

A spear sprouted from the creature's mouth. It reared back, choking and sputtering. A battered and bloodied Elwyn stood in the blasted opening of the wall. His jacket was torn, and his face was doused in blood.

Theo felt his heart start again as he saw him standing there.

"Get away from him," Elwyn snarled.

The creature's claws tried to wrap about the spear but couldn't get a grip. It beat its wings, rising off the floor.

It lunged for Theo, but Elwyn hurtled from the ground and into the air, both arms wrapping about the spear and thrusting it into the creature's mouth, pushing it back and away.

He did not fall but remained floating in the air. The wind whipped dust streams around his flying form as he pushed the spear with all his might.

The silver tip of metal pierced through the back of the creature's neck, yet still it struggled and flailed. Its talons locked its feet to the floor, and its muscles began to strain.

The creature forced its head up the length of the spear, its horrible eyes locked on Elwyn's as it dragged its way up even as it died. Its gnashing teeth came closer and closer to the boy's hands.

Elwyn hung in the air, every muscle straining, his face twitching with dried blood as he snarled at the monster. Theo's ears popped as the pressure in the room changed. Every molecule of air seemed to gather about Elwyn's body and with a boom Elwyn rocketed forward, throwing the creature from its feet. The flyer pinned the creature to the wall.

It slashed its talons one final time, and then life fled from its body. It hung from the haft of the spear, its lifeless body swinging inches from the ground.

Elwyn collapsed to the floor.

Theo gaped. He had just seen a devil fight an angel.

Elwyn groaned with pain. Theo dragged himself to his feet and swallowed down the sob of agony when he put weight on his leg. He limped over to Elwyn and turned the other boy over. The damage was even worse upon closer inspection. A large chunk of Elwyn's side had been carved away by what appeared to be a cruel and jagged butcher's blade. Elwyn's fingers clutched at Theo, his eyes rolling.

"Ambush. More than we expected," Elwyn gasped. "Please! Please, get to the professor, tell her she needs to send every winger she can. They're tearing the expedition apart!"

Elwyn shook once more and became still. For one terrible second Theo thought the boy had died, until he saw his chest rise and fall.

Theo considered his options.

He could run, hobbling back across the ribbon, leaving Elwyn as a distraction for the other monsters. Or he could throw a boy twenty pounds heavier than him over his shoulder and carry him over a bottomless abyss a hundred yards wide while being pursued by terrifying monsters that knew Theo by name.

He stared at Elwyn's slack face still caked with blood and grime. He turned and looked at the corpse of the monster that had almost torn the life from his body.

Theo made his choice. He crouched down, gripping Elwyn by his arms and hauling him onto his back. As the other boy's weight settled on him a haze of red pain cloaked Theo's sight. Every movement seemed to send hot knives into his wound.

He stepped forward and yowled with pain as he put weight on his injured leg. Elwyn moaned as a shudder of agony shook Theo's spine.

But fear drove Theo forward. Fear of that monster that whispered his name like a lover's. Fear of the creatures that could do something like this to Elwyn.

He jumped at every shadow as he stumbled forward. His ears searched for the sound of his whispered name or the scratch of a talon as he hauled himself step by step.

He dragged them both across the ribbon, leaving a trail of blood across the stone. A crowd formed as they watched the infamous Falling Boy haul Elwyn across, but the bridge was too narrow for anyone to come help him.

Theo's chest rose and fell like a blast furnace. The wind tore at his face and ripped sobs from his lungs, but he wouldn't let Elwyn slid away.

Yet his body was failing him. His blood coated his leg and Elwyn's soaked into his back. The wind's pull had become an unstoppable force, and with every step it felt like a boulder was thrown on Theo's shoulders.

The storm called for him, begging him to fall into the cool of its embrace. Pain would cease. Anxiety would end. Theo would be over.

Or he could keep trying to be a hero, Theo thought. He couldn't help but laugh a little through the pain. Him a hero? Impossible.

Impossible.

He dragged himself forward another step. And then another. The wind pushed him along, denied for now, but not forever.

It would claim him in time.

When he reached the other side, the crowd pulled him into their midst. But they could not pull Elwyn from his grasp until he whispered the boy's message into Litvak's ear. Only then did he allow himself to collapse.

When he came to, he was lying under a blanket looking at the stars. Someone had placed a pillow under his head. His skin felt like it had been scraped with an iron rake. His leg felt much bulkier than before, and when Theo raised the blanket, he saw that it was covered in bandages where the creature had slashed him.

It had known his name. A demon had wanted to drag him into the sky. Theo felt his stomach swirl with nausea and threw off the blanket. He climbed to a sitting position and saw that Litvak was kneeling beside him, her eyes closed, and her hands clasped in front of her in silent prayer.

Gone was her customary flight jacket and high boots. Her shoulders were slouched as if crushed beneath an immense weight, and for a moment Theo forgot his own pain and felt sorry for her. Then she opened her eyes, and the steel slid back into her expression and posture.

"What were you doing in the curtain wall, Theo?"

"I wanted to see if I could cross the bridge. I did."

"What did you find?"

"A monster. Professor, what was that thing?"

"What happened to Elwyn, Theo?"

"He was like that when he found me. I was fighting that—that thing. It was about to kill me, and then Elwyn showed up already covered in blood. He fought it, killed it, and then collapsed." Theo closed his eyes, traveling back to that scene, "he said something about an expedition, that I had to tell you something. He said that the expedition was in danger, that those things were in the storm. Professor, you have to send help!"

"I sent help three hours ago, Theo, when you told me the first time. You've been falling in and out of consciousness ever since." To Theo's great shock she put her hand on his shoulder. "You did well, boy."

55

"Where's Elwyn? Is he okay?"

"He's safe, he's in the infirmary. You saved his life. I sent the rest of the wingers down to find the expedition. It will be some hours yet before they return." She looked down, as if trying to peer through the stone and into the dark clouds below.

"Professor, what was that thing?" Theo asked once more.

"That was a stormcrow. And it's time you learned what we do here." She rose. "Come with me."

Theo clambered to his feet and put delicate weight on his injured leg. He followed the professor as she led him deeper into the castle. Theo saw crowds of people waiting at windows and near ledges. The crowds held lanterns made of paper and wood with small candles inside. They set them loose into the wind, and the lanterns danced and whirled as they spun down into the storm. Theo rushed to a ledge and leaned over and saw hundreds of the frail lanterns spiraling into the clouds and lightning far, far below.

"What are they doing?"

"Calling the expedition home," the professor said, as she led him past more and more of the candlelit crowds. No one seemed to be asleep tonight. The immense bulk of the great keep hung beneath them like an enormous bat. Two guards stood by its wide mouth; pikes firmly planted in the stone. The professor nodded at them as they passed, and Theo felt their eyes slide over him, assessing him, judging him. He hurried up to stay with the professor.

The tower was carved into the very heart of the rock the castle clung to. The air was clammy and ancient, and Theo felt as if the rock's immense bulk had settled on his shoulders. The professor led him to a flight of stairs that spiraled up into the rock. Grabbing a torch from a wall bracket, the professor led him up into the castle's depths.

At the very height of the staircase, when Theo was convinced he could walk no more, Litvak led him down a narrow hall carved into the rock.

They walked into the heart of the mountain until they reached a large room with a high ceiling. Rows and rows of seats lined the walls, each facing a point in the center of the room where a strange lantern rested upon a stone table. Litvak gestured to Theo to take one of the seats, and he collapsed into it.

Litvak produced a lighter from her pocket and lit the lantern. The lantern's light shone into a series of mirrors built into the device, which bounced it around and through a transparent screen, and an image flickered to life on the far wall.

It was a monochromatic sight, pale whites on dark blacks mixed with shades of gray. It was an image of the castle he had spent the last few weeks in, but it was decades younger. Its turrets and walls were the same, except they pointed up instead of hanging down into the sky. A castle planted firmly in the earth long before it had to cling to rocks in the sky.

"What you are about to see is heretical, but true. This knowledge has led to shattered families, hundreds dead, and the destruction of everything we once held to be sacred. There's no going back from here, Theo. Are you sure you want to know?" Litvak asked, her face ashen white and backlit by the ghostly projection behind her. She looked, for the first time since Theo had known her, haunted.

He nodded.

"The castle you now sit in is almost two thousand years old, and it once had a twin." Litvak began to pace as she spoke. "In those millennia we two schools had always been places of learning, twin lights drawing in scholars and students from across Poa. Our school was called Hypnos University and our sister school was the College of Kronos." The professor changed the slide, and a new image slid onto the wall. A castle, but different in style than the one that Theo now sat in. This one was far taller and was supported by flying buttresses and other supports as its towers reached for the sky, as graceful as birds in flight.

"This tile was a place of great peace where we strove to understand the universe. Two thousand years of learning, and then the world fell to pieces." The image changed once again. Theo saw an immense sky with the setting sun casting two castles into shadow, yet some deeper darkness was falling from the corner of the picture. The slide changed again, and then again, and now the image fell into the center of the frame, tearing a screaming hole of darkness through the setting sun and the night sky. The slides clicked through, and Theo watched as the center of this darkness plummeted to earth in between the castles, cracking the very foundations of the ground and sending shockwaves across the land.

The next few images were hurried and unfocused, as if the picture taker, knowing death was only seconds away, took what images could be taken. One malformed image showed darkness filling the new made cracks in the earth. Another captured great columns of rock thrown into the sky like toys. A final image showed Kronos castle cracking in two.

"The total deaths from the Cataclysm are still unknown. Records taken from the other side of the world say that it seemed like the very planet was screaming in agony. Imagine what it must have been like here?

"The universities died that day, but our work was just beginning. The other tiles declared that the cataclysm was the result of an asteroid strike, of a celestial accident. And they abandoned us to the immense crater that was all that was left of the twin jewels of learning. And that was the end of it, or so it appeared."

The slide changed. Hypnos castle, battered but unbroken, rising into the air, clinging to the underside of a mountain.

"We learned that the rules had changed. Gravity had lost its potency and our castle took flight with the survivors clinging to her like frightened children. And we ourselves had changed." The slide moved, and now it showed a man and woman floating off the floor, looks of utter astonishment on their faces. "Like our castle, some of us could fly. But even with our new gifts and in the midst of our great tragedy we were still scholars, and so we asked ourselves the question. Why? Why were the fundamental rules of the universe now broken? And why only here? We sent our newly gifted into the sky and into the ground to discover the answer. What we discovered shattered our very understanding of truth."

The last slide cycled through, and now a square frame of white light hung on the wall, like a window to a far-off land. Litvak turned, and her eyes burned into Theo as she spoke.

"The god Vovatum, creator of Poa, died seventy years ago, and his corpse fell into our castles and shattered the land." The sentence hung in the air like a tattered flag.

"God. All-knowing and all-seeing and all that, died?"

58

"Yes." And the word was a slamming of a tomb.

"How do you know?"

"Because we had seen his body plummet to earth. Because the very laws of his creation began to break down just after his death. Castles do not fly, Theo, and neither do people. It is simply a law of the universe, or at least it was."

Litvak reached into the collar of her shirt and pulled forth a silver chain. The chain was dull and worn with the long passage of metal against the skin. At the end of the chain was a gold circle with small triangles of bronze radiating from it. The circle had two lines in its face forming a right angle. It looked like the sun with a clock superimposed on it.

"My great grandmother once wore this chain, and at the end of every day she gave thanks to Vovatum that she lived in his world and was one of his people. She passed it on to her daughter, and to her daughter, and then to me. It is the only thing I still have of my family, an heirloom of devotion. And now it is meaningless, because our god is dead." Litvak said, and with a sigh she tucked the chain back under her clothes.

Theo looked at the professor, an old and lonely woman in her night coat. She had tears in her eyes as she looked at Theo, but there was far more fierceness than sadness in her gaze. She believed what she said.

But do I? Theo thought.

"You still have not explained, what was that creature that tried to kill me? How did it know my name?" Theo asked, Litvak's hand fell away from her symbol.

"It knows all our names Theo. It knows everyone's name. I told you that god died, but I didn't say what happened to his body. Immediately after the Cataclysm a storm formed in the hole his body had broken in the world. It is the largest storm in existence, covering hundreds of miles in every direction. It is unstoppable, all consuming, and forever. We call it the Godstrom.

"Those creatures live in it and are a part of it." The professor put a new slide into the magic lantern and Theo tried not to vomit as an image of a dissection appeared on screen.

It was the creature from before, or one very similar to it. Its gray and cracked skin had been pulled back and Theo could see its rippling musculature beneath. One broken wing was pinned to the table with spikes, delicate veins spread out through its thin wing tissue. Its blood was sickly green, and its eyes seemed to see Theo on the other side of the room.

"Stormkrow, a brand-new species. They are well suited to dwelling inside an eternal storm. Lightning has no effect on them, their eardrums can withstand the repeated effects of intense thunder, they can navigate and fly through gale force winds, and they know the name of every single person on the planet, because they are eating Vovatum's corpse."

"What?"

"It is difficult to even stomach. But yes, that is what we think is happening. They're carrion birds. Krows pecking at a divine cadaver. We believe some of his omniscience is passed with each consumption. Thankfully no such transference has occurred with his omnipotence. They can be killed, with great difficulty, though there are thousands of them."

"Do they have any consciousness?"

"No. They are mindless as maggots, as far as we can tell. They have not learned the names; they are merely repeating that which they have absorbed. Our scouts have observed them reciting the names of flowers and types of fauna, the names of cities, and on and on. They contain all the god's thoughts, but none of their own. Perhaps in time, with continued consumption, they will develop a kind of consciousness. But for now, they are less than beasts. They attack everything on sight, even each other. It is the one thing that has allowed so many expeditions to the storm to survive."

"But why send expeditions at all? There are monsters in the sky below you. Why not just fly away?" Theo asked before he could stop himself.

"I would think the answer was obvious, Theo. We need to recover god's body before the stormkrows devour it. Vovatum is dead, but we won't let him rot. Some hope we might even find a miracle down in that storm, and he'll come back to us." Litvak looked at Theo, and the tears now freely fell down her face. "It's a test of the faithful you see."

Litvak led Theo back through the narrow and darkened passages of the deep castle. She pointed to certain passages as they clambered back down the stairs. She explained that the libraries lay further in. The professor told him that he now had access to the library, that he had passed his trial by fire so to speak. Yet Theo was only half listening. Inside his head he tried to count his breaths.

He nearly had a psychotic break when he thought there was just a floating castle and flying people, and now they were telling him that there were real demons in the world and that they were eating a god's corpse!

His body moved mechanically as he walked, his movements jerky and imprecise. Litvak had to catch him once or twice as they went down the stairs.

He needed to learn to fly as fast as he could, get the hell off this rock and find his friends, Theo thought. This place was insane, and he needed to find them before the next shoe dropped.

They left the inner keep. The sun had begun to rise, and everyone was running to the place of arms. Theo and the professor joined the throng and began to push through it. Excitement rose in his chest, replacing the fear. The expedition must have returned.

"Everybody move!" Litvak roared, her voice slicing through the din. The crowds parted, and Theo and Litvak charged through the gap. Men and women were climbing through the launch bay. They had on flight gear just like Elwyn's. Equipment fell from them as they clambered onto the stones. They carried spears, and some of them had long sabers dangling from their belts, flecked with blood. Their clothes were slashed and torn in many places, and some of their members were splashed with ichor both red and green. Yet they grinned at the growing crowd, and they seemed to bring the dawn with them as the assembled people cheered and roared.

Litvak stepped up to them, and the members of the expedition wiped the smiles from their faces as they jumped to attention. As one they brought their flat right hands to their mouths, parallel to their lips. The professor returned the gesture with great solemnness, and then she broke into a grin. The crowd roared again, and some of their number rushed forward to drag the flyers into deep embraces, heedless of the gore that covered them. One of the expedition's members, still wearing her flight helmet and mask, moved off into the corner, far from the crowd. Litvak followed with Theo in her wake.

She had dark hair shaved close to her scalp and dark brown eyes. Her face was a mask of scratches and scars. The word "Striker" was sewn into her lapel. She and the professor clasped arms.

"How did you fare, Miriam?" Litvak asked.

"Poorly. We were attacked before we went 1500 fathoms down."

"That high?"

"Yes. In greater numbers than I've seen in a few years."

"How many did we lose?"

"Four. We lost Dolfo in that first attack. And then Dutch and Ginger another thousand fathoms down," Miriam said, her voice cool and casual as she spoke about the deaths of the men and women under her command.

"You kept going?"

"Had to. I wasn't going to lose three of my best just to go sightseeing. Besides, Elwyn was baying for blood after Dutch died. He would have killed me himself if we stopped. Poor bastard. We lost him too." As she spoke, she unclipped a water bottle from her belt and upended in on her head.

"Elwyn's alive, Miriam. He made it back to the castle five hours ago. A stormkrow followed him that nearly killed our young friend here." And she gestured at Theo, who smiled sheepishly at the other flyer. "Elwyn managed to kill it though."

Miriam's eyes shifted to Theo, and he tried to stand up to her cool appraisal. She did not look very impressed. "Yeah. Elwyn mentioned him. Falling Boy, right?"

"Yeah, Falling Boy," Theo said, a little happy that Elwyn had spoken about him.

"Striker," Litvak said, suddenly very serious, "what did you find down there? Was our intelligence good?"

"We found something. I'll let the eggheads work out what the thing is. Looks like some sort of jellyfish to me. We brought it along." She gestured back at the mass of equipment by the entrance to the place of arms. "Three people died bringing that thing back, professor. Make it worth it."

"I will." Litvak went to the largest piece of equipment, an egg-shaped package wrapped in studded leather as large as an oven. The professor fiddled with the mess of locks around the package's middle. The hatch clicked, and the egg hatched open on hidden hinges. The inside was hollow, though the shell was thick with brass and wires and other mechanisms that Theo did not understand.

With trembling hands Litvak brought forth the thing that three people had died to bring back. She laid it on the stone with care and moved back to admire it. It had four thin rubber tentacles attached to its body. The carapace was oblong and a dull gray with the slightest of shines. It had a slight mouth from which a bright yellow tongue poked out.

Its tentacles swung down from its body, ending in strange mandibles. Each one had three prongs, like the clawed foot of a chicken. More strange designs and protuberances covered these mandibles, as if the creature were afflicted with sores.

Without thinking Theo found himself reaching out for the strange mandible of the device from the clouds.

He ignored the shocked gasp of Litvak as his hands wrapped around the controller, just as it had so many times before. Without thought his fingers flew across the buttons, pressing them in patterns.

"Theo, what are you doing? Get away from it right now!" Litvak exploded; her voice appalled at this desecration of an artifact from the storm.

Theo complied, but as he placed the mandible back down the device exploded with brightness. A cone of light shot out of the device's top and etched a floating image in the air.

The crowd gasped, and the expedition members reached for their weapons. They leveled rifles at the patch of light floating in the air, the click of cocking guns piercing through the screams.

And then the light filled with color, and the colors spun into shapes. Theo's eyes bulged as the light filled with images of impossible places.

A castle appeared in the light, although this castle was tethered to the ground unlike their own.

The scene changed. Warriors battling in a floating temple.

Another change, monsters dueling in a vast arena.

Still more images appeared until they became incomprehensible, too awash with movement or light.

Theo stumbled away from the device even as Litvak stood stock still, gazing with open wonder at the flickering scenes. But Theo's own blood was pumping like rocket fuel as he endured the bombardment of the images.

The device's show stuttered to a stop, showing one final image carved into the air. This one image, unlike the others, stayed locked in place. It depicted a sphere circled by two smaller objects. These spheres swung in orbit, and Theo at once realized he was looking at a planet from space, this planet. Poa and its two moons.

The scene zoomed in and the assembled university beheld a cross section of a narrow part of that sphere. Fanciful images of castles appeared on the surface of the sphere. A dark mass loomed at the top of the image and slammed into the space between these castles, and the bottom of the image tumbled away. One castle fell with it, the other rose. A mass of swirling darkness climbed from the bottom of the image, reaching for the castle that flew. Within this darkness, points of light began to appear. The light shone bright and true in the swirling void. Slowly, beams of light began to connect these shining motes until a path reached from the heart of the darkness to the castle that floated above it.

The image hung in the air and did not move. The denizens of the castle, the last scholars of the Final University, stood in stupefied shock. And then Litvak's voice ripped through the air.

"Record that image now!"

At once, the crowd lurched into motion. Scholars still in their dressing gowns produced paper and pen and began sketching the device's image. The returned expedition produced cameras to record and to capture.

The scholars worked in frenzied silence for several minutes, doing all they could even as the image hung unmoving in the air. And then the gasps and curses started ripping through the crowd. Ink curdled and faded away on the page. Film and photos corrupted as soon as they were exposed to air. Only the device's image stayed true, as if jealous of the attempts at replicating it.

Litvak shouted over the rising clamor, commanding the scholars to memorize the image as best they could, to burn it into their brains more deeply than their own names. Yet as she spoke the device's light began to flicker and fade. Soon the image vanished and the device once more resembled nothing less than a strange rubber squid.

Litvak rounded on Theo, "Bring it back."

Theo stumbled away from her to the edge of the place of arms. He clutched the stone column there, grasping it like a drowning man. His chest heaved as he looked into the abyss, and for one terrifying second he thought of flinging himself into the depths. Litvak rushed to his side.

"Make it show that again, Theo," Litvak ordered.

Theo did not respond.

"Theo, what is that thing? Tell me how you set it alight." Her hand clutched his shoulder, her nails digging into him just as the talons of the krow had. "That thing it showed, it was a map, wasn't it? It was a map that leads right to the heart of the storm."

"It's not a map. It's an N64. A video game console," he said, his voice toneless and dead.

"What's that?"

Theo did not answer her. He looked down into the endless storm below. Monsters lived in those clouds that knew him by name. One of them had tried to kill him. A god's body was beneath that storm, rotting away and eaten by carrion beasts.

"Theo, what is that?" the professor demanded.

They had found an N64 in that storm. Theo hadn't seen one since he was a kid. He remembered summer nights spent on the couch playing games for hours and hours on such a device. He remembered all the happiness he had found in its bright lights.

What was it doing in a storm above a god's corpse?

"Theo, what are you talking about? What is that thing?" the professor said, her voice rising now.

Theo looked into the heart of the storm; his mind dominated by a single thought. Was one of his friends trapped down there?

Chapter 5: The Dreamer's Escape

...travel to another tile is almost like traveling to another world, an experience we are all now familiar with. The constant turning of tiles has led to a sort of societal stagnation. No new ideas are ever shared. A solution to one tile's problem never makes it out of the bounds of another tile, but problems and horrors stay locked away. A meeting of the tiles, due to their vast cultural disparities, can often lead to conflict. However, war seems to be a little-known concept in this world, as tiles are often not near each other long enough to ever get to a form of higher conflict.
(Letter 2, Paragraph 2, Lines 1-7)

Mel slept, and in her dreams all her friends were still alive.

In the dream they were back at the gates of the Renaissance faire that Huck had insisted they all go to for his eleventh birthday. He was obsessed with that sort of stuff. He had worked for weeks to write backstories for the characters he wanted them to play. Not everyone had learned their lines though.

"What's a bard again?" Finley asked, checking again to make sure the feather hadn't fallen off his hat.

"He's like a musician. He sings songs for the nobles and stuff," Huck answered, directing them forward, his foam sword held aloft. There was a slight whistle under his words as the air rushed through the gap where one of his front buck teeth had fallen out the night before.

"Oh, a rock star then! Why didn't you say that?"

"That's not what you are though. A bard is a storyteller. They tell the nobles stories about heroes and monsters," Theo corrected him.

"I don't know, guys. I think I'm just gonna tell them stories about rock stars," Finley said, miming a solo on his plastic lute.

"Fine," Huck said, laughing at his friend's antics. "You can be the bard of rockstars. Your feather fell out by the way."

Finley yelped and rushed back.

"Yosef the mad monk is not amused by this," Yosef intoned from the depths of his cowled robe.

"Course you did the reading, nerd," Mel said, pushing him forward.

"Did you not?" Gwen whispered from behind, drifting along in the spiderweb and batwing encrusted witch's dress her mom had made for her. "I was up all night trying to learn it."

"You don't always have to do what you're told to do, Gwen," Mel said. "Sometimes it's better to do your own thing."

"Isn't it more fun if we all play along though? We all have a part now at least," Yosef said, the cowl cloaking his face in shadow.

"Yeah, I would have no idea what's going on otherwise. And all these people around." Gwen shuddered. "It's too scary for me. But not Gwen the Witch. Bwahah!" she said and tried to raise her usual soft tones into a mad cackle at the end.

Mel wasn't impressed. "I prefer to come up with my own stories."

"I know," Huck said, still laughing as he looked back at her. "That's why I left yours blank."

Mel's eyes snapped open, the echoes of her friends' voices in her ears. For a moment she let herself imagine she was back on her bed in her room, tucked away and safe.

But then the horns started to blare and the camp shook to life around her. Bodies shifted down the barracks as her fellow sleepers awakened, but they didn't make a sound as they got to their feet.

Ash covered their shoulders and choked their hair. Half healed burns decorated their arms and their legs, and their hands were so calloused they might have been hewn from stone. They wore faded gray tunics streaked with grease and they had fallen asleep with the tools of their trade still in their belts. Hammers and nails, crowbars and measuring tapes.

Their faces did not move. They remained vacant, as empty as the windows of an abandoned house, and their eyes passed over Mel without seeing her.

The song had already taken hold of them.

Mel heard the first notes of the chorus creeping at the depths of her hearing, like the itch of an ant crawling up her leg. But she could resist it for now.

Another horn blared off in the distance, and the ashen men and women began to stumble out of the barracks like sleepwalkers, still without any sign that someone lived beneath their flesh.

Mel grabbed the arm of a woman in her sixties. The ash cloaked her like a second skin, but she had wrinkles around her mouth you only got from a lifetime of smiling. "Hey, what's your name?"

The woman's face remained frozen as she made eye contact with Mel, and Mel shuddered at the doll-like serenity in her gaze. "I don't think I have one, dearie."

"How can you not have one?"

"Well, if I did, I must have forgotten it." The woman giggled, her body limp in Mel's arms. "Silly me. I'm always doing things like that."

"How can you forget your own name?"

"I guess there was something more important," the woman said. And she started to hum. It was a funny little tune, the kind a child might hum to herself as she walked to class.

Mel pushed the woman away and clapped her hands over her ears, blocking out the song coming from the woman. The old lady smiled at Mel before turning to join the other workers, unbothered by Mel's antics.

Mel's feet began to move, and every step sent a jolt up her legs as if she was walking on limbs still asleep. But she could not stop her steps. She joined the sleepwalking workers as they trooped outside. The sky was thick with smoke and Mel could see only the man in front of her and the woman behind. But she did not stop looking for her friends in the smoke, desperate for any sign that they too were marching to their destination. But she saw nothing. They marched until they arrived at a checkpoint manned by guards armed with clubs.

The guards wore shirts of coarse brown hair. The rough hairs had cut into the skin of the guards and their chests were lined with scratches and half healed wounds. These hairshirts were not under the same stupor as the marchers. Their eyes were clear. They spread that same fervor with the clubs in their hands, encouraging the marchers with smacks and hits.

The workers walked past these guards without reaction and accepted different tools for the day's work. Screwdrivers and hand cranks for one man, wire clippers and gauges for one woman. To Mel they gave a shovel, and the song rose a little in volume as she grasped the shovel's handle. But she didn't throw the shovel away.

Mel's hands wouldn't let her. They just tapped out a tune.

The ground began to slope up under their feet, but the smoke made it almost impossible to see how high they climbed. To their left, a wall of steel appeared. Encrusted with rivets, but shining despite the smoke and the muck, it followed them as they marched ever upward through the smoke. And though the wall bent and sloped, it never ended. It climbed with them.

They rose out of the smoke that had entombed them, emerging in the sky. Behind them was a wasteland of ash and smoke. All that was once green in this valley now drowned beneath an ocean of soot. Foundries ringed the earthen ramp, churning out more smoke and metal in equal measure. Thousands upon thousands of sleepwalkers lined the valley, all making their way to this mound of metal. And any one of those far off specks could have been one of her friends.

Mel turned and beheld the monstrosity once more. The wall of steel she had marched all morning alongside rose and rose, and she craned her neck upwards to see where it all ended. As her eyes traveled further and further into the sky, the wall expanded and grew, mutated and morphed. The wall veered up and off, turning into a massive beam that stretched out into space, ending in iron fingers. The metal wall bent upwards and out, forming a chest and shoulders so far above the ground that clouds iced them like cake frosting. A neck stretched from that far off plateau and ended in open air. The chest had gaps in the ironwork, the left arm was still under construction, and scaffolding covered the figure like massive spider webs.

As always, Mel felt the air leave her lungs and her knees go weak as she looked at the Colossus. The statue was immense, taller than a skyscraper, more vast than a mountain. Tens of thousands toiled in numb silence around her. They hammered and marched and carried and the statue grew ever larger and more detailed.

The ramp leveled out as it passed closer to an unfinished section at the bottom of the giant's thigh. Mel could see the vast skeleton of iron girders and braces beneath the metallic skin, and now the song was stronger than ever. Her brain ached with the strain of resisting it.

The sleepwalking workers stumbled to the skin of the statue and their hammers rose and fell. Nails sunk into metallic skin as iron plates were hammered onto its massive frame.

A girl bumped into Mel in her eagerness to reach the statue, and Mel seized her by her arms. She spun her about, trying to see past the ash and dust that cloaked her face. "What's your name?" Mel demanded.

The girl did not answer. She wasn't that much older than Mel.

"Please, tell me what your name is," Mel begged.

"My name?" The girl forced out; her face wracked with confusion.

"Yes. Who are you? What are you doing here?"

"My name is…Aketa," the girl said, and her mouth dropped open in shock as she remembered. "My name is Aketa."

"Aketa, what is going on?"

"What do you mean?" Aketa said, tilting her head to the side.

"What is this place? How did I get here?"

"I'm—I'm not sure. I just woke up here one day, and I saw it. The thing that I had been dreaming about." Aketa turned to face the statue, and her body shook with ecstasy. "The Colossus."

"What is it? What's it for?"

"Can't you hear it?" Aketa asked, her eyes glowing with happiness, "Can't you hear the song? If you listen, you'll know. It will tell you. It wants to be built after all."

"I don't want to listen to that stupid song! How do I stop it? How do I get out of here? Where are my friends? What have you done with them?"

"Shush," Aketa said, wrapping Mel in a hug. "It's okay. You're safe here now. You don't need to worry anymore. Just listen." And she started to sing in Mel's ear. A lullaby sank into her bones and sent her mind adrift. And there was another song beneath it, one lower and slower that came from the depths of the metal giant, like an endless choir thrumming throughout the statue. And Mel could no longer resist. She slipped away.

Mel regained her mind slowly, in fits and starts. The sun rose and fell along with her hammer, and she saw the interplay of light across the metal. She felt the heat change, and she realized that she was growing cold.

She was forgetting something.

And then the beat drew her back in, and she fell into the deep and dark river of music coming from the giant beneath her fingers. Her hand slipped as she worked, and the hammer crashed into it. Yet she felt no pain. The finger turned purple as blood rushed into it.

She was forgetting something.

"Do you know where they are?" She found herself asking the man swinging the sledgehammer next to her, but she had already forgotten who she was asking about.

It was so hard to think! Her thoughts weren't loud enough to drown out the song.

She was forgetting something.

She was at the Colossus's chest. Here most of the Colossus was without its metal skin. Bones of iron girders and sinews of rigging and wire gave it shape. Men and women crawled across the girders, building new bones, stringing new veins inside the great statue. The wind plucked at their hands and at their clothes. It whistled through the giant's half completed chest, shaking its innards. The workers continued with the great labor, heedless of the danger.

The wind picked up, slamming into the bones of the Colossus, and she and the other workers clung to the girders beneath them. But no one paused their work. The hammers rose and fell. Rose and fell.

A hammer fell past her, nearly taking off her head. She looked up, the girl from before, Aketa, had fallen off her beam. She was a hundred feet directly above Mel.

Mel. Yes, that was her name. Her name was Mel and she needed to help.

Aketa clung to the girder, digging in with her nails even as the wind tried to pluck her away. Mel moved, scrambling along her own beam to the ladder that would carry her up to Aketa's.

Rain began to fall, and the girder grew slick, but Mel raced forward, desperate to reach the girl before she slipped away. She clambered up the ladder, calling out for the others to help Aketa. But none moved. They just continued to work.

Mel raced along the beam, dodging the workers who toiled on. She fell onto her belly and grasped Aketa's arms just as the other girl's hands gave out. Mel's arms shook with agony as she took all of Aketa's weight. Below them was only the abyss of the Colossus's endless insides.

Aketa looked up at Mel, tears streaming from her eyes. "Help me, please."

"I got you," Mel said, scrabbling to brace herself. "Just hold on."

A roar rose from the depths of the statue. It was the thunder of drums and the screech of trumpets. The song washed over them.

A smile overcame Aketa's face, and her panic vanished. "Let go. The Colossus is calling me, it wants me to join it."

"You're out of your mind," Mel said, pulling the girl still harder. "I'm not letting you go."

"Let me show you what it means to believe," Aketa said, and she dug her nails into Mel's arms. With a gasp of pain, Mel felt her hands loosen. Aketa fell away from her, a beatific smile on her face, still humming her song.

Aketa disappeared into the darkness of the Colossus.

When the song pulled at Mel's thoughts and offered her oblivion, she welcomed it.

It wasn't until the next day that she remembered who she was.

Mel lost track of the days. Mel lost track of time altogether. The song crept into her mind and wound its way around her thoughts.

The song found her in the morning when she woke up and hurried her to work.

She was able to slip out of it at the Colossus's kneecap, where the fires from the soldering irons burned well into the night. The flames reminded her of the camping trips she took with the gang in Yosef's backyard. They roasted smores by the dozens and tried to scare Theo with their ghost stories.

"Where's the nearest city? How do I get there?" She tried to ask one of the welders. But he ignored her, even while the sparks from his equipment burned holes in his clothes.

He hummed to himself as he worked, tapping his toes to the tune that slipped back over Mel and took her away.

She found herself again on the great rampart that climbed to the giant's waist. She tried to remember the last time she had been that high up, and Mel remembered when she had convinced everyone to go on that hike at Harper's Ferry. They had complained the whole way, no one louder than Finley and Yosef, but the looks on their faces when they made it to the top made it all worth it.

And then the song found her again and wrapped her in its embrace.

Days passed in this way, or maybe weeks. Mel had no way of knowing. The only way to track the time was by the changes in her own body. Her muscles hardened, her legs become as thick as tree trunks from all the climbing, her arms as tough as gnarled wood from swinging the hammer.

She became a creature of silence. She stopped talking to her fellow workers. They had nothing worth saying, and they would offer no help. Just as they had with Aketa, they would watch Mel fall without a sound.

Accidents plagued the workers. The wind tore them from the heights of the Colossus. Equipment crushed them at its feet. And Mel no longer reached out a hand to help. She would not make that mistake again.

All her thoughts were bent on escape. She did her best to conjure a plan in her moments of lucidity. She hoarded food in the barracks. She scouted the valley from the giant's edifice. She memorized the routine of the hairshirts.

But how could she escape the song?

It haunted her, always ready to pounce as soon as she woke.

In her dreams there was no song. Only the memories of friends. She dreamed of Huck's face as he told a story. She remembered the feel of Yosef's hand in hers, and the way Gwen would giggle so softly that it sounded almost like a sigh.

There were no songs in these happy places, no Colossus.

In her dreams she was free.

Mel's eyes shot open. She knew how to escape.

Chapter 6: The Dreamer's Survival

Perhaps the greatest unifying force in the tiles is the common language, which they call Divine. Although there are slight linguistic differences, almost every dialect spoken or written on the planet hews to a common root language. Without this universal language it is possible that the people of the tiles would soon be as different from each other as alien species. We're just lucky that the language is almost identical to English.

(Letter 2, Paragraph 4, Lines 1-5)

The sun set on her twelfth day of laboring on the Colossus and Mel made her escape. Clutching her bag of hoarded food, she disappeared as the workers trooped back to their bunkhouses.

The bag was half empty, and she had no idea where she was going, but she could wait no longer. If she stayed, Mel knew that the person she was would disappear forever, and she would be just like the other sleepwalking drones.

So she ran.

It was easier than it should have been. There were no fences around the workers, no razor wire to cross, no guard towers to avoid. The hairshirts had made no attempt to trap the workers at the construction site. In fact, it seemed they had done their best to leave the door wide open.

As Mel ran, she told herself stories about her friends.

She remembered when Gwen convinced them to go to the National Zoo. And that girl seemed to come to life wherever there were animals. Mel had had her sketchbook, and she did her best to capture the plumage of the birds of paradise in paper and ink. Yosef droned on and on about their migratory habits, while Finley and Huck tried to race in a cotton candy eating contest.

Mel recalled when she practiced with Theo night after night for his big speech in their world government class. Her friend hadn't slept in days, and he seemed seconds away from breaking down in tears or bolting, but when they locked eyes, he was able to smile again.

She saw Yosef as he tried his best to dance at the spring formal.

She heard Huck's laugh as they played chess in the library between classes.

She tasted the snickerdoodles Finley and Gwen swore could cure anything.

She wrapped these memories about her like a cloak, and the song disappeared. With silence in her ears for the first time in weeks, Mel vanished into the ash strewn wasteland around the construction site. She smothered herself in soot and moved only at night. During the day she heaped ashes on her body and slept in brief snatches. She strained at every moment for a sign of her pursuers. She tensed for the thud of their clubs, for the echoes of the song that had dominated her thoughts for days.

But there was nothing.

On the fourth day she realized no one was pursuing her, but she could not unclench her fists or rest her eyes, and her ears still ached for the song of the Colossus.

That night Mel allowed herself an extra bit of her food. One mouthful later and she already regretted her indulgence. She brushed herself off and stood, surveying her surroundings. The Colossus loomed behind her to the south. At least she assumed it was the south. It was impossible to tell, as the stars themselves seemed to be working against her. She knew only a passing amount about astronomy, mostly because Finley could never shut up about it, yet even she knew how to find Polaris, the north star. Except there was no Polaris in this sky.

She craned her neck, looking for that bright star that would lead her away. And then, in front of her very eyes, the sky changed.

The stars lurched into motion. Like a vast moving screen, the burning stars light years distant rolled to new positions. Constellations leapt into new formations; the moon jumped across the sky. The fixed points in the heavens no longer seemed so fixed.

Mel's stomach roiled as she watched. Battery acid surged up her throat and her head swam with vertigo as the stars danced. And then they stopped. The constellations locked back into place. The sky stilled, and in seconds it looked as if it had never moved.

Mel turned. The Colossus was still behind her, a black void in the lit sky. She grit her teeth, forcing the nausea away, refusing to throw up what food she had.

"Seeing things and hearing things? Good work, Mel. Way to cling to sanity."

Mel put the statue to her back and set forth, keeping the ash clogged river on her right side. She crunched her boots into the dry, cracked dirt, and resolved to put a dozen miles between herself and the Colossus tonight.

She marched for hours, ignoring the sky above, keeping her eyes planted on the ground below. Memories rose in her mind, but she would not let herself feel them. The memories had helped her escape the song, but even these happy thoughts were starting to cut at her.

She would not let herself remember the last hike they had all taken together as they made their way up Harper's Ferry. The last time they had all been together. She did not recall that Huck had stopped to sketch every flower, that Yosef had chatted to every passing hiker, that Gwen and Finley had argued like cats and dogs. Mel did not let a smile come to her face at this thought.

She just put one foot in front of the other. And tried not to think about the friends she might have just abandoned to the thrall of a statue.

She walked for miles through the wasteland, empty except for her, until a small row of shapes appeared in Mel's vision that gleamed like soldiers in armor. Her heart dropped into her stomach, and she searched for a hiding spot. The clouds parted and she could see in the moon's light that these were no soldiers, just rows of tree stumps poking out of the ash fields. They stood in rows one after the other like a field of headstones.

Mel crept toward the stumps and slipped into their midst, careful to avoid their spreading roots. The stumps were tall, almost level with her chest. She had to crouch only a little to vanish amongst them. The moon went once more behind the clouds, and total darkness descended. Mel navigated by feel amongst the stumps of the trees. Her hands guided her, reaching out from stump to stump. The dead wood was cool beneath her fingers, the roots slick beneath her feet.

The moon appeared once more, and Mel took the opportunity to rest in the hollow space between the roots. She stretched out, using the bones of the tree as a pillow. She allowed herself to close her eyes as she rested. She was so tired. She had not slept in the dark in many, many days. Even the hard roots beneath her head seemed as comfortable as a mattress, though one as cold as steel.

"No," Mel said, and her eyes shot open. She rocketed to her feet to stare at the stumps around her. The pale moonlight reflected off their bark, giving each stump an odd gleam. She knocked her hand against the roots, and it rang in a dull echo.

It was a tree made of iron with rust coating the stump like moss. And all around her were stumps that were just the same.

"I don't believe it. Metal trees. Or what's left of them."

Mel spun about, trying to picture what this forest would have looked like in its prime. A sea of steel trees, not at all bothered by wind or rain. Living metal, growing, spreading, shining in the sun. Now, it was just more skin for the Colossus.

Beneath her fingers, she felt a cut in the top of the stump. Someone had carved something into the iron wood. She brought her face close to the metal, attempting to decipher the crude and jagged writing in the dim light of the moon.

Farther than last time. Not far enough. - Aketa.

That was all. A shiver traveled up her spin. Aketa, the girl that Mel had tried to save, the one who had spoken of the statue with all the fervor of a priest, had tried to escape?

"What happened to you? What made you go back?" Mel whispered. "Did they find you at last?"

The night was silent around her, the field of cut down trees as somber as a tomb.

"Well they won't catch me."

Mel walked all night, until she stood at the very edges of the forest's graveyard. The river flowed further north, and Mel could see that it had carved a canyon in the northern end of the ring of mountains far ahead. That would be her way out.

Her supplies were almost exhausted, and her clothes were flimsy things, little more than rags, but she would not stop.

Mel turned back to the Colossus, still huge despite the distance she had put between herself and it. She could even see the glow of the welding torches as the workers toiled through the night. Thousands upon thousands laboring without sleep, and any one of them could be one of her friends.

"I'm sorry, okay?" Mel said, tears suddenly burning her eyes, dust choking her throat. "I couldn't find any of you. And if I stayed it would only be a matter of time until I disappeared. I had to get out while I could."

Silence swarmed about her, but Mel filled it with what she imagined they'd say.

"You left us to die," Gwen said.

"You left us to go mad," Finley cried.

"What kind of friend are you?" Theo demanded.

Mel clenched her fists so hard that her nails drew blood from the palms of her hands. But she would not stop the pain. The pain let her remember. The pain was the punishment she deserved for outliving another friend. "You didn't find me either. How do I know you didn't abandon me?"

"We never would," the voices seemed to say.

"One of us had to get away," Mel said, and she straightened her spine, but the pain lingered in her hands. "It's not a sign of true friendship or something for us to all die together. It's just stupid. I guess I'll just have to get used to you hating me for escaping."

She threw her bag over her shoulder and stepped out of the forest.

And then she heard a new voice.

"No one escapes," Yosef declared.

Mel heard a noise at the depths of her senses, a sound almost deeper than her ears could hear. It was the low moan of the mountains, the cry of the deep sky. It froze her in her tracks as it grew louder and louder, until it seemed to almost crush her beneath its crescendo.

With dawning horror, she turned her back on the river and the freedom beyond the mountains. She looked back on the massive Colossus so many miles distant. Mel told her body to run, her hands to clutch her ears, and her voice to scream, but all she could do was stare at the unfinished statue and listen to the song coming from its chest.

The world disappeared and Mel disappeared with it.

Mel dreamed of herself. She dreamed that she was walking through a forest of dead trees. It was a world of bleached colors, the bright blue sky now bone white, the green sludge of the river stone black.

The stumps of the trees were iron lumps with flat heads. Yet from the iron of these trees there came the ghost of a shape. It was a towering thing, this ghost. It reached to the sky, and hands sprung from it to reach the grasping hands of the other ghostly trees.

And among the branches of these phantom trees there was Mel. And from above she watched her body walk amongst the metal carcasses on the forest floor. Her body's face was slack, its movements were sluggish, yet its purpose was unerring. It traveled back to the Colossus. Mel tried to shout but found she could not. There was only the sound of the whispering trees.

Mel shook with rage and found she could move, and so she leapt to the next tree with a grace she did not have in the waking world. She shot after her retreating body, still attempting to yell after it, but it was clear her body was listening to a different call.

She caught up with her body and fell from the trees above, aiming for her own head. They collided and Mel found herself falling through her body and out the other side. She hit the cold mud of the forest floor, and turned to see her own body stumble forward, only to right itself and continue its march south.

Mel roared with fury, but still no sound came. She watched her own body walk away from her, taking plodding steps and jerking strides.

She raced back into the ghost branches of the trees above and leapt from limb to limb to catch up to her prey again. She soon hung in the tree above her own body. This would require exact timing.

Mel leapt once more, passing through her sleeping body, but this time at the exact right moment. Her body stumbled forward onto the slick branches, and she felt the wrenching pain as her ankle twisted beneath her.

The pain brought her back, anchoring Mel to herself like the clasp of a friend's hand in hers. Mel, both body and soul, slammed into the tree stump ahead, which was now a plain but dead tree. Mel cradled the injured appendage and wept both tears of pain and of relief.

She focused on the pain. She made that white hot burn her whole life as she clutched her own injury. Yet even still, she could hear the chorus at the edge of her senses. It lurked there, waiting for her focus to waver so that it could drag her back to work.

And all at once Mel realized just why the guards did not care who escaped. Why Aketa returned to the place that would consume her. She came back willingly, just like everyone else. They came back for the song.

Her stomach gurgled with hunger. How long had her body marched without her mind? Mel reached over her shoulder for the food in her bag. But the bag was gone.

Where had it gone?

Frenzied, she spun about. She needed that bag. Inside was all the food she had left in the world. The pain built ever higher up her leg and into her chest, until it felt like it would consume her heart.

And then Mel saw that she was being watched.

She froze, her eyes locking with the figure before her. It was a boy, perched on top of the stump in front of hers. His limbs were short, and his head was large. He had a small bow mouth, and a narrow scar along his chin.

For a moment, as her eyes still watered with pain, Mel thought it was Yosef looking at her. A child Yosef she had not seen in years, but as the tears fell, she saw she was wrong. The boy's face was different, slenderer, and he had a scar. And Yosef had gray eyes, but the boy's were bright yellow.

Those eyes of his watched her, unblinking and unafraid. Mel straightened up, and even with him perched on the stump she still towered over the lad.

"Hello," Mel said, her voice raw and scratchy from disuse.

The boy said nothing, only continuing to look at her. He swung his feet before him so that the dull tap of leather on dead iron filled the silence between them.

"I'm Mel," she said, pointing at her chest to emphasize the idea. She was terrible with small children. This was always more of Finley's area than hers. "Who are you? What are you doing here?"

The boy remained silent, cocking his head to the side to watch her.

"Are you following me? Are you one of the hairshirts?"

Silence.

"Hey, kid, I asked you a question. Answer me," Mel said, losing her patience. "What's your name anyway?"

The boy's only answer was to pick up a small sack behind his back and hold it in front of him. Mel's eyes lit up.

"My bag!" she said, rushing forward. The boy reared back as she stumbled toward him. She froze, and so did the boy. They stared at each other. Mel remained locked in place, and with the gentle movements of a frightened deer the boy returned to his original position. He was an odd-looking kid. His clothes were mismatched and faded, his pants too large, the shirt too small. The boy's eyes were bright yellow like an owl's, but the tree he sat on was made of metal, so Mel tried not to judge.

They stared at each other for a while longer, until the boy once more picked up the bag and tossed it to her. She caught it and tore into it. Her food was still there, meager as it was. Her extra set of clothes and shoes were still there as well.

"Thank you," Mel said to the boy and smiled at him. She was a bit rusty at smiling, but she thought it wasn't terrible.

The boy's face remained blank, but he raised one finger. He sketched out a shape in the air. His finger glowed with neon purple light as it moved, and where he drew the light remained. It took a moment for Mel to realize that he had just drawn a glowing, smiling face in the air. The face hovered for a moment, and then the light faded. The boy was just as impassive as before.

Mel raised her own finger and traced her own smiling face. "Yeah, I can't do that. Not the weirdest thing I've seen today though. How did you get here, kid? Where did you come from?"

The boy looked at her, his face tilted to the side. He pointed to the ground, and then brought his finger slowly back up so that it was level with his face, and then he pointed where he sat.

"You live under the trees?"

He nodded.

"Can you understand what I'm saying?" Mel asked, perplexed by the boy's quiet.

The child nodded once more. His face remained a mask of perfect calm.

"Is there a reason you won't speak?"

The boy nodded again, and his hands launched into motion. They moved into shapes and into symbols, a language of movement that Mel could not understand, and his fingers still glowed.

"Yeah, I don't know how to sign. I took Spanish instead. Listen, how do you do that glowing finger thing?" she asked, miming his shining digits.

He touched his head as he closed his eyes, and then he pointed to her own head and reopened them. He repeated the gesture several times. Mel shook her head in frustration.

"I have no idea what you are trying to say. Do you have someone that can talk to me? Is your mom or dad around?" The boy jumped to his feet, but as he did so Mel heard a dull rumble coming from his midsection. The boy stopped and patted his stomach. She thought of how little food was in her own pack.

"You're hungry huh?"

The boy gave a helpless shrug. His stomach gurgled again, and he flushed with embarrassment.

"Well, that really stinks," Mel said.

The boy nodded, agreeing with her.

"Fine, fine, fine!" She reached into her bag. "Here, have this." There was so little food left. At the bottom of the bag, wrapped in rags, was a hunk of molding bread. She tossed it to the boy. Surprised, he caught it. The boy looked at it and her for a moment, before tearing into the bread with childish gusto. He turned away from her and walked off into the dead iron trees.

"You're welcome!" Mel called out as she followed him. "Little jerk."

The boy ate as he walked and moved through the stumps with easy familiarity. The sun was high overhead, and the iron trees around them started to shine. Mel felt a desperate need to get under cover. Any moment the song could take over her again, and the thought sent a spike of ice through her heart.

"Wait!" she cried. "Wait, wait, wait." The boy kept walking however, polishing off the crumbs of the bread. She rushed forward, and in her haste, she grabbed his shoulder and yanked him around. His eyes grew huge as he looked at her, and he tried to stumble back, but her grip was tight.

"Your parents. Do they hear it too? Do they hear the song?" Mel demanded. The boy was silent. Mel grew louder. "The song! Do they hear it? Are they going to make me go back?"

The boy's eyes narrowed to little specks of light, and he shivered in her hands. He shook his head.

The spike in her heart melted. She had to be careful. She couldn't let her guard down. The boy kept watching her, wary. Blood rushed into her face, and she scratched the back of her head. She couldn't meet his eyes.

"Sorry. Are you okay?" The boy watched her for a moment more, before he turned and walked away. He turned and waved at her to catch up, and Mel rushed to join him. The pain in her ankle was still a dull deep ache, but even more overpowering was her exhaustion. It hung off her like great chains of iron, trying to drag her down onto the soft dirt below.

The boy came to a halt in front of a tree stump, a great iron flat head twice as wide as the other stumps. Mel struggled to imagine what such a living tree would have looked like as it towered in the sky. In her old life she would have marveled at such a thing, but scale had lost its meaning to Mel. The grotesque goliath seemed to loom over all else in her mind.

The boy raised his arms at his sides, and once more his fingertips began to glow with an odd purple light. His hands danced before him, crafting elaborate symbols that hung in the air for a second before fading away. Mel only recognized a few of the images. One looked like a tree in bloom, another looked like a setting sun, and it took a moment before Mel recognized that the boy was telling a story. The pictures flowed around him, creating a setting and a scene.

The great iron stump of the once proud king of the forest opened. The hole grew wider and wider, until it became a tunnel into the dirt. The boy's fingers stilled, and his song died away. He waited.

"Am I going to be safe here?" Mel asked.

The boy crept toward her as if approaching a rabbit that would dart away at any moment. His hand, when it found hers, had the softness of a child's. Mel clasped it in her own scarred and callused hand and followed as he led her down into the cave.

As they stepped into the mud, the song vanished. It felt like a lead weight had disappeared from Mel's mind.

They walked into the ground, following a tunnel that took them to a room filled with people rooted to the earth. Over a dozen people were in the chamber, each with their head thrown back, their eyes pointed to the ceiling. They sat in cradles of twisted iron branches, which rose from the ground in gnarled masses, seeming to have grown around the people in their depths. The people did not struggle, but only looked up at the cave roof from their iron nests.

Mel shuddered back, pulling away from the boy. The boy glanced back at her, surprised at her sudden reaction. With quiet steps he walked back to her and grabbed her hand again. He led her through the grove of the sleepers in iron.

Mel followed, her hand slack in the boy's grasp. She stared at the sleeping people wrapped in the roots. They were a strange lot. All wore purple tabards that bundled around their waists as they sat listless in their chairs. Most of them were old, many decades older than Mel herself. There were no other children.

The sleepers were slender and frail, their limbs emaciated with disuse. Most of the sleepers had the same nut-brown skin of the boy, as well as his wide yellow eyes and small nose. They were family, Mel realized at once, and the boy was not afraid of what he had probably seen before.

He led her to the center of the great chamber, where the oldest sleeper lay in her metal cradle. Her own eyes rolled about her head as she looked at the tangled roots far above. The boy released Mel's hand and walked to the old woman. He tenderly pulled at the woman's crooked claw of a hand, her fingers ending in long sharp nails.

The woman's eyes stopped their roving and closed.

"Welcome to our Hollow, young one." And while her body was frail, her voice was rich and strong. It poured over Mel as she continued to speak. "I hope you are not averse to dark places. It may be some time before it is safe for you to see the sun again."

"Who are you? What is this place?" Mel demanded.

"Safe. You might have noticed you ceased to feel the call of the Colossus here. You will not hear it again while in our presence."

"How are you blocking the song?"

"Why did you feed the boy?" the woman asked, her voice drowning out Mel's own questions even as the woman's face remained slack. "You did not know him. He was of no use to you in your escape attempt. You sacrificed the last piece of food you had, even after you had traveled for days with weeks ahead still. Allow me to apologize for that as well. Cisseus knows not to take food from starving strangers. It seems even the most diligent students misbehave."

The boy, Cisseus, gave a little shrug and looked at the floor. He had a flush to his cheeks now, but he still held on to the woman's hand.

"He found my bag for me. I owed him some bread."

"So you fed him merely to fulfill a debt?"

"I fed him because I wanted to. Nothing more than that," Mel said, looking at the boy before her. "Now tell me what I want to know. How do you block the song? And where are we, a tomb?"

Mel looked around again at the sleepers in their iron cradles. None stirred except for the twitch of an eye or the jerk of a lip.

"They are not dead, they are dreaming. This forest was once known as the Shining Forest
, and it was filled with growing things that the world could not damage. The earth could not shake its roots, and the axe man could not cut it down. But now it is dead, and we dream amongst its remains," the woman said, and at her words the air began to glow with that same purple light that had come from the boy's fingers. Flowers of electric green and luminescent purple sprouted from the dirt, and Mel could hear the echoes of birdsong even as nothing flew above.

"We are the Sheosirra, the dreaming people. And we have no tile to call our own. The Sheosirra are drifting, seeking, sleeping. We walk the Reverie to the hidden places of the world. And sometimes we can talk to the dreams of the world, to the birds, fishes, flowers, and trees. And if we are kind enough, persuasive enough, they might give us aid," the woman intoned, and now more creatures of light appeared in the air, each moving about as a living thing, but as insubstantial as a dream.

"And you are our guest, Melanie Omar. I am Harmodias, leader of these people." And the woman smiled at Mel. It was a crooked smile of missing teeth and ancient lines. Yet when she opened her eyes, they glittered with a young girl's mischief and joy. As they locked gazes, the creatures and flowers she had summoned from dreams faded away once more.

"Thank you for feeding my great grandson, the dunderhead that he is. Allow me to return the favor. Would you like tea?"

Chapter 7: The Messenger's Test

Magic exists here. I feel stupid even writing this, but in this place magic does exist. It is a strange and terrible thing, and the people here use it for both the mundane and for miracles. I do not know if we can learn it, but I will certainly try. I believe they call this magic the Cognitive Domains, and for some reason it seems familiar.

(Letter 4, Paragraph 1, Lines 1-4)

"Wake up!" the voice thundered from the end of the dormitory, and Gwen's eyes snapped open.

"On your faces!" the voice roared, and Gwen swept the blanket from her body and rolled off her bunk and onto the floor. She caught herself before her nose crashed into the stones. All around her she heard the thumps of dozens of other bodies slamming into the floor.

"50!" the voice cried, and Gwen's arms collapsed and rose as she counted her pushups aloud.

She called, "ONE!" with dozens of others joining the chorus.

"TWO!"

"THREE!"

She did not fully wake up until they reached thirty. At forty she started to feel the pain, and at forty-five every movement became an agony, as she fought against exhaustion and gravity to keep her arms pushing up and down, up and down.

"UP!" the voice called, and the bodies around her rose.

Each was puffing with exhaustion, and they did not look at each other. Gwen tried desperately to control her breathing. She sucked air into her nose and sent it swirling out her mouth.

"RUN!"

As one, the bodies in the room moved to the door. The dull slaps of feet on stone accompanied Gwen as she ducked into the racing crowd. She ran with the group as they hurried out of the compound and into the wilds that surrounded it. The wind's howling cold cut at her skin like knives. The dull slaps of her fellow runners vanished, and she ran to the beat of her own labored breathing. She angled her body so that the wind lashed at her left side and raced on.

The flat stone of the compound faded away to be replaced by harsh and jagged rocks. The stones stabbed into her feet and froze the wounds with their coldness, turning each step into a dull agony.

Gwen did not look around at her fellow runners. She did not see if they too felt such pain. She did not see at all, in fact.

They ran blindfolded, as they had so many times before.

The preceptors had trained them well, and they could run the five-mile course that surrounded the compound blindfolded better than those with sight.

The training had started on the first day. Gwen and the other novices had been led into a room without light and had been told to find their beds. After much flailing, cursing, and cries for aid, the novices found unoccupied beds with only a few minor injuries.

Over the weeks and months that followed, the preceptors removed light from more and more of their lives. Mealtimes were cast in darkness. Lessons were conducted in a void, with only the sound of a preceptor's voice for company. The novices were not allowed outside, and instead moved through the dark tunnels of the compound like rats crawling through walls. Gwen soon forgot the sight of the sun.

The tasks the preceptors set them became ever more difficult. Building puzzles in darkness, dissembling machines, practicing martial arts, deciphering coded messages, on and on. But Gwen did not know why.

"Make familiar that which is most foreign. Make every part of your environment an ally and an old friend. Only then can fear be conquered," the preceptors whispered to their students, and the pupils obeyed. Gwen and the other novices searched for patterns in the wind and learned to navigate the darkness based on the way it played upon their skin. Their feet became as sensitive as their own hands, able to pick out the slightest changes in the ground beneath them.

For miles she ran, traversing the steep ravines and rocky paths of the mountainside. She felt reborn, far removed from that weak girl that the preceptors had taken under their wings, as dependent on light as a newborn bird. She was stronger and more at peace now then she had ever been, and all they asked was that she obey without question.

She pushed herself harder as she neared the end of the run. She heard only her footsteps as she raced through the gate and to the fountain at the center of the courtyard. She collapsed at the edge, reaching for the water in the fountain, only to meet a thin layer of ice that had formed on its surface. She punched through, and cupped pure icy water. She drank and experienced bliss, which doubled when she felt a feather light touch upon her shoulder.

"Well done," the voice whispered. She now heard steps on stones as the other runners caught up and joined her at the fountain. A smile formed on her face, fierce and proud, that no one else could see.

"Follow," the voice rasped again. Gwen rose and noticed that no one else had. Her spine straightened as she understood the honor that was being bestowed on her. She followed the soft sweeping echoes of the master's passage into the bowels of the great compound, past dormitories, classrooms, and mess halls, journeying far deeper than Gwen ever had until they entered a room at the very heart of it all.

"You have shown great progress, child." The voice seemed to come from all around her, seeping from the floor and dripping from the ceiling, a rasping voice full of age and wisdom.

"When you arrived you were weak, dependent on light, and on others. But you have been trained. You are at last our perfect instrument for the tasks ahead. Now you are ready to learn your purpose. But are you willing?"

Gwen's pulse pounded through her limbs and her head, seeming to add a new echo to this strange room. A voice tickled at the edge of her hearing. It was a shy voice, one that felt familiar to her. It crept in at the edge of her thoughts and urged her to run, to flee, but she ignored it.

"I am," she said.

"Remove your blindfold, child. Step into the light."

With unsteady hands she untied the blindfold and opened her eyes for the first time in months. The light stabbed into her eyes, yet she forced herself to focus on the source of the light and saw that her agony came from a simple candle, too weak to even illuminate the room fully. Her preceptors remained in the shadows of the room, draped in their hoods and cloaks.

"Yes, child. We still use light when we must, and you will as well. There is paper upon the table, child. Read it to us."

Gwen walked to the table and picked up the paper beside the candle. Upon it were two scripts, one the system of dots and dashes embedded in the paper that the preceptors had taught her to read with only the feel of her finger. The other script was English.

"Not darkness, nor light; not peace, nor war; not hatred, nor love; shall stop the flight of the message."

The air shook as the preceptors all breathed in at once, as if soothed by the words. Yet the meaning was lost upon Gwen.

"I don't understand."

"It is a promise. Can you keep that promise, child? Can you be our instrument?"

And now that inner voice was screaming at Gwen, begging her to run from these madmen cloaked in shadows making her swear stupid sacred oaths. But it was easy to ignore that voice. They had taught her how to ignore it.

"Yes, I will be your instrument."

"Very good," the preceptor said. "Welcome to the *Herald*," and he spread his wings. The raven feathers beneath were darker than midnight, and his beak was as sharp as a knife. He gave a great ringing cry, louder than any crow call she had ever heard.

"Welcome, our new courier and messenger."

And they opened their beaks wide as their shouts of triumph and of joy squawked through the room. Gwen looked into the flame and wondered what the hell she had gotten herself into.

Chapter 8: The Messenger's New Employers

The magic of this world is organized into a system called the Cognitive Domains. How many domains there are in total is unclear. Based on what I've seen it seems it is a truly rare thing to master even one of these domains. Mastery of more than one may be an impossibility. In either case, skill with a domain gives one control over an aspect of the mind...
(Letter 4, Paragraph 2, Lines 1-5)

Gwen stood on the lip of a mountain and felt no fear. The preceptors had told her that she was ready for the next step, though they did not elaborate further. She was sent without ceremony to her dormitory, gathered what meager possessions she still had, and left without saying a word to her fellow trainees.

Now she stood on the edge of the world waiting for a ride. The sun had risen some hours before and now glared down at her from its celestial perch. Gwen had gone sixty-four days without seeing sunlight, and now it punished her, beating down on her like an immense club.

Gwen did not seek out the comforting embrace of the blindfold. Though she could see no one nearby, she was not yet sure that this was another test.

The cold winds continued to rise, and Gwen resolved to stand in this spot until she froze. She was certain that this was a test now, an examination of her ability to endure the elements or to follow orders. And her resolve not to fail was so fierce that it took her a moment to register the new vibration she felt in the ground below her. It was a slow and steady rumble that grew and grew until it felt like an avalanche climbing up a hill.

She would not move. She would not fail!

But she could not stop her gasp as a pair of horns crested the edge of the mountain. They were massive things, as long as Gwen herself. The horns were gnarled with age, pitted with grooves and pits of various sizes. A vast white head, with a snow crisp beard. A powerful neck of coiled muscle with high shoulders following it. A platform of wood and cloth rode upon the creature's back, as large as a room. The massive mountain goat climbed onto the rock platform to tower above Gwen.

Gwen had not moved. The goat turned its large eyes upon her and then with one rippling motion it shook the snow from its body. A wave of frost hit Gwen in the face, and nearly drove her to the ground.

"Well, what are you waiting for? Climb aboard!" a harsh voice cried from atop the massive beast. Gwen walked to the front leg of the goat closest to her. Feeling like a fly climbing the skin of an elephant, Gwen dug her hands into the thick fur of the goat and began to ascend. The hair was greasy and smooth on the outside, yet closer to the beast's skin it was dry and coarse, however it was difficult to notice anything besides the overwhelming smell.

She clambered onto the flat muscle of the creature's shoulder. On the creature's back was a small carriage made of delicate wood with numerous cloth fabrics that cloaked it like the feathers of a bird.

Inside was a short and wizened man wearing an immense fur hat. "Sit down, girl, sit down. We have a schedule to keep, and I will not have some young novice too simple to stand out of an oreamos's way besmirching my record!" the man said, in the same high, thin voice from earlier. His hat bobbed as his face contorted with passion.

The driver turned from her and took up the reins once more. He cracked them against the side of the howdah, and the oreamos shuddered into motion. It did a slow spin to face the ledge of the mountain again and stepped off the edge.

Gwen reached out for the sides of the basket to grab onto. The howdah rocked with the beast's shoulders like a swaying ship, and Gwen started to feel sick. She had always had trouble with motion sickness.

But she wasn't Gwen now, she was an instrument of the *Herald*, and she did not need to feel anything she did not want to. With an effort of will, Gwen forced her body back to equilibrium.

There was no pain, no nausea, no fear. Only darkness.

She started to look around the cabin and found the baleful eye of the driver as he looked over his shoulder at her.

"First time," the driver said. It was not a question.

"Yes," Gwen whispered. She couldn't stop staring at the driver. It was so strange to see another person's face again!

"You're doing better than most. Those that throw up in my howdah have to ride on the animal's ass."

"Thank you," the said, her voice barely louder than the roaring wind.

"Do you have a name?"

She hesitated. The preceptors had not told her what to say here. She decided to stick with the easy answer. "Gwen."

"I've not heard that one before. Strange name."

"I think I might be a strange person," Gwen replied. He laughed, shaking the hat on his head.

"That makes two of us then. I'm Epa. Nice to meet you, Gwen. We'll be at the Cradle in four hours. I'm going forward, this next bit is tricky if the oreamos tries on its own," Epa said, and with a grace that surprised Gwen he stepped over the front of the howdah and climbed up the creature's neck and onto its head.

Gwen relaxed into a cross-legged sitting position. It was refreshing to hear a new voice. She had spent the last several months with only the preceptors for company, and while they were wise far beyond Gwen's measure, they were not exactly conversationalists. With a jolt, Gwen realized he was the first person she had heard laugh in some time.

What a strange thing to miss! Laughter was absent everywhere in the compound of the preceptors. Only whispers sounded in that place, and the only expression of joy came from the release from pain, or at a job well done. She missed laughing with her friends. She missed Theo's quiet chuckle, and Mel's snorts of glee. Finley giggled like a schoolgirl, and Yosef's laugh was always long and loud and made everyone want to laugh harder. She missed them all.

And all at once the strange joy of hearing the laugh was crowded out with shame. She could not think of her friends. Gwen did not have friends anymore, only teachers.

And those teachers did not require laughter, did not need it in their teachings or in their lessons. Who was Gwen to say what was good or bad? What the preceptors needed or didn't? They had taken the light from her, what would they take next if she continued to fail them?

Gwen felt the walls closing in around her. She crawled to the edge of the howdah and threw the curtains open. She saw mountains capped with snow on the other side of an immense valley. The mountains looked delicate from here, like cupcakes glazed with frosting. Streams of flowing water moved across the valley, meeting in the middle to form a larger river that seemed so blue that it looked dreamlike.

A snowflake fell onto her nose, and she smiled. For a moment the sun shone on Gwendolyn Brooks, and she forgot what it felt like to be wrapped in darkness.

Then a voice whispered behind her, "You know, I'll never get over how your mouths do that. It's quite disgusting."

Gwen whipped around, and the bundle of furs and blankets at the back of the carriage rose up. The blankets and fabrics slipped off it as it stood, and Gwen could see that the creature beneath was dressed in torn and dirty rags. A cloak that had once been black draped the creature, yet it was now splattered with muck and mud. The shirt beneath was just as dirty, and it hung off the creature's narrow chest. Rising from the shirt was a strong neck of purple feathers topped with a beak of dull black, which was chipped and scratched, but the creature's eyes were whole and startlingly dark. They burned into Gwen, even as she dropped to her knees.

"Preceptor," she said. "I am sorry. I did not realize you were here." Gwen's voice did not shiver or falter, but inside her emotions roiled. She had been smiling, she had been thinking dangerous thoughts.

"Oh, stand up, I'm not one of the preceptors. You can relax." The raven-headed person fell back onto the furs at the back of the howdah, and his clawed hands began to pick at his taloned feet. Gwen did not move.

"Please get up. I do so hate the groveling. It's far worse for me than it is for you, you know. At least the groveler gets to do something. The grovelee just has to bask in it," the creature said, and he threw his arms wide as if a massive crowd was cheering for him.

"Awkward for everyone really. Worse than birthday parties. Oh please, stand up, why don't you? Fine, fine, fine. Here, I command you to stop groveling. Better?"

Gwen fell back into a cross-legged position. Her hands respectfully in her lap.

"You can look at me too, if you like. Seriously, I'm not one of the preceptors. I'm not going to beat you or throw you off a cliff, or whatever the hell they do to novices at that disgusting monastery. Look, what do you humans do? Oh yes." The raven jumped up and

94

strutted over to Gwen. He extended one clawed hand to clasp one of Gwen's. He pumped it twice.

"Lelial, nice to meet you. My friends call me Lelly. Charmed, I am quite sure," Lelly said, his eyes flashing with humor as he looked at Gwen. "I believe this is the part when you tell me your name as well."

"Gwen."

"Gwen, what a pleasure it is to make your acquaintance," Lelly said, and returned to his seat, smoothing his feathers as he did so.

"What is it you command?"

"Come now, do you think I really look like one of those awful preceptors?"

He did not, Gwen realized. Though the preceptors preferred to be enshrouded in darkness, Gwen had caught brief flashes of them during her recent ceremony. They also had the heads of birds, with the same clawed feet and hands that Lelly had. However, there the resemblance ended. The preceptors wore cloaks of deepest purple. They delivered sermons and lessons in whispers, and they punished disobedience with terrible swiftness. Lelly, on the other hand, looked disheveled and carefree. And, even more startlingly, he was in the sunlight.

"No, sir. You don't look anything like them."

Lelly nodded in approval. "Very good, not every corvid is a preceptor, Gwen. About time to get over that particular bit of prejudice, especially where you're going."

"I'm very sorry, but I'm confused. Could you explain what you mean?" Gwen whispered, still wary of the corvid. The preceptors were clever beyond words, but this Lelial was the strangest test they had set for her yet.

"I mean that Cradle, thank Vovatum, is nothing like the monastery, elsewise I wouldn't be caught dead in the place. You'll see more corvids like me when you're there. And not all of us are so uptight as the preceptors. So young Gwen, what brings you to our mountainous hideaway?"

"The preceptors are sending me to Cradle. They say that I am ready," Gwen said, her response easy and automatic, trained.

"Did they explain what you are ready for?"

"The Truth."

"Oh, what nonsense! Those preceptors really have their heads up their own asses, don't they? Calm down, calm down," Lelly said, as Gwen started to rise with her fists clenched. "They're not here, Gwen, you don't need to defend them."

"They don't require a defense. Only obedience."

"But obedience to what? Don't you think you have the right to know?"

"I'm an instrument. You don't need to care about me."

"I don't, not particularly. I hope you are not offended, we have just met, after all. I am quite sure you care not a whit for me," Lelly said, smoothing his raised feathers as Gwen returned to her seat on the floor. "I do, however, care deeply for fairness. I would hate for you to arrive at Cradle without having a full deck, as it were.

"The preceptors have told me all that I need to know."

"No, no they have not. That's what a teacher is, after all, a withholder of knowledge until they feel you are ready for it. But shouldn't you decide such a thing, Gwen?"

Gwen looked at the disheveled figure before her, so different from the figures that had controlled her every moment for the past few months. They had given her commands, they had given her wisdom, but answers were rare. That little voice in her head, the one that sounded like who she used to be, demanded she not waste this opportunity.

"I don't trust you."

"Naturally."

"But I do have questions, sir."

"You can drop the sir. I am a disreputable rapscallion and nothing more. And your answers shall not come for free."

"What do you want, si—?" Gwen asked, cutting off the honorific with difficulty.

"Not to worry, nothing drastic, nothing you would miss. While the preceptors want only obedience, I crave a much more tempting thing," Lelly said, leaning forward until his face seemed to fill the entire world. "I want stories. Tell me yours, and I'll give you answers."

He sat back. The landscape continued its slow march across the howdah's window. Gwen watched as Lelly moved on from smoothing his feathers and returned to cleaning his talons. He seemed absorbed by the work, but every so often his covetous eyes would flash again at Gwen's.

"Alright, but I would like to go first," she said and saw that while the rest of his movements were smooth his hands twitched.

"Of course, of course."

"What is the Truth?"

"The Truth is our goal. So much of this world is lost in barbaric nonsense. So much of this world thinks only of their tiles, and cares nothing for what happens or what is learned outside of it. They are lost in darkness, Gwen, and the Truth would solve all that. The herald is the vehicle of that Truth."

It was so hard not to scream at his non-answer. "I'm afraid that didn't make much sense. What does it mean?" Gwen said, trying to keep her tone respectful. It seemed to amuse Lelly as his beaked head twitched in a gesture she was starting to associate with smiling.

"That's two questions, Gwen. My turn." He craned forward, dropping all pretense of seeming disinterested in the conversation. "How did they find you?"

"I found them."

"Impossible. The *Herald* cannot be found. Are you telling me that you were the first one to ever find us?"

"That's two questions. I ask my original question, what do you mean about the Truth and the herald?"

"Fair play. I always pity the new novices. They keep you totally in the dark over there don't they? Teaching you nothing but to jump, and run, and fight when told, all for a purpose they barely even explain. I hope you forgive the *Herald*, Gwen. What we do is all for a higher purpose, I assure you." He leaned back, and closed his obsidian eyes, yet his voice deepened so that it filled the howdah.

"It is my favorite story of all, which is arrogance I suppose, as it is my story as well. In any case, the story starts as all tragedies do, with a cry for help. There was a tile long ago that was one of plenty and of peace. The people on this tile lived idyllic lives. They were happy, unstressed, and at ease. Simple in a way, stupid even, but very charming." His eyes opened, and he turned to the side of the howdah, gazing off past the snows and the mountains.

"The tile was called Drever. And to know that such a place of peace existed was a balm to troubled minds, even mine. My people found that tile and befriended its people. You must understand, Gwen, we corvids are a nomadic, unsettled folk. It is rare for one of us to call anywhere home. Yet they welcomed us, and then it all went to shit." And Gwen saw that tears were leaking from his eyes. "We made them sick. Some sort of disease, just a cough to us, but almost universally fatal to them. It only took about a month for most of them to die. And you know what the worst part was, Gwen? They never blamed us." Lelial wiped his tears away with one clawed hand.

"We were eventually able to find a cure. It turns out the people only two tiles over had access to a plant that produced a medicine with a near ninety percent cure rate. But the Drevers didn't know about that tile, or its herb, and neither did we. All that suffering and death due to our ignorance. That's when we decided that the people of this planet could no longer be ignorant of each other, and thus the *Herald*." Lelial composed himself. "I am sorry to wax on so. The journey to Cradle always brings out the sentimental in me. Do you still think that I am a preceptor?"

"Is that your question?"

"Ah, wary until the last. I do admire that in a traveling companion. It does give conversation an air of suspense. No, my dear, that is not my question. How did you find the *Herald*?"

"I'm not sure."

"That is not an answer."

"It is the truth though. I woke up on the mountain, in a little cave in the rocks. I don't know how I got there. I tried to go outside, but the mountain was too steep, too cold to go anywhere. I went back into the cave, and I thought I would die there." And Gwen could see it once more. A shattered hollow in the mountain, with nothing but dead animals and Gwen herself. Nothing around her to make a fire, nothing around to cover her, and she was wearing a dress of all things.

"I slipped in and out of consciousness all night, certain that I was having a nightmare. But I never woke up from it. I would have gone to sleep for the last time right there, but then I heard the novices. I saw the preceptors leading them on a march through the snow. I dug my way out and threw myself at them. I don't think I realized until later that they were bird people." Gwen saw that Lelly made a face at this slight, but he remained silent. "It was the only time I ever saw them less than composed. They took me in, and I've been in the monastery ever since. Until now."

"Sounds like quite an ordeal. Thank goodness you survived. How did you end up in the cave? Ah yes, it's your question, isn't it?" Lelly said. He settled back in his seat. Gwen stared at him, uncertain how much to reveal. He had been very forthcoming with his story, almost as if he had been preparing to tell her all along. This was unlike any test that the preceptors had given her before. Was she meant simply to listen? To figure out what was lies and truth?

"Tiles. You keep using that word. What do you mean by it?"

"My, my, Gwen, you are an interesting one, aren't you? Did you grow up in a cave?" he said, and his head twitched again in that strange expression of humor. "Ah, please excuse me. Slip of the tongue." Lelly reached out of the howdah and picked up a pile of snow from the shoulder of the oreamos. He shaped it into a ball as he spoke.

"Would you like me to explain what a planet is as well? I could explain the sun and the stars next if you like. Ah, I believe that thing you're doing with your mouth means you are upset, or perhaps...angry? I think you can see why I never could have been a preceptor. I am clearly not one for teaching," he said, and he held the ball of snow in front of her.

"This is Poa, and in the great void of nothingness that is the universe it is what we call home. And the god Vovatum decided to make dear Poa interesting." With one clawed hand he began to carve shapes into the planet's surface. The planet grew continents and oceans, but each was contained in jagged fragments that somehow made a whole picture, like puzzle pieces in the shape of a planet.

"The Tiles. Like parts of a vast mosaic, they break our world into patterns that, together, make up the surface of the planet. Yet while each tile is the same general shape, the people and environments in each are staggeringly different. The people of this tile live in a symbiotic relationship with enormous insects called humdrills. Yet here, just one tile over, is a blasted ruin of a land, filled with the wreckage of broken civilizations and faded cultures. However, that and the other tile occasionally share a border with a tile affectionately known as the Stacks, a place of smoke and industry and little else. In short, they have almost nothing in common, and when the people of these tiles meet, the results can be...messy. Yet from above, Gwen, does it not look neat and tidy?"

"It's too uniform. Unnatural."

"Quite. From above I suppose it does look a little too immaculate, yes? Almost as if Vovatum had intended to make a clock. But you must remember, Gwen, clocks tick, and when they do the tiles move," Lelly said, and he swept one of his feathered arms in front of the ball. Feathers expanded and flared, and for a moment Poa vanished from view. Yet when it returned it was different. The tiles had shifted. Lelial swung his arm again, and the tiles turned once more, and again, and again.

"Not so orderly you see."

"The surface of the planet moves?"

"Yes. It has finished moving for the moment, but every few days, weeks, months, years, the tiles will move."

"Where do they move to?"

"Elsewhere. They migrate much like our bird cousins do. A tile can shift from one side of the planet to the other in the span of an afternoon, and here is the great problem. Every tile is insular, for in its nomadic trek across the planet it is always meeting someone new, someone, perhaps, dangerous. Why reach out when in time the tiles will break apart once again? Thus, people of the tiles turn inward, satisfied to never move from where they stand for fear they might be left behind at the next great shift. This is why the Drevers never knew there was a cure just a tile or two over. They never spoke to each other. But all of that is starting to change, and you can help. That is why the preceptors have sent you to Cradle, so that you can help us ensure every tile is no longer alone."

Lelly pointed with one talon at a tile in the southern hemisphere. "In case you are wondering. We are right here" And his talon shifted ever so slightly. "And we are going here. Why don't you keep it? Just in case you should ever get lost." And he threw the snowball at her.

The planet Poa hit Gwen in the face, but she did not react. The mountain ranges and plains dripped down into the neck of her tunic, sending a shiver down her spine.

Lelly had confirmed what she already suspected. She was alone on another planet. And as she wrestled with this revelation Lelial tipped his head back and gave great screeching cries that Gwen realized was his version of a laugh. She heard cursing coming from the oreamos's head and with a clatter Epa clambered back into the howdah glaring at the source of the noise.

"Up at last I see! And throwing snowballs in my carriage," Epa snarled.

"I do apologize, Epa," Lelly said, delicately flicking a tear from his eye with one of his feathers. "You know I like to get a rise out of our new novices, break the ice so to speak. Yet this one seems frozen still. Disinclined to laughter it seems."

"Or maybe she just hates your childish pranks, sir," Epa replied. "I can't say I blame her. You've always been a bit too clever for your own good."

"You wound me, Epa!"

"Not as much as I'd like. Here, Gwen." And Epa unwrapped the scarf from around his neck and handed it to her. Gwen took it and began to brush the snow from her clothes, and the scarf soon became sodden with melted snow. She tried to hand it back to Epa.

"Keep it, girl."

"I'm afraid I can't do that," Gwen said, and without shifting from her seat she threw the now soaked scarf at Lelial. The corvid squawked as the heavy scarf bowled him over into the blankets behind him.

"I'll have to give it away," Gwen finished, and Epa roared with laughter as the indignant corvid pulled himself back upright. "Thank you for your lesson, sir. I've learned a lot."

"Seems our novice here is one for laughter after all, Lelly!"

"If I was a preceptor, I would have you whipped, girl! But as I am not, I'll happily say well done." And Lelial once more extended his hand to Gwen. She rose and clasped his clawed hand. One of his fingers extended out from the shake and he tapped its talon against the underside of her wrist.

"Looks like there's more to you than a mere instrument. But tell me, do you still think I'm a test, Gwendolyn?" Lelial whispered to her so that Epa would not hear. Before she could respond he reared back and pointed with one claw at a sight just over the Oreamos's head.

"Ah! Cradle at last, and just on schedule too. Well done, Epa," Lelial said.

Two mountains rose in front of them, twins both in height and in mass. Each reared from the other, but one thing kept them together. A massive bridge stretched the gap between the two peaks.

The bridge was almost a mile in length, and it hung between the two peaks without support. It was as straight as an iron bar, and just as ugly, made of hard and jagged stone, pocked and marked with the screams of the wind. It was a tall bridge as well, almost a quarter high as it was long. Immense windows dotted its face, though Gwen could not see into its depths from here.

"Ah, I believe that expression means anxiety. Relax. It's much nicer on the inside."

The oreamos continued its summit of the mountain, trekking through the deeper snows to a massive door at the base of the bridge. Epa warned them to hold on as the oreamos thundered into the hangar.

Inside was a massive room packed to the brim with crates, supplies, and packages of all sorts. Yet each pile was well back from the oreamos's path as it galloped to a large trough to the side. A pile of steaming brown mush sat in the trough with a barrel of water beside it. An oreamos was already at the trough with its head and horns nearly submerged in the mush. Gwen's own oreamos hurried to join, and the vibrations of its enthusiastic eating shook the howdah. Epa turned to his passengers.

"Best be getting out now. The beast will be eating for a while yet. You don't want to be here when he finishes," he said, jerking his thumb at large shovels leaning against the wall. Gwen's eyes widened in horror and she clambered down the oreamos's leg. Lelial joined her at the base of the creature. He threw one feathered arm over her shoulder.

"It seems the welcoming committee neglected to show. I suppose I'll have to shoulder this burden as well. Come along, I'll show you around," Lelly said, and he led her to a passage off the main hangar.

Cradle had the atmosphere of a military base. Every piece of it was designed for function rather than form. Men and women trooped up the halls, moving with the iron discipline and speed of monastery novices. The marchers were clad in dark green uniforms of heavy cotton fabric with fur at the edges of the collars and cuffs, far too warm for the moderate atmosphere of Cradle, but perfect for the snows and storms that waited outside. Each marcher had a tool belt at his or her waist, packed with equipment of all shapes and sizes like a flashlight, fire starters, maps, compass, telescope, and even flintlock pistols.

Each carried bags that were secured by at least three heavy brass locks. Bits of paper poked out of the corner of each bag. Before Gwen could examine further the marchers turned off the hallway.

"Ah, you've noticed our messengers. Such earnest young people. But don't worry about that. Your future can wait for a moment. Here, let me show you the Hub," Lelly said, and he led Gwen down a passage.

A dull thud met them in this space, and then another, and another. The same rhythmic crash of metal on metal, as if an iron wave was cresting and falling again and again. She saw that down some of the adjacent halls there were rooms filled with immense machines and workers hurrying about. As they flashed by a room, she saw a machine rear back before falling forward, producing that terrific noise. Lelly pulled her on, taking her further into the depths of Cradle until at last they arrived at their destination.

Here the ceiling was vaulted like a church. Workers labored at maps and ledgers across the room, speaking in hushed tones. Massive windows covered the walls and Gwen could see that they were now in between the two mountains, and atop the Cradle itself. A vista of swirling white snow lay just beyond those windows, but she could not hear the howls of the wind here. Technicians worked at banks of switches and lights, hands dancing across the panels. Some others took notes at machines that looked to Gwen like the kind that measured earthquakes.

Maps of various kinds littered the room. Some were topographical, showing mountain ranges and ravines across the planet. Still other maps showed air currents and wind patterns, and corvids traced delicate lines across the face of the maps, taking careful measurements with compasses and tools Gwen did not recognize. While the map keepers labored, they looked again and again at the sculpture in the middle of the room, making minute adjustments based on what it showed.

Gwen looked upon a model of the world. The globe was four times the size of her, and it hung from the ceiling like a chandelier. Mountain ranges rose from the face of the sculpture, and though some were no larger than Gwen's thumb, each was carved with frightening accuracy. Oceans danced across its surface; continents were etched onto its face. Cities stretched across the metal, along with roads, bridges, ferries, and trade routes spinning out from these. It was a map of the world, made of interlocking tiles like an immense patchwork quilt.

And it turned.

"Bit more impressive than a snowball, huh?" Lelly asked.

Gwen heard the dull thud of a cane on the stone floor and turned and saw another corvid coming towards them. While Lelly seemed to radiate untidiness, this corvid was elegant, orderly, and covered in feathers of pure white. Gwen knew at once this corvid was the real deal, and she fell to one knee in front of the preceptor.

"Our reprobate has returned, I see. At last, our peace and quiet shatters," the corvid said, her voice much smoother than Lelial's. She did not spare a glance for Gwen. "Have you brought what I asked for, Lelial, or have you brought nothing but excuses once again?"

"Grigori, how wonderful to see you again, darling. As ever, you charm and delight," Lelly said with a bow.

"Yes, I believe I do. And who is this that you brought into our observatory?" she asked, eyeing Gwen with one shining eye.

"Our newest recruit. Fresh from the monastery itself. Sadly, those savages neglected to tell her the purpose of all this. I was providing some help."

"Those 'savages' as you say do important and necessary work, Lelial. Work you need not concern yourself with. I trust the girl has been trained and has sworn the oaths?"

"I do believe so. Though, as I said, she does not understand the meaning of it all."

"She does not need to. She need only play her part; one I am sure she is eager to get to. Lina!" she screeched, and a young woman that had been standing at attention at the far side of the room rushed to her side. "Show our recruit to the messengers wing. See that she understands what to do. And you, Lelial, best have those maps I requested, or I will throw you from Cradle with a smile." Lina nodded, and Grigori turned back to the globe, dismissing Gwen without a thought.

And just like that, Gwen was back under the control of the preceptors. She had had four hours of freedom and a single smile.

Lina gestured at her from the door, and Gwen turned to leave. Lelly's clawed hand reached out and gripped her shoulder, talons digging into her skin.

"Wait," he whispered, looking at a device along that wall that seemed to be counting down. "Don't mind the old bird. I wanted you to see this." The room's energy shifted. The people working at the maps slowed, but those at the windows and at the switches and the seismometer became frantic, scribbling and flicking at breakneck speed. A klaxon began to wail above their heads, and the lights flashed around them. Grigori stood before the immense globe, her eyes burning into its depths, cane clutched in her hands. The room held its breath as the clock hit zero, and then the tiles moved.

Like a rock dropped into a still pond, ripples began to shake across the globe's surface. Its pieces sprung into sudden and violent motion, twisting and turning as they rattled across the surface of the planet into new positions. Islands became peninsulas, landlocked nations jumped into the ocean, mighty rivers shifted course, crashing over new landscapes.

And, just as suddenly as it had started, it stopped. Grigori stood before the globe with not a feather ruffled. She watched as Poa settled into place, and then uttered one single word. "Go."

The technicians zoomed back into action, throwing old maps aside and pulling out fresh sketch pads to capture the new shape of the planet, to measure its rebirth. Lelly's claw let go of Gwen's shoulder.

"Now do you believe me?" he whispered.

His arm swept out, pointing at the mountain range beyond the windows. And Gwen's jaw dropped. She had remained still, but the world had changed. The wind carved through a new landscape; snow fell on flowers that had once enjoyed summer. Gone was the candy landscape she had admired on the way to Cradle.

105

"I hope you understand what your place in all this is, Gwen. The world is an ever-changing place, a place of chaos. But you will show the world itself, and you will do it with this." Lelly handed her a bundle of paper, so like the kind that the messengers had carried in their bags. Ink crawled across its pages, forming pictures and lines of text. Some words were larger and demanded attention, others were as thin and delicate as ants. Gwen unfolded the paper, the motions well practiced. She saw the masthead at the top of the newspaper. *The Bird's Eye Herald.*

"You have been wondering at your place in all this? You deliver the paper, Gwen. You deliver the Truth," Lelly said, and he looked over his shoulder at Lina. "Show her how she does this."

Gwen followed Lina to the door, the paper still clutched in her hands. Lina took her through stone halls away from Grigori and Lelial and their moving world. The halls were lit with dull candles and the odd electric light. The stones were cracked beneath her feet, and all around Gwen was information that the preceptors had trained her to process and master. All around her was the task she was meant to carry out as the new instrument of the *Herald*, but she ignored all of it. She was in another place.

The Bird's Eye Herald. She had heard that name before. A laughing boy had come to her door, whooping about what he had done. In his hands he had cradled a bundle of rough papers painted and scratched with ink. He had laughed as he told her the title of the newspaper he had invented, one that had all the gossip of the neighborhood and every childhood secret he could find. And in his hands was the first edition of the brand-new *Bird's-Eye Herald.*

Gwen followed Lina as she took her further and further into the bowels of Cradle, to its innermost depths. She talked as she walked, but Gwen did not hear. All she heard was the laughter of that boy as he showed her his newest creation and asked her to help him write the first article. How could Huck's paper be here in this world? He had died, and all his laughter had died long before that.

Gwen snapped back to the present when she heard the first chirps and clicks. Lina led her into that sound, explaining. "We must deliver at night you see. Otherwise, everyone would see us coming and try to stop us, or worse, get spooked by us. Don't worry though, when you're riding one it isn't nearly as loud." Lina opened the door.

Gwen saw a room without a floor, revealing the far distant valley below. Hanging in this open space, clinging to the roof above, were massive bats. And when they noticed her, they began to screech.

And she remembered now, one of the first articles she helped Huck write was about how he had seen bats perch in the tree next to his bedroom window, and that the neighbors should watch out for vampires.

And now here were the *Herald*'s delivery vehicles, bats the size of trains. Gwen hoped, deep in the bottom of her soul, that they did not bite.

Below the whirs and clicks of the bats Gwen could hear Huck's high snorting laughter, and she could not help but join in.

Chapter 9: The Detective's First Investigation

I have tried my hand at learning several of the Cognitive Domains, but I seem to have no affinity for them thus far. The cogonauts I have encountered assure me this is not uncommon. They claim every person has the potential to learn a domain, but most lack the will. I do not feel I lack will, however, but something else.
(Letter 4, Paragraph 2, Lines 5-8)

"Okay, how about Barnaby? Seems you don't like that one. Hercule? No, I don't really like that one either, little too formal. Sherlock! No? That one's a classic," Finley said to the glowing flower hidden underneath his shirt. The flower flashed dully back at him and shook its petals.

"Fine, fine, fine. You're quite picky for a glowing flower you know? Look, I need to call you something, and you can't talk. How about you give me some help? What kind of name do you want?" Finley asked, and the flower flashed once more, and the afterimage of a familiar scene floated briefly in front of Finley's eyes. It was a picture of a young man in a gray suit surrounded by gravestones. The young man was tall and gawky. His mouth was open in shock, and his eyes wide with wonder.

"What are you a camera now or something? Doesn't matter, delete that one would you? I look like a goofball. That's the moment we first met, right? Why did you show it to me again?" Finley said, rubbing the spots from his eyes. The flower spun happily inside its cotton confinement.

"What can I say, you made quite an impression on me too, buddy. Still, it doesn't answer the question, what kind of name do you want?" The flower flashed again, and again that same image appeared, but this time Finley got the gist of the message.

"No, absolutely not. Finley is MY name. It can't be yours too." The flower shook again, giving off soft flashes of red and yellow lights.

"Because it would be confusing, that's why. Keep thinking."

"What in the Shepherd's name are you doing?" said a ringing voice in front of Finley.

Deputy Moro stood in front of Finley, frustration radiating from her like heat. She was young, only slightly older than Finley himself, if

108

he had to guess. Muscles bulged under her uniform, and every step was more of a stomp. Her eyes were as dark as her cap, and they glared at Finley for flashes of time before circling him and scanning the rest of the street.

"I'm discussing the case with my partner."

"No, you are not. You're just spouting gibberish."

"That's an important part of the discussion."

"Well, keep it down, you're causing a scene" Moro said, and she jerked her head at the people walking by. Each person had varying degrees of disgust and curiosity on their faces.

"Morning everyone. Don't mind us, police business." Finley said.

Moro gave a snort of annoyance and walked off again.

Finley hurried to catch up. "You know, I've always wanted to say that. How did it sound?"

Moro did not reply.

"That bad, huh? Well, I guess some practice will help with that," he quipped.

Moro's eyebrows continued to cloud like thunderheads. Finley considered that a small improvement over simple silence.

"By the way, I'm trying to find a name for my partner. Any suggestions?"

"A name?"

"Something by which to call it, yes."

"Why doesn't the thing have a name?"

"Not a thing, it's my partner. And it might, for all I know. It can't talk, you see. I've been listing names, but it doesn't seem to like any. Might be because they're names from my world." Moro turned to look at him again, her brow coming together. "Ah, Orsos must have forgotten to mention it. I'm from another planet. Finley Marsh."

"The name of your planet is Finley Marsh?"

"What? No, the name of my planet is Earth. My name's Finley Marsh, and I'm still trying to find out what this guy's name is. Course, it might not be a guy. I can't really tell with flowers." Moro turned away again, leading him further into the city. The silence lingered between them until Finley got the message.

"Well, let me know if you come up with any names. She's thinking about it," he whispered to the flower in his shirt. It spun round again.

Finley interpreted that as a shrug, and he gave his own. They walked further into the depths of Oshroar.

Moro led him down the backstreets of the city, far from the hustle and bustle of the main thoroughfares. The streets were cloaked in the shade of the buildings that loomed to either side. The roads themselves were stone worn down by the passage of thousands of feet across the surface.

Some of these feet had been made of stone.

Guardians trooped up and down the road. Some held burdens such as boxes of fruit, cartons of books, or equipment of various kinds. Still other Guardians carried people in tall carriages that kept them level with the tops of the buildings. Finley craned his neck to see these lofty travelers. They too wore clashing, colorful clothing. They perched on the Guardian's shoulders like birds of paradise, looking down their beaks at those who walked below. Finley had never seen a more uncomfortable way to travel.

The Guardians themselves were far less noticeable than the people they served, despite their impressive size and bulk. Each one was made of local stone, and they blended into the background of the buildings and alleys with ease. The Guardians all had the same harsh stone face with only the suggestions of facial features: a slab of a jaw, the harsh cut of a mouth, cavernous eyes with burning embers in their depths. They varied in size, they varied in function, but they all moved the same. Their motions were slow and smooth, careful and plodding.

The flower burrowed into his shirt and began to dull in what seemed to be its version of a nap. He was calm, Finley reminded himself, he was collected, and he was on a mission. He could figure out why he was in this alien world later, but for right now he had more important things to worry about.

Huck. He had to learn what happened to Huck. The desire burned through him like fire. And the only way to learn more was to play the part of detective.

Moro led him further and further through the labyrinth of alleyways and side passages. The great bulk of the Shepherd loomed far overhead, its outstretched arms keeping the entire city within its grasp. It gazed down on its city with an expression Finley could not identify.

"What is that thing, if you don't mind me asking?"

"The Shepherd."

"Yes, I gathered that much. But what is it? Who built it? What is it for? Is it supposed to be a statue of someone?" Finley rattled off the questions and caught the look of annoyance that Moro threw him. "I'm new in town, and Orsos never gave me a straight answer."

"I didn't expect to play tour guide."

"It will at least pass the time as we walk. Or I could keep trying to figure out my partner's name…"

"No, no. You don't need to do that. The Shepherd has always been there, I suppose. Ever since they founded the city he's been there. He doesn't do anything except sit there and watch over us. So, no I don't think he's for anything either. Although sometimes, if you stand just right when you're watching over the gate to the city his hand will just cover you up with some nice shade," Moro said, her voice trailing off wistfully.

"That's it? He's just for shade? Why not build a giant umbrella then?"

"I didn't say he was just for shade, did I?" Moro retorted. "He does loads more than that just by being around. He's what the Council says is the reason for all their decisions. They all say something is 'in the Shepherd's name' or 'done in the Shepherd's shadow.'"

"So he's like a king."

"More like a patron, a sort of Guardian. He's always watching over us, so we have to do him proud, have to act well in his name, that sort of thing."

"Interesting. He's a giant conscience for the whole city."

"If that's the way you want to think of it."

"Do any of the temples or priests claim to speak to him? Or speak for him?"

"They can't, can they? Because we would hear him speaking too. He's got a great big mouth you see," Moro said, and as he looked at her he saw her crack the faintest hint of a smile.

"Moro, did you just crack a joke? I had no idea you had a sense of humor."

"Don't know what you're talking about, Marsh."

"Uh huh. Who built him?"

111

"No one knows. Or at least, no one knows for sure. He was here long before we got here, long before the City. And we've always been well off in his shadow. Crops rarely fail. We've never been in a war, at least not for long. Even the tiles turning always seems to work out. We never end up next to one of those roaming states you read about in the *Herald*, or near one of those freak nature places. It's like we have the only peace and quiet in the entire world. Or at least we did until recently."

"What about the Guardians?" he asked, keeping half an ear turned for any thundering steps behind him.

"They came with the mountain and the Shepherd, and they've been with us ever since."

"How do they work?"

"They just do. They come from the Shepherd himself, cast in his image so to speak, and they're here to help us. We're on our way to the people that oversee them right now. The oldest religion in the City, they call themselves the Crooken. Save your questions for them."

"Yes, of course," Finley said. So, it was something that everyone relied on that few understood, like electricity back on Earth.

"My mother told me a story once about the Shepherd, when I was just a little girl. I was a lot smaller then, and I got picked on. I came home from school, all busted up and crying and she took me outside and told me to look at the Shepherd. She said that he was one of the first people that ever walked the world, and that he was Vovatum's first follower. Except she said that back then the Shepherd was one of the littlest people too," Moro said, her voice slipping into a higher cadence, her tone becoming softer, gentler.

"Everyone was huge back then, bigger than mountains, because there was so much more food and space than there is now. Everyone could be as big as they liked. But the Shepherd was still the smallest, so he got picked on all the time just like me. They beat on him, and they told him to do the stuff that no one else wanted to do, like carve up canyons, or catch meteors. But the Shepherd was a tough kid and never let it get him down. He took all the worst jobs and tasks they gave him and did it with a grin, which only made everyone madder of course. But he kept doing it anyway," Moro said, a grin on her own face.

"One day they beat him worse than ever before, so he couldn't do any work at all. He found a mountain all by itself and he curled up and cried just like I had, until he heard a little voice in his ear. The voice said, 'Don't cry now. I have important work for you to do. And the Shepherd said, 'Leave me alone. Can't you see I'm too hurt to do any work?' and the voice said, 'I said stop crying. I'm Vovatum, your god, and I need you to do something for me.' So, the Shepherd sat up and asked the voice what he was supposed to do. And the voice told him to look at a group of people walking towards the mountain, but these were the smallest people the Shepherd had ever seen, they were like ants to him.

"And Vovatum said, 'These are my people, and I need you to watch them for me, since I can't be around all the time.' The Shepherd was amazed and said, 'But why me? I'm so small and useless.' And the god said, 'That's why I want you to do it. They're small too, and you'll understand them, and watch over them, and help them, because only someone who was once small and weak can help someone feel strong. Would you please?' And the Shepherd said he would. And that's how the city of Oshroar started, my mother said. We were Vovatum's people, but the Shepherd watched over us, and one day we would be big and strong like him too," Moro said, finishing her story with an embarrassed flush.

"Is that why you became a warden?"

"No. I became a warden because I grew up big and mean and in this job, I could hit people and not get in trouble for it."

"Of course. How silly of me."

They emerged in a plaza at the Shepherd's feet. Temples warred for dominance over the square. They struck at each other with elaborate architecture, flying buttresses, filigree, and an army of statues. Worshippers and priests and priestesses moved about the plaza discussing matters of spirit and body.

Moro led Finley across the plaza, paying little mind to the routes and routines of the priests and their flock. He tried to apologize to the priests as they passed, but not one would meet his eye.

"What a shy bunch," Finley remarked.

"They don't much like wardens. Think we're a bit too big for our britches."

"How shocking. Will any of them speak to us?"

"The ones we're going to will. Don't pay any mind to this bunch of birds. They're only the front men."

"Is it one religion here, or are there many?" Finley asked, scanning the vestments of the priests as they passed. He saw icons of stars and moons and other celestial bodies. He saw more complex logos of various animals, and even more abstract sigils that he could not decipher.

"There's a bunch of them. I lost count a while ago. They fall in and out of fashion in town. Sometimes they raise a ruckus down in the lower ranges, but mostly they stick up here and out of our way. It's only the richies that really pay attention to them, treat it like it's some kind of sport. Pay it no mind. We're talking to the only ones worth mentioning."

She led Finley to a narrow path at the far end of the plaza. Here the temples and buildings were pressed directly against the Shepherd's skin, crowding for space in the mile long gap between its feet. They took the path, and the buildings began to disappear and were replaced by narrow canyon walls. They walked into the depths of the mountain and the light began to thin as the walls of the canyon rose higher and higher. They walked on until they came to a door carved into the rock of the mountain.

It was a plain, simple door made of rough-hewn wood and iron nails. Moro knocked once, and the sound boomed down the narrow valley behind them. The door opened and a wiry old man filled the doorframe. He had silver hair, and great bushy eyebrows he kept caged behind thick black framed glasses.

"Oh hello," he said, his voice warm and surprised. "We weren't expecting any visitors today."

"Warden business, sir," Moro said,

"Yes, of course. Please come in. Although I must ask you to take your shoes off, I've just swept up the place."

As he slipped his black wingtips off Finley scanned the place. Unlike the grand opulence of the plaza, this temple was austere. The room was small and round, with a raised ceiling, made of the same rock as the canyon. Rough carvings were gouged into the rock, depicting scenes from myth. Iron candelabras held yellow candles that

114

gave off shimmering and cheerful light. A hallway led off from the top of the room, though it bent so Finley could not see what it led to. Other than the candelabras and the door, it looked no different from a cave. The man matched the setting, wearing a simple brown robe smudged with dirt and dust.

The stone was cool beneath Finley's socks as he left his shoes by the door. Moro left her boots on. The old man's eyes flicked down to the boots, and his lips pursed.

"Hello," Finley cut in before the man could speak. "My name is Finley Marsh, I'm a special detective with the wardens. Pittsburgh branch. Do you have time to answer some questions?"

Finley saw Moro glance at him for a moment, wary of what he might do. But the moment passed, and she relaxed, staying back as Finley stepped forward. She seemed willing to let the alien take the lead. For now.

"I suppose I do, sir," the man said with some confusion. "I'm afraid the other clerics are in the midst of services just now, and I must begin preparing the mid-day meal for them, so if we could make it quick."

"Of course, really it should take no time at all. Can we start with your name please?"

"Fodor Marton."

"And Mr. Marton, what are your duties here in the temple?"

"I am in charge of all the domestic details, food and cleaning and what not."

"And you've been in the position for how long?"

"Ever since I first joined the clerics, some thirty years ago."

"And do you like your job?" Finley asked. He figured he should start with the easy questions in interrogation. The detectives in the stories always tried to set the suspect at ease first. He pulled a little notebook and a pencil from his inner pocket. He had swiped it from a desk jockey back in HQ, figuring the part of detective needed the right props.

"I do. I would not have been here for as long as I have if not." Finley doodled across the page as he listened to Fodor, making a show of diligently listening. He scratched an address into the paper before ripping the note off the pad.

115

"I'm sure, Fodor, I'm sure. And I gotta say this is one of the cleanest temples I've ever been in. And very nicely decorated as well. Could you explain those carvings along the walls?" Finley asked, gesturing to the images etched into the rock.

He moved closer, and saw the same icon repeated over and over, that of a man sitting high atop a mountain above a growing city. One carving had him standing at the crest of the mountain speaking to the sun. Another had the figure crouching low over the city, shielding it from some terrible storm. Again and again the image of the Shepherd appeared on the carvings, and always the city slumbered in his shadow as he protected it from some great evil. But Finley was looking for something else, however, and he found it in the image above the door frame.

Here were figures in mourning carrying a departed loved one with them. Here they laid the departed to rest in a field filled with gravestones. Here the stars fell and danced above the graves. The flower stirred below his shirt, and Finley raised his hand to quiet it, knowing the time was not yet right.

"I'm afraid I just clean the carvings. If you want the stories about them, you'll have to ask the clerics. They know much more about them than me," Fodor said, giving a little shrug.

"Yes, of course. I am very eager to learn about that one," Finley said, pointing to the image of the Ghostlights above the door.

And as their eyes followed his finger to the carving, he dropped a small wad of paper from his hand to the ground below.

"Where are you from, detective?"

"Special detective. And I'm from very far from here. I'm sure you've never heard of it. But I've been in town for a few days, and I've seen some things I can't explain. Could you help me out with that, Fodor?" Fodor pulled back some, but nodded nonetheless. Moro still stood off to the side. Finley met eyes with her over Fodor's shoulder. She seemed amused by his little show, but she let it continue.

"My partner here tells me that this is where the Guardians come from. Is that right?"

"Yes, it is our duty to handle the distribution."

"And who set you that task?"

"The Shepherd himself of course."

"Do you help in this process, Fodor? Do you direct the Guardians?"

"Not everyone has the gift," a new voice said behind Finley. He and Moro turned and saw a man and a woman emerging from the tunnels. The man was short with a vast barrel chest perched on stubby powerful legs. The woman was taller than he, with a high proud forehead and large hands clasped in front of her body as if in prayer. Both were dressed in simple brown sackcloth, yet they walked with purpose and power.

"Wardens. How may we help you today?" the man said, and his voice was rough and low.

"We have questions," Moro said, and Finley saw her muscles flexing beneath her jacket.

"Do you now? And what makes you think you have any right to ask them?"

"What right?" Moro said, flaring up. "What right?"

"Merely the concerns of any citizen," Finley said, sliding in front of Moro to stop the storm. "Why, a policeman without questions to ask would be like a priest without prayers to lead. Allow us to introduce ourselves. This is Warden Moro and I am Special Detective Finley—"

"We know who you are," the woman said, and Finley's eyes flashed to her. She looked at him with distaste, as if he were a rat upon the street, and it was a familiar look.

"You're the priestess from before, the one from the graveyard. Sister Sinoh, you look even more radiant than before," Finley said, and he swept into a bow.

"The last time we met you had just barged into a funeral," Sinoh said, her nose wrinkled with disgust.

"I apologize for that. My arrival was not at all what I intended, in many ways."

"Orsos arrested you for your offense, and now you are a 'special detective' for the wardens?"

"What can I say? I'm a fast riser."

"Really? I find it more likely that Orsos seeks ever more creative ways to aggravate me."

"Well, we might have that in common. I do have questions that need answering, Sister. And I will not leave until they are answered."

The man beside Sinoh puffed up at this remark and moved to Finley with his arms outstretched. Moro brushed past Finley to meet the man as Fodor cowered in the corner of the room. Yet before the two could meet, both Sinoh and Finley reached out for their respective champions, restraining their movement.

"There is no need for anger, Gaspar. We will play their little games, for now."

"Thank you, Sinoh," Finley said, as Moro eased back to his side and Gaspar moved to stand beside the Sister. The four eyed each other across the room. The flower stirred inside Finley's cloak, but remained hidden, for now.

"The Guardians," Finley said, skipping the preamble. "Everyone uses them, but no one knows a thing about them, except for you."

"Yes."

"Could you illuminate me? Why are the Crooken the only ones that are said to have the knowledge about the Guardians?"

"It is our right, and no one else's. Hardly anyone has faith and the strength necessary to serve the Shepherd and learn its secrets."

"Hence why I've come to you. People are dying, Sister Sinoh, and if I want to save them then I'm going to need some enlightenment."

"Ask away, Finley, I'm eager to hear what has brought you to my door."

"How do the Guardians work?"

"By faith alone."

"I don't buy that for a second, Sister."

She smirked. "Not many do. Yet it is the truth."

"I've seen wonders, Sister, that you would not believe. Yet I have never seen stone move by itself. How do you make them?"

"They are miracles, Finley. I do not expect an uninitiated to understand how they are created."

"What powers the Guardians? Who gives the commands?" Finley said, trying a different tact.

"The Shepherd created them, Finley, and he moves them now. They are aspects of his form, of his mind, created to help and guide his flock."

"His sheepdogs, then," Finley said, watching for her mask to crack. Yet her face remained haughty and superior.

"I beg your pardon. What is a sheepdog?"

"Earth reference, pay it no mind. How long do the Guardians last? Do they need much upkeep or repair?"

"The Guardians will last as long as this mountain stands, detective. So quite a long time. The Guardians in this city served my mother, and her mother before her, and on and on, since the first humans walked this land. They will always be with us."

"Someone is murdering them," Finley said, and he watched, waiting for her eyes to widen and her cheeks to flush.

Her face remained still.

"Ah, I see you are a believer in this insane theory that Orsos has been spreading. Guardians are not people, Finley. They cannot be murdered. The warden is simply using the few broken Guardians he has discovered to further his own ends and carry out his mad crusade against some of the more...erratic portions of our populace."

"You're aware of the four broken Guardians in the morgue then?"

"Of course. The Guardians are meant to last forever, but we are a chaotic and messy people, us humans, and this is a chaotic and messy world. Sometimes the eternal breaks. I told Orsos as much when he first discussed the matter with me," Sinoh said, her hands clasped tighter before her.

"I've never heard of a Guardian breaking," Moro said at Finley's side.

"It is not common knowledge. We feel it would be unwise for people to find out that the thing they rely upon most is not as stable as they thought."

"And it would make you look pretty bad too, wouldn't it?" Finley said, watching Sinoh. She withdrew her arms, clasping them in front of herself again.

"You are a cynical boy."

"I just know a lie when I see one," Finley said, turning away from the scene and pacing the room. His bare socks slipped a little as he walked across the cold stone. He could feel the eyes of the others on him as he walked, but he let them wait. He was warming to the part now, and it seemed like he was actually good at being a special detective.

119

But what did this have to do with Huck? Why did the Ghostlight care at all about any of this? He strained for the connection but couldn't spot it yet.

"Nothing lasts forever, huh? I can buy that. You wanting to save face in front of the entire city I understand too. But why are you so quick to rule out foul play? I saw the bodies myself, Sister. They were not broken by falling masonry or a runaway carriage. We have evidence that something or someone turned them off; flicked a switch and they were dead as doornails. I want to know why someone would do that, and how. And I want to know why you are lying to me."

Sinoh watched him now, and her eyes reflected him like dark pools.

"What has Orsos told you, Finley? Do you even know where he is right now? He did not send you to me because you have some rare genius, or because he knew you could get me to open up. No. He sent you as a distraction, dear boy, but I see through it. Gaspar, where is our dear warden?"

"He's in the lower ranges, Sister. He and his men are kicking in doors across the city as we speak. At last count, he has arrested almost one hundred men and women," Gaspar said, rattling off the information with ease.

"Mass arrests then. He knew I would oppose such a thing in the council. Is this really the kind of man you wish to support, Finley? One who uses you to carry out tyrannical rule?"

"Are you trying to convince me that Orsos is an evil guy? I don't need convincing. The man threw me in a cell for being in the wrong place at the wrong time. He threatened to kill me if I got in his way, but he hasn't lied to me, Sister. And I'm more than just a distraction," Finley said, tamping down his worries. He pushed it all far away, until only the mystery was there, the one that might lead him to Huck's killer. And he had a winning move still to play.

He whistled long and loud and the glowing flower rocketed out of his shirt sleeve. The Ghostlight flew into the air with a flourish and threw a shining light into every inch of the room, resting above his head like a star.

Fodor gasped behind Finley as the flower pulsed with light. Gaspar shielded his eyes, and even Moro cried aloud. And Sinoh, for the briefest of seconds, dropped her iron mask. The light of the flower reflected in her eyes as she looked without blinking at Finley.

"A Ghostlight," Fodor whispered behind him.

Finley grinned. "It's my partner."

"Release it at once!" Gaspar growled. "You know not what you play with, boy. You tamper with forces beyond your understanding."

"True. All too true. I do have a habit of sticking my nose in places it does not belong. But I'm not holding the flower against its will. You like me, dontcha?"

The flower buzzed over his head, shining a deep blue.

"That's right. And if the Ghostlight likes me, maybe you should too? Let's try this again, answer my questions, and you can be my friends. Otherwise, you'll miss your chance to speak with my partner."

Gaspar's glare slipped from his face as he gazed in rapt awe at the Ghostlight spinning about the room. Fodor was muttering prayers under his breath.

"That's right. They never stick around people, do they? Hundreds of years and no one has ever been able to touch them or even speak to them. This fella has been by my side for the last two days. I may be new to your religion, but judging by all the imagery, I'm guessing my little buddy is important to you." Finley watched as the cleric's hands twitched at his sides, warring with his need to break Finley for his arrogance and his need to reach out and seize the light.

"It is the spirit for the fallen, returned to shine a light for the lost," Sinoh said, her eyes never leaving Finley's face.

"Well then, I'm here to guide you home, Sister. Answer my questions, and I'm sure I can convince my partner to give you what you ask," Finley said, his heart racing as he watched Sinoh's eyes slide from his face to the light hovering above his head.

Time to take advantage of their shock.

"How many Guardians are in the city?" Finley demanded, but Sinoh remained silent, considering the flower. Gaspar rasped out a response, as the flower shifted into a deep purple light.

"At last count, 12,543 active Guardians."

"How many fall apart every year?"

"None."

"Every century?"

"None," Gaspar said, his face vacant as he looked at the light.

"Have any ever died?"

Gaspar's eyes flicked to Finley's for a single second, before switching back to the Ghostlight.

"No."

"Can they be deactivated? How do you deactivate them?"

"I don't know," Gasper said, his eyes flicking towards Sinoh.

"How do you make a Guardian?" Finley asked, and Gaspar was sweating now. His face was flushed with excitement as he looked at the Ghostlight.

"Gaspar, that is enough," Sinoh said, her voice as still as a clear pool.

"Sister, he has a Ghostlight. Our scholars have tried to study them for centuries, and we have never gotten this close. They're supposed to be the guides of the dead. It could help us speak to the ancients, to the Shepherd, to my dear Soran," Gaspar said, his voice dropping to a whisper at the end. "We could learn things; we could learn how to—"

"Gaspar, you will control yourself," Sinoh said, cutting him off, her eyes shifting once more to Finley's face. The calm had vanished. There was anger in her eyes at last.

"It is obvious that this is just another of Orsos's tricks. A ruse to draw our attention while he inflicts martial law on our city. Do you really believe that such a sign from Shepherd would appear to this man and not to one of us…to you?" Sinoh said, speaking to Gaspar without looking at him. The man's face warred with itself. Awe was soon replaced with the flicker of suspicion.

"How could this outsider, this interloper, obtain what we never have? Such a thing is impossible. Why would the Shepherd not choose one of his faithful?" Sinoh said, and now the look of suspicion in Gaspar's face became the dark light of malice. His eyes returned to Finley, hatred in them now.

"No. It would have been one of us. You're right. Just another trick," Gaspar said, a look of divine anger appearing on his face as he looked again at the Ghostlight, searching for the mirrors and lights it must surely be. "Would you like me to throw them out?"

"No, no. That would be far too dignified. I grow tired of their tricks." And her hands clicked at her sides. Moro moved in front of

Finley, shielding him from Gaspar. She reached for the nightstick dangling from her belt, but as she raised it the walls opened their eyes.

Dull green orbs opened in the panels carved in the walls, and as one they all moved to glare at Finley.

The walls shook and groaned as the carved figures of men pulled themselves from the depths of the mountain, clambering out of the walls to form up in front of the clerics. The Guardians stood in rows, filling the small room with their bulk. Dust and grit spilled from their shoulders as they moved into position, but their eyes shone without flicker, and Finley could hear the crunch of their tightening fists.

"You threatening us, Sinoh?" Moro growled. "Guardians can't kill people, remember. They're here to protect us."

"But as you well know, Moro, they can certainly hurt people. For their own good, of course."

Moro turned to Finley. "We might want to leave."

"You think?" Finley said. The Ghostlight started to whistle and flicker blue.

Finley and Moro retreated. He fumbled for the door as they moved away from the now marching wall of sacred rock. They stumbled into the valley, inches ahead of the encroaching landslide.

Finley raced down the narrow canyon with Moro at his back as he glanced left and right in desperate terror that here too the walls would grow eyes of sinister green.

He pumped his legs, desperate for the light of the plaza and the many witnesses there. The Ghostlight glowed above his head, sending their crooked shadows onto the canyon walls that echoed with the marching stone feet behind them.

They burst through, and Finley fell to the hard stone tiles of the plaza as Moro gasped at his side. The brightly colored priests of the plaza lifted their robes as they walked by, but Finley saw the smirks lurking at the corner of their mouths. They looked down the canyon towards the temple beyond, but there were no Guardians in sight. With a gasp, Finley turned over onto his back to look at the Shepherd towering overhead and thought what a fool he was for thinking that this was all a game.

"Oh crap. I left my shoes there."

Chapter 10: The Detective's Intro to Interrogations

I am leaving these letters at whatever Herald station I can find. I hope at least one of you will find them, and it will begin to answer your questions. I know not why we were separated when we landed, but I hope we will find each other soon.
(Letter 5, Paragraph 5, Lines 6-9)

Finley did not like to lose. Even as a child he had felt burning anger at every lost kickball game, at every trophy without his name on it. However, the world was quick to punish a sore loser, and so Finley had begun to adapt. He had faked his good cheer, his nonchalance as others walked off crowned with glory.

Yet there was one kind of loss that Finley could never accept. He hated feeling like a fool. It happened with riddles and challenges. Brain teasers and puzzles. It didn't matter. He knew he could solve them, but sometimes, for whatever reason, the answer would elude him, and he had to ask for help. And he hated that almost as much as losing.

Finley contemplated this flaw in his character as he trooped back to the Warden HQ, Moro following in his wake. His sock-clad feet slid and slipped on the cobblestones as he walked. She grumbled at his side, stamping her boots into the pavement, as if punishing it for the embarrassment they had suffered. Finley wished that he had that luxury of stamping but knew that he would look foolish stamping in socks. He contented himself, instead, with a stream of low-grade profanities. He tried every curse he knew, in every language, but eventually he ran out.

"How do you swear on this planet?" Finley asked Moro behind him.

"Oh, the normal ways. You've covered most of them to be honest. You can try 'Shepherd scorned' if you like. Usually, we use that after a bunch of bad luck, or for someone we really hate."

"Well, that suits me perfectly then. Shepherd scorned am I. Shepherd scorned are those uptight, self-righteous Crooken. Shepherd scorned is this whole situation!" This last one he hurled at the great statue that towered over the city, stopping in the middle of the street to do so.

"Are you done?" Moro asked, coming to a stop next to him.

"I think so," Finley said, deflating next to her. "Sorry about that. Those were the only pair of shoes I had on the whole planet. I left all my others back on Earth, and I have no idea what the whole footwear situation is here."

"That's what's bothering you?"

"Yup."

"You're not upset by the whole being chased out of the temple district by unstoppable Guardians then?"

"Well yes. I do admit that put a bit of a damper on my day. But the shoes are what are really pissing me off right now."

"Ah, very mature on your part. The reveal of your partner did not go over as you expected, did it?"

"No, it did not." Finley admitted. He couldn't help feeling like Huck would be laughing at him right now, despite missing an opportunity to learn more about his death. The Ghostlight, meanwhile, refused to return to its hiding place under his jacket. Instead, it twirled between Moro and Finley, orbiting them like a moon caught between two planets.

The chase had not put a damper in the flower's happiness. Finley looked at it, envying its good mood, and then he caught himself getting jealous of a flower, and descended even deeper into the foul depths of surliness.

"I was hoping for shock and awe, not shock and anger. People don't like to give you answers when they're angry, mostly they just want to break your face in."

"I noticed. You had quite an effect on them. I've had a few run-ins with them before, but they've never acted like that. It's almost impressive how badly you upset them."

"Oh please, give me a challenge. I am the king of being insufferable! I could make a door want to maul me. I could convince a pacifist to attack me. I could make your dear statue wake up and squash me," Finley said, throwing back on the smile as he spun about, the flower orbiting him as well. He came to a stop, yet the flower still spun about him, urging him to join in the fun.

Finley reached out and caught the flower. It glowed with warmth in the palm of his hand, nuzzling into his grip for a second. He pushed it a little to his right, until it was exactly where he wanted it. He closed one eye and gazed once more at the Shepherd.

"Moro, I've redecorated your idol," Finley said, laughing as he stepped to the side, urging Moro to step into his place.

"What are you blabbering about now?" she said, bewildered, stepping forward.

"You need to bend down a bit. You're too tall to see," he said, and he positioned her so that her head was level with his and pointed at the Shepherd as well.

"See! I put a flower in his hair. I think he looks rather dashing," Finley said, cackling to himself. Moro looked once more at the Shepherd and had to admit that Finley was correct. From this exact angle, it looked like the floating, glowing flower was pinned in the Shepherd's hair.

"Yes. How creative," Moro said dryly, straightening once more. "And what was the point of all that?"

"Oh, you need to make your own fun, I always say. Lifted my spirits right up. He looks like a lovestruck Shepherd with our pal in his hair, doesn't he? 'Come live with me and be my love' and all that?" Finley said, and then he saw the look on Moro's face. "No, no, not you, Moro. Sorry. I was quoting. Do they have poetry here?"

"They do. I am not a fan."

"To each her own then. But it got me thinking of a name for you, pal," Finley said to the flower. It unfroze and floated over, colored a delicate blue. "How about Marlowe?"

The flower shifted a deeper blue, bobbing up and down. It deepened to purple as it stopped bouncing. Finley held his breath, and then gave a great whoop when the glowing flower spun into the air above them and gave off a pulse of white light.

"Marlowe it is then. Right, that's settled. I don't know about you, Moro, but I feel much better. One mystery down, another to go." Finley set off down the road, Marlowe still floating around him.

"Now that we have a name for you, we need to give you a rank as well. I'm a special detective, so you can be my special deputy." Marlowe flashed red at this.

"No, you can't be a special detective too." The flower flashed again.

"Because then neither one of us would be special, would we? You can't have herds of special detectives running around, then they're all just detectives. If you're a special deputy then you get your own rank and title all to yourself." The flower's color shifted to yellow at this. "It's thinking about it," Finley said to Moro.

"Can you actually understand what that thing—"

"Not a thing, it's my partner."

"Whatever, can you understand what the flower is saying?"

"A bit of both really. Mostly it's guesswork, but occasionally it sends images into my head. It seems to be able to play back memories from different perspectives too. It's shown me the image of our first meeting a couple of times. Anyways, the images help clear up the meaning."

"How lucky for you," Moro said, shuddering. "Care to share any of the terrific discoveries you both made in there? Or were you too busy running away to make any?"

"You were running as well, Moro. Everyone was. Seemed very popular at the time," Finley said, and Moro fell into step behind him. Yet she kept silent. Finley waited for her to prompt him for information again, but she seemed content to wait.

"You're ignoring me. You think that if you don't engage with me then I'll just fess up to what I found out to kill the silence. Well, it won't work. I am perfectly comfortable with silence. I love silence. It's a great time for silent reflection." Moro heeded this advice, and silently reflected as they walked down into the lower ranges of the city. Finley trooped along beside her, his gaze avoiding hers. The flower floated beside him. A minute passed, and the flower began to glow a dull pink. Another minute trickled by, and the flower was now glowing bright red. The long slow hands of time moved with glacial deliberation past another minute, and by then the flower was giving off a dull whine and with a great burst of "FINE," Finley launched into an explanation.

"We learned a great many things in that tomb of a temple. We learned that no one knows a thing about the Guardians except those Crooken, a fact they encourage and take advantage of. We learned that they're willing to kill to get our partner here. But we learned the most from what they refused to tell us," Finley said, his words rushing forth like a river through a bursting dam.

"Which was?"

"Gaspar. He was the weak one, anyone willing to show off how tough he is, those are always the weakest ones. Same with kids, same with adults. When he saw Marlowe here, I went after him, and he revealed quite a bit. However, it was not so much what he answered, but what he was not allowed to say. Did you notice what question Sister Sinoh cut him off from answering? 'How do you make a Guardian?' He was going to answer, but she set the guards on us before he could reveal it. I never expected to find out all the answers in our first questioning, but now we know the weak link in the chain. If we can get him alone, Gaspar will talk. Marlowe has a hold on him."

"Are you suggesting we bring him in for questioning?"

"Nothing so blunt. I expect he will seek us out himself. I left him a means of getting in contact with us."

"Which was?"

"I left a scrap of paper with an address in my shoe."

Moro turned to him, her mouth a flat line and her eyebrow raised. "You what?"

Finley grinned at her, and Marlowe glowed a beautiful gold as it twirled about them both.

"Oh yes. While Fodor was looking at the carving of the Ghostlight I dropped the address into my shoe. Either he or Gaspar will find it when they throw them out. I don't imagine for a second that Sinoh deigns to pick up shoes," Finley said, an impish smile on his face.

"You knew we were going to get chased out of there?"

"Well, no, I didn't know that," Finley said, his smile dimming slightly "I also didn't mean the note for Gaspar either. I meant to leave the shoes behind when we left, and then Fodor would come running to give them back to us and he would notice it then." And now the smile slipped from his face entirely as he pondered on the slim chance this plan had.

"What address was it?"

"Huh? Oh, it was just the address of a construction site I saw on the way into town with Orsos. I memorized it. That was back when I thought I was going to need to break out of warden jail and hide somewhere."

"So, you left a note in a smelly shoe for a janitor in the hopes he would meet you at some random address in the city. But that brilliant plan fell apart, so now you're hoping that a totally different man found that same smelly shoe note after he chased us out of his temple with an army of raging Guardians? And you think that man, who just tried to kill us, will then come to that address to see your ghost friend again? Is that about right?"

"Well, obviously it doesn't sound like a brilliant plan when you say it like that."

"It's not a plan! It's a series of random accidents you bumbled your way through that ends with a miracle that you're just hoping will happen."

"A lot of brilliant plans start out with accidents. It's all about, about," Finley was struggling now, the flower turning red with him, "creating opportunities."

"Creating opportunities?"

"Yeah."

"Did it sound like a better plan in your head?" Moro asked, not unkindly.

"It did, yeah. Not my best plan by any means. Certainly not my only one though."

"I'm sure."

Finley was getting a better handle of the city now that he had walked its streets for a day or so. Oshroar was a town of overwhelming extravagance. Each building competed with the others for the eye. Some did it with massive proportions: towering windows, rippling curtains, and pillars and columns that reached towards the sky. Other buildings stood on artistry alone, with panel upon panel depicting pastoral scenes or glorious battle. Perhaps one such Oshroaran building would have impressed, but taken as whole, Finley found the city's upper reaches grotesque. It was a side effect of the easy labor that each and every citizen had access to, Finley suspected. After all, it would take but a moment for a citizen to call forth a Guardian for a quick remodeling.

"There was one more thing we discovered, Moro. Did you notice, for instance, that when I asked him how many Guardians there were what his answer was?"

"He said there was something like 12,000 Guardians in the city."

"Does that number match the one you wardens have in your records?"

"Roughly, give or take a dozen or so. The ones in the walls at that temple were certainly a surprise. I don't see how that answer revealed anything particularly important though."

"Because that wasn't what he said. He said that there were 12, 543 active Guardians in the city. Active. That means there are inactive ones, and he didn't give a figure for those."

And Moro's face slowly lit up as she contemplated his word choice. "Active. He did say active. By the Shepherd, he said active! We only know about the ones we can see, the ones that move about and work. I've never heard of a Guardian without a job though, without something to do. They're always in motion."

"I thought as much. No one pays attention to the thing that always works, after all."

"But where are the inactive ones?"

"I have no idea. Clearly some were stored in the walls of the temple, but they could be anywhere else."

"In the walls, but that means..." Moro said, and fell suddenly silent. Her fists clenched at her sides, and her boots came down with new force on the cobblestone. Her head was pointed straight ahead, but Finley could see that her eyes were trained on the walls they walked alongside.

"Yes. It does. They could be anywhere. We should head back to the Warden HQ," Finley said, still trying to affect his usual swagger. But he could not stop the trickle of cold sweat that worked its way down his back. The walls were unmoving. For now.

They moved from the excess of the upper reaches into the low ranges of the city. Here the buildings were more uniform in shape and style. Washing lines with dripping clothes reached across alleys, flowers and pots and clinging vines worked their way along the walls and atop ledges.

And it looked like a hurricane had ripped through. Doors were in battered shards, as if they had been kicked in by stone feet. Windows were shattered, glass strewn about the street.

Children were weeping, calling out for parents who would not answer. The adults in the street whispered to each other, casting furtive glances at the warden by Finley's side.

"So this is what Sinoh was talking about," Finley said. "What did Orsos do?"

"He arrested the bad guys."

"And who are they?"

"You're new, Finley. I don't expect you to understand."

"I'm a fast learner," he said, and he watched as Moro made eye contact with a woman trying to gather up the shattered remains of her potted plants. It looked as if someone had smashed them. She gathered the loose soil in her hands with the tender care of a mother. The woman met Moro's stare with a look of absolute blankness.

"Being a warden is a pretty easy gig. Not much crime in Oshroar, and if there is its usually petty, stupid stuff, overturned fruit stands and graffiti. The people don't lack for much. I've heard of other tiles so bad that parents can't leave their babies alone for longer than a minute or so. Kid snatchers," Moro said, meeting Finley's questioning glance.

"Here though? You can leave your door unlocked. You can send your kid from one end of the city to the next and not have a second thought. No one's hungry, everyone has a place to live, and most people aren't too miserable. Because we are guarded, but not by wardens. The Guardians keep us safe. They work the fields, they build the city, they carry us from place to place. All we wardens do is the stuff that takes a brain. Solve the odd mystery, settle the occasional dispute, mostly it's paperwork, clerical stuff. Not much glory to it, but I ain't complaining.

"But about a year ago there started being a little less peace and quiet. They called themselves the Broken Ring. Not much more than a street gang at first, but they had a message that was hard to shake. They said we were prisoners.

"Except we weren't in a normal prison. We were in a prison 'of our own wretchedness.' That got people's attention, and soon they were a bit more than a gang, soon they were a movement. They even had a uniform, a broken metal collar around their necks. Certainly eye catching, and some of the kids in the streets took to the style. We started calling them bolt heads and went back to work. But they

131

wouldn't let up. They broke into every public event, disrupted every service, ruined every game, always preaching the same message, that we were slaves."

"Slaves to who?"

"To them," Moro said, and she pointed at a Guardian placing a door once more into its frame. The street was flooded with Guardians of all shapes and sizes. Blocky Guardians repaired the damaged homes, smoothing out the knicks and bruises the houses had sustained with the palms of their massive hands. Nimble Guardians, small, barely larger than children, collected the broken pottery and the other detritus that had spread in the ruckus of the mass arrests. Other Guardians went right to the people themselves and extended their hands, awaiting orders. Some of the citizens took them up on the offer, asking the Guardians to attend to one task or the other. Yet more, far more, turned away from the Guardians and did the work themselves. The Guardians remained in that attentive pose, waiting for orders that did not come.

"The Broken Ring think the Guardians are your jailers?"

"Oh no, they think the Guardians are our jail cells."

"Interesting. So they frame themselves as your liberators, I imagine?"

"Yeah. Their attitude didn't sit right with a lot of people."

"It seems to have taken hold of these people however."

"They started making some headway about a year ago, but even still they were just a gang. Until Evy Homme happened."

"Who is Evy Homme?"

"Who was Evy Homme. She was a little girl, just started her first year in school. She was walking home one day after class when she and some friends took a detour through a recent construction site. Typical kid stuff, they knew that the Build Guardians would freeze up if they saw the kids were in any sort of danger. Happens about a dozen times a day. But on that day, one of the Guardians slipped up and crushed her."

"What?"

"The Guardians are an ancient, all-helpful force, but sometimes they mess up. We get a few each year. A Guardian steps on a foot, or someone wanders into their path without looking and the stone can't

132

stop in time. But this time it was a kid, and this time it was slow. The Guardian lost control of what it was carrying, a pallet of almost a metric ton of bricks and mortar, and some landed on her and crushed her spine. She lingered for a week before she died. It was awful," Moro said, and Finley could see the emotions war within her. The natural horror of the death of a child in conflict with the cold professionalism demanded of someone in her line of work.

"The Bolt Heads jumped on it. Turned the whole thing into a circus and made her death out to be their symbol. The bastards. Whole ranges of the city refuse to use the Guardians at all, and those parts of the city are starting to slip back into some sort of dark age."

"What does Orsos have against them though?"

"Lots of reasons, but I'm guessing he thinks they're the cause of this whole dead Guardians situation. Makes sense, doesn't it? They're the only people in the city known to be Guardian haters. They seem like likely suspects to me."

"Moro, I realize that I am new to your city and to the wardens, but this doesn't look like an investigation to me. This," he said, gesturing to the carnage still being wiped away by the Guardians, "looks like hatred."

"You might be right about that. Evy Homme, the martyr of the Broken Ring, she was Orsos's daughter."

"Shepherd Scorned. Let's go," Finley said, and he picked up the pace.

Dead statues. Tyrannical police. Weird priests. Was he trying to solve a mystery in Huck's weird videogames? What the hell did this have to do with his friend's death?

Finley wanted to take out Marlowe and shake the Ghostlight until it answered, but he knew that was pointless. More than likely it would just show him more weird images and demand he call it Special Commissioner or something equally ridiculous.

They returned to find Warden HQ under a sort of siege. A crowd had formed, and they jeered and yelled at the wardens inside the building, but they didn't go any closer. A wall of living rock stood outside the doors of the HQ. Battle Guardians, standing so close together that Finley could hardly see the building on the other side of their immense bulk.

Moro led the way to these hulking brutes, and they parted as she approached, their burning eyes kept ever on the crowd across the street. Finley slipped in behind her before the wall closed again. The roar of the crowd fell away as the Guardians slid back into place, their immense stone frame blocking the sound.

The HQ itself was in a state of barely controlled chaos. Wardens rushed to and fro, filing paperwork, taking statements, and booking line upon line of the recently arrested.

Marlowe became shy at this great press of people and took up residence in Finley's hair. It burrowed into his brown curls, and now glowed a soft pink from its place above his right ear. Moro, meanwhile, pushed her way through the crowd to the desk sergeant directing the madness.

"Where is Orsos? We need to report to him," Moro said, shouting to make herself heard over the din.

"Interrogation cells. I'd stay away from him for now though. He's in a mood."

"It's about to get worse," Moro said, and moved off again, Finley following in her wake.

The interrogation cells were deeper than the cell that Finley had spent a night in, deeper even then the morgue where the dead Guardians lay. They were far below the madness above. Here it was almost peaceful, a place of stillness, the stillness of a tomb.

Battle Guardians lined the walls, their green orbs casting the hall into verdant light. No wardens walked the halls here. Perhaps they were all needed above. Or perhaps Orsos wanted no witnesses in this place. At least none that could talk.

As they walked closer, they saw that here the stone was replaced with thick glass. A woman sat in a chair in the room. A broken steel collar graced her neck, almost hidden by her auburn hair. She wore red workman's overalls over a rough gray shirt. Her shoulders were down, her eyes were closed, and her head bobbed to an unheard tune. She could have been sitting in the park, rather than in the bowels of the wardens' HQ.

Orsos stood in front of the glass, staring at the woman like she was a bug beneath a lens. He did not break his gaze as Finley approached.

"What do you have to report?"

"Orsos, love what you've done with the place down here. Very ominous."

"What do you have to report?" Orsos ground out.

"Well since you've asked so nicely, we spoke to the Crooken. We even ran into an old friend. Sister Sinoh sends her regards," Finley said, trying to affect his usual jocular tone. "They were tough to question, I don't mind saying. They would not tell us how the Guardians are made. They indicated that there is a way to turn one off but would not reveal it to outsiders."

"You have learned nothing."

"Not exactly. They let slip that there are inactive Guardians somewhere in the city, Guardians that don't work, ones that we don't know about."

"Fascinating," Orsos said, and now the man turned to look at Finley. His face was devoid of all emotion, as blank as the stone walls. "How many inactive Guardians are there?"

"We don't know. We think some are hidden in the walls of the Crooken temple, but other than that they could be anywhere. Sinoh made the Guardians come out of the stone. Until they opened their eyes, we had no way of knowing they were there."

"Do you suspect that they had anything to do with these murders?"

"No. They have too much of an interest in keeping the Guardians alive and eternal to ever want to murder one. They wouldn't give away the means of how to murder one either. They seem to love their secrets more than they love the Shepherd himself. But you knew all of that when you sent us, didn't you?"

"Of course. I have known Sinoh for decades. She is no killer. I simply wanted her distracted, and I can think of no distraction more powerful than you Mr. Marsh."

"Ha. ha. I don't appreciate being moved around like a game piece on someone else's board. You asked me to solve a mystery and you sent me into the lion's den hoping I'd make an appetizing distraction."

"Mr. Marsh, you give yourself too little credit. I sent you in merely as a distraction, and lo and behold you have returned with valuable information. I could not be prouder. But if you dislike your part in these events, I would be happy to return you and your light to your cell. We have kept it clean just for you."

"Oh, come on. You only know the things you do about these murders because of me and my partner. Marlowe is the reason you even know they were all killed the same way. The Ghostlight is named Marlowe, by the way," Finley clarified at the look of confusion on Orsos's face. "And Marlowe only sticks around because of me. So stop it with these pointless threats. You put me in a cell, and I'll tell it to snuff itself out. You keep threatening to have my head kicked in by a Guardian and I am walking." Finley was getting more indignant by the second. "By the way, that Hawksbill? I slipped its watch hours ago. You need to get a better guard dog."

"Do I now?" Orsos said, and Finley heard the slow and thundering beat of a Guardian's footsteps coming up the hall.

"I have the worst goddamn timing." Finley turned to face the approaching Guardian. Hawksbill stomped up the hall, its massive shoulder scraping against the chests of the Guardians that lined the walls, producing a terrific grinding sound. It ground to a halt directly before Finley, towering over the man.

"It seems you never slipped Hawksbill at all, Mr. Marsh. It is quite relentless in its pursuit. I think it would take you a dozen sleepless nights to put any sort of distance between you and it. Then again, it never sleeps."

"If you're going to have your goon grind me into a sticky pulp just get it over with, please."

"I don't believe I will. After all, you do tend to produce the oddest results Mr. Marsh, and I quite like having you as the wildcard in my deck. Hawksbill seems to have grown rather fond of you as well. It seems to have brought a gift for you," Orsos said, and Hawksbill's massive fist levered up, its palm opening to reveal Finley's black leather shoes.

"Thanks. What would I do without you, Hawksbill?"

"You'll never have to know." Orsos turned back to the glass window that separated them and the leader of the Broken Ring.

Finley slipped his shoes back onto his feet, noting with interest that the paper he had slipped inside was gone. He rather doubted that Hawksbill had taken it.

"What's your plan with her?" Finley asked. "Gonna send her on her own wild goose chase too?"

"I am going to question her," Orsos said, the muscles jumping in his jaw.

Moro made eye contact with Finley from the other side of Orsos. She gently shook her head at him. "Sir, I don't think that is the best idea."

"Why not?"

"It is a question of propriety. Your connection to her would—"

"She is mine to question!" Orsos snarled, the rigid lines of his face falling out of order.

"You can't go in there. It would taint any sign of impartiality or fairness."

Orsos threw his head back and let loose a mad cackle. "Are you a solicitor now, Moro? I think you need to remember that your job is to hurt whoever I point you at, not question me."

He stepped toward the door, but Moro blocked his way. "My job is to be right here, right now, sir."

Oroso's hands clenched and jumped at his sides. Finley saw his neck flush scarlet, and the veins on his skull throb with rage.

Marlowe flashed a bright yellow light, blinking frantically at Finley to do something.

"Why don't I take over the questioning, Orsos? I seem to be on something of a hot streak, interrogation-wise?" Finley said, already spinning into motion. "I'll introduce myself to the Ms...?"

"Kaja Runde," Moro said, not looking away from Orsos. The Chief Warden face switched from rage to consternation as Finley danced around him.

"Ms. Runde," Finley continued. "Wish me luck. Come on, Marlowe." And he slipped inside the cell containing the leader of the Broken Ring. He slammed the door behind him and wished that there was a lock on both sides.

"Ms. Runde, my name is Special Detective Finley Marsh, on loan from the Pittsburgh Office. This is my partner, Special Deputy Marlowe." The flower flashed a bright red from its space near the burning chandelier. "Fine. Special Detective Marlowe. They just recently received a promotion. I am here to ask you some questions in regard to some murders we believe you are connected to. May I sit?" Finley asked, and when Kaja did not respond he sat anyway.

"Are you thirsty? Have you eaten? Come to think of it, I am simply ravenous." Finley turned to the one-way glass. "Can we get some water and some sandwiches in here please?

"Someone will be along shortly." Finley turned back to Kaja to find her eyes open and her head cocked to the side, studying him. Her eyes were a startling green, and they shone in the white light from the chandelier.

"I must apologize for the state of these cells. You should know that I myself was a prisoner of such a cell only a day ago. Yet here I am now, a free man with a new job and new partner. You can have the same sort of abrupt change in circumstances, Ms. Runde, if you answer my questions clearly and without delay."

"Are you a lunatic?" Kaja asked.

"That is of minor importance. Let me clarify what is of extreme importance. Four people are dead. The method of their death is unclear, but the circumstances of their deaths has led us to believe that you are the culprit. You must answer my questions."

"Where's Orsos?"

"I'm sure he's attending to things far more important."

She grinned impishly at him. "Of course."

He plowed forward. "While we wait for him, why don't you help me solve the murders of four people?"

"Guardians are not people."

"So you know that the victims were Guardians?"

"The Warden HQ is not as airtight as you believe. We learned of the deactivations several days ago."

"Deactivations?"

"Murder is a misnomer, as is the term victims. Guardians are not living creatures, therefore they cannot be murdered, as they cannot die. They can only be switched off, like a device."

"You seem to know a great deal about the Guardians. I have had a devil of a time learning about them. Perhaps you could teach me."

"Why would I share any information with my captors?" Kaja asked her head tilted to the side, her mouth perking up into an amused pout.

"Who said I am one of the captors? Besides, I am interested in your organization. Yet I don't see a pamphlet on you. Could you, perhaps, try to convince me that your Broken Ring is worth my time?"

"And what would you bring to the Ring in return, Special Detective?"

"Much and more, Ms. Runde. Much and more."

"My organization has made a point of studying our jailers," Kaja said, her wrists idly pulling at the chains that kept her lashed to the table. "We know a great deal about the Guardians that much of the city has forgotten because we bothered to ask the questions in the first place."

"Your organization sounds like a group of diligent investigators. Should I be offended that I have not yet been offered an invitation?"

"You're from 'out of town,' as you said. Perhaps you will get one in time. We would welcome you," Kaja said, and for the first time in the conversation, she gave him a true smile.

"Please tell me more about your organization, Ms. Runde. I have heard the rumors, but I would like to hear it directly from you. What is it like to be a Bolt Head?"

"That is not our name," Kaja said, and her eyes flashed even as the smile stayed on her face. "We are the Broken Ring, and we are here to free you."

"Ms. Runde, let me assure you, I am free. I may leave this cell when I wish. I may walk this town as I wish."

"You are not free. You cannot go home," Kaja said. Finley stared at her, doing his best to keep his face fixed even as shock burned through him.

"Clarify, please."

"I have never heard of a place called Pittsburgh. I assume that you made it up. You claim to be from there, but you cannot return to a place that is not real." Kaja's voice fell upon Finley like hammer blows.

"Let us put aside my home for now," Finley said, trying to reclaim the conversation. "How are the citizens of this city not free?"

"They are locked in a cage and attended by powerful servants. Servants so powerful, so ever present, that they have lost the ability to function without them. A cell lined with velvet."

"A clever turn of phrase, but I don't buy it."

"Do you know how to farm, Mr. Marsh?"

"Excuse me?" Finley asked, surprised by the non sequitur.

"Do you know how to farm? Do you know how to till a field, plant crops, and harvest them?"

"No."

"Could you learn the skill?"

"Maybe. I could learn to do a bad job of it."

"Yet learning is always accompanied by pain. No learning has ever been easy, ever been free, or ever been finished. It is an agony to learn and to practice and to refine. Would it not be easier, even simpler, to ask for the help of another?"

"Yes, it would. I do it all the time. They're called farmers."

"There are no farmers in Oshroar."

"What?"

"What I said. There are no farmers in Oshroar. There are no plumbers or engineers or any work that demands a degree of labor. In Oshroar there is no need because…?"

"Because the Guardians do it all."

"Yes," Kaja said, and there was a note of sympathy in her eyes as she watched Finley process the information. "The Guardians do it all, and more. They carry us from place to place. They guard our walls and clean our homes. Every year we cede more and more of the tasks of life to them, to free ourselves of any burden. Soon, we will have them open and close our eyes for us and clean our filth when we grow too pathetic to wipe it away. They are jailers, and we entered the prison willingly."

Pieces clicked together in Finley's mind. The ridiculous religious organizations that competed like sports teams. The buildings that rose and fell with the whims of the architect. The pageantry in the streets and in the clothing. It was a city in search of distraction from the tedium of perfect leisure.

"What you describe is a kind of paradise. A life without pain."

"A life without pain is a life without accomplishment. This is a city of slugs and wastrels. We were more once. We built marvels and worked miracles. And then we built the machine that ended the need for anything else." Kaja's eyes stabbed into Finley's and her voice shook as she finished her diatribe.

"I thought the Shepherd built the Guardians."

"A fairy tale meant to placate children. The citizens of ancient Oshroar, when they were still men and women of purpose, built the Guardians. In the centuries since we have lost all knowledge of how our ancient forebears did such a thing. Now we are dumb children sitting in the ruins of a house our grandparents built." Kaja spoke as if she herself had watched such a collapse over the slow centuries.

"Fascinating. Is this the standard spiel you give your prospective recruits or is this a special one just for me?"

"You doubt my claims?"

"I think anyone that speaks about ancients this and ancients that is trying to sell me something. 'The good ole days' and all that nonsense. Personally, I don't see what's so bad about a land of peace and plenty. Besides, what does this have to do with the Broken Ring? What does this have to do with that tragically dead girl you use as a mascot?"

She was close to the explosion now; he could feel it.

"Evy was murdered," Kaja snarled, suddenly dropping the revolutionary façade.

"By things that can't murder or be murdered, apparently. Unless I'm wrong, of course."

"You don't know what you're talking about," she said, and she looked as enraged as Orsos was out in the hall. Thank goodness he walked in here instead of him. They would probably have set the building on fire from anger alone.

"Enlighten me then. How did you murder the Guardians?"

"You cannot murder—"

"How did you deactivate the Guardians?" Finley said, plowing through her answer.

"There is no way to deactivate them," Kaja protested.

"How can you be so sure?"

"Because we have searched." Finley's attention was snagged by the dull blue flashing of Marlowe. The flower was floating in the corner of the room, directly behind Kaja Runde and out of her line of sight. It seemed to be staring at the woman. Finley looked at his partner, and once more it flashed a dull blue.

"Please repeat that."

"We searched for ways to deactivate Guardians. We were unsuccessful." Marlowe flashed blue again.

"State your name one more time, please."

"What?"

"Standard police procedure. Clerical thing. Please state your name."

"Kaja Runde." Marlowe flashed a dull blue.

"Please tell me that there is an elephant in this room."

"For Shepherd's sake what are you talking about?" Kaja said, exasperation filling her voice.

"State it, please."

"There is a bright pink elephant behind you. It is about to stomp you flat," Kaja said, her tone thick with sarcasm. Behind her, Marlowe flashed a dull red. Finley sat back in his chair, and he could not help but grin.

Memories and truth. What else could Marlowe do?

"I think you earned that promotion, buddy," he said, under his breath.

"Did you deactivate the Guardians?"

"No. I did not." Blue light.

"Did someone in your organization?"

"No." Blue light.

"Do you know who or what deactivated the Guardian?"

"No." Blue light.

"Marlowe, can you do that picture thing you did for me earlier? Put an image of the murder method into her head, please."

Marlowe flashed green and yellow and shot to the space above the table. It whirled for a second, and then with a burst of light the flower shot an image onto the table: M. Guyot's head, complete with the glowing divots around its skull.

"Show off," Finley said to Marlowe before turning back to the stunned Kaja. "You seem to have done a great deal of research into how to murder the eternal. Tell me, what do you make of this image?"

"This is—this is not possible. What are you?" Kaja said to the glowing flower above her.

"Marlowe is my partner, now tell me what I need to know. What caused these markings?"

Kaja tore her eyes from Marlowe and down to the image of Guyot. She ran her fingers over the slight markings that dented Guyot's skull, and the image appeared on the backs of her hands as she drew.

"This is how it was done. This is how you turn them off. You go for the head. But what could make such a marking in solid stone? It must be heavy, blunt perhaps, to make these markings. But the markings are equal in spacing, as if they were all done at once. It could not be some sort of weapon that a person could swing. Guardians are tall too. Few can reach their heads from the ground. Perhaps the attack came from above?" Kaja said, her voice growing more excited as she spoke. Her eyes jerked across the image, focusing on one part of the image and then jumping for another. "How long does the deactivation take?"

"We don't know," Finley said, growing apprehensive at Kaja's fervor.

"It must be immediate, or else the Guardian would have tried to stop it. But why is it a feature of them at all? They are meant to last forever. So why would the ancients build in a deactivation feature? Is that what this is, an eons old safeguard in case they ever ran wild?"

"I'm happy to see you are so motivated to help solve this case. I was unaware the murder of Guardians so affected you," Finley said, sarcasm coating his voice. He waved to Marlowe, and the image of Guyot disappeared.

"They are not people. You cannot make me feel guilty for glorying in the fact that we have learned there is now a key to our jail cell. This method, whatever it is, is how we can free the city! You must let me examine the bodies. I can help you learn what killed them."

"Pass. You may not be our murderer, but that doesn't mean I trust you with the method. You'll sit here nice and quiet until I have more questions for you. Ms. Runde, you have been extraordinarily helpful. When this is through, I'll ensure that the city gives you a medal for all your efforts." Finley gathered up Marlowe with a sweep of his arm. He made for the door, before Kaja's voice stopped him.

"I had hope for you for a second, Mr. Marsh, but it seems you are also on the side of our jailers." She looked around at the locked room. "Our real jailers."

Finley did not turn around. "Ms. Runde, you are mistaken. I'm not on a side, I'm just passing through. And I think your whole argument is ridiculous. Your problem isn't with the Guardians. It's with the people of Oshroar. They're the ones that wish to be comfortable. But it's a hell of a lot easier to break a stone than to try to fix people, isn't it?"

"And what are you trying to fix, Marsh? Why are you helping Orsos?"

Finley shrugged. "Maybe I just care about justice."

The Ghostlight flashed a bright red. Kaja's grin split her face in two.

"No, that's not it. That's not it at all. You don't give a damn about justice, do you?" Kaja said, shaking her head, the grin still on her face. "Every part of you screams of desperation, from your bad jokes to that stupid swagger. Do you think I don't notice how bad your hands are shaking?"

Finley clenched his fist at his side.

"You don't care about the 'victims' at all. Orsos promised you something didn't he? Bribed you with some reward. Or maybe he just convinced you to be part of his vendetta. Tell me, Special Detective, is it justice when it's done for profit? Or is it just self-gratification?"

"That's it! That's it exactly, I just do it for the kicks," Finley said, his voice thick with sarcasm, even as his heart beat out of control.

The light flashed red.

"Seems your partner disagrees," Kaja said, her voice etched with mirth. "I do too. You're not having fun right now, are you? Tell me, how close are you to crying?"

His shaking hand reached out for the door. "I've shed enough tears. You have a pleasant afternoon. I'll tell Warden Orsos what you've said."

"Is he out there? Is he still too scared to face me? He didn't used to be such a coward. Tell him that I still visit our daughter's grave, but I never seem to see him there." Finley turned and saw that Kaja's shoulders were bent, and her face was twisted with cold anger.

"He didn't tell you? Him and his damn secrets. Evy Homme was our daughter, but we seem to have chosen different ways of mourning."

Finley, the light riding upon his shoulder, turned and left the cell.

Chapter 11: The Scholar's Ascent

The god of this world is a strange and many faceted thing. Most of the tiles pay tribute to a divine figure named Vovatum. While there are many faiths that worship this divinity, each one agrees that Vovatum is a young god.
(Letter 6, Paragraph 12, Lines 8-13)

"Sustained human flight can only be achieved through absolute mastery of both your physical and mental form. You have already made great strides in your pursuit of physical mastery. When you first came here you were, to be frank, a weakling barely capable of walking, let alone flying. Six weeks of flight school seems to have trimmed fat and added muscle to your form. Now the real work can begin. You may have thought you suffered under the tender care of professor Litvak, but I can assure you that you have not. I will push you in ways you cannot and will not comprehend because we are going to do something impossible, turn you into a flyer," Elwyn said from his bed in the hospital wing of the floating castle that had once been named Hypnos University.

He was held together with stitches and bandages. His left eye was useless, blinded by repeated lightning flashes when his goggles cracked six hundred fathoms below the event horizon of the storm. His left arm had been so badly broken that the doctors had wished to amputate it, only to flee from the room once Elwyn had heard of their decision. Now, after six operations, it sat in a thick cast cradled against his chest, perhaps one day it would be usable again.

Worse still, several of his vertebrae had been injured when he had to charge through a whole murder of krows. Elwyn had been confined to a wheelchair since his awakening and could no longer move his feet or his legs. Theo was terrified to think that he may have contributed to his friend's possible paralysis when he carried him across the bridge.

Yet despite all this, Elwyn made sure to dress in his battered flight jacket every morning, even if he had to drape it over his busted arm. He was propped against multiple pillows and surrounded by flowers from well-wishers, but he gave off the atmosphere of a carnivore at last sighting helpless prey as he looked at Theo.

"Yes, of course. Looking forward to it," Theo piped up. He met Elwyn's eye for a moment, but then quickly looked away. The older boy had intimidated him before, considering that he had swooped in like an angel to save Theo from tumbling into the storm. Now the winger positively terrified Theo. He kept feeling an odd swooping sensation in his stomach he usually associated with free fall whenever he met the other boy's remaining eye.

"I'm sure you are. I have been instructed to turn you into a winger as quickly as possible. I have been asked to cram a lifetime of study and instruction into one month. After I finished laughing at such a request, I was asked once again, very, very politely. It seems you've made some powerful people very anxious, Theo. How did you go about doing that?"

"Just bad luck I suppose."

"I heard you made that thing we found give quite a light show. What do think it is?"

"Litvak thinks it's a map to the heart of the storm. She's calling it the N-Device."

"Why that?"

"I've no idea," Theo said, trying not to think about its real name. The N64. "She won't let me near the thing."

"Why? She think you're going to run off with it?"

Theo thought of all the nights he had spent with friends playing on such a device. He had longed for one then, but Mom and Dad always said videogames were bad for his delicate constitution.

"Let's just say I had a bad reaction to it when I saw it. And it didn't seem to like me very much either. I've heard she's not letting anyone near it. She's studying it. Personally."

"She can be a bit enthusiastic, our professor."

Theo nodded, but thought 'zealous' might be a better word.

"Still, that's good, right? Finally, a map to where we're all going. Some friends of mine died to bring that thing back. I just hope it was worth it. It was, yeah?" Elwyn asked, and his voice had changed from drillmaster to that of a child seeking assurance.

"We think so, Elwyn. We think so," Theo lied, and he was frightened of how easy it was. Once, he had agonized over each and every lie, big or small. Now they were as easy as breathing. But what was the alternative? Could he reveal to his friend that he and his companions had fought and died to bring back a child's game station from another world?

"I'm glad," Elwyn said, closing his eye and adjusting the patch on the other one. He scratched beneath its dark surface, and then let it fall again. "You can relax, Theo. I only play the big bad drill sergeant because it's the only way I know how to teach. Truth is, I owe you one pal. You carried me across the ribbon by yourself in a storm and you barely know how to freefall properly. A grubber like you carrying a winger like me. I'll never hear the end of it from the other aeronauts," Elwyn said with a laugh. "Sorry. What I mean is, thanks for having my back out there. It means a lot to me. Know I'm going to have yours."

"Are you kidding? You saved my life first, and then you did it again. You don't owe me anything."

"Well how about we agree that we keep saving each other then? We seem to be pretty good at it."

"Elwyn, come on, you're a hero. A literal flying superhero. But me? Since I fell out of the sky I've been interrogated, attacked by monsters, and nearly got zapped by a godly artifact. And since you met me you nearly got crippled trying to keep me alive. Maybe we should stay away from each other. I don't want to infect you with my bad luck," Theo said, his arms wrapped across his chest in a tight hug, his eyes looking anywhere but Elwyn.

"Please don't make me get out of this bed so I can knock some sense into you. I mean it! Look, do you think this is the first time I've gotten hurt helping out a friend? You're my pal, and I've got your back whether you want me to or not."

"You're not just hurt, Elwyn, you nearly died."

"I've done that about twelve times, buddy. I'm probably going to do it a few more."

"Well it's new to me!" Theo said, his voice louder than he wanted it to be, but his pulse was racing now. And in the back of his mind he started to count his breaths.

"I don't," Theo shuddered. "I don't like seeing my friends hurt. It's too much...pain."

Elwyn tilted his head, his remaining eye as sharp as the spear he had stabbed the krow with. "You've lost somebody, haven't you?"

Theo nodded, numb.

"So have I. Do you know what it taught me?" Elwyn said, leaning towards Theo, reaching out with the unbroken arm to clasp his elbow. "It taught me to hold out to what I still have. It taught me that fear isn't worth all the time we give it."

Theo blushed. He couldn't look at the other boy. He didn't want Elwyn to see him cry.

"The heart can't be stopped, Theo. It's pointless to even try. So unless you want to outfight me or outfly me, I'm here to stay," Elwyn said, his grin wide and bright despite the scars.

"Are you sure you want to be my friend? All I do is get myself into trouble," Theo asked forcing himself to look at Elwyn even if he was as red as tomato.

"I like that about you, Falling Boy. Makes it so it never gets boring," Elwyn said with a grin that pulled his eyepatch up, and Theo could not resist that smile. It brought back that swooping sensation in his stomach. Theo didn't let himself think about what that sensation meant.

"Alright then, hero. I guess we're friends," Theo said, grinning back.

"Good. Now enough with all this nonsense. I've got to teach you how to fly, and I'm not going to go easy on you. Sound good?"

"Sounds great. What do you want me to do first? I don't see any wind tunnels in here, or any gear."

"First I want you to calculate the volume of this room while you do fifty pushups."

"What?"

"NOW!" Elwyn roared, and without a thought Theo found himself on the floor belting out pushups as his head craned about to get the dimensions of the room. The room was at least fifty feet long, and just as wide, but the height of the ceiling was difficult to tell from Theo's constantly rising and falling position. His neck ached as he looked about the room, but his arms pushed up and down without trouble. He guessed the room was ten ft high, and Theo began the calculations in his head, yet the numbers kept jumbling up as Elwyn shouted out the count for the pushups he was on. At pushup number forty-eight, however, Theo had his answer to the question.

"Twenty-five thousand cubic feet," Theo wheezed as he fell to the floor a final time.

"Correct. How did that feel?"

"Like I was squeezing my brain through a straw."

"Yes, I imagine so. That is the easiest question I will ask you over the coming days. Now, I would like you to count the individual stones in the walls of this room while singing the fight song of Hypnos University. Go."

And so it went, with Elwyn imposing brain twisting and heart bounding challenges upon Theo. He had him recall the name of every person he had met in the castle while shadow boxing across the room. Next there were increasingly more difficult math equations that Theo had to calculate while jumping from bed to empty bed. By the end, Theo felt like his whole body had been beaten with iron bars, and that his brain was less than mush. Elwyn looked very relaxed, and sipped his tea with his good arm as he watched Theo collapse onto the adjacent hospital bed.

"Let me know if I should send for a nurse," Elwyn said.

"Ha. Ha," Theo groaned.

"Yes, the training can be difficult, even painful. It won't get easier."

"Whoopee."

"Have you figured out what its purpose is yet?"

"I honestly couldn't tell you my name right now."

"How disappointing. I was under the impression that I was speaking to a scholar, not an imbecile."

Theo moaned and raised himself into a sitting position. "I know you're just saying that to get a rise out of me."

"And I know that it's working," Elwyn said with a smile. Theo rolled his eyes when he saw this but forced his brain into motion all the same.

"None of the challenges repeated themselves, so there was no common theme there," Theo thought out loud as Elwyn nodded along. "But you always made me do two things at once, three things at once at the end there. So you must be testing my ability to multitask, my ability to do something physical and mental at the same time."

"Very good. A gold star," Elwyn said, sipping his tea once more. "But why would such a thing matter in the pursuit of flying, do you figure?"

"I have no idea."

"A bird is born to fly, but we are not so lucky. The first flyers could barely rise a few inches off the ground without toppling over. And the first ones to fly above the storm quickly went mad. The human brain repels the idea of flight, it is just not equipped to handle a world without branches and mud and dirt. We are not suited for this task, but we undertake it anyway," Elwyn said, and there was fire of devotion and ambition in his uncovered eye as he spoke of flight.

"The only thing we have going for us is our minds. In the air you will need to perform maneuvers requiring staggering amounts of calculation and planning. At the same time, you must control even the smallest motions of your physical form, or risk careening into the abyss. If you slip, if you miscalculate, you will surely die."

Elwyn spoke of immense dangers, but there was longing in his voice. To him flight was more than just a means to an end. It was a higher calling.

"Is that the secret? Is that how you fly?"

Elwyn smiled, his eyepatch quirking up. "No."

"Then what is?"

"You already know it, Theo. You knew it when you walked across the bridge with me on your back. You've known it since you landed on our funny little castle."

"No, I don't."

"Yes, you do. Do you think any normal grubber could do what you've done? Walked across a handsbreadth of stone with a dying kid on your back? It's impossible, which is exactly the point. You flew across, Theo."

"No, I didn't!"

"Tell me, what were you thinking about before you crossed over the bridge?"

Theo thought back. He forced himself to relive that moment, the moment a demon attacked him with his name on its lips. He thought of the helplessness, the fear. He thought about his friend dying, blood trickling out of him while Theo watched, before deciding that even a failure like him should at least try to save Elwyn.

The rush of shame and frustration as he almost slipped again and again into the abyss. Fear was not new to Theo, but since that moment it had never seemed to leave his limbs, filling them with lead. It had only gotten worse since they had found the N64, since he had learned that one of his friends might be trapped down in the storm, sending messages with video game systems.

"I was thinking about myself. I didn't like what I was thinking about," Theo said, trying to make his voice light, blank, and unaffected. "Is that what causes flight?"

"Of course not. Are aeronauts filled with doubt as we fly? Of course! Everyone is. But that is not why we can fly," Elwyn said, his face clouded with concern and frustration as he looked at Theo. "Dig deeper, please. What else were you thinking about when you crossed the bridge with me on your back."

"I was thinking about saving you, and how it was impossible for someone like me," Theo forced himself to admit, looking away from the other boy.

"Exactly!" Elwyn said, his face glowing with happiness. "That is the key to flight. Impossibility."

"Excuse me?"

"Theo, people cannot fly. Do you see any feathers under my arms? Do I have hollow bones? Of course not. I'm not meant to fly. But the professor shared the secret with you. Impossible is no longer the hard barrier it used to be, even when it comes to the cognitive domains. In fact, impossibility is how we achieve miracles."

"You've lost me."

"Paradoxes, Theo! Paradoxes are how we fly. By contemplating something that is unthinkable we release ourselves from that which is possible. Let me give you an example, the first example that was ever given to me. It's a fable. Once upon a time, there was a winger walking her son near the edge of the castle. Suddenly, a krow tore its way out of the clouds and snatched her child away from her.

"The krow said to her. 'Eliza, your child is as good as dead. But I want to play a game with you.'"

"I thought krows couldn't talk?"

"It's a story Theo, don't question it. Anyway, the krow said, as its claws crept along the face of the child. 'I will return your child to you, if and only if you can correctly guess what I will do next. But if you guess wrong, if you can't tell me what I'll do, I'll send your child into the sky.'

"The winger watched her son, who was such a brave lad that he had not made a sound even as the krow scratched at his face. She never looked at the krow as she gave her answer.

"'You will not give back my son to me,' the winger said at last." And Elwyn's eyes gleamed with cleverness as he revealed her answer.

"The krow looked at her, shock rippling across its face. To kill her child would fulfill the guess of the winger, but then she would have guessed his action correctly, meaning he would have to give her the child. If he gave her the child that would break the guess of the woman, meaning that he never had to give her the child. And so, the krow thought on and on, so wrapped in the dilemma the winger had placed it in that it did not notice the knife until it had sliced through its neck.

"The head tumbled away, and the winger soared forward to save her son.

"But what could the krow have done? To fulfill is to break, to break is to fulfill. This is the Krow's Dilemma. The winger knew this, and so she gave the krow that which would choke it and allow her to fly, that which cannot be understood. If you understand this yourself, then you will be able to fly."

Theo rocked back on his heels, and then onto his toes, and then he did it again. And again. He felt a shout building from his toes and from the tips of his fingers. It came boiling up from his legs and down his arms. It collected in his chest, and then rose like a geyser until it exploded from his mouth.

"That's it! That's the secret to flight? A children's story? A stupid riddle? I've spent weeks on this stupid castle falling and falling again and again. I have bruises in places I didn't even know existed." Theo was thundering now, building up a head of steam and walking about the room as he did so, his arms flailing about. "I tumbled through the sky, Elwyn! I almost fell into the storm. And then I was attacked by a demon that knew my name. I watched you almost die. And you're telling me, that all this time, I could have flown away from all that if I had just asked myself a brain teaser?"

He stopped. He felt exhausted all of a sudden, and the many missed nights of sleep suddenly caught up with him. He sat on the hospital bed next to Elwyn's and watched the blood rush out of his unclenched hands.

"Yes, my reaction was very similar when I was first taught the concepts of flight. It's a stupefying concept to say the least, and one closely guarded by the few who have mastered flight. I believe I tried to hit someone when I learned it, it's difficult to recall. The truth is all the secrets of the universe lose their majesty after you learn that god is dead and your home is floating above his corpse. But it's still the truth. The secret of human flight lies in the contemplation of paradoxes."

"Why?"

"Because the rules are breaking down, Theo. The limits of possible and impossible no longer exist. People can finally fly, which is and always will be an impossibility. We know this deep down in our bones. We know it deep in our souls. We know it. Now we must unknow it, if we wish to fly," Elwyn said, and he drew himself up into a sitting position, a battle scarred, but unbroken master of flight.

"The purpose of the paradox is to unhinge the mind from rational thought. It is the rut in the road that knocks the wheel of the mind from its grooved path. The paradox is meaningless, unknowable, and unsolvable. Make the mind the same, and you can embrace the impossible. Only after you have done so will you begin to fly." Elwyn closed his eyes, and without effort began to float off the bed, as if gravity had switched off for him. He drifted over the sheets, his face a mask of calm repose.

"Do as I do, Theo," he said, and Theo clambered onto the opposite hospital bed, his legs crossed below him. He closed his eyes and thought of that impossible thing that had sent him floating into the air, and the dilemma of the krow. He thought of his friends, how they might need him to save them from a storm without.

"You must contemplate the unknowable within you. It will feel like you are swallowing a red-hot wire, inch by inch. It will seem—"

"Impossible," Theo said with a smile.

"Precisely. Are you ready to begin?"

153

Chapter 12: The Scholar's Mission

Biology is a fickle thing on this world, when it really shouldn't be at all. There's humans all over it of course, and we'll ignore how humans could possibly evolve on this planet to start with, because the real question is where did all the other species come from? I've seen bird people and otter people and gemstone people and more and more. It defies logic, which I guess is the point.
(Letter 12, Paragraph 1, Lines 1-5)

"One thousand fathoms below the castle the wind starts to pick up. It will blow you off course. It will tear away loose equipment. It will stab dust into your eyes. We call this space the neutral zone," Striker said. She paced in front of the blackboard at the front of the classroom. Her feet didn't quite touch the ground.

One month had passed since Theo had begun his training in flight with Elwyn. Theo could not sleep. His thoughts were plagued with bridges over running water, rocks that were too heavy for gods to lift. Food had lost its taste and texture, and he frequently found himself colliding with walls that he had not seen. It was thrilling and painful at the same time. Joyful and sad.

Paradox.

But with this pain came flight. Its progress was slow, but Theo was a motivated learner. He achieved concentrated floating by the third day. He was able to fly from one corner of the hospital to the other by the end of the second week. Now, most of his waking hours were consumed with flying laps around the towers of the upside-down castle while Elwyn lectured and ate applesauce from the comfort of his wheelchair. Theo had found a joy in buzzing Elwyn as he flew around the towers. It was a delight to learn again.

Yet his flight was not always smooth. Theo did not have the mental discipline of the seasoned winger. At times, his focus would shift for that single split second and he would once more realize the sheer impossibility of what he was doing, and he would plummet from the sky.

In these moments of doubt, it was the rope and harness around his back that saved him. Elwyn would yell for the orderlies to retrieve him from the sky, and Theo would rise like a hooked fish. The shame would burn through Theo as they pulled him from the depths. Yet Elwyn did not let him linger long with his injured pride and would instead send him once more into the air, to fly again and again until he got it right.

He could not achieve sustained flight for longer than twelve minutes. Yet here he sat, in a little-used classroom off the barracks. The room was littered with misplaced pencils and crumpled notes. Theo believed this is where they taught the young children before they graduated to the big kids' classes. It was only sort of funny.

Inside was only him and the famed expedition leader Striker.

"Deeper than one thousand fathoms, conditions become much trickier to predict. We call this upper portion of the storm the Anvil, as many expeditions have broken here. Weather is the greatest danger. Calm will become rain, become sleet, become hail that falls so thick and fast that I once saw ice punch holes in a winger who had survived fifteen expeditions into the storm. The whole process took 97 seconds," Striker said, and she delivered the tale of this winger's death without remorse and without emotion.

"I have survived twenty-five expeditions," Striker said, turning to glare at Theo, and her eyes were filled with a cool fire. "I am not bragging. I am not boasting. Surviving such a thing has as much to do with skill as it does luck. Do you consider yourself a lucky person, Theo?"

"Not really."

"Then you will have to rely on skill alone. Are you skilled?"

"Ha!"

"You do not lie. That is a worthy quality to have on an expedition. We will have no room for liars or boasters."

Theo's heart dropped out of his chest, fell through the floor, and kept on tumbling to the storm.

"I'm sorry what?"

"You will be joining us on the next expedition," Striker said, delivering his death sentence like it was the wind condition.

She resumed her pacing. "I have read the reports that Elwyn has written on you. He says you possess a keen mind for theory but struggle with application. He believes that, with time, you could become a capable winger. Time, however, is no longer a luxury we can afford." She picked up the chalk underneath the board. She traced a line to a point in the center of the storm, far below the castle. At that point she drew a neat little X.

"Tell me. What do you know of our enemies? What do you know about the stormkrows?"

"Wait, wait, back up. Why am I going on the next expedition?"

"Our enemies demand your focus, Falling Boy, not your questions. What do you know of them?"

"I—I read the autopsy reports of those that were captured. I also read the dissertations on their nature, their habits, and their environment. Their ability to survive frequent lightning strikes is fascinating, and I have some thoughts on—"

"Again, theory. Not application. What do you know of our enemy? Do you know how to kill one? How to survive one?"

Theo saw the vision that was ever close to his thoughts. The creature of cracked stone and bottled lightning with foot-long talons and his name on its lips.

"Yes," Striker said, her eyes staring deep into his own. And to Theo, they looked to be empty, pitch-black holes that had watched winger after winger devoured by fiends. "You know our enemy. You have met it, survived it. It is for this reason and this reason alone that I have agreed to take you on the coming expedition. I care nothing at all for your theories. I care only about your ability to survive."

"I have until now." But that didn't seem likely to continue, Theo thought.

"We suspect that the body of Vovatum is only ten thousand fathoms below us, a distance of about twelve miles. A short distance to walk, and a far shorter distance to fall. But we do not fall. We fly, and to fly successfully and safely, we must fly slowly.

"The storm will fight us for every foot of sky, trying its best to blow us off course or strike us from the heavens. Rest assured, if the storm cannot kill us immediately it will try to lead us astray. Whole expeditions have wandered for weeks in the Godstrom without ever getting closer to the ground."

"You speak of the Godstrom as if it were a living thing."

"It is a beast." Her hands came together in a massive clap of sound. It echoed in the room like a peal of thunder. "It despises us and loves its krows. To enter beneath its clouds is to invite death. Even the best winger would be obliterated in seconds if they tried to simply fly through the heart of the Godstrom. But a monster so big does have its blind spots. Ones that a careful expedition can soar through, along with any…passenger they might bring along."

She picked up the chalk again and drew another X next to the first one. And then another, and another, until the board was littered with Xs like fresh fallen snow.

"Below two thousand fathoms there is a period of relative calm in the storm. The wind dies down, the rain stops. You count your losses, and you thank whatever part of god that still lives that you are alive. This relief is an illusion. Below two thousand fathoms is when you begin to encounter demons.

"They can decimate an unwary expedition in minutes. The lancers, those like Elwyn, will take the brunt of the enemy's attack then. They are trained on how to confront and kill the beasts. You are not. You will be in the center of the formation, protected alongside our scientific equipment. You will not fight."

Theo nodded. He felt a brief flicker of shame at being tucked away with the equipment like an unused football, but he quickly quashed it. Better unused then sliced to ribbons.

"Below this point, the journey becomes considerably more difficult. The krows will continue to peck at us as we fall, but they will be joined by debris."

"Excuse me?"

"There are still pieces of this tile swirling about in the storm, as well as the remains of the original Universities. The mud and stone and brick of all that was once in the tile clogs the airways at the lower depths. The krows tend to back off here. Even they have difficulty navigating the treacherous airs. We might even find temporary shelter. The Detritus will serve as our base camp as we continue down into the darkest trenches of the Godstrom." She continued to add to her diagram of the storm as she spoke, marking the depths of these obstacles, tracing the path of their proposed flight.

"This is where you will come in. Over the generations, hundreds of expeditions have mapped the upper reaches of the storm. We have collected thousands of artifacts and have uncovered scores of mysteries and secrets. We have done the good work. Yet we have never penetrated the lowest reaches of the Godstrom. We have never reached the bottom, where God's body fell."

"Why?" Theo croaked out, imagining a storm filled with the dead.

"The Godstrom is a creature of malice, but at its lower depths it becomes a thing of sheer terrible force. The air will be so thick with lightning we will go blind. The winds will tear the flesh from our bones. Even the krows cannot live in the darker depths. Yet we have heard...whispers. Not all who journeyed into the deep did not return. Some washed up in the higher altitudes weeks, sometimes years, later. By the time we found them again their minds had cracked open, and they had gone mad. From their ravings we were able to learn only a little."

"Like what?"

"They whispered of terrors in the deep. They spoke of something—something terrible."

"What was it?" Theo found himself whispering.

"It has many names. The Elder Krow, the Coffin Maw, but the aeronauts prefer a different name. The Leviathan. The first stormkrow, and the one that reached the body of Vovatum first. It is said it gorged itself and become a creature so vast that you could stand on its head and not see its tail." She spoke with the same calm and clipped tones while she described this cosmic horror. Yet Theo wished she would whisper instead. He did not want to call this terror to life.

"But adventurers always tell such stories when they are in their cups. Let us put aside the terrors of madmen for the moment. Instead, let us focus on what we know, and what they once knew."

Striker reached into the depths of the bag beside the blackboard. "While these survivors had gone mad and could share only a little information with their broken words, their writings were another matter entirely." Striker tossed a tightly embossed moleskin notebook at Theo. A name was etched into the cover *Aldwin Dryn*.

Theo flipped it open and saw the tightly curling script of a long dead aeronaut. He paged through, and he skimmed the accounts of a routine expedition that had become extraordinary as it continued deeper into the storm than any other before. His last complete entry was just before their first foray into the lower depths. It contained his hopes they would find some piece of the divine below.

After this, his writing became convoluted. Entries would flow into each other, losing focus in the middle. Some writings were directly on top of each other, blotting out the entry below. Others were half finished and filled with repeated words. They became rambling, strained, frantic. His pen had slashed across the page, carving insane symbols and equations. The writing looked like a scream.

"Although Aldwin lost his ability to write as he lost his mind, his gift for mapping remained. We were able to piece together where his expedition traveled in the lower depths. At the end, we suspect they were only dozens of feet from reaching the bottom before they were destroyed.

"Based on the logbooks we have recovered from those mindless survivors, we have determined there is a path to god. One of relative calm amidst the chaos of the lower Godstrom. We call it the Pilgrim's Path.

"The survivors stumbled upon the Path, but they were not able to remain on it for long. It would take a thousand lifetimes to walk the whole path unaided and by accident. Luckily, we have found a solution." She drew once more on the chalkboard a familiar cartoon. It looked like jellyfish with the feet of a chicken, the N64.

"Litvak has determined that the device we recovered, and you activated, is a map. It spent decades in the storm, powered by the repeated lightning flashes at its heart, and in that time, it charted the width and breadth of the Godstrom, including the Pilgrim's Path. This was the image it showed us in the light. Finally, we have a chance of reaching god. I will be leading the expedition to the lowest depths of the Godstrom, and you will accompany us to work the device."

Her words lingered in the air. Theo waited for them to fall, but instead they floated there like sunbeams.

"Why?"

"Because I have failed," Litvak said from behind them.

Theo spun around. The professor's face was gray from exhaustion, her eyes were scarlet red, as if from a fever.

"What do you mean?"

"The device has defeated me," Litvak croaked. "I have devoted a lifetime to studying godly artifacts. I have spent decades in prayer, but it seems that god no longer wishes to talk to me. He has picked you."

"What?" Theo asked, thunderstruck.

"It is no coincidence that the device activated for you, it is providence," Litvak said, stepping closer, and Theo realized the light in her eyes was not one of exhaustion, but of fervor.

"But I don't even believe in your god?"

"It doesn't matter. Least of all to him."

"He's dead, remember?" Striker said. "Trust me when I say that you are not the first choice for this expedition, but it seems you are the only one. You will serve in a support capacity only. You will not fight, you will not scout, you will only work the machine. Do you understand?"

"This is all nonsense; do you understand that?" Theo said to both women, turning from one to the other. "I can barely float, and now you want to send me into the Godstrom to operate some sort of mystical map? The N-Device?"

"But that's not its real name is it, Theo? N64. God has made you his prophet and sent this device as a sign."

"Professor, I think you need to sleep. You're clearly unwell."

"Thank you for your concern, Theo, but you should care for yourself. After all, you leave tomorrow on a great journey."

Theo turned from her, giving up trying to convince the zealot. He faced Striker. "Why the hurry? Why the sudden burst to get to the finish line? Can't we wait awhile longer, until Elwyn is healed? I'm sure that he wants to go on this expedition," Theo said, scrambling for a reason not to disappear into the storm.

"It is unlikely that Elwyn will ever fully heal. We shall not wait for an impossibility," Striker said.

"I thought we were in the business of impossible things!" Theo said, his voice raw and ragged. He was on his feet, unsure how he got there.

"Elwyn knows he may never recover. I know that he may never recover. Why don't you?"

Theo rocked back on his heels and his breath caught on his chest. "I don't care if your god is dead. I have seen miracles. Elwyn will recover."

Striker watched him, her dark eyes burrowing into his own. "You've never lost someone before, have you?"

"I've lost more than you know."

"Perhaps. There will be loss in what we are about to do, Theo. But that sacrifice, if we must make it, will not be without meaning. We might even discover the formula for miracles," Striker very slowly and very hesitantly placed a large hand on his shoulder. It settled like a cool weight on him.

"Are you trying to comfort me?"

"It has never been my strong suit."

"I can tell."

Litvak spoke from behind him. "Your fall and the Device's discovery are linked, Theo. It is the only thing that makes sense."

Theo paled, and the thought that had tormented him for weeks, the thought he would not allow himself to have, thundered into his mind. If he had appeared above the storm, had someone else appeared below it?

And were they waiting for him?

"Does the expedition have to happen now? Does it have to go with me? I'm not ready. I'm just not," Theo said, turning from Striker to Litvak.

"No one ever is, but you are needed now," Litvak said.

"What has happened?"

"You were there, Theo. One of the krows reached the Castle. Even after scores of years and hundreds of expeditions no living krow has ever found our home. Since that attack, three more of their scouting parties have been destroyed before they could make landfall. We have not told the whole castle yet. We do not want to start a panic. But we will not be able to hold them off for long. Soon the people will learn, soon more krows will come," Striker said, and Theo knew that they were both picturing the same thing, a sky filled with krows. A horde of monsters battering down the gates of the clinging castle, a chorus of the defenders' names on their lips.

"The Final Expedition will need to slip out before the siege begins or we might never have another chance. It is simply too great a risk to take. Pack your things, you leave tomorrow at first light."

Theo slumped, all energy leaving him, he turned to Litvak. "What if I get everyone killed?"

"Then you can ask Vovatum for forgiveness when you meet him."

Elwyn was in the midst of his physical therapy when Theo came to him. He was trying to write his own name when Theo entered. Theo said nothing as he sat on the hospital bed next to Elwyn. Elwyn's battered hand trembled as he scratched the pen across the page. He could not let it rest on the page; else Elwyn's shakings would draw frantic zig zags across where he was trying to write. Elwyn had to write in slow pulls of the pen, like a child learning his letters.

He grinned at the doctor as he wrote, and he tried his usual banter on her as he carved out his name. Her eyes drifted away from his hand and went to his face. Theo saw his shaking increase as she looked away. His knuckles were white as he clutched the pen.

"I hope you don't mind the interruption," Theo said.

"Not at all! Wonderful to see you, Theo. I'm sorry Dr. Larson but perhaps we could cut it short today?" Elwyn asked, and he grinned at her.

"We will call it an end for today, but only because you have been working so hard." She made Elwyn promise he would do one more set of writing programs before he slept that night. He agreed readily and grinned until she left the room. The instant the door closed behind her, his smile turned off like a light. He glared at his still shaking hand as if it were some vile thing that had replaced his real hand in the dead of night.

"You shouldn't lie to her, Elwyn."

"I'm fine."

"You shouldn't lie to me either," Theo said, and Elwyn turned his venomous look on him for a second, and Theo forced himself to meet it. They locked eyes, and Elwyn turned away.

"Sorry. I hate this feeling, this weakness. It's unbecoming of an aeronaut."

"I don't think you're weak."

162

"I do. I've thought about death for years. I accepted that I would die in the storm, fried by lightning or chewed up by some monster. Wingers are supposed to die in the sky, not lie broken in a bed."

"I don't think you're broken, and you won't convince me otherwise."

"Now if only I could convince myself."

"Elwyn, you taught me how to fly. Maybe I can try to help you with your lessons. Here, why don't we start small. Mimic my movements." Theo lifted his hand, fingers raised, and then he slowly dropped them until only his middle finger remained upright.

"This is what I think of your so-called weakness." Elwyn's jaw dropped open and for a moment there was silence, and then, from somewhere deep within him, Elwyn began to laugh. And with his hands now shaking with mirth, he raised his left hand to Theo and managed to raise the middle finger just a fraction.

"You're a fine teacher! I didn't know you had it in you. I'm a little ashamed my training never provoked this response."

"Oh, I definitely thought about it, I was just too tired to do it."

"Well, at least I did something right," Elwyn said, and now he really looked at Theo for the first time. "They told you, didn't they?"

"Yeah."

"I'm sorry I wasn't there for that. I wanted to be, but Striker insisted she do it herself. She's a capable winger, and a fantastic commander. You're in very safe hands. I'm actually jealous. You might be on the final expedition of them all."

"I would happily switch with you if I could," Theo said, his face downcast, trying not to notice the gleam of enthusiasm that had entered Elwyn's eyes at the mention of the expedition.

"We couldn't even if I was able. I'm not a brain like you, Theo. They're going to need your big ideas down there in the storm."

"I don't think I'll make a difference. I have no idea who came up with this whole mapping nonsense, but that is simply not what it does!

"It's a toy, not some magic fix-all that will lead us to a god. It won't work, and it will get us all killed. And it will be my fault." Theo wrapped his arms about himself. The panic was there, the panic was always there. No amount of breathing exercises or mental gymnastics could throw it off for long. He could fly now, and he would still never be able to outfly it.

"You still don't have much faith, do you?"

"In a dead god? No, not particularly."

"Not in Vovatum. In yourself. You have no faith in you. Theo, I have seen you fall from the sky, and I have seen you fly. You've even made this broken winger laugh. It's not hard for me to have faith in you," Elwyn said as if he were talking about the weather, as if he were speaking plain truth.

"I hope you find your faith in the storm, Theo. You are more than what you believe about yourself," Elwyn said, and he closed his eyes. Theo looked at the other boy for a moment longer, realizing that was the best goodbye he was going to get. Then he got up and walked to the door.

"You'll need a call sign, by the way. All wingers get a sign, so that we can use names that the krows don't know. The members of the expedition will give you one. My advice? Don't try to force one. It all happens naturally. And in the end, it always seems to suit, like fate."

"What's yours? You don't use it when you're on land," Theo asked without turning around. A single, high, warbling note came from behind Theo. He turned and looked at Elwyn as he finished his whistle.

"Whistler. I'm always happiest when I'm flying," Elwyn said, and he grinned at Theo again. "I'll be waiting for you to come home."

The next morning, the members of the Final Expedition found Theo in the place of arms. He floated a few inches above the ground, his few belongings strewn on the ground around him.

Theo heard their whispers on the air, but kept his silence, and opened his eyes. There were thirty-five people in the courtyard, and no two were alike. The Expedition had gathered all sorts for this voyage into the storm, and although Theo continually thought of himself as strange and odd, in this crowd he was just part of the background.

Striker was the obvious leader of the bunch. Her every move sent ripples through the crowd, and conversations hushed when she spoke. She was the only winger Theo had met thus far that used their call sign both on land and in the air.

A short winger stood always behind Striker's left shoulder. The man was all corded muscles and menacing looks. His arms hung down to his knees, and he glared at all that came too close to Striker. Theo had heard of this man. Duan Ju, call sign Shaver, Striker's shadow and second in command.

The head of the expedition's scientists, Younette D'Albert, gathered her scholars around her like lost lambs. Her call sign was Wheeler. She was a tall woman, half her head shaved, a monocle dangling from one eye. Theo supposed that he would be under her direct command for this expedition.

Peering off the edge of the place of arms and into the void below was the new lead lancer, Titus Gunden, Fencer. He was a broad man with long red hair and beard. Over his shoulder was the handle of an immense broadsword that would have taken five Theo's to even lift.

Younette ambled up to Theo, still floating a little above the floor. "So you're Elwyn's prodigy?" she asked, as she helped Theo to his feet. "I've heard tales of you. Monsters and falling and all that. It sounds terribly exciting," she said, her words pouring over each other, so eager was she to say them.

Theo took a step back.

"You'll be working with my group for the expedition. I was told you're not a strong flyer, little unusual, but we can adapt. We'll store you with the supplies," she said, and she indicated the great leather diving bell in the corner of the place of arms.

"How kind," Theo said, already feeling a twinge of claustrophobia as he looked at his home for the next few days. "How do you carry it?"

"The packsmen take turns," Younette said, and she indicated the ropes and harnesses attached to the top of the equipment bell.

Theo turned to the packsmen and found them all already glaring at him.

Was this woman trying to get him killed?

"You'll embark when we get a few fathoms down. Too dangerous during take-off, they might bounce you to death. Are you good to fly a few fathoms?" Younette asked, an eyebrow raised. Theo could only nod. He felt the creeping shame moving up his spine, but the crowd moved before he could speak.

Striker gathered the expedition around her, and a hush fell among the other members. "I have no speeches. You all know what we mean to do. We will be making for the very heart of the Godstrom. We will journey on the Pilgrim's Path, a safe passage through the lower depths. We will face the krows, we will survive the storm, and at the very bottom of it all, we will find god. Take your positions and take flight."

The place of arms burst into sudden motion. Wingers all around Theo belted on packs and fell into neat lines in front of the edge that led into the storm. Some of the wingers bore weapons, rifles and pistols, while others had spears and long sabers. Still more wingers carried great packs filled with food and water and medicine and supplies for the journey. Others, such as Younette and her bunch, had machinery strapped to every available part of their bodies.

All wore the brown leather flight jackets with gold buttons that Theo had never seen Elwyn without. They had fur on the inside and were filled with many pockets. They were battered old things, ribboned as they were with the cuts and scratches and wear and tear of many expeditions. Theo donned his own spotless coat. He put on the canvas flight hat as well, a skull cap with ear flaps that also had a thin fur lining. His goggles came next, essential in the lower reaches of the storm where the wind would try to flay his eyes. The clunky breathing apparatus and flight mask came next.

"Check equipment!" Duan Ju called out. The front person of each line, Younette in Theo's case, checked her own equipment with swift and sure hands, tugging at each strap, tightening each piece. The person behind her checked her pack for any loose belts or misplaced bit of gear, and so on down the line. Theo was in the middle of his line, and he copied the motions of the person ahead of him as he checked the man's pack for any malfunction. He felt the tugs and pulls of the woman behind him as she checked his pack.

The lines of men and women fell back into stillness as the last checks ended. And Theo felt a great burning anxiety in his chest. He wanted to run, he wanted to leap. Instead, he waited with the rest. For what he did not know.

Striker took off her mask as she walked to the edge of the place of arms. She raised her head to the sky and to Theo's astonishment she began to sing.

"Hark, hark, upon the storm,
pilgrims soaring forth.
Proud and merry, strong and daring
Hearts flying true."

Her song trailed away, and she lowered her head. Striker raised her mask to her face once more, and without turning, leapt into the storm. The crowd surged forward, still holding to their lines.

The leaders jumped from the place of arms, tumbling down. Their seconds followed without an instant's pause, and now Theo could see his own turn coming, rushing up to meet him.

The man ahead of him jumped, and now Theo could see the figures falling into the great gash in the sky that was the Godstrom. Perhaps one of his friends was at its depths, sending him messages through an N64.

Theo thought of the days where he was too afraid to crawl out of his own bed, and how impossible it was that that boy meant to fly.

He ran towards the edge and leapt.

Chapter 13: The Messenger's Discovery

I was recently forced to travel through the Tile of the Grave. The place once had a proper name, but it has disappeared beneath the weight of the bones that the Eternal Empire left here. There is a small order of monks that tends the ever-growing graves. I have never met a more persistent people.
(Letter 13, Paragraph 3, Lines 4-9)

"The trick to riding a chiropt is to remain calm. The bats are sensitive creatures, and they will sense your fear," Lina said, watching Gwen's face carefully. She often watched for her reaction now, ever since she had broken into a laughing fit when she first encountered the immense bats the *Herald* used to deliver the paper.

Laughter was a foreign sound to bats, them being incapable of producing the noise themselves. They had assumed she was screaming. Lina had managed to remove her before any incident.

Still, first impressions matter.

"The chiropts are native to a tile far to the South from here, at least for now. The corvids recognized their use several decades ago and have been breeding them at the Cradle ever since. We tried to use giant owls before that, but there were a great many accidents. Riders kept falling off when their owls turned their heads to look directly at them," Lina said. Gwen's grin stretched so wide that her cheeks started to ache.

They were alone in the bowels of the Cradle, in a classroom meant for many more students. Since Gwen's laughing fit, the higher ups had seen fit to place her with just one partner who would train her up, so that she might have more personal attention. Gwen suspected it was because they thought she was damaged goods.

"Flyers are secured to the back of the beast with various straps and on a saddle. The creatures have been trained to respond to the slightest bit of pressure when you're clinging to its back. Think of the bat like an extension of your form. Bat and man working as one," Lina continued, and now Gwen could no longer suppress her glee. It burst from her face as a snort, and it continued in little giggles that sent tears pouring from her eyes.

"Can we please stop it with the chatter?" Lina said, turning to look at Gwen. The smile melted from her face, and she looked in confusion at the empty desks behind her, and then turned back to Lina, shrugging her shoulders.

"What is so funny?" Lina said, her hands clenched at her sides and her brow clouding like an approaching thunderstorm.

"The whole situation really. You're hilarious," Gwen said, her face once again in the mask the preceptors had taught her to form. Her voice, however, was light and airy.

"And what is so funny about me?"

"Nothing. Everything. I don't know. You might be the funniest unfunny person I've ever met in my life."

"You are aware that makes exactly zero sense, correct? I am trying to teach you things that will keep you safe and might even save your life."

"You just told me that the bats can sense my fear, owls have killed people, and that I'm going to become a batman. That's funny!"

"You might be the worst novice I have ever met. I honestly don't know how I'm going to train you," Lina said, her hands coming up to massage her temples. "I had big plans before I met you, you know? I was close to being named assistant editor, and now here we are."

Gwen let the mask slip off her face, all amusement vanishing. She cradled her head in her hands. "Look, I'm sorry. I—I don't really know what's going on. My friend died and the next thing I knew I was in another world being forced to train and live only in the dark by the preceptors." And she pulled her head up, scanning the room for any sign of them, only relaxing when she had examined every inch. "I do that for months, and then I come here and find out I'm just a papergirl. Forced to fly around on giant bats and deliver some stupid newspaper Huck and I made up when we were kids. I know I'm not the best student right now, but I'll do better I promise." And the tears were coming now, and Gwen couldn't stop them. "Please don't be mad at me."

Gwen sobbed into her hands. She hadn't let herself cry in a long time, and the tears seemed to have no end. Her hands shook and every breath was a struggle, but when she heard the footstep in front of her she jerked backwards. The chair toppled away from her as she lifted her fists, slipping into a fighting stance.

Lina froze. The other girl had a handkerchief in her hand, not a weapon. Lina lifted her other hand, letting Gwen see that it was empty. She brought it down with glacial slowness onto Gwen's shoulder, and the warmth settled Gwen, anchoring her back to this moment. She dropped her fists and accepted the hankie from Lina.

"Your friend died?" Lina asked, her voice low and gentle.

"Yeah," Gwen said, wiping her eyes. "Just before I came to the monastery."

"I'm sorry."

"Okay," Gwen turned away from her.

"The preceptors can be...brutal teachers. I'm sure they weren't what you needed after something like that."

"The preceptors are wise and good. They—"

"They can't hear you, Gwen. They can't see you."

And the shudder ripped its way up her spine. She wound her arms around herself, trying to suppress the shivers.

"Why would they do that? Why would they take the light away from us?"

"Because they wanted to show you what happens if you don't listen to them. They wanted to control you."

"Guess it worked."

"You decided to listen to them, Gwen. But that also means you can decide to stop."

"What would I do then?"

"I guess you'd do whatever you want. You could be yourself again."

Gwen let out a watery little laugh. "I've never really done that to be honest."

"Well, I'd love to meet her, whenever you're ready. I'm guessing she's probably a strange person, and we need more of those."

"You know, I've been getting that a lot lately." Gwen tried to smile for real, but it still felt wrong to pull her face into a position that so disgusted the preceptors. She relaxed her arms. She reached out to shake Lina's hand. "Gwendolyn Brooks. Your student."

"Lina Azny," the older girl said, shaking Gwen's hand. "Your mentor."

"You seem like you know a lot about ignoring the preceptors."

"It took a while, but yes, I think I managed to throw them out."

"What's the secret?" Gwen asked, desperation creeping into her voice.

"There is no secret. I can only tell you what helped. Gwen, this world is vast and strange. I fly on a giant bat through the clouds. I see places no one has ever seen, and then I give them their mail and their paper and fly away. It's an exhilarating way to live. The monastery, the preceptors, in the face of all of that, they are so very, very small. I didn't kick them out of my head. I just realized that they didn't matter, and that they weren't worth the effort of remembering them." She turned with a smile to Gwen. "Also, it helps to be a little bit strange yourself."

She was an unassuming young woman. Her clothes were ironed in severe lines. She held herself ramrod straight when she was silent, but when she spoke, she relaxed into a slouch. She smiled by default but tried to seem aloof and disaffected. Unlike the other mysteries currently racking her brain, Gwen found this one charming.

"That I am well suited for."

"I'm happy to hear it. We have much and more to do, and we best get to it," Lina said and made for the door.

"Where are we going?"

"To the hangar bay, we're going flying."

"We're just gonna skip the lesson?" Gwen asked, racing to catch up with her.

"For now. Besides, all the best things in life you learn in the air," Lina said, as she led her through the cramped halls of the depths of the Cradle and away from the classrooms.

In the days since Gwen's arrival, she had explored as much of the Cradle as she could. The Cradle appeared to be divided into three main levels. The bottom-most level was maintenance, an iron underworld of twisted steampipes and whirling metal. Here were the sweat soaked and bleary-eyed workers who crawled all day through a scorching world to tend to the great machines that kept the Cradle functional.

The next level was for messengers, legions of marching men and women training and preparing for the great deliveries and explorations carried out across the ever-shifting planet. The massive hangars where the chiropts slept were here as well.

Above this chaotic world was the scientific arm of the *Herald*. Weather equipment and mapping devices dominated this floor tended by legions of clerks and mechanics. However, most of the brain power in the building was located in the copy rooms, printing presses, and bullpens of the *Herald*. Writers clacked away at typewriters and printing presses, receiving information from carriers and informants across the world. Editors prowled these halls like lions, looking for weak copy.

Here were the stars of the *Herald*. Whole rooms came to attention when they walked by and lapsed into whispers after they had passed.

The reporters.

It was the position of greatest honor in the *Herald*, and the most dangerous. They were the eyes and ears of the *Herald*, they investigated, they interrogated, and they wrote endlessly of the deeds of great kingdoms, the follies of empires, and the works of scientists, artists, and leaders from across the ever-shifting globe.

The idea appealed to Gwen.

Lina led them through the underbelly of the Cradle, taking turn after twisting turn until finally they arrived in a small hangar bay. It was cluttered with refuse and debris. Only one bat rested here, clinging to the lattice work upon the ceiling and fast asleep.

"My own private hangar!" Lina said with pride.

"How glamorous," Gwen whispered.

"Yes, I thought you might think so. When I first started here, I was assigned to clear this room of rubble. No human had stepped inside in several decades, and the higher ups wanted it cleared."

"Why were you assigned it?" Gwen asked, still whispering, fearful of waking the great bat that dangled far above.

Lina continued to speak in her normal voice, "Ah, that. Well, it might have been a form of punishment. 'Attitude Correction' I believe was written on the official forms," Lina said, avoiding looking at Gwen's shocked face. "I was a bit wilder back then I will admit."

"What did you do?"

"Oh, that's hardly important," Lina said, her face flushing.

Gwen waited.

"I may have thrown a punch at one of my instructors. I felt he was being unnecessarily cruel to his chiropt."

Gwen's heart began to beat a little faster, even as she imagined Lina throwing a punch with her gangly arms. Lina walked up the scaffolding to stand directly beneath the slumbering bat. She reached one hand up and began to scratch it about its ears. It leaned down into her hand, snorting gently awake.

"Don't look at me like that. It got me nothing but bruised knuckles and a room to clean from dawn to dusk. The instructor still got to teach, still got to be cruel to his animal, and he got sympathy from the higher ups. I learned then that teaching is what I want to do in life, if only to save the world from bad teachers," Lina said, gesturing for Gwen to come onto the scaffolding as well. "Speaking of, might as well begin with the lesson. Gwen, this is Clementine."

Gwen walked up the steps, bringing her heart rate back under control, moving each foot with care. Even so, the metal steps clattered beneath her. The bat's massive black eyes opened and looked into her own. There was something ancient in that gaze, something hot and primal, but not unkind. Lina beckoned her forward, and Gwen raised her own hand and pressed it into the dense dark fur on Clementine's head. The hair was coarse and rough, and scratched at her skin, but as her hands sunk deeper into the matted fur it became soft and warm. She felt a low rumble in her fingertips as the colossal bat vibrated with sound. It purred.

She grinned at the massive creature. Its eyes meeting her own.

"Hello, Clementine," Gwen said, and the creature kept right on purring.

"See, not so scary once you get to know them, are they?" Lina said, by her shoulder. She climbed higher into the scaffolding, up another ladder, and then another, until she was level with the hanging chiropt's back. Gwen followed and saw the crisscrossing apparatus of hooks and straps and holsters that the giant bat wore. The structure was made of tough leather and brass wires, and it was pulled taut against the creature's spine. There were leather bags and pouches of many sizes across the saddle, and even, Gwen noted with some surprise, a holster for a rifle. In the midst of all this chaos was a series of loops and bands that could only be for the securing of a human to the massive flying bat. There was space for two. Gwen gulped.

"This next bit can be tricky," Lina said. "And it will require some of that hard earned dexterity the preceptors drilled into you. I'll go first and show you how it's done."

Lina whistled long and low at the bat, and it went rigid as a board. She stepped off the scaffolding and grabbed onto the rungs along the sides of the saddle and harness. She then performed a tricky bit of maneuvering that involved placing her chest along the spine of the creature, and then her feet above her head. Her feet and legs went in looped straps that he pulled taut with a few quick gestures of her hand. With her lower body secured, Lina slipped her arms into the holsters above her head, so that she was hugging the massive chiropt with her head and neck resting atop a low pillow. She was looking down the spine and above the head of the upside-down bat. The whole maneuver had taken thirty seconds, and to Gwen it had looked like a spider settling itself on a wall.

Lina raised her neck to look at her. "It's a lot easier than it looks."

"Really?"

"No, not really. But you'll have lots of practice. Come on up, there's a spot in the saddle for you as well."

"Won't all the blood rush to your head while you wait?"

"Yes, but don't worry. Again, lots of practice. But you might want to hurry," Lina said, her cheeks already going red.

Gwen took a breath and composed herself. She forced herself to feel every inch of her, from the tips of her shaking fingers to her sweating toes. She felt her heart pumping blood, calm and steady for now, but only a hair's breadth from beating wildly out of control. She imagined a whisper coming from the dark, ordering her to practice obedience, urging her to give away all thought and all control, to surrender such distractions to it. The whisper was safe, the whisper was powerful, and it was wrong.

She lurched into motion, her hands shaking with adrenaline. Gwen stepped off the platform and onto the harness of the chiropt. She clambered past Lina to reach the saddle directly above her. Gwen copied her movements from before, sliding her feet into the stirrups and her hands into the braces below her head. She tightened each strap until she was pressed tight against the harness. She reached her hands out and clenched fur, and beneath it she felt the rolling muscles of the bat twisting and shifting like ocean waves.

Lina clung to the bat below her, and she could see down her back and past her shoulders to the walls of the hangar below. Gwen felt the beating of her heart against her chest, and below it the slower and deeper beat of Clementine's. The whisper was still there, but she could barely hear it over the chorus of heartbeats. She looked up and saw Lina turning to check on her.

"All set?" she asked.

"All good back here."

"Ready to fly?"

"Just go before I pass out."

"Alright then, hold on tight, and try not to vomit on me."

"What?" Gwen asked, but too late. Lina threw out her hand and hit a lever dangling off the side of the scaffolding. A terrible grinding noise game from below them. A line of white space appeared on the floor, and with it came the cold howling of the wind. Snow shot up into the room, and Gwen grabbed the goggles Lina threw over her shoulder to her and put them on. The white line grew and grew until the floor itself disappeared and Gwen was looking down into the swirling white. Lina yelled something back at her, but it was lost in the roar of the wind. Lina pressed her knees roughly into the beast beneath.

Gravity disappeared. The icy wind pulled at her skin and at her hair. It slammed into the glass of her goggles, driving them down into her face. It forced the scream back down her throat and shook the breath from her lungs. They fell farther and faster, plummeting towards the stones of the valley below. And then the white void of ice and snow to either side of them was blocked by two great curtains of taut brown fur and skin. They swept up, and crashed down, and for a single instant the wind was silent, but it returned, only to retreat as the chiropt Clementine flapped her wings again, and again.

They pulled up from the valley floor, so close that Gwen could reach out and touch snow. They swept up the sides of the mountains, the beat of Clementine's wings thunderous in the valley. And Gwen found herself laughing with triumph until she was out of breath once again. They flew out of the shadow of Cradle and into the bright sunshine. She looked around the valley as they soared above it and saw the trickling waterfalls that littered the rocks. The air was still icy and cold, but now the sun beat at their backs, and Gwen felt a warmth in her chest that she had not felt since her arrival to Poa. She closed her eyes and enjoyed it.

She felt a gentle tap on her head, and she saw that Lina wanted her attention. She was splayed out across the back of Clementine, and each of her limbs was at work. Her hands were pressed against the sides of the beast, and the wings moved at the pressure of her fingers, palms, wrists, and elbows. A slight press of a finger and wrist, and Clementine turned her wings ever so slightly. They soared away from the river and over a forest of deep green. Another barest touch of her arms and hands adjusted their path again. Clementine responded to each slight change as if it were a shouted command.

As Lina's hands moved Clementine north, east, south, and west, so her feet and legs controlled her elevation. Raising her feet along her spine sent her shooting into the sky, while pressing them down sent her plummeting to the ground. So the training went, Gwen learning through observation what each touch did, what each movement meant. Weeks before, the distinctions between such slight changes would have been incomprehensible to her. Yet her time with the preceptors had changed her perception of movement and stillness. Such things mattered far more in the dark, when one must be aware of each limb with exquisite detail.

Gwen saw the science of it now and understood that while she had been enjoying the thrill of flight, Lina had not relaxed for a single moment. Every inch of her body was under her command and moved at her signal. No twitch could go unaccounted for, or else Clementine would move in unplanned and perhaps disastrous ways. Just as she strained to fly, Lina strained to direct her. It was a symbiotic relationship, neither one moving without the other.

Lina took them further afield, flinging them over rivers and fields of soft green. They passed over ruins made of bronze, and a meadow that was filled with the slow-moving shells of snails larger than carriages that left slimy green trails behind them. A thundering herd of oreamoses separated one snail from its companions, cracking its iron hard shell with their hooves and gorging on the snail within.

Yet, for all the wonders of the animals below, it was the changes in the landscape that were most startling. A field of green trees would flow beneath them, before a massive windswept canyon met it. The mighty river below would roar and pound until meeting the massive flanks of a glacier. Giant fields of porous stone flowed into the level sands of a desert. The land did not flow, it did not transition or change in a natural manner. It was without rhyme or reason, randomness on a global scale.

It could not happen naturally, Gwen thought to herself. Nature is more systematic and orderly than that. Environments change for a reason; biomes are shaped by what is possible. Yet it was not so here on Poa. It was a patchwork world. A jigsaw made of different pieces of a planet, endlessly jumbled up and reshuffled. It was unnatural. And if nature had not shaped it, what had?

Clementine took them back to Cradle, and as they flew back Gwen could see additional chiropts falling from Cradle and winging off into the creeping darkness, each one laden with packages and papers and mail. Lina had Clementine swoop once more into the hangar. She clambered up into the rigging of her nest, jostling Lina and Gwen as she moved about so that they were facing the dismounting platform. Gwen watched as Lina undid her straps and holsters slowly, so that she could better observe how it was done. Once she was dismounted, Gwen too went through the same process. She hoisted herself onto the platform and turned suddenly at a series of small popping noises coming from behind her.

She found Lina stretching her back and knees, the pops coming from her limbs as she cracked them back into position. Gwen watched with some amusement, until she felt a great swell of sickness building inside her. It seemed to come from her fingers, and her toes, and the tip of her nose. It shot down her limbs and collected in her stomach, so it felt like she had a swirling ball of acid building inside her. She lumbered to the edge of the platform and vomited into the valley below.

"Don't worry about it," Lina said. "It happens to everyone the first time you fly. Takes around five or six good flights before you find your sky stomach."

Gwen turned around and found her doing deep leans from side to side as she continued to stretch after the flight.

"That was awful."

"Well the end always is. But how was the rest of it?"

"That part wasn't so bad," Gwen said, as she slumped down against the railings. "That part was pretty wonderful. Are you okay?"

"Oh, I'm fine. I always need to stretch out like this after a flight. It puts a real strain on your back. There's a reason why all the flyers take so many ice baths," she said, as her head leaned side to side in a series of neck rolls. "We'll all have intense arthritis when we reach old age, but I believe flying is well worth it."

"The way you flew was...impressive," Gwen said.

"Thank you. That's kind of you to say. I'd like to teach you how to fly as well, Gwen."

"I thought I was too strange?"

"I'm willing to take the risk. I think this organization needs a few more oddballs like you and me. But please, I have worked hard to ensure my prim, proper, and rule following persona is unquestionable amongst the higher ups. I'd hate for them to think I have a rebel streak at this juncture," Lina said, straightening from her stretches so that her posture was ramrod straight once again.

"But you are prim and proper. That's no cover," Gwen said, smiling a little.

"Yes, well, some disguises come more easily than others. But in either case, I think they wanted us to drive each other crazy when they made you my partner. They wanted to tuck us away in some far corner and let us destroy each other. I do not imagine they anticipated for even a moment that we would get along."

"I didn't either, to be fair," Gwen said.

"Nor did I. A rather unexpected surprise. Let's see what other surprises we can achieve together. Who knows? Perhaps we might run this paper one day?" Lina said, and Gwen could see the gleam in her eye when she said this. She had ambition, this one. She was going to the top, but did Gwen want to as well? She did not know. She was just rediscovering herself, after all. But at this moment, after a magnificent flight and a nauseous end, helping an ally seemed like a wise thing to do.

She could feel it now. The flight and the laughter were beginning to clear out her head. For weeks she had been trapped in a sunless world with nothing for comfort but the whispers of tyrannical instructors. In that place she had been reduced to her barest essentials, thinking of nothing more than the next moment, the next movement. Gwen had not questioned her place in such a world, but now she could not help but marvel at the world of Poa, so chaotic and unnatural, but gripped in elements from her own childhood. She found herself wanting more than whispered approval from dark corners. She wanted answers.

"Sounds like a plan, Lina. Although you might have to forgive the occasional strangeness from me now and then."

"I look forward to it. Come on, let's say goodbye to Clementine now, I'll show you how the mail is sorted." Lina walked to the side of the platform and whispered something into Clementine's massive ear, as she stroked her sides. As they left, she brought forth a crate filled with fruits of all kinds and sizes for Clementine. The bat tucked into the delicacies within, producing an such unearthly racket that Lina quickly ushered Gwen away. They left the dusty halls of Lina's personal hangar and set out into the mid-levels of Cradle.

Here, the letters and papers reigned supreme. Vast clattering machines swung about the halls and storerooms of the midlevel, carrying bundles of papers in every direction. Gwen watched in amazement as some letters simply zoomed across the room, as if summoned by magic. Yet when she examined closer, she could see small holes drilled into the walls from which pipes directed the terrible outer wind to industrious effect, creating zooming wind tunnels that shot letters to and fro. Swarms of mechanics and scribes rushed about the room, dodging the machines and each other, pulling a machine there, tipping a bundle of letters here, swiping a flying letter there.

"Every day we send couriers out to our various depots throughout the world. People from all over the planet drop their letters at those depots for delivery. The couriers bring the letters here where we sort them according to their destination," Lina shouted above the clattering of the machines as she led her from the sorting room to the even more vast mail room, where immense crates and stacks of letters waited in neatly identified areas for delivery.

Every few minutes a troop of deliverers and couriers marched in and filled their mail bags with stacks of letters and then set off for deliveries all over the planet.

"Each courier has a route, so to speak, that they deliver on. Now the route is not determined by tiles, but rather by longitude and latitude. If we based it on tiles the whole system would be chaos, after all, the tiles move all the time. So we divided the planet into sections and assigned them. We have thousands of couriers and their seconds on standby delivering letters almost constantly," Lina continued to explain as she led Gwen through the packaging rooms where larger parcels waited for pickup.

"We try to deliver each letter within a week, of course that's not always possible to pull off due to weather and on the ground conditions. Timing also plays a significant factor. We have to fly at night, after all."

"Why do you have to fly at night?" Gwen asked.

"Because people try to shoot us down."

"Excuse me?"

"Lelial explained that we are trying to tie the world together with information, right? But not everyone is so open to the idea. We've had to deal with many tiles that desperately want to keep the world away. There is an ongoing debate about what to do about this situation. Current thinking holds that we should leave well enough alone, and that soon they'll open themselves up when they see the world advancing without them," Lina explained as she stopped in front of a room marked with a little plaque sign that read simply 'Lost Letters.'

"It's not those tiles that keep me up at night though, Gwen. No, I am terrified of those tyrants both large and small that feel that their people should remain unburdened by knowledge, even as their people cry out for stories and songs that are not the tools of tyrants. So we send flyers anyway and are met with fearful adversaries. The Coral King of Ihika Isle, the Iron Council of Domedes, the Eternal Empress of the Locked Kingdom. They shoot us with arrows, they patrol the skies with monsters, they fill the air with poisonous gas. The Truth is a dangerous thing, and not without its sacrifices." Lina stopped speaking, and Gwen watched her gather herself in front of that door. "And here is where we go to remember."

She threw open the door. In the room beyond, Gwen saw stacks of undelivered mail spread throughout the room. Some had the sheen of new mail, while others were rotting with age and mildew. The air carried the hint of decaying paper and fading ink. And it seemed the air carried the whisper of words unsaid, of hushed voices and stifled breath. It was a room for waiting.

"What is this place?" Gwen said, her voice automatically becoming a whisper.

"This is where we keep our failures," Lina said, as she stepped into the room. Her fingers floated above the undelivered letters, as if afraid to touch and disturb their slumber. She walked amongst the stacks and in her eyes there was the glow of pride, but also the shine of unfallen tears as she looked at the work of generations of couriers who had tried to deliver the mail and had died in the process.

"Every letter we have failed to deliver we bring here. Men and women of immense bravery flew upon the winds to carry these words, but in the end they too fell. We bring their bodies back to Cradle, and we bring their letters back here."

"What do you do with them?"

"We wait. I say failures, Gwen, but I do not say defeats. We will deliver these letters, even if we must wait a thousand years. There is a trial among the reporters, one that is an open secret throughout the *Herald*. To become a reporter, you must pass the Trial of the Lost Letters and deliver one of these bundles to those that still wait."

Lina sighed. And she allowed her fingers to brush one of the letters beneath her hand. It was the briefest of touches, and then she turned away.

"Come on, that's enough lessons for today. Let's get something to eat. Tomorrow we will tackle the care and maintenance of a chiropt's equipment," Lina said, and she led the way from the room.

Gwen turned to follow, when a letter by the corner caught her eye. It was jutting out of a stack of yellowed missives by the door. The paper was lined with inked swirls and spirals that once would have covered every inch of the envelope. Now most had chipped away and the beautiful etchings were mere suggestions. Gwen found her hand reaching out and pulling the letter free. Her eyes traced the envelope following its spirals until she reached the intended address. At the top, in handwriting she knew well, was her own name along with the names of her friends.

She tilted it to the side to send the letter tumbling out. She caught it before it fell and opened it with trembling fingers. It read, in faded ink:

Dear Friends,

The first thing you must understand is that this world does not make sense. The second thing you must understand is that you can force it to. I pray that you have not joined me in this place, yet I fear you might have.

The next section of the letter had rotted away, so that the letters on the page were impossible to decipher, even as Gwen's fingers clutched at the faded and yellowing paper, even as her eyes begged for words. All that remained was a signature at the bottom in the crooked, frantic hand of a friend.

Yours, Yosef League

A tear fell and landed next to the *Yours*. And another soon followed. Gwen moved the letter away, folding it carefully and sliding it once more into the envelope traced with the remains of spirals. She tucked the frail letter away in the folds of her thin coat and wiped her eyes. Gwen stilled her breathing and slowed her racing heart. She focused on what she could sense and feel. She heard the faint roar of the wind beating at the walls of Cradle. She tasted the ink on the air, and the scent of tears. She heard the whispers of words unsaid and unread all around her, and then she walked out the door to catch up with Lina, who had not noticed her absence.

She nodded along as Lina spoke about the care of the chiropts and the role of careful equipment upkeep. She matched her stride and made her face a mask of careful polite interest. She did not make a sound, but allowed herself a small, almost imperceptible smile.

It was more than she had dared to hope. In the unending void of the monastery, she had known she was all alone, with nothing to rely on but her own skills. Even after she had left, she did not allow herself to even contemplate that one of the others had come to Poa with her.

But now Gwen knew the truth at last. She was not alone in this strange new world.

Yosef League, her friend, was here on Poa with her, but she knew not where. Perhaps even Yosef did not know. But she knew what Yosef must have done next when he had found himself in this strange land. He had reached out.

Yosef was writing them letters, sending messages in bottles into the ocean of mail that was the *Herald*. And if Yosef was here, why not all the others? Was she the first to find such a letter? How many others were there? She did not know. But one truth filled her with an unfamiliar warmth.

Her friends were out there, waiting for her. And she would find them, using all the resources of the *Bird's Eye Herald*.

Chapter 14: The Messenger's First Delivery

I think I'm being followed, and I'm sure it is not one of us. I have had to change tiles several times, and I never stay in the same place for longer than a few weeks. Please, find me before my pursuer does. I think they are trying to kill me.
(Letter 16, Paragraph 4, Lines 1-3)

Clementine twitched beneath Gwen's fingertips. The immense bat lifted its right wing, sending them soaring through the air towards the great river that ran through the heart of this tile. Gwen felt the muscles beneath Clementine's skin stretch and pull as she flew through the sky.

Gwen tapped both feet against the back of the beast, and Clementine pulled up, sending them shooting into the sky. Lina was shouting something to Gwen above the wind, giving her more instructions and more tips. But Gwen was not paying attention. It was much more fun to listen to Clementine. Gwen could hear the steady beat of the chiropt's heart as it thumped blood through its chest and down the thin skin on its wings. She could hear the chiropt's breaths and the low rumble it had in its throat, like it was preparing to sing.

The tile was spread out below them like a painting. The river glowed red with the light of the setting sun. Trees nestled along the riverbanks, their long branches dipping down into the water. The trees moved with a will of their own, but all with the same motion. Each tree, all at once, swayed and shook its branches along the surface of the water, like children dipping their hands in a lake. The sway sent the water leaping into the air, creating a fine mist that hovered over the river.

Gwen smiled and found that it was getting easier and easier to do so. She whispered a command to Clementine while making a rolling gesture with her left hand. At once Clementine tucked in her left wing and rolled on that side, and now they were diving towards the river below and the playing trees. The wind rushed by Gwen's ears pulling at the grin on her face, but she could not stop smiling. Lina was slapping at her calves behind her, the only part of her that she could reach, but she did not stop the dive until she was close enough to count the individual leaves on the trees below her.

They soared along the river, moving with its flow. And Gwen could feel the trees flinging water up towards them. She could taste the water as it landed on her face. Clementine slowed as Gwen relaxed upon her. Now they moved as slowly as the river below.

"You are going to regret getting Clementine wet," Lina said behind her, the wind no longer snatching at her words. "We have to fly through subzero winds to get back to Cradle, you know?"

"Oh," Gwen said, the smile falling from her face. She tucked her toes along Clementine's side, tracing them up. Clementine began to rise, leaving the river below.

"Sorry about that," Gwen said, a flush appearing on her cheeks and forehead.

"No need to apologize to me, but you might want to say a word to Clementine when we return. She wasn't due for a bath for another three weeks, and she is not a huge fan of water," Lina said, her words carrying a gentle reproach but also the hint of a smile.

"I will," Gwen promised. "How am I doing otherwise?"

"Passing well I would say. I was worried we had not adequately reviewed how to pull out of a dive a little while ago, but you seemed to have remembered at the end."

"Are you always su—such a mom?" Gwen said, stumbling over her words. She was trying to remember how to be funny again but was worried that the preceptors had killed her sense of humor.

"Only when it may end in my premature death," Lina said, laughing. Gwen glowed with pride at the sound. "Really all forms of death tend to bring out my matronly aspects. You have to avoid getting so close to the ground unless coming in for a landing though. We stay in the high skies the rest of the time. Almost no one outside of Cradle knows about the chiropts, and therefore may not take kindly to seeing a monster diving at them."

"Clementine is not a monster. She's a sweetheart. Aren't you Clementine?" Gwen said, snuggling into Clementine's fur with her face and head. She could not pet the beast, as such a motion could easily send the highly trained animal into a maneuver.

"She is exceedingly adorable, but I seem to recall a young messenger having a bit of a reaction to seeing Clementine and her brethren.

Reduced to a laughing fit, I believe. Most tend to attack or run screaming," Lina retorted.

Gwen blanched at the thought of arrows piercing Clementine's wings. "I'll keep to the clouds. This tile seems deserted, however."

"It mostly is. It's one of the more pastoral tiles. The standing population is around 5000 souls I believe. It's why I chose it for today's training exercise. I had a sneaking suspicion you were going to attempt some less than covert maneuvers."

"Flying is so fun, Lina!" Gwen said, bursting out with enthusiasm.

"I know! You and Clementine are almost totally in sync. You might even start to dream as each other soon."

Gwen hid her smile in Clementine's fur. She and Lina had spent weeks in the classroom and in the hangar discussing and learning everything there was to know about what it took to soar on a chiropt. They had covered aerodynamics, chiropt maintenance, and basic navigation. Although the tiles were in constant flux, making navigation by landmarks a difficult task, Lina had instructed Gwen in how to read the stars and chart a journey by their movements. This allowed the *Herald* to fly at night, which was why so few knew how the *Herald* was able to accomplish its mission of spreading the Truth. A mission that Gwen was soon to take part in.

"Now that we have practiced some of our more...advanced maneuvers, let's get on with the mission. The town of Autumnmond is not far from here. Keep following the river north and we should be there by the time the sun sets."

Gwen gave the hand signal indicating that she understood the instructions and pressed herself once more against Clementine. It was getting easier and easier to fly her. She could read Clementine's gestures and expressions as well as a person's now. She could tell when the beast needed feeding, when she needed cleaning, and when she needed Gwen to let the leash off and just let her fly. Those were the moments Gwen liked best. She treasured the thrill that rushed down Clementine's spine whenever she could fly without restraint, when the skies were hers and hers alone.

Gwen gave Clementine the lead now, and the chiropt gave a ripple of pleasure. And now the great wings beat against the wind, and the chiropt rose on the gusts into the air so that her wings just traced the undersides of the clouds. The sun set ahead of them, and they steered into its dying light.

Gwen relaxed and let her mind slip away from the mission. From here she could see the curve of Poa as the landscape sloped away. And she could see how segmented it was, so like the puzzles they would all do as kids. Landscapes collided with each other, desert winds scything over sun drenched meadows, oceans emptying to form coral canyons. An unnatural thing. A dangerous thing. And Yosef was out there in that mess and had done the thing he knew best, reached out.

From her discussions with Lina, she had learned that the *Herald* was one of the few global organizations of this world, with the ability to deliver anywhere at any time despite the shifting tiles. The high cabinets in the research department of the *Herald* were packed to the brim with stories on every tile the *Herald* delivered to. There were desks devoted to hotspots all around the planet, each with a dedicated team of researchers monitoring the situation on the ground, all to assist the messengers as they picked up and delivered the mail. And what the research department did not know, the reporters would discover.

Yosef must have learned these things when he landed and decided to use its network to reach out to anyone else that had arrived on the planet. Gwen had checked the records and determined that Yosef had not joined the *Herald*, and thus had never had full access to its resources. But he could rely upon the network to deliver his letters. And so he had written to each of them, all those that had been present at the funeral. For that was the last thing Gwen could remember, the last flashing moments of Earth. And then she had woken up here, and she now guessed so had all the others.

Yosef must have tried to find them using the *Herald*, but something must have gone wrong. For no letter had ever been delivered to Gwen in her time on Poa, even in the heart of Cradle. How could he have thought the letter would be delivered if there were no addresses for any of them? If they were lost in an unknown world? The thought Gwen tormented her to no end, but Yosef had always been a step ahead of the rest of them. Perhaps he had discovered something about this world they had not, or maybe he had hoped that one of them would make their way to the *Herald* and would find his letters as they made their way through the system.

Yet something had gone wrong. For what else could have brought his missive to the Lost Letter department where the failures of the *Herald* were kept? And now, Gwen feared that one of their number was on a hostile tile, one ruled by a leader who desired no outside intrusion. One who had sent a messenger of the *Herald* tumbling from the sky and had nearly destroyed Yosef's letter.

It had been five months since Gwen had arrived on Poa, give or take. Could she have survived in such a wild place for so long? Could one of their friends? Frightful as the *Herald* was, at least it sounded better than the wild tiles Lina described.

Gwen's knuckles whitened on Clementine's harness. She had to master all that Lina and the *Herald* could teach. A chiropt would be an invaluable tool for searching the world for the others, and she was only just now starting to master flight. Lina still had much to teach her about the systems of the *Herald*. She would need those resources to conduct her search. Everything could be used, and each would be of help. Yet Gwen stayed for another reason, one that she kept in her heart of hearts.

She was certain, more certain than stone, that the paper had secrets. The corvids played the part of benevolent bosses and reluctant taskmasters well. They spoke of the Truth and of enlightening the world, and perhaps they intended to. Yet their methods contained an urgency, a desperation, that spoke of some higher motive. And the name, the name was key.

If Yosef and the others were all here, then it was no coincidence that the *Herald* shared the name of the newspaper Huck had created as a child. They had departed at his funeral and were brought here to this new world to find his childhood dreams waiting. But for what purpose? What had sent them here, and why?

So she waited, and she tried to master the nightmares she had begun to have of her friends trapped in a savage place.

"We're getting close, start to bring us down," Lina said behind her, and Gwen eased herself back into control of Clementine. She brought them down into a gentle dive. Below she could see a clearing in the middle of the swaying woods. A dock and pier jutted out into the water, and many slender canoes dangled from long lines. A winding path worked its way from the dock and into a small town. Houses just as graceful as the dancing trees lined the path in twisting patterns.

Clementine alighted on the ground, and Gwen began to pull at the straps and bindings that kept her lashed to the great beast. She loosened her gear until she could slide from the creature's back and onto the solid land below. She pressed herself against the wet grass along the river's bank, the first grass she had seen in many months. The heady scent of the earth filled her nose, and the rushing of the river warmed her like song.

Lina grabbed the mailbags on the sides of the saddle while Gwen instructed Clementine to wait. Clementine bundled down under the eaves of the swaying trees and tucked her head into her wings. Gwen could see her bright eyes follow them out of the clearing, before they closed, and her chest rose and fell under the gentle caress of sleep.

Lina guided them through the outskirts of the swaying forest to the lights of the village ahead. The sun set behind them and night covered the land, but Gwen and Lina were used to a world without light.

They crept from bush to bush, tree to tree. Their eyes roved, looking for any change in the darkness around them, but they did not rely on just their eyes. Gwen heard the world move around them, the rustling of branches, the chirping of crickets, the movement of the wind.

She fell into the patterns of the roving gusts, following its flowing path through the obstacles she could not see. Lina moved with her, falling into the same patterns and movements.

They approached the village from the trees, ever careful of a fellow late night wanderer. Yet the town was still as stone. Lina stopped with her back to the last house at the end of the curving lane.

She whispered to Gwen in the bird's voice, the language that the preceptors had instructed them in, a low swooping tongue that always arrived at the listener as a whisper no matter the distance.

"The pillar box is in the center of the town. We will sweep the area for watchers and then deliver and pick up the letters. I want you to focus on how I access the pillar." Gwen nodded.

Lina led the way through the streets, moving from the deeper shadows below the houses to the gaping mouths of the alleys in between. She flowed like water across the lane, as calm and cool as a leaf on the wind. Gwen followed in her wake.

The main square of the village lay ahead. Market stalls, closed for the night, lay resting in the center of the square like slumbering cattle. The shops that occupied the corners were shuttered and vacant.

Lina gave the signal that the area was clear and led the way to a tall pillar on the other side of the square. It was several feet taller than Gwen and much wider. It looked to be made of stone, but its color was a blue so deep that it seemed to suck the surrounding darkness into its depths. It had a large gaping mouth at chest height, but its throat was blocked by a metal screen that only the turn of a handle could move. All around the mouth were tiny drawers carved into the stone. Each drawer had a series of numbers and letters etched onto its face as well as a curving half-moon of pure white.

"This is a pillar box, and it will soon become your second-best friend in the world, after Clementine of course," Lina said as they approached the pillar. "There is one just like it in most every town across most of the tiles, and they all look and work the same. The people nearby can place whatever mail they desire into the mouth of the box and work the crank to deliver it into its depths. They cannot reach further in the pillar from this mouth, however. The screen is just the first gate that blocks any attempt to break into them. Only messengers can get into the pillars."

"Why all the security?"

"People need to trust that no one can see or steal what they want the *Herald* to deliver. Security, reliability, and secrecy are the chief virtues of our delivery service."

"How do we get in? Is there a key or something?"

"No key. Keys can be stolen or copied. Locks can be picked. We needed something more secure than that. Notice anything familiar about the stone?"

Gwen peered closely at the pillar and its construction. It was hard to make out any details on its surface, as it seemed to resist any attempt by the lingering light of the stars or the moons to illuminate it, but it looked as if it was hewn all from the same familiar piece of stone.

"It's the same stone as the outside of Cradle."

"Correct. Each pillar is made by us and installed in the delivery location. The stone is unique, only available at the Cradle mountains, and only our engineers know how to mine it and shape it. We control the entire construction process, and we alone know its secrets." Lina reached out to the stone and began to jab the rock in different spots. She pressed a space near the mouth, reached up and ran her finger in a line near the top of the pillar, and pressed her palm against the space beneath the delivery slot. Her hands whipped out, almost too fast for Gwen to follow, as she worked several other combinations on the surface of the pillar.

A moment passed, and then the mouth of the pillar gapped wider and elongated. A part of the face of the pillar fell outward on greased hinges at a place where there was no seam before. Lina stepped forward and reached into its depths. She pulled out some twenty letters and packages and placed them in her pack.

Lina closed the mouth of the pillar. "Were you able to follow the sequence?

"I got most of it. Is it the same for every pillar?"

"No. It's a different combination for each one. Again security—"

"Is the name of the game. How many combinations do you have memorized?"

"None of them. The combination is written right on the pillar. Look closely, look with more than just your eyes. Try to figure out the sequence to unlock the drawers. The first symbol is right here," Lina said, and she lifted Gwen's finger to a spot at her eye level. Gwen focused on the spot on the stone. To her eyes it seemed indistinguishable from the spots around, the same rock as all the rest. Yet there was the slightest difference in the grain of the stone under her touch, the softest change in the sound her finger made as it swept across this bit of surface. Together, the sensations seemed to point towards another bit of the pillar about six inches above.

Gwen traced this part as well, eyes closed as she focused all her attention on what she felt. Her finger swept the surface, finding the second point and following this one's markings to the next, and the next. Yet the fifth spot eluded her. The fourth string in the combination gave no clues where the fifth was, or how it could be found. Gwen opened her eyes, defeated, she had lost the combination.

"I've lost the thread of it," Gwen said, her face colored with shame. She hunched her shoulders against the berating she was sure would come in a birdlike whisper.

"You did well. You got much farther along than I thought you would. The preceptors taught you how to enhance your attention. Yet that can get you only so far. There are multiple combinations that can be pressed on the pillar. You were following the one that would activate the tinder kept at the base. If you had managed to follow it for another three steps, you would have destroyed every letter in the pillar."

"Why would you have such a thing on a mailbox?" Gwen asked, aghast. Lina made a face at her and shrugged. "Right, security."

"Only a fully trained messenger can open one of the pillars. You'll need a Cognitive Domain to see what lies hidden here. You require Observation," Lina said, before stepping forward. Her hands flicked out, as quick as darting snakes, triggering the combination. At once there was a soft click, and each of the drawers slid out.

"Time to deliver the mail," Lina said and indicated the bag on Gwen's shoulder.

This part Gwen knew well. She darted around the pillar, slipping each letter into its destined drawer. When she had delivered all of the dozen letters, they had carried she stepped back so that Lina could add copies of the *Bird's Eye Herald*. Afterwards, she input another of the combinations onto the face of the pillar. At once, each one of the drawers snapped shut and would remain locked until the sun rose in the morning.

Lina nodded at her, and in silence they strapped their packs to their sides once more. They left the pillar box behind and retraced their steps across the square. Gwen was still going over what parts of the combination she had been able to glean when Lina's hand shot out and grabbed her wrist. She pulled her into an alcove, hiding them in deep shadow.

"What are you doing?" Gwen said.

"Silence," Lina whispered back to her. Her eyes were wide and roving. Her mouth was open, but she did not breathe. There was a light at the edge of her pupil, a dull pulsing purple. The light spread across her eyes, creating a film that covered them like a cataract. Gwen lurched back in horror, even as Lina's hand stayed clenched around her arm. The film rose from Lina's eye, lifting off the surface until it floated just a centimeter above. And Lina stared through this lens to the world beyond.

"A woman is screaming six hundred meters from here. She's in pain," Lina said.

"What?"

"Her house is waking up. A man has gotten out of bed and grabbed the sword underneath. Doors are opening all over the neighborhood. A crowd is forming. Fifteen of them have weapons. They're coming here."

Gwen turned to where she was looking, attempting to peer through the heavy shadows that cloaked the square. Gwen closed her eyes, attempting to focus with her other senses. A crowd that big would make a great deal of noise. Yet there was nothing. The town was empty.

"Lina, what are you talking about? There's nothing there."

"There will be. They just left the neighborhood on the outskirts of town. They've gathered up the screaming woman, the man with the sword as well. The man is crying. They will be in the square in the next two minutes," Lina said, her voice a flat monotone. No more emotional than if she was commenting on the weather.

"How are you seeing these things?"

"I'm not seeing them. I'm observing them," Lina said, and she turned to her. The film in front of her eyes twirled. There were hundreds of shining sparks inside the film. They appeared and fizzled out, flashing for an instant and then breaking apart to form new sparks. Lina blinked, hard. And the film vanished.

"I'll explain later," Lina said.

"I hope so."

A minute passed in silence as they stood in the alcove like furtive lovers. And then Gwen could hear them, the screaming, marching crowd, racing towards the square.

The mob thundered into the market. They were an odd assortment. Some wore the clothes of farmers and laborers while others still wore their pajamas. Many were carrying weapons: old swords, pitchforks, rough spears, and a hunting bow made up the group's arsenal, that and their torches.

The group stopped in the center of the market beside the dribbling fountain. The light of their torches lit up the square, yet there were shadows still.

They must be here for the pillar box, Gwen thought to herself. They must have figured out that the delivery was tonight. Or maybe they had spotted them when they flew overhead or crept into town. Now they were here in numbers, ready to find the intruders who had had the temerity to deliver their mail. Lina had always said that there were those that meant them harm.

And she was unarmed! Gwen looked down and saw that one of the cobbles was loose beneath her feet. It would take only a moment to work the brick loose, and with that she could do some damage.

"What's happened?" One of the crowd roared.

"Annete's boy has gone missing," one of the torchbearers said.

"Joshua?"

"Another one?"

"They say he stumbled off in the night. Just like Justian the day before yesterday. Or Ivan the day before that. Vanished before the sunrise."

"Where is he!?" the woman cried, her face tortured. Her husband clung to her, his sword shaking in his hand even as tears fell from his eyes.

"We'll find them, don't worry," a woman with a torch said.

"We have to comb the town."

"We'll need more men for that."

"They'll be here soon," another said. He seemed to be the leader judging by the way the others looked at him. He was a wide, squat man with massive shoulders. There was a terrible sunburn on the back of his neck, and Gwen could hear him scratch at it as they waited in the dark. Bits of skin flaked off him with every turn and glittered in the light of the torches.

"They'll all come! This ends tonight. Sixteen people vanished in the last month, not a trace nor sign of any of them," the man snarled. "Even my own daughter, my Joanna, vanished! No more. We will find out who has taken them!" And now the man was roaring, and the

194

crowd shivered with more than the cold. Rage shook their limbs, and the torches rose higher, and they roared back at the man.

"Wait, wait. Taking them? My own girl saw Joanna leaving the town from her bedroom window. And she was all by her lonesome. She wasn't being taken by anyone," a man with a torch said.

The leader rounded on this man. He loomed over him, heedless of the torch's heat as the fire crackled near his hair. "Are you saying Joanna abandoned her family?"

The man cowered back. "No."

"I didn't think so," the leader said. He leaned back, shouting at the assembled crowd to make himself heard over the crying mother and father.

"Search the town! Find any sign of what's taken them."

With a roar the crowd lurched into the motion, men and women with torches leading the way as they fanned out from the square.

Hidden in the sounds of the chaos, Lina whispered to her, "Time to go."

"What?" Gwen said, but Lina was already sneaking away. Gwen grabbed her arm and pulled her back into the alcove, back into what remained of the shadows.

Lina turned back to Gwen, but her eyes still roved the square looking for threats. "We made the delivery. It's time to move on."

"There are people missing. We can find them. You can use that eye thing you just did and find that boy," Gwen said, and she forgot to whisper as her body shook with the urge to run after the crowd to help find the boy.

"We can't do that, Gwen."

"But we can! We're right here, and we're faster than that crowd. Come on, he could be in trouble."

"We are not allowed to interfere. We have to move on."

"It will only take a second," Gwen said, shifting her feet and stretching her shoulders, ready to spring into action. She had to find the boy!

"We will not do any such thing. We will go back to Clementine and fly away. That is our job. It is not our task or our right to interfere on this tile. We simply deliver the mail," Lina said, looking at her. She was as still as a statue, and just as cold.

"What are you talking about? You've talked for hours about how great the *Herald* is and now you just want to let people disappear?" Gwen said, and now her blood was up, and she could feel it rushing through her chest and up her arms.

"That is the job! We are not god, we are the *Herald*, and we do not interfere. Our job demands secrecy," Lina said, and her voice was rising now as she turned from Gwen. "The *Herald* cannot survive if we try to heal every wound. We uphold one task, and perhaps…" And now Lina's voice dropped until she was speaking in a whisper. "Perhaps one day that will redeem us for all we failed to do."

Panic gripped Gwen's heart and squeezed. Her mind played host to a parade of horrific images. Screaming parents, lost boys, all familiar sights to her. "We can find him!" Gwen said, her mouth moving as fast as her rabbiting heart. "Come on, Huck could be in danger."

She froze.

"Huck? Who's Huck?" Lina asked.

"I mean Joshua. We must find Joshua."

"It's not our job to save people, Gwen!" And as the words left her mouth people came streaming back into the square.

"We found him!" a woman cried, and she was leading a mob of people carrying a person above their heads. It was a boy, and he was struggling against their grasping arms, but they would not let him go.

More and more of the town poured back into the square. And Gwen and Lina ducked back into the narrow alcove.

The mother and father of the boy rushed forward, hands reaching for their crying son. But the father of Joanna blocked their way.

"Put the boy down but hold him tight."

"He nearly took our eyes out, Elias. Be careful."

Three strong men and women held the boy fast, and now Gwen could see him clearly. While his arms and legs pulled with desperate fervor, his face was as blank as a doll's. His eyes seemed clouded over, as if gazing at a landscape no one else could see.

Elias crouched down in front of him, heedless of the boy's screaming parents as they fought to get by his side. The crowd pressed in on them, eager to see what he would do.

"Where were you walking, Joshua? Where were you going tonight?" Elias asked, his voice empty of all emotion. Members of the crowd shouted out the same question.

The boy did not respond. His expression did not change as Elias loomed over him.

"Where did the others go? Were you going to find them, boy?"

Again, no answer. The crowd was growing more agitated now. The torches swung closer and closer to the boy, but he still showed no reaction.

Elias's face twisted with anger as he lost all trace of calm. "Tell me where Joanna is! Are you the one who took her?"

"Stop! Stop!" Joshua's mother cried. "He hasn't taken anyone. He's sick. He has visions. He sees things that aren't there. That's all."

"What do you see, Joshua?" Elias demanded. "Did you see the others you've taken?"

"He sees a statue. One made of metal. Something he—he just made up. That's it, just a statue! He says he dreams about it, and sometimes he moves when he sleeps. But he didn't take anybody. Now get away from him!"

But the crowd had lost all sense. They surged forward, torches lowered, mouths open with screams. They hurled abuse at the boy, along with their desperate pleas to tell them where their missing people were.

And Gwen's feet were moving before she could think. Her senses focused before she knew she had made the decision to intervene. She saw the gaps in the crowd, she heard the thunderous beats of their hearts, and with one fluid motion she blew through their ranks like a gust of wind.

Ducking torches and leaping over outstretched limbs, Gwen flowed to Joshua's side. Her hands found the arms that were keeping him captive, and with the iron strength of a *Herald* novice she broke their grips.

"That's enough," Gwen murmured, her eyes downcast, seeking what remained of the shadows.

The crowd reared back from her. Elias clutched his injured hand to his chest, his mouth still open in a howl of anger, but Gwen could see the tears pouring from his eyes, tears that had begun to drip as soon as he said his daughter's name.

"The boy is sick, but he's not dangerous. Everyone needs to back away," Gwen said, forcing her voice to rise above a whisper. She dragged her head up, but she could not manage to meet the sunburnt man's eyes. Instead, she looked for Lina, but there was no sign of the older girl.

"Who is she?" someone whispered in the crowd, and it passed like a virus through their midst, growing louder and louder with each echo.

"I need you all to step back and let his parents through. Please."

"Who are you!" Elias roared. "Are you the one that took them? WHERE ARE THEY?"

"I didn't take anybody," Gwen said, and the torches burned into her eyes like flares, but she would not let herself blink.

"Then who are you?!" someone in the crowd shouted.

"I'm nobody," Gwen muttered, and she could feel it building around her, danger lapping at her senses, sucking the strength from her bones. "Just let the boy go back to his parents. That's all I ask."

"Or what? You going to vanish us too? Tell us where the others are, girl. Tell me where Joanna is," Elias said, the acrid smell of his sweat scorching her nostrils, his hammering heart filling her ears with thunder. And Gwen stepped back, bumping into the boy still muttering in his sleep behind her.

Whispers ripped through the crowd and began to rise in strength. The free ground between Gwen and Joshua and the crowd was diminishing every second. The mob came closer and closer, the air grew hotter with the burning of the torches, and the smell of blood, ash, and sweat was choking Gwen now.

"I said stand back," Gwen said, and she could not hear her own voice over the roar of the crowd. "Please don't take another step forward." And she closed her hands into fists now and brought them before her. She looked into Elias's eyes for the first time.

"You took my daughter away from me, and you expect me to be scared by threats?" Elias said, and his voice was as dead as a tomb.

The world stilled for a moment. The faces of the crowd were hidden from Gwen, cast into a hellish twilight of shadows by the burning torches. Elias took a step forward and Gwen held her breath.

"Grab the witch!" a voice cried behind her, and she felt hands reach from the crowd. Some aimed for Joshua, and others reached for Gwen.

She reacted without thinking. She reacted as she had been trained. Gwen shifted to the side so that the grasping hand scraped the fabric of her clothes. Her own hands reached out, finding the sides of the man's fist. With a single motion she broke his wrist, twisting his hand up and up until she felt the small muscles and bones give out. Her other hand shot out into the man's throat. The man gave a gurgling cry of pain, and with a whistling gasp fell onto the ground.

The other hands were pulling Joshua away into the depths of the crowd, but he was resisting, driving his own elbows into guts and into eyes, even as his face remained slack and blank.

Gwen stepped forward, evading the other reaching hands. Her fists flew out, finding the nerve cluster at the top of one woman's shoulder, another the solar plexus of a man with a torch.

Gwen closed her eyes, the words of the preceptor's words whispering in her ears. "Light can fool you, child. Light can trick you to your grave. But the sound of a step, the intake of a breath, the beat of a heart. These things cannot be faked. These things can be your targets."

She heard the pitchfork one man stabbed at her. She heard it whistle through the air. It was simple to duck it, to flow beneath it until she was inside the attacker's guard. She did not see the man's face as her hands broke his nose and knocked the breath out of his gut.

She did not need to see these things. She knew her movements, she knew their effects, and she knew the sounds they would make. What more did she need?

She was already moving to her next target, dancing amongst the writhing members of the crowd. Gwen kept track of Joshua's breaths in the tumult, the breathing of a sleepwalker in the midst of a bad dream. They were only feet from each other, but the crowd was rushing in, filling every space with bodies. Gwen dropped another woman as she moved, and then another man after that. The preceptors had taught her how to fight in darkness. They had taught her how to use the shadows to strike and then to get away. Yet there was no escape here, and the preceptors had never taught how to defend against an army.

A hand found Gwen's short hair, pulling a chunk free as she spun away. A surging leg caught her spinning foot, stumbling her for a second. A fist caught her side as she dodged a swinging torch, and Joshua's breath moved farther away, laced with pain as the crowd tore at him too. Gwen lunged forward even as clawed hands grasped at her shoulders and her ankles, pulling her back. Joshua was feet away but separated by a wall of people. Gwen opened her eyes to look into his, and saw her own empty expression reflected back at her in the empty glass of his gaze.

There was the sound of a massive drumbeat and a screech upon the wind. Gwen sagged with relief.

Clementine flew in from above the rooftops, her wings buffeting the crowd. They stumbled back, crying aloud in terror at the monster that had appeared before them. One woman raised her torch, her arm ready to throw. But the figure with glowing eyes on the bat's back made a motion, and the enormous creature screamed. The roar of ultrasound battered into their senses, sending men and women to their knees, and all traces of fight in them broke.

The town of Autumnmond ran all their rage forgotten in the face of this new threat. They ran for the shelter of the forest and soon only Gwen and the parents of Joshua remained.

Their eyes were wild as they looked around the square. Their hands were empty as they swung about, grasping for something now out of reach.

"Where is he?" the father cried, his body shaking with sobs. "Where did he go?"

"Joshua! Joshua, where are you?" the mother screamed.

Clementine touched down, snuffling with pride at her accomplishment. The mother and father paid no mind to the giant bat. Gwen thanked her as she climbed onto her back. Lina waited farther up her spine, strapped into the pilot's place. She did not speak to her as she strapped herself in. Lina gestured with her feet, and Clementine kicked into the air, flapping her wings to achieve flight. They spiraled into the sky until they were far above the town. Clementine turned, and they flew south along the river, back to Cradle.

But they could still hear the screams of Joshua's parents as they searched for their missing boy.

"You need to use Observation thing. We can find Joshua before he gets too far."

"I think we've done enough harm here. Our interference will only make things worse, for Joshua and for his family."

"How could you be so heartless?" Gwen said, her adrenaline still pumping through her system, sending words pouring forth she was used to keeping locked away.

"How could you be so foolish?" Lina asked, and her voice flared with anger. Clementine responded to it with a shudder as they flew. "You've ruined that family. Who will ever trust them again? First their son vanishes and then a giant bat appears at their call. They'll be outcasts forever. And their son will still be missing."

"It's better than doing nothing like you did," Gwen retorted and now Clementine's flight pitched and rose as she responded to the emotion in their voices and the shaking in their limbs.

When they spoke again, they made sure to remain still.

"How do you know that you made things better by interfering? For them or for us? Their boy is still missing, and you've just sent the paper back decades in this tile. The next time we come here we'll be greeted with arrows!"

"Which do you care about, the boy or some damn newspaper?"

"I care about both. The best way we can help everyone is to do our jobs, to do as we have been trained to do. We deliver, we observe, we return, we report. That is how we change the world."

"And what if we have to watch people die?"

"We cannot intercede in their lives, Gwen. We're messengers, and nothing more."

"You told me you had thrown the preceptors out of your head, Lina," Gwen said, her voice dead of all emotion. And the darkness was coming back, wrapping around her so tight it felt like her lungs were in the grips of talons.

Clementine's flight stuttered as Lina's hands gripped the fur beneath her fingers until her knuckles turned white.

"Do you understand that you were going to die?" Lina said, her voice shaking with anger even as her body remained still. "Do you even care about that?"

"I'm an instrument of the *Herald*. A messenger and nothing more," Gwen said, and even Clementine's warmth could not dispel the familiar chill that gripped her limbs.

Lina looked back at her for the first time. The other woman's eyes were bloodshot, her skin ashen. "We can still save people. We just need to be—"

"Selective. Of course. You are correct. The preceptors are wise. I will do better, be more...effective."

Lina flinched back as if stung. She opened and closed her mouth several times, started to speak, thought better of it, and tried again. "We will need to accelerate your training. Mastering the Domain of Observation is the next step. But you'll need a master cogonaut to teach you. I—I don't know how."

"Whatever is necessary, ma'am."

Gwen looked back at the vanishing town of Autumnmond. If she focused, she could still hear the screams and shouts of the vanished boy's parents. Joshua, a charming boy, consumed by his dreams.

He had looked, in that moment, just like Huck. And she had failed to save him again. Grief closed around her throat and stabbed into her eyes, but she did not let her tears fall.

Instead, she did as she had been taught, and closed her heart to it.

Her hand touched the letter from Yosef League, kept hidden away in the folds of her coat. Yosef would be better off without her help. He needed his friends, not an instrument.

Chapter 15: The Scholar's New Name

I was one of the first to meet him, I believe. He was hiding under the slide one day at recess building castles out of twigs and mulch. As I recall, I kicked the castle over. We did not become friends for many more years. I don't know if he ever forgave me. Perhaps that is why I am here.
(Letter 17, Paragraph 4, Lines 6-10)

It took a day to fly down to the event horizon of the Godstrom. Flying, as Theo was happy to learn, was much much slower than falling. The thirty-five members of the final expedition flew in a spherelike formation, lancers above and below, supplies and packmen in the next ring, with the scholar scientists in the middle. They moved at a slow clip, flying down a quarter of the speed a person could fall.

The speed allowed for maximum flexibility as they flew. And let each expeditionary focus entirely on their assigned task.

The packsmen were responsible for keeping aloft any equipment the expedition might need including, food, water, ammo, spare weapons, medical supplies and more. Some flew with these bags attached to them with ropes and pulleys. Others kept them stashed in packs. They were the expedition's mighty shoulders.

The weatherbreathers, meanwhile, took measurements of the air and its qualities as they flew, ever watchful for the sudden shifts in air pressure that would herald the sky changes that could wipe an expedition from the air. They were an odd bunch and kept mostly to themselves. Each weatherbreather was loaded with so much of the latest in mapping and tracking technology that they looked as if they were being consumed by an engine. The other members of the expedition tended to fly away when near them, for fear that they too would be gobbled up by the mapping machines. But they alone could pierce the chaotic miasma of the Godstrom to find the narrow paths of safety in the higher reaches of the storm. They were the senses of the expedition's body.

The charters circled Striker providing constant updates to the movements of the various parts of the expedition. The charters were the nimblest of the wingers, darting from person to person with unerring grace. Striker was always in the bottom hemisphere of the expedition, her eyes on the storm below. The charters were her voice, and the only means of communicating with the expedition's pieces.

The lancers patrolled the sphere, but the largest part of their number was fifty fathoms below the main body of the expedition. Here were the dragoons, the deadliest of all lancers that flew as the ever-ready fist poised to smash whatever band of krows might emerge. Elwyn had once been part of such a band, but now he lay a thousand fathoms above in his hospital bed.

His brothers and sisters soared through the air kitted out with half a dozen weapons each. They had no official equipment. Each lancer equipped himself or herself as he or she saw fit. Some carried rifles fixed with wicked bayonets. Other lancers equipped themselves with long sabers that slashed with terrible force when wielded at the lancer's full speed.

Theo carried no weapon of any kind. While each other member of the expedition bore some smaller weapon, usually a knife, pistol, or shortsword; Theo was unarmed. Striker had felt, poor flyer that he was, that he would be far more of a danger to others than to the enemy if he had a weapon.

As ever, he was alone. Theo was quartered in the weatherbreather's bell, the vast leather tent that held their larger equipment. It took three packsmen lashed to the bell at all times to carry it through the sky. On most expeditions it took only a team of two, with a rotating third packsman to carry the great bell. But, as they took no small pains to remind Theo, this time it took three.

For much of the first day Theo's time was taken up with beginning his examination of the N-Device. It had defeated Litvak, but he was determined not to lose to it as well. He had an advantage, after all, he knew that it was really an N64.

The device, unlike its earthly counterpart, seemed to require no electricity to operate. It took only the press of the button to activate. Theo flicked the switch, and once more the N-Device came to brilliant life. It projected a light that became an image hovering in the air before Theo's face.

Theo worked its controller as the Device produced scenes from its archives. A whirling kaleidoscope of lights and sounds produced brief flickers of games from Theo's childhood. His favorite games and settings flashed by, each as welcome as an old friend. Yet Theo had no time for such scenes. He cared only for the map.

The weatherbreathers had assured Theo that while their maps were as precise as human science could produce, there were inaccuracies. Such inaccuracies had terrifying results for unwary expeditions caught by a sudden shift in the storm. But the N-Device's map was perfect in every way, providing a godlike omniscience of the storm. Little wonder that the weatherbreathers treated the device as something divine, with all the fear and respect it deserved. They had avoided Theo since its activation, regarding him not as a colleague or fellow scholar, but as a sort of helpless prophet.

And Theo did feel helpless. Although he had been responsible for the Device's initial activation, he had been unable to activate the map a second time.

Back then, Theo's fingers had seemed to move of their own accord, flicking across the familiar controller of the N64 once more. He had closed his eyes and found himself as a young child bathed in the soft light of the TV in his basement. Mom had ordered pizza for him and his friends. The sugar of the warm soda Dad kept beneath the stairs coursed through them like rocket fuel. Everything was funny, and nothing was sad or worrisome. They took turns, passing the controllers back and forth. The games changed, and the food arrived. Pizza grease dripped onto the old sofa. Yosef leading them always, Huck getting everyone to get along, Finley and Mel battling to see who could be the funniest, Gwen in control of the music.

Back at the University, Theo had let himself fall back into the past, into that perfect moment, and it seemed his remembering fingers had opened a map to a dead divinity.

Now, when the expedition was only hours away from entering the storm and the lives of dozens depended on him, Theo could not reproduce the miracle.

Theo threw the controller away from him in disgust. He wanted to scream, but he was quite sure that the other expedition members would hear him, and it turned out that the one force more powerful than his terror was his social anxiety.

He made his way to the door that kept him locked in and knocked at it. A porthole let Theo peek out into the endless sky beyond. Every now and then a small figure would fly by in the ever-shifting pattern of the expedition's descent. Theo pressed his head against the glass and waited. He did not have to wait long. With a groan of old hinges, the door opened. Keeper, one of the packsmen who pulled the bell, was grinning on the other side, his flight mask dangling from his face. It was a biting grin, traced by the thinnest goatee Theo had ever seen.

"Well, well, if it isn't his majesty? How can I help you, my liege?" Keeper asked, his voice raised above the rushing wind.

"I'd like to get out please."

"I think not. You're not properly attired for the fine weather we are about to have," Keeper said, pointing at his own face and goggles. Theo flushed, turning back and grabbing his flight helmet and putting it on. Once he was buttoned up, he turned back to the portal. This time Keeper nodded and floated away from the door, sealing it behind him.

Theo stepped out into the open air. For a second his stomach lurched, and he could feel himself begin to tumble, but he soon found the floating mind that Elwyn had drilled into him, the one that allowed for the possibility that a person could fly. With that impossible thought in his head, Theo's fall stopped.

To him, flying felt almost like being a computer. To fly, one had to develop various subroutines and programs that were automatic and took place all the time. If even one of these routines failed, he would tumble from the sky.

One such subroutine was in constant contemplation of the impossible. This part of his brain floated in a world of paradoxes and allowed for flight in the first place.

Another subroutine, of just as much importance, oversaw maintaining his body's movement through the air. The subroutine had to adjust for the wind, had to adjust for the weather, had to adjust his body for each development, a twitch of an arm here, a twist of the leg there.

Flight was, as Elwyn had said, a continual fight with his brain and his body to remain in the air. His brain wanted to remember the facts of reality that ruled that a man could not fly. And his body longed to return to the simple comfort of something to stand on. It was an exhausting process, like running a marathon and composing a symphony at the same time.

He felt the wind gather beneath his feet and along his legs and chest. He felt his fall stop as gravity began to ignore him and his impossible thoughts. He could fly. For fifteen minutes. After that he would be falling just like a stone again.

He had none of the casual flying grace Elwyn had. Elwyn soared, Theo trundled through the air like a tractor trailer caught in a tornado. Still, flying poorly was better than falling quickly.

Theo shot up until he was flying beside Keeper next to the great bell that housed the expedition's equipment. The storm lurked below, so near that the whole world seemed to have vanished within its depths. Keeper was lashed to the bell, two other flyers, Toddler and Sidewinder, were similarly strapped to the bell. Now that Theo was out though, Keeper was unclicking the straps and buckles that kept the bell attached to him.

"When can we expect you back? Do I have time to stretch my legs, my liege?"

"I'll stay airborne as long as I can, Keeper. I'm sorry you three need to carry me."

"Not as sorry as my back is. Go on and wing off, we'll see you again in fifteen minutes. I can set my watch by it," Keeper said, stretching as they flew. Theo turned away.

Theo flew up, his muscles and brain already starting to ache with the strain of flight. Wheeler, Younette D'Albert, floated with her cluster of weatherbreathers. Her eyes were wild and wide beneath the thick lenses of her goggles. A billowing red scarf trailed behind her back like a flag. She zoomed forward until she was flying beside Theo.

"Any luck with the N-Device?" she said, over the roar of the wind. The wingers had a special way of speaking, a certain lift to the voice that made it clear in all but the harshest of winds.

"No," Theo said, and his voice was thin above the wind. He was still learning the tricks that were so natural to the other wingers.

"I hate to disparage another scholar's methods, but you must work faster. We can chart our way through the high storms, but once we reach the lower depths our maps will be useless."

"I'm trying everything I can to get it to work. It's like it doesn't want to function now, like it has a mind of its own."

"Godly artifacts can be finicky, but you are a scholar of the Final University. You must work the problem until you have a solution. We will likely die if you continue to fail. So try your best not to, please," Wheeler said, flying in a gentle corkscrew next to him, her voice light and airy, as if her possible death was only a minor inconvenience.

"Should we turn back? Should we scrap the expedition?"

"It's too late now, I'm afraid. We slipped out right before the siege began. If we go back, we might never have another chance."

"I haven't seen any krows though. Are we sure that they will threaten the castle?"

"Oh, there have been several krow sightings," Wheeler said, whipping the scarf behind her back. "But we were able to avoid them for now."

"I didn't know that."

"You miss things when you're in the bell all day. Listen, Theo, don't tell anyone else about your failures with the Device. There are not many others who are sympathetic to the challenges of a fellow scholar. All they want to hear is that you are making progress."

"But that would be a lie."

"Is it? Failure is part of learning, my friend. The most important part. Who knows, you may discover the secret of the device as you continue to fail," Wheeler said with a little smile. She peeled away and flew back to be amongst her weatherbreathers.

Theo pulled away, flying to the height of the sphere. He could still see the Castle far overhead, little more than a spot against the setting sun. The professor was waiting up there, preparing the castle for a siege. Elwyn was up there, probably tearing the hospital ward to pieces with his eagerness to be part of the defense. And perhaps, Theo thought, with worry for Theo himself.

The captain of the lancers was zooming nearby in the midst of his route. He was a massive man, easily twice the size of Theo. He seemed to beat the air into submission whenever he flew, not so much as carving through the air, but battering his way through. Fencer gave him a nod and a clap on the shoulder as he passed.

"Falling Boy, good flying today," Fencer said, his great red bread twitching as he spoke. Many of the lancers had taken a shine to Theo after he had rescued Elwyn from the curtain wall.

"I heard you met some krows in the night?"

"Aye, a small murder of them, no more than a dozen. We will see more once we drop into the storm. It is their home after all."

"So they're waiting for us?"

"Aye. But more are going up to the siege."

They lapsed into silence, looking up at the castle far above them.

"What do you think their chances are?"

"It will be tough, but they're a tough lot. They'll give those krows hell. In fact, we left some of our deadliest lancers up there as a surprise just for them! Whistler is going to tear them apart, even if he has to do it with his ass hanging out of a hospital gown," Fencer said, and he roared with laughter until there were tears collecting inside his goggles. Theo found himself chuckling along.

"Don't worry so much, Falling Boy," Fencer gave a great clap to Theo's shoulder. "Keep your mind on the mission, that's the best thing we can do for them. In and out of the storm and back in time for the siege." Fencer nodded at Theo and resumed his patrol, arcing down and around the sphere of the expedition.

Theo swooped up and up, and he felt the air pulling at his clothes and at the skin of his mouth, until he let the wind flip him onto his back and he was once more face down to the storm. He fell, zooming past the weatherbreathers and the bell until he was closing in on the command center near the bottom of the sphere.

Striker was below, giving orders to a charter and sending her winging off to the forward lancers. More charters flew beside Striker, waiting for orders or to deliver a message. Theo joined them, waiting for Striker to notice him. Two more charters came and went before Striker turned and gestured for Theo to fly down towards her.

"I heard we ran into some krows a while back. Did any say my name?"

"You'll have to learn to ignore the names, Theo. If you are distracted even for a moment by what they say, then you will surely die. It is why we all have a flight name that the krows will never know."

"But I haven't been given a flight name."

"Give it time. You cannot force one or choose one. Terribly bad luck to try to force a name. How goes your work on the N-Device?"

"Making progress," Theo said, mindful of Wheeler's advice.

"Good. Go get some rest, Theo. We will reach the storm soon. And I want you out of the bell when we hit the horizon. The storm cannot be hidden from or protected against. You must dive into its depths yourself."

He flew up, exhaustion pulling at him. His back spasmed with the ache of keeping his body in the air. His left eye could not focus, and he could feel a migraine building above his ear. He made his way back to the bell. Keeper saw him coming and slipped back into the slings and straps needed to carry the bell. He did so with many sighs and groans, but otherwise kept his mouth shut.

Theo opened the bell himself this time, turning the great wheel on the outside and opening the door against the protests of its groaning hinges. He slipped inside and collapsed onto the floor, letting flight go.

He groaned; his face pressed against the tough leather of the floor. He had remained in the air for twenty minutes that time, a personal best. Yet all around him were wingers expected to fly for weeks on end. He could not imagine the strength of body and will that took. Even twenty minutes in the air had reduced Theo to a puddle on the floor, unable to even keep his eyes open. His last glimpse before he slipped into sleep was the N-Device resting and waiting for him to try again.

Thunder rolled below Theo. It seemed an army of giants was beneath his feet, and their gnashing, grinding teeth made a thunderous clatter.

He shot up onto his knees. Through the porthole, he saw that a wall of dark clouds and lightning had devoured the horizon. Only the barest hint of blue sky lingered far overhead. They were about to drop into the storm.

The rolls of thunder grew closer. And closer. His hair stood on end, static building around the tips of fingers. He could feel the world hold its breath, and Theo did the same.

The sky split with light, and a thunder swallowed Theo whole. The shockwave drove him to his knees. White hot pain raced along his face. He tasted iron in his mouth. He spat, and blood painted the door.

He stumbled forward, pounding his fist against the door. The sound was pathetic compared to the roars of the breaking sky.

"Let me out!" Theo screamed.

There was a flash of light, and Theo closed his eyes, certain that a bolt of lightning was about to descend and consume him.

A moment passed, and he was not dead. He turned and saw that the N-Device had activated itself. A beam of light shot out from its depths projecting a screen of black in the air. White words provided all the light in the darkness, displaying a single message: "PLAYER ONE PRESS START."

Theo shot forward, scrambling with the controllers on the device until he could find the purple player one controller. He brought his thumb down on the start button, even as another crack of thunder sent him cowering to the floor. He looked up, and the screen had changed. The words had vanished, replaced by a rectangle of white slowly filling. One word appeared above this bar. "LOADING."

What had he done?

But before Theo could move, he heard the terrible groan of rusty hinges above the roar of the storm. He turned; Keeper had opened the door of the bell. The man was in the air outside, belted up with goggles and mask on, but Theo could see the wild animal terror behind his eyes.

Theo shot forward, belting his mask and goggles into place, walking through the rain now shooting into the small cabin. The porthole had cracked under the pressure change and now a spider web of breaks was on the glass. The storm beyond struck at the air with almost malicious violence.

"What do you need, your grace?" Keeper roared over the wind. "The storm is no place for royals who can't fly."

"I can't stay in here. You three need to be able to maneuver through the storm, so you can't have me weighing you down."

"Be my guest. Welcome to the Godstrom!" Keeper said, clearing the door. Theo turned once more to see the barest hint of white in the black bar of the N-Device. Then he launched himself into the storm.

Theo had seen hurricanes on TV. He had seen how they covered up whole swaths of the ocean before making landfall. He had watched the testimonials of the survivors who had had their lives destroyed. He had seen these things and thought he knew what a storm was.

Now he knew the truth.

At once he was soaked to the bone. His mouth and eyes were dry, safe behind the mask and breathing tank. Yet the wind plucked and tore at these protections, clawing at his face and at his chest. Thunder boomed and roared, so loud and deep that if not for the plugs and protections of his helmet, he was sure to have his eardrums blasted beyond repair.

He felt as if he were an ingot upon an anvil as the sky brought the hammer down again and again, shaking his very bones to rubber. Yet the lull between the sounds was worse than the thunderous booms, as the sky seemed to suck all the oxygen out of the air before once more slamming down.

Lightning accompanied every hammer blow, flashes of terrible force miles long. The air hummed with the electricity thrown by these bolts, and the cloying scent of ozone clogged his nostrils and throat. Bolts of blue lightning cracked all around him, providing the only light in the dark depths of the storm.

Theo saw bodies tumbling through the air. He looked down and could not see the command center below him. Keeper and the other packsmen were struggling to carry the bell through the wind.

Theo moved to help with the bell, and then he felt the air hum with power, and he shuddered backward right as a bolt of lightning cracked through the air between them.

Blinded, Theo tumbled away, losing focus, forgetting the impossible. He could feel himself lose control of his flight and then all at once he was hurtling down.

Falling, again.

But this time he wasn't lucky enough to be above the storm. This time he was inside its gaping jaws, and they were close to devouring him whole.

A wave of wind and thunder threw Theo through the clouds, soaking him even further. He picked up speed as he hurtled down through the storm and towards the body of a god.

"Come on, come on," Theo shouted to himself as he tumbled, trying to bring his limbs back under control, slipping once more into the flight position, locking his arms and his legs.

He shook his head, trying to clear his vision, but he could see the lightning even with his eyes closed.

"The dilemma of the krow, the dilemma of the krow!" Theo roared at himself, filling his head with impossibility after impossibility, but again and again the image of the N-Device slipped into his head.

How had an N64 found its way here? Why would it be able to map a storm? All it did was play games.

He remembered night after night spent staring into its depths as he fought his way through worlds where victory was only a button's press away. Who had owned the N64 though? He couldn't remember. So odd that now one so similar was here in this new world.

No, not similar. The same.

Impossible.

Theo's eyes shot open, and he felt the air glide along him rather than bash him. He slid through the sky, not a tumbling boy but a bird on the wing.

And he wasn't falling. He was diving, and he could pull up.

Theo tilted back, and now he brought his hands before him like a spear shooting through the air.

And now the world changed, no longer zooming past him but hurtling with him as he shot up, back towards the expedition and the device from his childhood.

And now the lightning changed. They were not the bolts of an angry god, but glorious torches that shone the way through the darkness of the storm.

And now the wind did not shake him like a broken leaf. It lifted him up.

And the rain still soaked him to the core, but as Theo soared through the deluge, he realized it was not a drowning but a baptism.

Theo flew up and found himself once more in the protective sphere of the expedition. After the shock of storm entry, the lines had reformed. Lancers still flew their patterns around the great sphere. The weatherbreathers still kept to their position in the center of the sphere, lanterns dangling from their shoulders. Charters zoomed from group to group, timing their passage for the cascading waves of wind so that they could ride each swell. The packsmen still lugged their supplies and the great bell.

Keeper tossed Theo a wave, and indicated the bell dangling beneath him, as if asking if Theo needed to retreat to its shelter.

Theo gave a great shake of his head and went winging off to the lower center of the sphere. A ragged purple banner flew near the command center. Charters were zooming in and out every minute as Striker gave orders and changed plans while they flew ever deeper into the storm.

She flew as if on a Sunday stroll, flight jacket unruffled, voice under tight control. Charters flew to her gasping for breath and shaking with nervous energy but flew away with a piece of her calm resolve.

Theo flew to join her on her left side. She paused as she noticed him, and then continued to give commands. Theo looked down to the gauge on his wrist, a circle faced strap much like a watch, but this was not divided into seconds and minutes, but into feet and fathoms. It had been at a thousand fathoms as they entered the event horizon of the storm, but now the hands had ceased to tick and were locked at a thousand. It must have cracked as he had tumbled through the sky.

"How far down are we?" Theo said, holding up his broken altimeter.

"About twelve hundred fathoms down from the Castle, two hundred fathoms into the storm. We're lucky. Conditions are mild today. We'll make good time. We should be able to reach two thousand fathoms before the day ends."

"This is mild?" Theo said before he could stop himself.

"Indeed. It could have been much worse. This rain could have been hail. We will have to move quickly in order to take advantage of this stability. How much longer can you fly?"

"Actually, I feel pretty good." He was soaked to the bone and shivering in his flight suit. His ears rang with the aftershocks of the thunder blows, and stars burst behind his eyes with every lightning strike. Yet his flight was stable. He felt focused and calm, like a chord strung tight and ringing true.

"Soon the krows will come. The lancers have seen them gathering in the clouds at our perimeter. They will attack once they feel they have enough numbers. Return to the bell and protect the Device with your life. If we lose it then this whole expedition is for nothing. Take this," Striker said, pulling a long knife from a sheath on her thigh. She unbuckled the sheath and handed it to him as well. "Did Elwyn teach you how to fight?"

"Only the basics," Theo said, holding a weapon while flying always made him nervous. He belted the sheath on and slid the knife into place.

"Stabbing them will have the desired effect. But I recommend that you fight only as a last resort. Let the lancers do their work and try to stay out of their way."

Theo moved to fly off, but Striker grabbed him by the arm. "I saw you fall there, Theo, but I knew you would find your way back to us. Only you seem to be able to work the device, and I am starting to suspect that it is for a reason. Wouldn't you agree, Pathfinder?"

"Pathfinder," Theo said to himself, and it did not sound like a lie. It sounded like a promise. He grinned at Striker beneath his mask, and she nodded back to him, buckling on her mask and goggles once again. She turned to a Charter waiting on her wing. She called him over.

"Tell the Expedition we have Pathfinder flying with us." He nodded and zoomed off to spread the message through the sphere. Theo turned away, repeating his name to himself as he flew higher, going to rejoin the Packsmen carrying the bell and the N-Device.

When he reached the bell, he looked inside its depths and saw the slowly filling bar on the N-Device's screen. It could be a long time before it was filled, and he would allow no interruptions to its progress.

He joined the Packsmen flying above the bell, zooming forward to fly alongside Keeper. The man was chained to the great mass of the bell, straining with the effort needed to carry it down into the storm. He nodded to Theo as he joined them.

"Are you heading inside, my liege?"

"No. I don't feel like being carried right now. Do you need help carrying this thing?"

"You honor us," Keeper said, his voice as sharp as a knife. "Are you sure you can handle the weight? This isn't for day flyers and royalty."

"How about we try and find out," Theo said, and reached for the other carrying harness lashed to the bell and slipped it on. At once, he could feel the weight pulling him down into the storm, digging in across his back and shoulders. The bell wanted so desperately to fall, but Keeper and the packsmen dug their heels in and pulled up anyway. Pathfinder joined them.

Chapter 16: The Scholar's First Battle

You must understand that I know only a little about this place. I was involved with only the beginnings of its creation. Since then, it has grown and mutated into a thing beyond my comprehension. I fear no one alive knows its true depths or purpose.
(Letter 17, Paragraph 6, Lines 24-27)

The only warning of their coming was the flap of crooked wings and the screech of long dead names.

The krows climbed up from the deep storm, their eyes lit with gleaming lightning strikes, their claws outstretched, gnarled and broken from years of conflict.

Names were on their lips, and they were dread things. For the krows did not speak in a voice that matched their monstrous appearance. They spoke like your mother, like your father, like your friend. They called to you in a voice of love. And a part of you wanted to go to them, wanted to fall into their arms and their gaping mouths.

Charters raced ahead of the pack of monsters, calling out formations and flight patterns. One charter was too slow, and Theo watched as a krow latched onto his foot. It pulled him down into the seething mass of flying maggots. It whispered his name as its claws ripped into his stomach.

His name was Leon, and Theo learned this as he watched his first person die.

The lightning struck, the thunder roared, and the krows climbed higher. Their voices rose as they did, overwhelming Theo with their hatred.

"Theo," they screamed, and he met their eyes, and his mind went blank.

And then the lancers arrived. They zoomed past Theo, unholstering weapons as they flew.

"Pathfinder!" Fencer roared as he flew past. "Awaken from your slumber, there are monsters to kill."

A berserker's grin was on his face, and his beard was a soaked tangle beneath his chin. Yet his sword, when he drew it, was sharp. He flew at the head of his lancer brothers and sisters, and as they fell into the

217

gaping maw of the krows, they gave a battle cry that for one brief moment drowned out the thunder.

"Hypnos!" they roared.

The two foes met in the air with terrible force, but the lancers had gravity on their side. They crushed through the lead ranks of the krows, sending smaller monsters flying.

Theo watched as Fencer's broadsword swept through the air like another bolt of lightning. The cracks and bangs of Shaver's pistols rang through the sky, sounding tiny in comparison to the lightning. Yet these lesser sounds still sent krows to their doom. A thin woman named Butter bore a trident to the battle, impaling krow after krow onto the points of her deadly weapon. She leapt through the krows like a jackrabbit, landing on one krow to stab it, only to use its corpse as a springboard to jump onto the next.

Green blood joined the pounding rain, pouring down onto the ascending krows.

It was the most lethal dance Pathfinder had ever seen, but it was grinding to a halt. The lancers were too few and though each dealt death with every spinning movement, the krows were an unending geyser.

Each strike of lightning illuminated more of the monsters as they roared up into their dying brethren, pushing the mass higher into the Final Expedition's formation. And as the lancers broke the rising krows like a rock breaks the rush of the ocean, still more were riding the swell over the fighting lancers, bypassing flanks to go right for their backs.

Pathfinder cried out, horrified he was about to see red blood join the storm. And then he heard a trumpet's call.

A tiny silver horn blared out; a faint echo mixed in with the cracks of thunder. As the horn's note faded, Pathfinder watched as a new wave of lancers ripped through the cover of the clouds on their sides.

They emerged like demons from the smoke, lightning reflected in the blank glass of their helmets. A woman with a purple scarf led them carrying a sword.

Striker led the attack into the krows unprotected sides. And now the lancers made the krows pay for their mindless savagery. The new fighters dove into the flanks of the horde of krows like feasting sharks.

218

With an animal's simple-mindedness, the krows seemed to realize all at once that the conflict was lost. First one, then two, then whole packs of the creatures peeled off the main body.

Striker ordered the lancers to let these fleeing creatures go as she led the lancers further into the dwindling mass of the krows. Now the lancers and remaining krows broke into separate smaller duels.

Fencer and a krow with exceptionally long talons spun through the clouds, sword locked against claws. Thunder boomed and the two combatants separated. Lightning flashed in the space between them, and Fencer was flung into the wind.

The krow seemed unaffected, bathing in the yellow light as it crackled over its skin. It hung in the air, its eyes turned up and found Theo's.

"Theo," it crooned, and a shudder rocketed down his spine.

With a lazy flap of its wings, it rose higher as Theo descended. Its claws were splayed to its side as it grinned at him.

Theo's hand reached for the knife belted to his side. As he pulled it out, he realized that its blade was half the size of the long talons of the krow. The straps around his shoulder that connected him to the bell pulled at him like chains.

With a screech of talon on leather, the krow latched itself onto the bell below and began crawling up its face. Its long talons punctured the side of the bell, carving jagged gashes in its outer shell.

"Theo," it cried again, and as it climbed, the white light from the N-Device poured out of the tiny window of the bell. Its light hit the krow's face, sending its glowing eyes into shadow.

It turned, looking into the bell and at the device within, and its voice fell silent.

Pathfinder found his courage.

He dove down and plunged the knife into the back of the krow. The krow gave a mangled roar.

It pulled its claws from the skin of the bell and slashed at Pathfinder.

Pathfinder dove below the claws, leaving the dagger in the back of the creature. He tumbled back, the wind extending the dive, but he was still connected to the bell.

One hand moved to the straps to try to disconnect himself while the other searched his belt for a weapon.

The creature lunged forward at Pathfinder. He brought his arm up in desperation to block the blow.

The krow's claws made a terrible screech as they connected with the iron face of his altimeter. The creature's dive tore it past Pathfinder, but it collided with the straps of leather that connected Pathfinder to the bell.

Pathfinder dove to the side, soaring over the outstretched bands. He zoomed past the creature before making a hairpin turn. The krow gave a strangled cry of his name as the great leather bands wrapped its arms around its side, lashing it to his chest.

Pathfinder flew on, circling the creature again and again, but only managed to wrap the creature twice before the bands ran out of slack.

With a sickening jolt Theo realized the error in his plan. Now he was tied to the struggling creature, and it still had one arm free.

Its gaping, gnashing mouth spit his name again and again while its one free claw slashed at Theo. It tore up the right side of his body.

Pain erupted on his side like white fire, and for a moment Theo was convinced he had lost his arm. Only the trickle of blood along his fingertips let him know that he still had a right hand.

Thunder boomed below them, and the wind battered both the krow and Theo against the surface of the bell. His head collided with an iron rivet and the glass in his right goggle lens cracked.

He could feel the rain rushing into the ruins of his suit, washing the blood away even as it spilled out of him.

The krow's left arm was trapped against its side, but its forearm had broken at a sickening angle. An iron rivet had carved a terrible slash across its cheek that leaked green blood. Yet its eyes were focused on Theo.

Its mouth was filled with broken teeth, but its voice still spoke like a lover's into his ear. "Theo, are you going to find me?" it whispered, and it raised its right claw.

Theo roared with anger and fear as he spun away from the creature, unwrapping it from its leather bonds.

Its broken left arm loosened even as its right armed slash missed. It pulled against the bands, seeking more slack. But it was still trapped against the bell.

The creature broke eye contact with Theo and turned its talons to the bands that encircled it.

Theo lunged forward, reaching over the distracted creature's shoulder for the knife still embedded in its back. Theo grabbed the knife, ripping it out as the creature realized its mistake.

"Th—" it said one final time as Pathfinder drove the blade into its throat, cutting off the rest of his name. The creature's eyes widened even further, and Pathfinder watched as the lightning inside those orbs faded into nothing.

The creature slumped, and it slipped from the loosened bonds that had kept it lashed to the bell. The wind collected its corpse like a floating leaf, and Theo watched it vanish from sight as it plunged into the clouds.

Theo looked above and below for more krows, but to his relief the few that remained were being mopped up by the lancers.

With shaking hands Theo sheathed the knife at his side. He brought his right hand to his side, searching for the cut that the creature had given him. He found the tear the creature had torn through his clothes, and the lesser cut it had given to his skin.

His hand found three jagged cuts that stretched the length of his rib cage. He dared to look down and to his relief did not see the white of bone beneath the blood red. They were only skin deep.

He floated up, his head feeling as light as the feather he imitated. There was pain, but it seemed to be happening to someone else.

At the top of the bell, he found Keeper carving an ear off a krow before sending it tumbling into the wind. The man's eyes were wild but there were no cuts on his body that Theo could see. There was an empty harness next to Keeper where the third packsman should have been.

"Are you okay?" Theo asked.

"Never better, your majesty," Keeper growled.

"What happened to Sidewinder?"

"Krow took her," Keeper said, adjusting the straps on his shoulders. His face shook with strain as he pulled against the weight of the bell beneath him. With a start Theo realized what was wrong. He pulled against his own straps on his pack, settling the weight of the bell on his shoulders as well.

"Sorry," Theo said, indicating both the bell and the empty harness.

"No trouble."

"I didn't know her well. Did you?"

"Yes."

Theo nodded, his thoughts still drifting like clouds. He scanned the rest of the formation. Striker was once more in the center of the sphere, and charters soared around her, each vying for her attention. More charters flew from scholar to scholar assessing the damage that had occurred.

Fencer was further below at the bottom of the sphere, his blade dripping with green ichor. Even from far above Theo could see the rage that shook the man's shoulders as he zoomed ahead of the formation. Several of his brother and sister lancers flew in his wake, weapons out and eyes sharp.

Wheeler and her ilk were far above. Theo could see that they were unharmed. The krows had never risen higher than the diameter of the sphere. She and her fellow weatherbreathers were still taking their frantic measurements. Perhaps they had never stopped even as the krows had clawed at their flanks.

A thin charter flew up to Keeper and Theo's level, her chest heaving.

"Status?" She gasped.

"One casualty and three dead krows," Keeper rattled out.

"Who?"

"Sidewinder is gone. Her body's in the Strom. But the krows couldn't take it after she fell."

"Are the lancers okay?" Theo asked before he could stop himself.

"We lost Bouncer."

"We need another packsmen here. Two if you can spare them. I can't take the weight for long." Keeper said.

"I can take it. You don't have to do it alone."

"I'll send someone as soon as I can," the charter said as she flew away to another group of flyers.

"No, you can't," Keeper said.

"I can and I will. I'm not going to let you fly this bucket of rust by yourself."

"Kid, you're barely conscious right now. Your hands are shaking."

Theo looked down. His right hand was still covered in blood, though the rain had prevented it from drying. His left hand was uninjured, but this was the hand that killed the krow, that stabbed into its throat.

Both shook.

"Your right side is bleeding. Go inside the bell. There are medical supplies on the second shelf. Do you know how to wrap your wounds?"

"Elwyn taught me."

"Good boy. Go inside," Keeper said, but Theo did not move. "Pathfinder, go inside. Your replacements are on the way." Keeper indicated the two packsmen flying their way.

Theo unstrapped himself from the bell with his shaking hands. They slid and shivered as he worked the rain slicked buckles. He handed the harness to the new packsman, who quickly buckled in as Keeper held the weight of the bell by himself for a span of seconds. Theo dropped below to the hatch of the bell, the shaking in his hand becoming full body shivers.

"Kid, I heard you fighting the krow. Was that your first one?"

"The first I've killed."

"It gets easier. But nothing else about this does. Do you understand?"

Theo looked at the ear of the krow that Keeper attached to the loops of his belt, and the packsman who had replaced Sidewinder.

"I understand."

"You did well, for a rookie. Now go rest. Get that device working so this was all worth it. Yeah?" Theo nodded, opening the door of the bell and making his way inside.

"It spoke to me," he said, before he closed the door.

"They speak to all of us."

"No, it wasn't just my name. It was…I don't know."

"Stay sharp, Pathfinder. This was only the first wave, and the others won't be so easy."

223

Theo shut the door.

The next attack came three hours later. A pack of krows shot out of the clouds near the top right hemisphere of the expedition. The lancers caught them before they could break into the formation. Theo was back on the bell when the attack came. He watched as the sphere constricted and the lancers pulled reinforcements from all across the expedition to meet the threat. Theo heard the krows call out names under the rolls of thunder, but he did not hear his own. The lancers made quick work of the threat, and the krows did not cry for long.

Theo's hand never left his knife.

The third attack came the following morning and Theo only learned about it after it occurred. He was eating his breakfast in the bell as the krows ambushed a dragoon lancer named Turner fifty fathoms below.

He had been separated from his band by a gale force wind that had blown him a kilometer away from the main body of lancers. By the time the lancers had discovered he was missing, the charters far above had already found his severed limbs floating in a rising wind. Theo was unable to keep down his breakfast when he heard.

The fourth attack came two hours later. And the fifth only an hour after that. By the end of the sixth attack two more members of the Final Expedition had fallen from the sky. Now they were only thirty strong. Theo had killed two more krows and had stopped keeping count of the attacks.

The hours blurred together, and he could only track the time with the change of his shifts. Two hours on the bell, two hours off winging from group to group to help the desperately depleted charters. Then a further four hours inside the bell tinkering with the N-Device or desperately trying to sleep.

By the end of the third attack Theo counted himself lucky if he could sleep for longer than twenty minutes without waking up clutching at his knife.

He longed for his shifts outside the bell, laboring to keep the thing afloat, or helping the charters. At least in those moments he felt like he was of use. But as Keeper took pains to remind him, that was not his role.

His place was here, kept safe inside the bell that others worked to carry through the sky. His duty was the device in front of him, but it was one he continued to fail at.

For hours he was trapped with a device that mocked him with its refusal to collaborate. The only way to keep track of the moments was the slow creep of the loading bar of the N-Device. It crawled across the screen, unhurried by the blood that spilled again and again outside the walls of the bell. Nothing he did could provoke it to move faster, or to reveal another screen.

When Keeper opened the door at the end of another four hour shift he practically flung himself outside. Even the threat of monsters that knew him by sight and name could not stop him from venturing forth from that stifling room where the air glowed with stabbing white light.

Theo did not know what attack this was. He did not know what their elevation was, as his altimeter was still broken. He did not even know what day it was. Theo watched through cracked lenses as Keeper added another krow ear to the ring at his belt. He had thirteen now.

Theo had not even had to draw his knife this time. But his hand had stayed near the hilt as he watched Keeper rip into the krow with blood curdling efficiency.

It had been like watching a dissection.

"Why do you collect them?" Theo asked, his voice hardly above a whisper.

"It's not a collection. I'll leave them in the Strom when we climb back up to the University."

"So why do you do it?"

"Does it bother you, your majesty? Is it not to your tastes?" Keeper said, his voice as sharp as his knife.

The weight of the bell pulled at their shoulders and burned along the curves of their backs. The wind pulled and clawed at the thing, trying to rip it away from them and pull it into the heart of the Godstrom. When he had first placed the burden on his shoulders Theo had felt like he was being beaten across his back and shoulders with iron bars. Now, he hardly noticed.

"It did before. It reminded me of an animal, but even animals don't rip a body to shreds for no reason."

"What changed?" Keeper said. Theo shrugged as best he could.

"You're not angry when you do it. I thought that was rage in your eyes when you sliced the ears off. I thought you were collecting trophies. But that's not it is it?

"No, it's not."

"So why do you do it?"

"Because I'm afraid," Keeper said. Theo waited for him to continue, thinking he had misunderstood. But the man said nothing more.

"I don't understand."

"This is your first expedition. I barely remember my own first. We were in the storm for six days, but when we returned to the University I felt as if I had lived a thousand centuries. Those sorts of feelings do not go away," Keeper said, adjusting the bundle of ears at his waist. Some still dripped green blood onto his clothes.

"It felt like there was someone screaming in my head that only I could hear. I tried everything to make it go away. Some of the other wingers recommended prayer, but I always thought that was rather silly considering Vovatum is dead and all. Some suggested drinking, and I can admit I took to that option quite hard in the days after our return. That became weeks, and then months, and then we were told we were going back in.

"I've never been so afraid before or since. When we flew down the first pack of krows nearly overwhelmed us. There was one that—" And Keeper cut himself off when he looked down to find his hands at his knife. Theo watched the man force himself to relax, the muscles unclenching and releasing. "In any case. At the time it felt like the krows could hear the screams that were inside my head, that they were the only ones that could hear them. So I starting taking their ears."

"You wanted to prove you weren't afraid."

"I wanted to prove that the fear wouldn't stop me." Keeper looked at Theo now, and Theo felt like the man's gaze went all the way down to the pit of his stomach. "I know it's not healthy. I know it's not to most people's tastes, but it's the only way I've found to keep flying in all this madness."

"So you're recommending it?"

The other man looked at him for a moment, and then his spine bent backwards, and his hands came to his chest. There was a great whining sound coming from the man, and Theo moved forward in fear. He stopped when he realized that the man was laughing. Great gasping whines and giggles came from the man with severed ears at his waist. Theo found himself smiling, a scratch in his throat that might have been a laugh, but no sound came forth.

"No, no, I wouldn't recommend it, your majesty. It only works for me, and only barely," the man said, as he got himself under control. "Ask around, you'll find a dozen unhealthy coping mechanisms in this bunch. I know flyers who have become so superstitious they can barely pass over a cloud without looking around for curses. I know others who gamble anything they can get their hands on. Others turn to drugs, or the drink, or sex. Whatever works."

"Whatever works," Theo repeated.

"It's okay to feel it, your majesty. It's okay to feel that little scream building inside your head. It's only natural in all this mess. The trick is finding a way to let the scream out a little. Otherwise, you'll just go crazy, and we've lost too many scholars to the storm and to their own minds for us to let that happen to you." Theo remembered the journal of Aldwin Dryn and the crazed ramblings splashed across its pages.

"I didn't know you cared."

"I don't. I'd just hate to lift the bell all by myself," Keeper said, adjusting the pull of the straps on his back. "Time's up, your shift's over. Go report to Striker and then think on what I've said," Theo slipped the bell off his shoulders as another packsman ducked in to take the burden. He started to fly towards Striker in the center of the formation but turned back before he left.

"What will you do when we get to the bottom though? What will you collect after we find god?"

"Who knows? Maybe I'll cut my own ears off." And Keeper flashed a smile at him sharp enough to slice. Theo flew away.

He reported to Striker. He lied about his progress on the N-Device. He tried to forget the sound a knife makes when it cuts through bone and cartilage. He flew back to the bell. He tried to sleep.

227

Theo tossed and turned for some time before giving it up as a bad job. He removed the blanket from the N-Device, the one that he used to block its light when he tried to rest. The loading bar had not moved for the last several days.

"What are you?" Theo asked of the machine. "You're just a kid's toy. You're not a map to anything, and certainly not one to a dead god. So how did you get here? Who sent you to me?" Theo shook his head ruefully. "You're a puzzle you know. I wish Finley was here. He'd have figured this out ages ago."

The loading bar ticked forward.

"What?" Theo said. He looked in desperation at the bar. Its movement had stopped.

"Finley." Nothing changed.

"Finley Marsh!" Still nothing. Nothing, nothing, nothing. And the naming of his lost friend brought it home to Theo like a great weight crashing onto his head and neck. The fear and heartache he had kept at bay through sheer adrenaline clawed at his heart as no krow had yet done.

Theo put his head into his hands. His shoulders shook, and his lungs gasped, and it wasn't until the tears fell into his mouth that he realized he was crying. A scream was building in his head.

He tried to remember Keeper's words, but the thought of getting anywhere near a krow's ears revolted him.

His body curled in on itself until he was clutching his shins with his head against his knees.

He thought of Elwyn so far above him, and the scars that now littered his body. Theo remembered the pride in the other boy's eyes when he had taken flight for the first time.

"I'm gonna fail you too. Just like I did with him," Theo said, thinking of Huck.

The light changed in the bell.

Theo looked up. The light of N-Device had changed.

The loading bar was still there, and still frozen. But new text was beneath it, giving him advice. Giving him a clue.

Just like in a videogame.

"WOULD YOU LIKE TO CONTINUE YOUR GAME, ALDWIN DRYN?" The N-Device projected across the wall of the bell.

"Of course," Theo whispered. "Others must have found you, floating through the storm. Other expeditions, other lost souls. But they didn't know what you really were. So what did they call you?"

With a gasp Theo pulled himself from the floor to stumble to his bag. There was a book in the bottom, the journal of Aldwin Dryn. Theo slipped away into the pages, tracing the descent of a man losing his mind, searching for what he was certain was there, for a clue to the N-Device.

And for the first time in days, Theo didn't count his breaths.

Chapter 17: The Detective's Arrest

What does it say about this world that no one seems to have noticed that Vovatum is dead? Cogonauts world over are reporting fluctuations in the cognitive domains, as the very rules underpinning the universe begin to break down. The Herald's deliveries have started to become chaotic, often arriving months after the tile has moved to a new location. Even the Circus acknowledges that many of the stories they are responsible for have simply gone missing.

Yet no one seems to grasp what this really means. They deny the evidence of their own eyes. Only the Final University accepts that the world has changed, but even they shy away from asking the real question. What happens to Poa without its god?

(Letter 17, Paragraph 7, Lines 7-12, and Paragraph 8, Lines 1-End).

As a rule, Finley Marsh did not often hang out at construction sites at night. Nor did he often hang out at construction sites during the day. But, he supposed, a new position often brought along its new locations and fresh locales.

Thus, the newest Special Detective of the Oshroaran Wardens found himself waiting near the central column of the Spiral Tower construction site. He was not waiting alone, however. Moro skulked in the deeper shadows one level above him. For such a large woman she made little sound as she moved from column to column. Her eyes searched the gloom like search lights for any sign of their quarry, but her hearing was even more phenomenal. She seemed able to hear even a mouse's pitter patter from across the road.

Finley had adopted a more sedate posture of careful observation. He sat upon the many bags of cement stacked near the central column. Marlowe, the other Special Detective of the Oshroaran Wardens, slumbered on his shoulder pulsing a pale pink light.

Two hundred yards away the Guardians still worked to complete the tower. They had not stopped as the sun set, and Finley knew they would work without ceasing into the morning. The construction Guardians were massive things, towering dozens of meters over the site. They moved stone blocks the size of carriages like they were toys. But despite their size they worked without making a sound, so Marlowe's sleep was uninterrupted.

The city also slumbered around them, but Finley could see the city turn and thrash in its sleep as he watched the candlelight still burning in windows all around the construction site.

"I can guess what they're talking about," Finley whispered to the flower nestled into the side of his coat. "Frankly, I would rather be talking about mass arrests too instead of waiting in this creepy place."

The flowers continued to sleep beneath the flaps of his coat. The sleeping perplexed Finley. After all, what sort of flower needed to sleep so much, let alone at all? Yet he tended to avoid following this thought. If he went down this road he would soon start to wonder if the flower breathed, or ate, or drank. Did it eat food? Did it absorb energy from him to survive? Better not to wonder about such things. Besides, he had much more troubling things to turn his thoughts to.

"Marlowe, I'm slightly afraid that we have hitched our wagons to a totalitarian horse. Or perhaps it might be more accurate to say that we have climbed aboard a wagon pulled by the horse head of a burgeoning police state? In either case, it's a bad horse, and we are in a bad spot. Besides Orsos I know maybe five other people in this city and two of them hate my guts. The third is always annoyed with me. The other is a janitor, and the last is you. And as much as I love you my dear friend, I worry that you cannot employ, feed, or house me. Am I correct?"

The flower turned slightly in its sleep and gave a dull purple pulse.

"I thought as much. Therefore, we are left with relatively few options. Orsos presents a problem. If we turn against him he'll definitely throw us into a cell to rot as he has done with everyone else in his way. Or perhaps the idea of a cell is my optimism at work. After all, Orsos has Hawksbill dogging our steps. I don't think Orsos is above having us crushed.

"Escape. Escape might be the option that is left to us. We could slip out of the gates as the sun rises and be miles from here before Orsos or Hawksbill could find us. We would roam this new world as a traveling investigating pair. We'd find out how we ended up on this strange alien planet, and kindly ask them to undo their mistake. I would be charming, you would be menacing, I'm sure they would agree. Just two detectives on the hunt. Doesn't that sound fun!"

Again, the color of the ghost shifted so that the flower shone a dark blue. Finley wondered if that was the Ghostlight equivalent of snoring, or perhaps having a dream.

"Just us and the open road. On an alien planet, with alien magics, no money, no maps, and no friends. I'm sure nothing would go wrong. We could leave tomorrow. We could leave right now and be away from this dreadful place where the statues try to kill you, and where law is bent to the whims of a tyrant."

The Ghostlight stirred beside him, and Marlowe rose in the air, humming slightly and shining with a soft golden light. A picture formed in Finley's head of the broken Guardian laid out on the slab in the morgue.

From above, it looked like a map of a city. The broken lines of the Guardian were the streets and rivers that carved the city into wards. Its broken limbs were the hills beneath his feet, its great head the Shepherd far above. And though the pieces were broken, it was undeniably all part of the same whole.

He looked up from the slab and saw Huck standing on the other side of the table. He didn't look like a corpse. He just looked like his friend.

The vision faded, and Finley could see the flower floating directly in front of him. It twirled once and then sank lower. Marlowe nuzzled into his neck, slipping into the folds of his collar, and stilled again. The light slowly faded, and Finley petted the flower as it slumbered.

"I think I understand. You want me to fix the thing that's broken. Maybe Huck would want that too," Finley said, still petting the little snoozing flower.

"You know, for a Ghostlight that never talks you can be quite eloquent."

There was a faint hiss from above. Finley looked up. Moro was gesturing at him, indicating an opening in the construction not too far away. Marlowe shook itself and rose to float over Finley's shoulder. A minute later, Gaspar walked around the corner. His face was hidden in the shadows of his cloak, he had switched out his vestments for simple tradesmen's clothes, and there was just a hint of dirt on his cheeks, but it was unmistakably Gaspar. There was no disguising that gait, full of arrogance and anger, every step a strut.

232

He was clearly not designed for clandestine work. Finley found it hard not to laugh at the touch of dirt on his cheeks. Perhaps he assumed everyone outside the temples was dirty. Gaspar could not even spot the man sitting right next to the glowing flower.

"Give us some light, eh partner?" Finley asked. The Ghostlight gave off a flash of green light. Finley watched as Gaspar reared back a step before hurrying over to them.

"Hello, Gaspar. I'm so happy to see that you decided to visit."

"Marsh. What are you trying to pull, having the Ghostlight out like that, using it as a torch?"

"My partner's name is Marlowe, and it does what it likes."

"Is every word that comes out of your mouth a heresy?" Gaspar asked, his eyes burning into Finley's face. Yet he could not hold the stare for long. His eyes wandered ever back to Marlowe, and when it did, his whole body dropped the anger and the arrogance for just a second. And then he would look again at Finley, and they would come rushing back. Finley tended to have that effect on people.

"On the good days? Yes. Now shall we put aside the bluster, brother? It's late after all, and I hate to think what will happen when Sinoh finds out where you are."

"How do you know she didn't send me here; how do you know this isn't a trap?"

"I didn't, not until you just confirmed it wasn't. I can tell that covert work doesn't come naturally to you, Gaspar. While I seem to have taken to it like a duck to water."

"The move with the shoe note was sloppy. Fodor nearly threw them away. It was only in passing that I saw the note inside."

"What you call sloppy, others might call inspired," Finley said, rolling his eyes at the spot where he knew Moro hid. "In either case, you're here, aren't you? And why are you here, Gaspar, if this isn't a trick? What brought you to an abandoned construction site in the middle of the night?"

"It's certainly not you, boy!" Gaspar snarled. "I have not come to trade barbs with that wriggling snake you have inside your mouth. I have come here seeking divinity, and not your feeble attempts at japery. I have come to speak with the Ghostlight."

233

"And I'm its interpreter. So, I'm afraid you'll have to tolerate some degree of japery. And the fun part is, you'll never know whether it's mine or Marlowe's."

"Why did you give it that name? I am unfamiliar with it."

"I was inspired. It's an old name in the land that I'm from. It suits it somehow."

"Yes, yes it does," Gaspar said, and his eyes glazed over as he looked at the Ghostlight. There was a covetous look to him, as if Marlowe held the secrets of the universe beneath its petals. And who knew, Finley thought, perhaps it did.

"Although Marlowe and I grow closer by the hour, I fear I'm unfamiliar with your city's history. Perhaps you might regale me with a tale of the Ghostlights?"

Gaspar tore his eyes away from Marlowe to glare at Finley. "Maybe Marlowe would find such a tale flattering?" Finley added. Gaspar looked back at the Ghostlight before turning away and putting his back to the pair of Special Detectives. He faced the shuttered lights of the city instead, and Finley heard him take a deep steadying breath.

"The Ghostlights predate the settlement and construction of Oshroar and can only be found here."

Marlowe drifted closer to Gaspar's back as he spoke. It bobbed and weaved, giving off an air of curiosity.

"Many attempts have been made over the centuries to make a connection with the Ghostlights. Some have even foolishly attempted to capture them. Both of these approaches have failed time and time again. They cannot be contained by any means known. A Ghostlight seems able to come and go as it pleases from our physical reality. Marlowe is the first Ghostlight I have ever heard of that has not fled at the presence of people." Gaspar turned to look at Finley. "I must know, how did you get it to stay?"

"You want to know my secret, then give me one in return. Right now all you're doing is boring me."

"I'm starting to understand why the Ghostlight has chosen you, Finley Marsh. Perhaps it has come to personally ensure that a heathen like you is punished. Perhaps it wants to watch me punish you," Gaspar said, stepping forward. Finley did not move.

"I think it has more to do with my winning charm. Get on with the story, Gaspar, the night is getting old."

Gaspar spat at Finley's feet before turning away to directly address the Ghostlight. Every line of his body relaxed when he looked at Marlowe, as if the light shining from the flower bestowed safety that could not be broken.

"There is one legend about the Ghostlights that is my favorite, and it is perhaps the most complete tale we have of them. The legends tell that when the first founders arrived at the Shepherd's feet that the Ghostlights numbered in the tens of thousands. They gathered around the Shepherd like snow upon the mountain, though they never interacted with the people who had settled in his shadow. The first Oshroarans found that the land was abundant here, and there was a peace that they had not felt in generations. They thought at last that they had found a place of safety from the horrors of the world.

"Of course, such a thing could not last. A great plague struck these settlers some fifty years after their arrival. It was a terrible sickness. It stole the minds away from those that contracted it, making them as simple as children, as lifeless as sleepwalkers. The town of Oshroar was filled with these walking corpses, and it seemed to be the end of a once proud community. And then came the Ghostlights. They came down from the shoulders of the Shepherd, called by the cries of those trying to wake their sleeping kin, and where they went the people were healed, their minds returned. Thus, the town was saved. This was the gift of the Ghostlights.

"Many such tales litter the early stories of our founding, but as the city developed the Ghostlights began to lessen in number, until the sighting of any one was a rare thing. They could be found, for those still seeking them, in places of death. They floated in cemeteries and in the houses of the sick. Though they chose not to heal these people, they brought comfort to those soon to depart this world. Some even say that they usher these souls to the other side, to the land where the Ghostlights go.

"I have spent my life in the study of the Ghostlights, even as this city forgot them. I joined the Crooken to learn more about them, the only religion old enough to remember them at all. And now here you are, a newcomer, and you have a Ghostlight following you around like a loyal pet, and you have the temerity to name it. Life is full of cruelties it seems, and mysteries without answers."

"Yeah, but that's why we have special detectives and clerics to answer the questions we find so unanswerable," Finley said, watching as the flower circled Gaspar in curiosity, examining every inch of the man. The story had captivated Marlowe, like a child listening to a bedtime tale for the first time.

"I think perhaps you are right about Marlowe being flattered by my story. I have many more, if you would linger with me, I would fill your days with stories."

"Nice try. Marlowe is my partner, not yours," Finley said, a flare of jealousy burning in his chest. "And I think we are ready to have our questions answered, Gaspar, about the Crooken and the Guardians."

"No. You have had your story for free, but for more information I want what was promised me."

"I promised you nothing."

"Yet your partner did. The very fact a Ghostlight is before us is a promise of something more. Do you not understand you clattering fool? It wants to show us something! It knows what waits beyond death, and it can speak to those that linger there until we join them. I will not share what I know, until you have them share what it knows."

"An exchange of information then?"

"Yes."

"I thought the point of faith was to believe there are answers but to be content with never knowing them?"

"Not to me," Gaspar said, and his voice was as cold as a winter wind, and his eyes were hard as flint. His fists were clenched at his sides and the veins on his neck stood out against his flushed skin. Finley was suddenly very glad that Moro still hid in the shadows. She would protect him if the cleric lost his temper.

Maybe.

Probably.

Best not to risk it.

"I can only ask it, Gaspar. I can't make Marlowe show you something that it does not want to show. And I can't make it share what isn't there. Are you sure you want me to ask?"

"DO IT!" Gaspar roared. The Ghostlight shot away from the cleric. It floated in the air between them, turning from one to the other. Finley saw its petals drooping, and its light dimming until it cast off no more than a dying candle.

"It's okay, it's okay. He's not going to hurt me. I don't even think he can hurt you," Finley said, his voice soft and his hands patting the air. "He's just scared, and sometimes people get angry when they get scared. But you can help him, partner. He says he wants to see a vision, like the pictures you've put in my head. If you want to, can you do the same for him? Can you show him a glimpse of your home?"

The flower floated above and away from them, until it shone like a star over their heads. Finley's gaze fell into the light, until it seemed that the shadows around him vanished, and the stones beneath his feet fell away, and all that was left was a sun of shining brilliance, one without heat or pain.

He waited in this blank space for some time in perfect silence. And then he heard footsteps behind him, though he could not turn to look. Slowly the steps came forward until they were passing Finley. A rail thin young man walked by him wearing a red wool sweater and Chuck Taylors. He tried to smile, but it did not seem to fit his face. He tried several variations of the smile. One that pulled his lips away from his teeth, one that showed no teeth at all, but was merely a quirk of the lips. He tried many kinds of smiles, but none reached his eyes.

The young man bounced with anxious energy, hopping from foot to foot, his gaze shifting from point to point. He checked his watch again and again. But then the boy seemed to see something out of the corner of his eye, and his face stilled with a smile frozen on. Finley heard a little ring of a bell, and then he watched himself walk onto the scene.

It was a younger version of him, only a year or so younger, and he seemed to have dressed in a hurry, as his hair was in disarray and his shirt was misbuttoned. His mouth raced ahead of the rest of him.

"Huck, so sorry I'm late!" the younger Finley said.

Huck swiveled to face him, his face serious and his arms akimbo. He waited until Finley froze, and then lifted his hands like he was calling forth lightning from the heavens. "Meteor strike!"

237

The younger Finley grinned and made his hand like spear on his forehead. "Rhino stampede."

The two held their positions for a moment, before bursting into giggles.

"I don't know, Finley. I think a meteor beats rhinos any day of the week."

"Ah, but these are some tough rhinos, buddy. Someone didn't raise them right." The two boys bumped fists. "How you been, Huck?"

"Good. I'm good," Huck said, his voice very soft.

"Have you been waiting long? Again, I'm sorry I'm late, my mentor was lecturing me after school, and I lost track of time when I got back home. Here, let's grab a table," Finley said, and the two kids sat in a booth that appeared in the blank light.

"No, I just got here. How are you though, Finley? Everything okay?"

"Oh, I'm fine. You know me. Always running about and causing a bit of chaos."

"You must be a terrible example to those kids," Huck said, his face lifting into a more natural smirk.

"Oh, I can't imagine. I have no idea why they would let someone like me work in the early education program. Just a bunch of little hooligans watching a big hooligan making a fool of himself and knocking things off shelves," younger Finley said and laughed.

"I'm sure you'll make a wonderful teacher, Finley. You have a great way of making a person feel listened to. I'm sure the children love you," Huck said, his voice earnest and his eyes filling with light for the first time.

"Thanks, buddy. How are you, Huck? It feels like it's been ages since we talked. Everything okay at home?"

"Oh fine, everything's fine. My parents asked me to say hello to you by the way, or at least mom did."

"They're wonderful. Give them my love. Is your mother still the biggest card shark this side of the Mississippi?"

"Actually, she doesn't play cards so much anymore."

"Really? She was the one that taught me how to play bridge, and poker when my parents weren't looking. Why did she stop?"

"Not enough time, with Dad and all," Huck said, and a silence fell over the conversation. The silence had a shadow in the shape of a man. When Finley spoke again his voice was much softer.

"How is your Dad?"

"He has his good days, but a lot of bad days in between them. And even the good days aren't so good anymore. He doesn't know who I am most of the time."

"That's horrible, Huck. I mean that's really horrible. But I'm sure a part of him remembers you, the best part."

Huck gave a terrible wrenching laugh, and this time Finley saw his own younger self's reaction to it. The young him recoiled at the sound coming from his friend. It was a scornful sound, that laugh, as if he were trying to hurt someone, but whether that person had been Finley or Huck himself Finley still did not know.

"Yeah. Yeah, some part of him does remember. But that part thinks that Mom and I are his jailers. That part of him hates us. It's better when he forgets."

"It was wonderful of you to stay at home, Huck, to help your mom with your dad. Even doing online classes. That was a terrific thing to do."

"Yeah. Thank you. Sometimes I wish I hadn't."

"I'm sure it's awful."

"It is. But it's worse for Mom," Huck said, and the barbed anger started to fade from his eyes. "She's...not doing well. I don't think she'll survive for long without Dad. He's destroyed her before he goes."

"Huck…"

"I hope it happens soon. Better it happens soon. Get it over with."

"You don't mean that. I know you. I know that's not what you really feel," Finley said, reaching out across the table slowly to hold Huck's hand. The other boy looked at him with tears in his eyes. He opened his mouth as if to say something, and then closed it. He pulled his hands away from Finley, using the corners of his sweater to dab at his eyes.

"Yeah. Sorry about that. It sort of builds."

"It's no worries, bud. Let it all out," Finley said. And even in that moment he knew how empty the words were, how pathetically hollow they sounded.

"Hey, are you still writing those stories? The Awesome Planet ones?" Finley asked. And it tore at the older Finley to see the desperation in his younger self. How eager he was to change the subject, to speak about anything else, or even to run from that room and all that terrible sadness in his friend until he could no longer feel it clawing at his own heart. And it was so obvious, to him, and to Huck.

"Oh yeah," Huck said, forcing life back into his voice, though his eyes were still red, and the ends of his sleeves were still wet. "Yeah, I'm trying to whenever I can."

"I always loved them when we were kids."

"Really? Even the ones about the bees?" Huck asked slyly.

"Okay never that one. You know how I get about bees, I have that thing, that small hole fear thing."

"Trypophobia"

"Yeah, trypophobia. You wrote that one just to mess with me, didn't you?"

"Maybe," Huck said, and this time the laugh he gave was close to his normal one.

"I knew it. I absolutely knew it. Gave me nightmares. Any new ones to send me screaming into the night?"

"I think so actually. The new ones seem to have gotten a bit darker as of late."

"Yeah?"

And slowly the shadows crept in, and the darkness fell, and the younger Finley and Huck swam in the last remains of light until they too vanished. And then Finley saw the lights of the city return. Marlowe's own glow was dim and small, and it floated down to return to it spot on his neck. It cuddled into his collar and stilled.

Gaspar was standing across from Finley, his eyes still fixed on the point where Marlowe had been. His hands were open as if he were about to embrace someone. Yet his eyes were brimming with tears, and his mouth was a slash of misery on his face.

Finley reached up to touch his own eyes and found that he too had tears collecting in them. He did not brush them away as he waited for Gaspar to collect himself. He watched the cleric reform before him, like a puzzle moving into its proper shape.

"Did you have your vision?" Finley asked, his voice a quiet rasp. Gaspar's eyes met Finley's, and for once they were not filled with hate.

"Yes."

"Was it the one you wanted?"

"No."

"Mine either," Finley said. "It seems you were right, Gaspar, the Ghostlights can give us visions of those that are dead. But I wonder, was yours, like mine, just a memory?"

"Yes. Just a memory, our last together."

"I'm sorry."

Gaspar looked at him with wonder. "You are, aren't you? I can honestly say that I'm surprised."

"It's been a surprising day. Was that what you wanted? What you expected?"

"Neither."

"But we were both shown something, Gaspar. That proves that your legends are true. The Ghostlights are a link to the dead, just not in the way we hoped. Still, you were right." Gaspar gave a quiet laugh at this.

"Yes, I suppose I was. But I rather wish I had been shown nothing at all." Gaspar began to turn away.

"Where are you going? You still have information I need."

"It has been a long night, Marsh. You will have your answers on a different night."

"NO," Finley said, rushing forward and grabbing onto Gaspar's shoulder. "I delivered what you wanted. I gave you a vision that no one else could offer you."

Gaspar ripped his shoulder away and he spun, grabbing onto Finley's lapel and lifting him off the ground. Finley's left hand found Gaspar's hair, while his right frantically signaled Moro not to strike yet.

"You showed me nothing, it was that thing, that monster. I did not want to see that! I did not deserve to see that! A memory is worse than nothing."

"I warned you, Gaspar, that you might not like what you see. The Ghostlights will allow us no illusions."

"You sanctimonious cur! I'll shatter your face!" Gaspar roared.

241

"If you do, I'll have Marlowe show you visions until you go mad. You'll spend the rest of your miserable life trapped in your worst memories, with nothing but shades and shadows for company," Finley said, making his voice cold and pitiless, although his heart beat like a frantic rabbit beneath his ribs.

Gaspar gave a shout of misery and threw Finley away from him. Finley stumbled and flew, falling onto the stones, Marlowe toppling from its spot on his collar. The flower zoomed away but came hurtling back as Finley gave a cry of pain as his head collided with the solid stone. The flower pulsed a worried violet as it hovered over Finley.

"I'm okay. Just a scratch. I'm okay," Finley pulled himself to a sitting position. "See, no blood," Finley said, brushing his hand against the back of his head and showing it to the flower. Marlowe shifted into a blinding red. Finley looked at his hand. There was, in fact, blood.

"Well, that's not so good. But I'm fine, I'm fine. Relax, partner," Finley said, attempting to calm the flower. "You're worrying my partner, Gaspar. I don't know what it will do if you upset it. And I have other friends that you don't know about, other mythical creatures who call me pal. So, start talking before I get a unicorn to come down here and beat your...Gaspar?" Finley asked, stopping short when he saw Gaspar on his knees in front of him. The man's shoulders were slumped, and his hands were lined with bleeding cuts. With a start Finley realized that the man had been beating his hands against the ground.

Gaspar's shoulders were shaking with sobs. Finley turned away, looking off into the night, giving the man his privacy.

The night was quiet around them. The city had drifted off to sleep and turned off the lights. With a terrible racking breath, he forced himself to speak.

"I saw my friend, Gaspar. Marlowe showed me my dead friend. His name was Huck, and I buried him before I came to your city. But that wasn't what Marlowe showed me.

"Huck and I fell out of touch before his death. We were incredibly close when we were kids. We called each other's parents mom and dad for most of our lives. We were like each other's shadows. And then, suddenly we weren't. I'm not sure how it started," Finley said, and the flower floated behind him nuzzling the cut on his head. Finley felt the warmth of the flower on his wound, as if he were standing in the light of the sun.

But then the flower flashed red.

"That's a lie," Finley said, looking for some sign of approval from the Ghostlight above him. "His father was diagnosed with dementia. Do they have dementia on this planet? Or does it go by another name?" Finley risked a glance at Gaspar, but the man did not look back. His gaze was fixed on the ground before him.

"Dementia is a disease of the mind, a lot like the one from your story. The sufferers, over time, begins to lose their mental capacities. They forget things. Little stuff at first, like where they put their car keys, or leaving the pot on the stove. But soon the big stuff starts to go too. They might forget that they're sick. They might forget that they're being taken care of, and that they're loved. And then they might start to forget everything else.

"Huck's dad had it, a really bad case of it, too. He was diagnosed incredibly young. And Huck had to watch his father fall to pieces in front of him, had to watch his mother break herself to care for him, had to give up his life to care for them both. My friend was an incredibly kind person, but soon all he had left was anger and resentment and confusion and that was what scared me.

"I was terrified that all his unhappiness would latch onto me, so I started to distance myself. I called him less and less, visited less and less. I think, before he died, he thought that I had forgotten about him," Finley said, his voice breaking. And now the burning in his eyes matched the pain on the back of his head.

"That's who I saw just now. I saw the last time I ever saw him. He died soon after. And I think it might be my fault. I think…in the end it was just too much. You can't imagine what that did to me.

"But I was given a sign! A sign that his death might have been something more than it seemed, that it might have been murder. And Marlowe can help me learn more. But for some reason it thinks your city is worth saving.

"Believe this, you're going to tell me what you know, you're going to help me solve this mystery. Because it is the only way I'll figure out what happened to Huck and make things right.

"I don't know what you saw, I can't even guess, but I'm the only other person in the world who understands what just happened to you. So, you might as well talk."

Finley looked at Marlowe, which twirled about him looking for more cuts and bruises that it could tend to. When it was not casting its light over him looking for more wounds, it turned furtively to look at Gaspar, its light shining on his face, before turning back to Finley.

"I don't think Marlowe knew what it was doing. But I think you and I just discovered what the Ghostlights are for. They're here to remind us that this world is all there is, and we are all we've got. I couldn't, wouldn't, help Huck then, but I can help you now. You couldn't help your love, but you can help me. Tell me what I need to know about the Guardians. Tell me what I need to know to give this City answers. Tell me what happened to Huck. It's the only answer you or I are going to get tonight," Finley said, wondering if he was pushing in the dagger too hard. But he had no time for subtlety, he had no time for the slower, kinder path.

He needed to get out of here. Every minute he spent in this place in front of Gaspar and Moro felt like a press on an open wound. He needed to be alone.

"It seems that all my faiths are breaking tonight, Marsh." Gaspar groaned. He pulled himself upright to look Finley in the eyes. "The Crooken do not know how to murder a Guardian, for we do not know how to create one at all."

"What?"

"The Crooken have lost the knowledge of how to build a Guardian. Now we are simply maintainers, tending to the creations of better men and women than us."

Finley felt as if he had been dipped in ice cold water. "What about Sinoh?"

"No Crooken has the knowledge. This is why she seeks the one who is murdering the Guardians." Gaspar met Finley's look of shock. "Did you think you were the only one hunting for the killer? Mr. Marsh, you are one of many. Yet Sinoh would kill before letting an outsider discover the secret of Guardian death."

"Because if you know how to kill one, you might be able to learn how to create one."

"Precisely. It is why Sinoh allowed me to join you this night. I convinced her that the Ghostlight would allow me to speak to one of our ancient predecessors, to discover this lost knowledge. Of course, this has backfired."

"How could such knowledge have been lost? I thought your entire faith was built around these Guardians."

"The world fades, and we fade along with it. The secret of the Guardians' life is the Cognitive Domain known as cognition, the highest and noblest of all the domains. And we have forgotten it. Once we were masters of that domain, able to give life to all that we wished. We could make the wind speak and serve, teach the stones to dance, have rivers rise and walk at our command. No more."

"What are you talking about? What is the domain of cognition?"

"The Cognitive Domains you purblind fool, the forces that shaped the universe at its founding, the ones that Vovatum himself taught his followers at the dawn of all things. The Crooken were entrusted with the highest art, the one that gave shape to each of the other domains, Cognition itself, the ability to give thought to the thoughtless."

"So that's how the Guardians were made. They're just stones you put thoughts into. And you used this power to make slaves?" Finley asked, unable to contain his shock and anger.

"To make Guardians to save us from the ravages of the world."

"To tend to your every whim."

"To make the world easier, better, for god's chosen people."

"Yeah, I bet he's pretty pissed you lost his super special power," Finley said. Gaspar surprised him by not exploding with anger. Rather the man went cold as a winter pool, and a pensive look fell over his face.

"Perhaps. We have sent agents all through the tiles to reclaim Cognition, but none know the way of it. And now, irony of ironies, it is being used here, in our own city, against us. Perhaps it is divine punishment."

"We suspect that the killer is looking for Cognition just as we are, but it seems they are much further along than us. Whoever they are, they have discovered how to kill that which cognition animated. And once you know how to destroy something, soon you may be able to create as well."

"Orsos thinks that the Bolt Heads are the ones responsible for the killings. Have your own mysterious hunters come to the same conclusion?"

"In a sense. If it was the Broken Ring they could not have acted alone. Mastery of Cognition is beyond any such as they. We are speaking of a power that can bend the very heart of this planet to your whim. A mere political movement could never wield such power."

"So who do you suspect?"

"Our agents think that—"

And then the world roared around them.

Stone tore loose from its foundations. The air shook with the scream of twisting metal.

Finley and Gaspar looked up and saw the clenched fist of a construction Guardian thundering towards them.

Finley dove, grabbing Marlowe as he passed. The half-completed wall to the north buckled and turned to dust as the arm of the Guardian smashed through it.

Its fist slammed into the ground where Finley had been standing and a shockwave sent Finley hurtling through the air.

He collided with the half completed southern wall. Jutting rebar only inches from his face. His bleeding head hit rough stone and the world flashed white.

For one shimmering second there was no pain, and then it rushed in. White hot fire raced down his spine and a wrenching moan escaped him.

The world cleared, and Finley looked up to see the second raised fist of the construction Guardian. Its eyes were lambent red instead of their normal green as they spotted him.

The fist came rushing down, blotting out the night sky, and Finley closed his eyes.

There was a terrible crash as stone hit stone, and Finley's eyes shot open.

A different Guardian stood over him, holding back the massive fist of the Construction Guardian. Finley heard the screech of stone being pushed across stone, and he could see the feet of his savior being pushed backwards.

Finley lurched to the side, still clutching Marlowe to this chest. He turned back to see the face of his savior and saw the spiked pauldrons and glaring eyes of Hawksbill. It held back the fist of the Guardian, its own crossed arms blocking the massive one.

"This isn't one of those 'only I can kill you situations,' is it?" Finley asked. Hawksbill shifted its weight and sent the falling fist hurtling to the side. The great arm punched through the southern wall, and as the dust fell, Hawksbill lumbered up the length of the Construction Guardian's limbs to deal with it face to face.

"Finley?" Moro shouted. Finley turned but could not find her in the clouds of dust that the colossal fistfight had produced. He stumbled towards the sound. He could feel blood trickling down his neck, and the dust around him shook with the shockwaves as fists of stone met each other behind him. His hands vibrated, and with a jolt of recognition Finley remembered what he was carrying.

He opened his hand, and Marlowe flew out, sending beams of yellow light through the clouds of dust. Finley followed the light, hoping that Moro was smart enough to do the same. He stumbled forward, one hand pulling his coat in front of his mouth to keep the dust out of his lungs. He tripped and fell to his knees. The wall had collapsed here, crashing into exactly the spot where he and Gasper had been standing. The concrete at his feet had shattered from the force of the colossal punch. Finley felt fabric with his right hand, sodden with some sort of liquid.

It was a scrap of Gasper's clothes, and it was drenched in blood.

Finley followed the cloth and found the rest of Gasper.

His knees went weak, and his stomach surged as he looked at the remains of the cleric.

"Finley!" Moro roared. She was not far. Finley stumbled to his feet. He didn't know the words to any prayers in this world, but he tried his best to form one that Gasper might have approved of.

"Shepherd bless and keep him. Ghostlights guide and lead him," he whispered to himself as he stumbled through the clouds of dust towards the sound of Moro's voice.

He found her beyond the construction site. She too was covered in dust. Falling glass had cut her face and collected in her short hair. Marlowe floated beside her, scanning her just as it had Finley.

247

"Come on! He's the one that got the Guardian to start construction early. I saw him commanding it," Moro roared as she saw Finley. "He's getting away!" she said, pointing to a figure fleeing down the main street. Before Finley could speak, she shot after the fleeing figure.

Finley forced himself to follow. Every footfall sent a lance of pain to the wound on his head. Yet he forced himself to run on. Finley knew he was no match for mad Guardians, but just this second, he felt like he could win a footrace against a murderer.

Thoughts raced through Finley's head, far faster than his feet could move as they chased after the murderer.

For what else could he be?

Guardians can't murder. They can only do what they're told. But you're not supposed to be able to tell it to kill someone.

So how had that man provoked it?

He pelted after Moro, Marlowe followed in his wake, sending flashing white lights into the sky to herald their coming.

Finley saw curtains opening all around him and lights turning on, but they soon became a blur as he picked up speed. The adrenaline coursed through him, and the pain faded away to be replaced by the thrill of the hunt.

Finley turned right, following the shouting Moro as she thundered up the thoroughfare. Finley could see their quarry farther ahead up the lane.

The man turned behind him to look at the roaring Moro and the flashing lights of Marlowe.

A mistake.

The suspect twisted to the side and fell. Finley quickened his pace, and Moro moved in for the kill.

The ground in front of her erupted in a shower of stone, and out came one of the smaller maintenance Guardians. It looked like a spider made of dark brick, with eight glowing red eyes in the center of its head.

It leapt onto Moro. But Moro seemed to see it at the last minute, and she slipped the crushing blow meant for her head so that it only cut across her right cheek. She spun away, the Guardian landing past her on its eight stone legs.

Its legs beat a strange, pulsing rhythm as it swiveled to face her. The harmony grew and grew, an ever-increasing drum beat. And then it leapt.

This time she was ready, and as the creature extended its stone pincers to crush her head in its jaws she rolled to the side. As the creature flew over her, she snatched one of its stone legs.

With a roar of anger and pain she swung the creature over her head and brought it down onto the hard stone of the road. The Guardian made a crater in the brickwork as its small body collided with the road.

It was motionless for only a moment, before its stone limbs rotated in their sockets. Its eyes had turned a dull green. It stood up once again, and Moro raised her fists in front of her, ready for another charge. Yet the Guardian only stared at her before it shook itself like a dog shaking the rain out of its fur. It turned away from her and climbed back into the hole it burst out of. It took the time to repair the damage to the road as it left.

The suspect's pace had not slowed, and he continued to thunder up the road. Finley changed course, rushing to Moro's side right as she collapsed to her knees.

Her hands clutched the wound in her face, trying to stem the blood that was pouring into her eyes. But she seemed to hear his footsteps as he raced to her side.

"Get after him. Don't stop," she said between gritted teeth. "I'll follow."

Finley reared back and then followed her command, racing after the man, who was now more than a hundred yards ahead. He could hear Moro calling for backup as she moved to follow him, though now she was much slower.

"Get ahead of him and blind him," Finley said to Marlowe as he panted for breath. The Ghostlight shot forward, moving like a bird in flight. It flew down the road, between the legs of the fleeing murderer. Marlowe stopped in front of his face. The man's pace stuttered to a halt at this strange glowing flower. Marlowe stared at the man for a moment, its little black veins pulsing inside its petals, and then the sun rose in the middle of the road.

A bright flash of burning light burned the shadows from the world, and Finley shut his eyes a second too late. The afterimage of the man backlit by the rising sun of Marlowe floated in front of his eyes. Yet he grinned as he heard the man give a cry of pain.

Finley blinked the spots out of his eyes while his vision slowly cleared. He saw the man flail his way down a nearby alley. Marlowe sank to the hard gravel of the road, fluttering like a dying candle.

"It's okay, partner. I got it from here," Finley said, and he moved to follow the man down the alley. The darkness of the alley coated him like a blanket and soothed his screaming eyes. Yet it had covered the murderer in that same darkness.

Silence. Finley paused. The killer was in this alley still, waiting. Waiting for him to do something stupid.

Why not let him make that mistake?

"I have to know. Does that hurt as bad as I think it does?" Finley asked. "I mean, that must have been like staring directly at an eclipse for hours and hours. You'll be lucky if you ever see again. Hell, you'll be lucky if you don't get cancer and have tumors growing out of your eyeballs."

Finley crept down the alley, moving his eyes from side to side. His ears were tuned for the slightest sound, but he kept talking.

"And to think, the last thing you ever saw was a pissed off little flower burning your retinas to ash. I imagine a loathsome little low life like you doesn't have a family. But you might have a mother, maybe a dad. You'll never be able to look at them again you know? But that might be a blessing. You won't have to see the disgust on their faces whenever they look at you. A murderer and a man with burnt out eyeballs? Not even love goes that far."

He heard a noise. It was the slightest shift of fabric on metal. The garbage cans up ahead? The drainpipes farther up? He kept talking, kept using all that skill he had in annoying the hell out of people.

"And such a sloppy murderer too. Really amateur. Bush league. D-. Were you trying to prevent Gaspar from telling me something? Were you afraid what secrets he would whisper in my ear? Well too bad, buddy. He told me all I needed to know, and now you made him a martyr. They'll build statues for him. The hero cleric who died trying to save his city. Tell you what, when they finally let you out of prison about four centuries from now you can beg for scraps in front of his memorial. I'm sure you'll get a few pennies. After all you'll be a pathetic sight, wrinkled with age and blind as a bat," Finley said, his voice dripping with scorn.

"You'll be a novelty! The ugly, failure of an assassin who turned his target into a hero and let the other one beat his—"

Finley heard him move a second before he saw him.

The man roared as he shot to his feet from his hiding place amidst the rubbish cans. His face was contorted with rage, spittle flying from his mouth. There was a knife in his hand that scraped against the bricks as he lunged.

Finley dodged to the side.

The man stabbed the wall behind Finley, breaking the blade against the bricks. Finley's elbow hit him in the neck and folded him like old laundry. Finley put his boot into the man's stomach twice as he fell.

The man groaned and then stilled. Finley kicked him one more time for good measure. He pulled the knife from the man's hands and tucked it into his jacket pocket.

He was in the middle of frisking the murderer as Moro and Marlowe rounded the corner. One still bleeding, the other a pale shadow of its usual glowing self.

"What the hell happened?" Moro asked. "Did you hit him?"

"No need to sound so shocked. I am slightly more dangerous than I seem. Self-defense classes. Huck's dad made me and him take them after Mel beat our butts too many times," Finley said, Marlowe landing on his shoulder. "Of course, Marlowe here did most of the real work. It blinded him. All I had to do was make him angry enough to charge at me."

"I imagine you had no trouble with that."

"Ha. Ha. How are you?"

"I'll be fine once I get some bandages on my face. I'm mostly stunned. Guardians have never attacked a person before."

"That makes twice in one night then. He seems to have some sway over the Guardians. That construction one killed Gaspar."

"I wouldn't believe you if one hadn't just lunged for my face." Moro leaned down and turned the man over onto his back. She studied his face for a moment, before her hands patted the man down just as Finley had.

"Do you recognize him at all?"

"No. Did he have any identification on him."

"Nothing. But he has this around his neck," Finley said, pulling down the man's shirt to reveal the necklace on his throat. It was an incomplete iron loop. There was a gap in the circle, and at each end there was a broken metal ring welded to the iron.

"The Broken Ring. So Orsos was right."

"Maybe. I'm not so sure. Why would they send an assassin wearing their insignia? And how could they have control over the Guardians? They hate the Guardians. They want them destroyed."

"Making them attack and murder people is a great way to get everyone to abandon them."

"True. It's certainly got my blood riled up. Let's wake him up and see what he has to say."

Finley squatted next to the man and poked his face. The man's eyes fluttered. Finley poked him again, harder, and then once more for good measure. The man gasped and opened his eyes. His pupils were the tiniest things Finley had ever seen, mere shadows in the green of his eyes. The man's eyes roved about but did not focus on anything until Finley spoke.

"Hello. My name is Special Detective Finley Marsh. This is my partner Special Detective Marlowe and Constable Moro. We have questions we would like you to answer."

The man's eyes locked on Finley's face but did not focus. His lips opened and closed like a fish, but no sound emerged.

"You are a suspect in the murder of a cleric and the attempted murder of three wardens. You are also a suspect of an attempt to murder using the Guardians. That last may not be a crime, considering no one has ever been able to pull off such a thing. Congratulations, you are very special," he said, and then addressed Moro. "Does he have the right to remain silent?"

"What the hell are you talking about?"

"Fantastic. Bad for you, sir, good for us. If you behave and answer my questions you will be escorted to a dark cell. If you misbehave or are silent then I will feed you to Chief Warden Orsos. Am I understood?"

The man gaped at Finley. His eyes blinked again and again, but even in the darkness his pupils would not un-dilate.

252

"I can't see."

"We are aware. I am afraid you made a mistake when you killed Gaspar. My partner had begun to take a liking to the man. It turns out the Ghostlights are quite testy and prone to vengeance. But if you answer my questions, perhaps I can talk my partner into returning your sight to you," Finley said, shrugging his shoulders for Moro to see.

"Please, please let me see."

"In time. What is your name?"

"Marocs."

Marlowe flashed a dull red above Moro.

"A lie. I would like your real name please."

"Turok."

A flash of red.

"Another lie. Allow me to help you save your breath, Mr. What's Your Name. You cannot lie to us. So, I'll ask my question one more time, and you'll answer truthfully, or I'll leave you to your darkness. What's your name?"

"Kazacz. My name is Kazacz."

A flash of blue.

"Now we are getting somewhere. Kazacz, why'd you try to murder me?"

"I wasn't trying to."

Another flash of blue. Finley shook his head. The man was clearly the assassin, he had shown he had an ability to control the Guardians. After all, hadn't that spider Guardian only attacked Moro because this man was in danger? Unless there were other assassins? Ones that Moro did not see. Finley's mind spun with the possibilities, and he opened his mouth to speak, but before he could Moro cut him off.

"Did you try to murder the cleric, Gaspar?"

The man's head spun to face the sound of Moro's voice, but then quickly turned away.

"No."

There was a flash of red light. Ah, Finley thought. A misdirection. He would need to be more careful. He nodded to Moro.

"So I wasn't the intended target. You were after Gaspar. How did you know where to find him?"

The ground shook beneath their feet. Finley turned and saw an immense dust cloud rising from the construction site. There was the rumble of an avalanche as what sounded like tons of stones falling to the ground shook through the air.

"Ah, it seems Hawksbill has dealt with the Construction Guardian. But back to the matter at hand. How did you know where to find Gaspar?"

"We have eyes that no one can see," Kazacz said. And it seemed the sound of the Construction Guardian's destruction had given him new strength. His voice had lost its waver and was now calm and confident. He closed his eyes as he spoke, and a look of peace came over him, as if he had vanished from this alley, as if he had vanished from the world. "We knew he would be there before he did."

"Who is we? Are you a member of the Broken Ring?"

The man did not speak. He opened his eyes and his blank stare passed through Finley to another place, another time. It was like he was a different person, as if someone else looked out from his skin.

But Finley would not let him escape.

"Who are you? How did you get the Guardians to listen to you? Are you the one who has been murdering the Guardians? Speak!" Finley said, his voice rising, his spittle flying onto the man's face.

"But I murdered no one," Kazacz said, his voice serene and untroubled. "It was a construction accident, a tragic twist of fate. The good cleric wandered into a building site, little knowing that it was scheduled for an early destruction. That will be the story the city will come to believe. After all, Guardians cannot kill, can they? But of course, people will wonder. Why did a cleric die? Why would the Guardians do such a thing?"

"How did you force the Guardians to kill?" Finley said, overriding the man.

"I forced nothing. I spoke to it, and it wanted to help me. That's their job, you know? They are here to help. Once I explained to it how Gaspar's death would help me, it was only too eager to oblige. So eager, maybe they dream about killing us all."

"That's impossible. The Guardians cannot kill a human being. It is written into their very foundation," Moro said.

"And yet, accidents happen. Again and again."

254

And Finley remembered the accident that had begun this terrible thing. The death of a young girl by the errant hand of a Guardian. With dawning horror Finley grabbed hold of the man.

"Are you a member of the Broken Ring? Did you organize the death of Evy Homme? How do you control the Guardians?!" Finley roared.

"Through faith."

"I want answers. Speak the truth. I'll know if you lie," Finley said, his hands almost choking the man. And it was all catching up to him at once. The chaos in the streets and Orsos's rage. Finley's own desperation to learn about Huck's death. The death of Gaspar, the sickening crunch his body made as it shattered, played over and over on a loop in Finley's head.

And there was a new sound approaching. It was the crunch of stone on brick. The thunder of a great weight coming closer and closer, leaving an echo of its footsteps in his bones.

"It scares you, doesn't it? Not knowing. Be at ease. If you choose to, you can shed that fear, and disappear into sleep. And who knows what dreams may find you?" Kazacz said.

A shadow crossed the edge of the alley. It blotted out the windows in the street beyond. The shadow walked closer, the tread of its steps growing louder and louder. The dust of its conflict with the construction Guardian streamed off Hawksbill's shoulders like a shroud. It paid no mind to Moro and Finley. Its own eyes were locked on Kazacz.

"Report, Hawksbill," Moro said, but the Guardian paid no heed to her command.

"Halt, Guardian," Moro said, her voice much louder now as the Guardian's grinding footsteps filled the alleyway. She moved to stand in front of it.

Finley turned back to Kazacz. The man's eyes had closed. His face had smoothed and become still. His voice, when it came, seemed to come from the bottom of an ancient well.

"Do not be scared. God is almost ready," Kazacz said. And to Finley's horror he saw Hawksbill brush aside Moro as if she were made of nothing. He watched the massive stone hand reach out and pick up the bolthead almost gently. Kazacz did not offer a hint of struggle as the giant's hand closed about his face. Finley saw the Guardian's stone fingers start to flex. He closed his eyes, but he could not stop himself from hearing what happened next.

He reared away, stumbling to the other side of the alley. Moro flailed back as she tried to choke back her cry of alarm. Hawksbill stood perfectly still. Its red eyes fixed dead ahead. What remained of Kazacz hung in its hands, and as its twitches stopped, Hawksbill's eyes became green again. With glacial slowness the Guardian gathered Kazacz into its arms and walked away.

With slow pounding steps it made its way out of the alley, turned right, and vanished from their view. Finley and Moro remained rooted to the spot, unable to pull their eyes from where their suspect had just been. Finley felt his hand quivering at his side, and he could not steady it as the adrenaline and the fear crashed through him like a wave. Marlowe hovered over his head; its glow of light dulled to stone gray. Finley looked down the alley, towards where Hawksbill had disappeared.

"I'll call—I'll call it in," Moro said, moving into the fresh air beyond the alley.

"Why would Hawksbill do that? Why would he say that? What did that mean? 'God is almost ready?'" Finley asked.

Marlowe flashed blue, sending Finley's shadow up the alley wall until it seemed to tower over him.

Chapter 18: The Dreamer's Game

Where are you? I have lost count of the years. I have lost count of the lives I have lived, and the deaths I have escaped, but I have never found any of you. Did you abandon me here? Did you leave me in this hell to rot?

Or is it more horrible than that? I torment myself with these thoughts, with the images of you laughing and laughing at poor Yosef as I grow older and lonelier every day, writing letters to no one. I wish I had never come to this land. I wish I had never met any of you.

(Letter 18, Paragraph 1, Lines 1-3 and Paragraph 2, Lines 1-3)

"Do you take milk with your tea?" Harmodias asked.

"No," Mel replied.

"Very well." Harmodias poured the iron kettle into the crooked tin cups. Steam frosted the surface of the metal so that Mel could no longer see her reflection in its depths. She was glad for it. She had seen far too much of herself reflected in metal lately.

They were in an antechamber off the Chamber of Sleepers. The room was sparse. Little alcoves lined the walls. Inside were pens and papers, pots and pans, a tea set, and the various other implements of the smallest kitchen Mel had ever seen.

A fire burned in the largest alcove. Its smoke rose through the chimney dug into the earth. It would emerge somewhere far above them in the remains of the Shining Forest. Harmodias sat across from Mel in a chair of normal wood. She steeped her tea in silence, her eyes gazing over Mel's left shoulder. Cisseus lay on his stomach off to the side playing with pens and paper.

Mel let her wait. She forced herself not to guzzle the tea. A perfect cup needed to steep for three minutes at least. It required patience on behalf of the drinker. Rushed tea was weak tea. Rushed tea was wasted tea. And Mel was of the firm belief that tea must never be wasted.

So despite her days in the wilderness, and despite her time laboring on a metal giant, she forced herself to wait. Harmodias sipped her tea, and Mel flashed a savage smile. The old woman had jumped the gun. Those final ten seconds were the most important.

Finally, Mel reached out. She brought the mug to her face. The smell hit her nostrils first, and then the heat caressed her skin. She waited one more second, just to prove to herself that she could. She took a sip.

Perfection.

You had questions?" Harmodias asked, a smile tugging at her cheek, even as her gaze remained locked over Mel's left shoulder.

"Yes." The questions stacked up in her mind. She skipped the larger ones like what planet she was on, why this world had magic, what the hell was going on, and various other concerns she knew the woman across from her would be unable to answer. She decided to lead with the most pressing concern.

"Do I get a reward for feeding the boy?"

"A reward?"

"Yes. I helped someone that was precious to you," Mel said. The boy in question looked up from his pen and paper, but Mel couldn't see what he was drawing.

"You gave him bread; you wish a reward for that?"

"I may not know much about you Sheosirrans, but I know gratitude when I see it. The boy looked shocked when I gave him even that moldy old bread, and I bet you did too when you heard it. So, what do I get as a reward?"

"No. I am afraid you will not receive a reward. However, I am more than happy to grant you a gift."

"What's the difference?"

"A reward is transactional and temporary. A gift is the beginning of a relationship. One interests me not at all. The other presents a fascinating opportunity."

"What kind of relationship?"

"One that may benefit us both. An example, you have fed my wayward grandson. And I have given you tea. An auspicious start I would say."

"I haven't had many successful relationships with people that live in trees."

"Melanie, we do far more than live in them, we rebuild them."

"What's that mean?"

Harmodias paused. She poured more of the boiling water into her half empty mug. She placed her finger in the water and stirred. The only sounds were those of the boy as he scratched away at the page.

Mel glanced at him. Cisseus was completely absorbed in his work. He was lying on his stomach, his legs kicking in the air behind him, the tip of his tongue peeking out at the corner of his mouth. Mel craned her neck to see what he was drawing, but Harmodias spoke before she could recognize it.

"What do you know of us? What do you know of the Sheosirrans?"

"Nothing. I've either been hypnotized or running since I got here. You can safely assume I know little about anything."

"Then you have no prejudices. Perhaps I should begin with what people say about us. People say that we were cast out from our home tile, and we are cursed to wander forever. Those that invite us in, we steal from. They say we salt their fields and befoul their flock. But that is not the worst thing about the Sheosirrans. The worst is that once they have destroyed your home, and your family, and your body, then they will destroy your mind." Harmodias gave a nasty smile that revealed the sharp points of her canines. She continued to stir her tea with her long nail as she spoke.

"In whispers, they claim that the Sheosirrans are dream eaters. They will slip into your thoughts and learn your secrets. They will have your mind devour itself, pulled to shreds by what you tried to keep hidden from the world in your own head. They will give you dreams you'll never wake up from, and in your sleep, you'll do as they command. That is what they say."

Mel gulped. She looked at Harmodias and took a sip of her tea.

"In my experience 'the people' are mostly idiots," Mel said.

"That is my experience as well."

"So, what is the truth then?"

"Oh, large parts of it are true. We do eat the dreams of people. But only very bad people, Melanie," Harmodias said, her grin even wider now. She reached below the table and pulled a fork from her lap. She raised it high, like a dagger she was about to plunge into Melanie's heart. The boy looked over at the commotion but did not move.

Mel stumbled back, her arm pulling the iron mug back to throw it at the witch. Her feet were already taking her to the door, and she was halfway through before she realized that Harmodias was kidding.

259

The old woman cackled, great peals of mirth echoed around the tiny chamber as the old woman snorted and stomped her feet. The boy covered his ears and turned back to his drawing.

Mel sat down again with a noise of disgust.

"Are you done?" Mel asked.

"I do apologize, Melanie," Harmodias said as she wiped her eyes. "We so rarely meet outsiders. I couldn't resist." She pulled another fork from her lap, before reaching into one of the alcoves to retrieve little slices of brown cake. She gave a serving and a fork to Mel before tucking into her own.

"There you go, the gift of food returned. As you said, there is a kernel of truth to every story. It is true, the Sheosirrans have no home tile. We are a wandering people and small in number."

"What happened to your home?"

"There are differing accounts. Our people believe that the tile became uninhabitable to our people. Some twist in the Cognitive Domains made it impossible for us to continue to live there."

"Is that why you are wandering? Are you trying to find your home again?"

"Heavens no. The ancients abandoned that place for a reason. It would do us no good to return to such a place. Thus, we wander. However, very few others are so restless on Poa. Most keep to their tiles for their entire lives. Besides the odd visit from the Circus or from the *Herald* they are content to live tucked away in their corner of the world."

"I'm guessing that makes the Sheosirrans pariahs," Mel said. Harmodias stabbed her fork at her in confirmation.

"Correct. Thus, the frightful rumors that have spread faster and further than we ever could. Almost everywhere we go we are met with unkindness, if not outright hostility."

"It sounds like a hard life."

"It is. Especially for children." Harmodias looked at Cisseus with deep fondness as she said this. "I am grateful you helped my great grandson. Few would. Most would throw stones at him rather than feed him. I am not sure you understand what you did when you fed him, but the rest of the world would much rather we starve to death. I do not believe anyone outside of his family has ever shown Cisseus kindness."

Mel swallowed, the cake suddenly seeming as dry as ashes in her mouth. "I just gave him bread. Seemed like the right thing to do."

"Sadly, that makes you a rarity, Melanie." She stabbed at her cake with great force, ripping the treat into shreds. "Still, the work continues."

"What work?"

"We endure the shambling hatreds of the unwashed masses for a simple reason, Melanie. We are called to a higher purpose. What do you know of the Cognitive Domains?"

"Nothing."

"The Domains are the primal energies of creation, or at least the bits of them that humans are able to control. They are many in number and each can give the user great power."

Mel's heart beat quicker at the mention of power. She concealed her eagerness by taking a slow sip of tea.

"The Sheosirrans are the sole masters of one such domain."

"I've seen it haven't I?" Mel asked with sudden insight. "Cisseus knows how to work one of the domains. That's why his fingers glow, why he can carve symbols in the air, and all the other mystic stuff."

Mel looked at the slight boy as he drew on the floor. His little feet made clouds of dust whenever they came down to kick the floor. Mel craned her neck to see what he was doing. The boy noticed and pulled the drawing out of her sight. His silent look asked her to wait.

"Why are you telling me this?"

Mel tried to catch Harmodias's eye, but they never quite met. The eyes across from hers were gray with years. With a practiced eye Mel traced the cheekbones that formed the lines of her face. She followed the hollows at her temple and the curve of the woman's jaw. She would make a magnificent portrait, Mel thought.

"What do you know about dreams?" the crone said.

"Just what I know from my sleep."

"And what do you dream of?"

Her friends' faces flashed in front of her eyes, and Mel suppressed a flare of guilt in her chest. "What business is that of yours?" she spat.

"Because dreams are power, perhaps the most dangerous power on this planet. After all, how could you escape the Colossus without them?"

Ice pooled in Mel's stomach. "What are you talking about?"

"That's how you were able to break free, was it not? You used one of your dreams as a shield against that wretched song. Do you really think anything else would have saved you from that?"

The ice spread from her stomach, shooting up her spine and into her heart. "You should watch what you say, you old bat. I'm not above elder abuse."

"I am not trying to frighten you, Melanie. I am trying to invite you."

"Why?"

"You helped my great grandson."

"I don't believe that for a second. I gave the kid some bread. Anyone would have done the same."

"You are not just anyone. You are a fighter, you are a dreamer, and you refuse to be a victim. You are Sheosirran in all but name."

"I am not one of your people."

"I think you'll find that it is the people who decide that." Harmodias said with a smile. "It is my right as the leader of my people to bring any I deem worthy into the fold. I have deemed you worthy. My invitation is not a small thing. If you join us, you will be us, and you will suffer as we do. But in return you will have a family."

"I already have a family," Mel said, her words coming out as a low growl.

"Then where are they?"

Mel had no answer for her.

"Trust me when I say that I know what it means to lose the ones you love. I have had sons and daughters and grandchildren return to the dirt, all because we were not strong enough. So I promise you power as well, the power to shape the very thoughts of the world. I will show you the Reverie," and when she said the word like it was the name of a family god.

"I don't know what to say."

"For now, say nothing. Think it over. But perhaps you should see what I'm offering first. Cisseus, will you take us there?"

The boy looked up and nodded. As he stood, he rolled up his drawing and tucked it into his belt. He stretched without a sound. Mel watched with some trepidation as his fingers began to light up with that purple light from before.

The boy began drawing in the air, and the symbols he drew seemed to grow and grow until their purple light consumed the room.

The world around them changed.

There was a sun far above them, yet its light was not yellow or orange, but a shade of pale purple. Massive columns of steel carved with flowing lines loomed over them and the light of the purple sun shone on their surfaces.

The light seemed heavier somehow, fuller and more substantial. Mel could almost feel the light shift around her as she lifted her hand to touch the column. She could even see the light change around her fingertips as the purple rays broke off into shades of red, yellow, and green.

She looked up, and she saw that the column splintered at its height. Offshoots from the columns tangled in the air above them, creating a dappled shade on the ground below. And it was only when she saw the dull copper leaves dangling from these branches that Mel realized that the columns were iron trees. She was in a forest of steel.

"What was in that tea?"

"Oh, give the boy some credit. This is all Cisseus," Harmodias said, smiling as she nodded towards the boy.

"Where are we?"

"I would think that is rather obvious. We are in the Shining Forest."

"The Shining Forest is dead. Chopped down. I walked through its stumps only yesterday."

"In the waking world it is gone. But we are in the dreaming world now, Melanie. And though only its deepest roots remain, in the Reverie the Shining Forest still towers overhead."

"The Dreaming People. I thought you were speaking metaphorically," Mel muttered to herself.

"Hardly. The Sheosirrans are the masters of the Reverie. We are the gardeners of the sleeping world. We have made it our mission to tend to those places, like the Shining Forest, which have died in the waking world, but dream on in this one," Harmodias said. She gestured to the forest around them, and Mel could see it stretched in every direction, an endless forest of iron and metal that lived and grew. And as Mel watched a bird flew from the air to alight upon Harmodias's shoulder. She stretched out a crooked finger to stroke its wings.

"If it dreams, it cannot die. And sometimes, if you are very polite, you might even ask that dreamer to shift in its sleep. Do you understand, Melanie, why we do what we do?"

"I do," Mel said. She closed her eyes. A deep sense of peace was spreading through her. It was the smell of new pencils and the sound of her friends' laughter. It infused her like tea in water, filling her to the brim with serenity she had not felt in a long time.

She opened her eyes.

"You still haven't said. Why me?"

"Because we owe you, Melanie, for what we have done to you," Harmodias said, and she pointed behind Mel.

Mel turned. The bark of the tree seemed to grow cold beneath her fingers, and the light of the purple sun began to dim.

Far away, beyond the sweep of the Shining Forest, past the flowing river and the great plains, there was a colossal metal man.

"A dream not your own has taken root in your mind. Even now it worms its way into your waking thoughts, creating a compulsion. To return. To work. To worship the Colossus. It is only our power that keeps you rooted here beneath the Shining Forest.

"You are not the first. For the last five years we have chased rumors of such things from tile to tile. We have heard whispers of whole cities vanishing, of tiles emptying, as each and every one of its people dropped everything and walked away. But these things did not happen without warning. According to the whispers, before their disappearance everyone in the tile would have the same dream.

"We came here and found a nightmare. Thousands and thousands working without stop or pause, compelled by a dream that is not theirs. Still, we had hoped that our worst fears had not been realized. And then we found you. Melanie, I am so sorry. Only a master of the Reverie could place such a compulsion on you, on these people. One of the Sheosirrans is behind this, and we need to know why."

And Mel was shocked to see that the old woman was weeping. Great trickling tears cascaded down her face as she looked at Mel with

264

her dull yellow eyes. "We have traveled all this way to correct this most grievous crime, but we need a guide to the top of the Colossus. Please help us fix what has gone wrong."

Mel sat in her room with the boy, Cisseus. He was cross legged in front of her, an air of concentration on his face. His hands were in front of him shaping signs, although his fingers were not glowing.

Mel attempted to mirror them. She waved her own right hand as he moved his left. She tucked her fingers into her palm, before releasing her pinky and her ring finger. These stuck out at angles. She struggled against the muscles in her hands and in her wrists as she did so, unaccustomed to the movement and the formation. The boy's hands moved without strain. His fingers and hands seemed to have far more joints than hers. His little hand reached out and smacked her hand as she got the position wrong.

"Hey!" Mel yelped.

The boy said nothing, merely repeating the gesture he was trying to teach her. Mel tucked all her fingers into her hand except for the middle one and showed it to him. The boy's head cocked to the side, and he looked at her with wide and confused eyes. His little eyebrows climbed to the top of his forehead.

"I guess that gesture isn't a universal one. This means that I'm frustrated with you."

The boy nodded and mirrored the gesture back to her, understanding on his face.

"Great. My teacher just flipped me off," Mel said. She put her head in her hands. "I'm terrible with kids."

The boy nodded again. The drawing was still in his belt, but he would not let Mel see it. Instead, he had spent the last day trying to teach her the hand movements needed to access the Reverie while Harmodias finished her work in the dream Shining Forest. The same hand movements served as his sign language.

Mel hadn't had much success. "Face it, kid. I'm really bad at all this stuff."

The boy shook his head at this, his eyebrows clouding over his eyes in frustration. He looked at his hands as they moved easily from form

265

to form. He watched the motion as if trying to decipher how he did them so easily.

"Why don't you speak? You're not deaf," Mel asked. Cisseus looked up at this, his mouth quirking to the side and wrinkles forming around his nose in annoyance.

"Sorry if that's a mean question to ask, but we've been hanging out and you've barely made a sound. It's getting on my nerves. Can you speak at all, or do you just not want to?"

The boy looked exasperated at this. He moved his hand next to his head and opened and closed his hand to mimic flapping jaws. He shook his head as he did so.

"Right. I guess you can't explain," Mel said, and the boy nodded at this.

As he put his hands back into his lap his eyes opened wide with surprise. He looked up and smiled at Mel. He gestured frantically at her to raise her hands up, palms to him. He did the same for her. He clapped, and then his right hand shot out to meet hers. He clapped again, and his left hand found its marks on her palm.

Mel did not move. The boy rolled his eyes at her before reaching out to hold her hand. He moved it so it hit his own palm, and then looked at her, checking for understanding.

"Yeah, I know how to play patty cake, dumbass. Is that super important right now?"

The boy nodded vigorously. He sat back down, resuming his stance with his palms up. He clapped, and the game began.

To humor the boy, Mel joined in and the sound of clapping and slapping soon filled the little room. The boy's face was a mask of intense concentration, and Mel, despite herself, soon found herself matching his mood. Their hands moved faster and faster until, as Mel gave a cry of frustration, her hand was a beat too slow.

The boy raised his hands above his head and gave a silent cry of triumph.

"Alright, if that's how you want to play it. Round two, right now," Mel said, growing heated at the boy's display. The boy shook his head and began to stand, moving as if to walk away and leave the room.

"Uh no. Not so fast. Sit your little butt down. We're playing again." Mel growled.

The boy sat down, his face shifting back to one of fierce concentration. Mel readied herself, raising her hands again. The boy stopped her with a lifted finger. Cisseus raised his right palm so it met hers, but he did not clap when he brought his hand back. Rather his hands came together and made one of the signs that he had been teaching her over the last day. The middle finger came behind the ring, the pinky came in, and the hand tilted. He kept the pose for a second, and then his left hand clapped hers. He stopped, looking at her for understanding.

"Oh clever. Maybe you're a pretty good teacher after all," Mel said. The boy beamed at her, and they settled in to play.

Thus the day went. Their hands flew, meeting and colliding again and again. The only sounds in the room were the claps when their hands met. Each round focused on a different pose, a different symbol of the Reverie. The boy's hands moved from pose to pose with the grace of flowing water. Mel's own attempts to copy were shoddy and clumsy. Her joints cracked again and again as she moved her hands in ways she had never tried before.

Yet she did not stop. As each round progressed the symbols became easier and easier to form until she was shifting from one to another with few mistakes.

She had no idea what they meant, but that would come later. And it was a relief to think about something else, to have her thoughts shift from the song that had invaded her mind, the friends she might have abandoned.

It was enough that her hands were beaten into shape as the game of patty cake became more and more intense. The boy was ever faster though, ever surer. His gestures were without error no matter the speed. He beat her round after round, still without making a sound.

He did not crow with triumph as he had before. But Mel could see the light glinting behind his eyes that signaled his immense satisfaction after each of her defeats. Mel would never beat him fair and square, but she was okay with that. She had ways of making the competition unfair.

"So you can't talk at all, huh?" Mel asked as they settled in for a final round. The boy's attention remained fixed on the game.

"That's a shame. Talking is good for all sorts of things. Like talking trash." The boy's eyes flicked to her, before returning to their shifting hands.

"And I learned from the best. A boy named Finley Marsh, who could make your hair curl with a sentence. I'm finally gonna take the gloves off this time. You don't have a chance against me. Even if you beat me in a dream, you better wake up and apologize. Cause you're just a little kid. Itty, bitty, teeny, tiny." With every word she could see the boy's checks flush and the wrinkles around his eyes tighten.

"You'll probably stay this size forever. A mousy little brat who stinks at games." The boy was losing the rhythm. She could see his hands moving off beat, his gestures becoming less precise.

"Tell you what, when I beat you I'll only make you bow a little when I walk into the room. I know you can't get much lower to the floor, but let's find out." Cisseus slipped, his hand sliding off hers and the next one missing her palm entirely. He froze, his hand still outstretched his eyes open wide with shock.

Mel jumped to her feet, her arms over his head. "And the student has beaten the master!" The boy's hands lowered, and he looked at them with a sense of betrayal. Mel loomed over him, still basking in her come from behind victory. She looked at the boy wallowing in defeat.

Did she feel bad that she had psychologically destroyed a boy in order to win a children's game? Not really.

Mel's grin widened. Once you've been enslaved to the whims of an immense metal statue and escaped, you learned to take what victories you could.

The boy was still looking at his hands. He was flexing his fingers, uncurling them and refurling them as if testing to see if they still worked. Mel felt a twinge of guilt in her stomach, but only a twinge.

She sat back down anyway. Cisseus would not look at her. "Hey, chin up. I'm sure you'll grow up one of these days. You probably won't stay so mousy forever."

The kid looked up at her. There were little tears brimming at the corner of his eyes. And now that twinge of guilt was like a knife ripping into her gut.

"Sorry," she grunted. "I've always been a bad loser. You're my teacher, and I shouldn't have talked to you like that."

The boy looked at her, and his chin gave a little nod. He did not let his tears escape those large, yellow eyes of his. He turned away from her, looking into the far corner of the room as he mastered himself.

"At least we know something now," Mel said, and the boy looked at her from the corners of his eyes. "We know you're really good at this domain stuff, and I'm really good at getting into people's heads. I guess we both have something to learn from each other."

Cisseus face was solemn, his mouth still and flat. The tears had vanished from the corners of his eyes. He nodded once at her, as if they were sealing a sacred pact. And perhaps they were, Mel thought.

"Want to play again?"

The boy shook his head and rose to his feet. He pointed to his head and then back in the direction of the other sleepers. He turned and walked away. Mel hurried after him.

The other Sheosirrans trudged through the halls, leaving the Chamber of Sleepers. Their movements were sluggish and imprecise, their eyes hooded. They did not react to Mel and Cisseus as they walked among them.

Cisseus waved to a few as they passed but held to his course as he led Mel back to the Chamber of Sleepers. Harmodias was still there, sitting rather than lying on the cradle of metal roots they used as beds. She too looked exhausted. The boy rushed to her side and attempted to help her to her feet, but the old woman waved him off. With great difficulty she hauled herself to her feet.

"I apologize for leaving so quickly. We are in the process of adding the finishing touches to our restoration of the Shining Forest in the Reverie. I needed to be there to guide the final dreams. I believe you still had questions," Harmodias said, her voice filled with phlegm and ragged from disuse. The woman looked like she was about to keel over. Mel crossed her arms and started talking.

"Yeah, I have a few. My first is why? Why go to all this effort to rebuild a dead place?"

"It still dreams, Melanie Omar. Can a place be dead if it still dreams?"

"Yes. Things die. It's the nature of the universe. Why are you not planting new trees, shaping new forests? Instead, all you've done is bury this one in a dream."

269

"We do far more than that my dear. I can assure you that the Shining Forest lives on, in memory if nothing else. We tend that memory."

"I still don't see the point."

"Have you ever dreamed of a place that was not real?"

"Yes."

"Then you have dreamed of our works. The Reverie is where the forgotten things live on, long after they have vanished. And when you dream of these places, you walk through the art of the Sheosirra."

"Why? What do you get out of it."

"I can't answer that for you, Melanie. I can only guide you to an answer. Or rather, Cisseus can." She turned to her grandson. "Take us there again. Show her what you have been working on."

The boy nodded, stepping away from her. His hands glowed with purple light as they shifted through the forms that called the Reverie to them. Mel recognized some of the movements, but the sequence was too complex to memorize. The world began to shift around her, but this time Mel was ready.

The light changed first. It flickered on and off all at once, as if the entire world was blinking. Mel could feel herself becoming lighter, more insubstantial as they moved to this other plane. She was less solid here, she could still feel her limbs, could still move her muscles, but her body vanished from her sight. It faded away like a shadow in the expanding purple light of the Reverie. As she watched it happen a second time, she realized that this had happened to her before. When she slipped out of her body in the forest, when the Colossus had tried to pull her back, she had become this wraith.

The ground rose around them, until they were no longer beneath the earth. The Shining Forest bloomed to sudden life, and they were once more in the dappled shade cast by the bronze and gold leaves far overhead.

"The seed has been planted here. The Shining Forest will live on in this place long after we have left its shade. Dreamers will once more walk among the roots of iron and metal," Harmodias said. Unlike Mel, she seemed more solid here, more herself. Her back straightened, and her hands unclenched. She was at home in this place.

"Now we must move on." The Colossus was ahead, miles and miles distant, but no less imposing than the mountains of the world.

"You said a Sheosirran was responsible for that," Mel said.

"Yes. We journey to the statue in two days. We will discover why a child of the Sheosirran has used our domain to corrupt and control."

"We can't go back!" Mel erupted. "The closer we get the more powerful it is. We'll find ourselves slipping away. I'll slip away. I won't go back to its shadow."

The thought of the friends she might have left there swept over her, sending hot shame crawling across her skin like worms.

"You will never escape it if you do not break its hold on you," the old woman said. "Understand, I cannot make you join the Sheosirra, but you will not be able to last for long away from us."

"Is that a threat?"

"It is the truth. You need us, and we need you now. Our scouts have not been able to approach the site in the Reverie. We will need to travel in the waking world, and we do not know what awaits us. Only you do. We must break the statue's compulsion on you. We must free all that have been enslaved by a dream not their own. Melanie, please help us do this."

Mel stared at the old woman. As ever, Harmodias looked through her and past her, as if she saw through to her soul. Perhaps, in the Reverie, she could. She walked past Harmodias to stare at the statue. Even here, even now, she could hear the faintest echoes of its song playing upon her ears.

The shame was still there. Gwen and Finley and Theo and Yosef. What would their hatred feel like when they found out what she had done?

"What if it can't be fixed?" Mel asked.

"We will never know until we try."

Mel closed her eyes. Could she be redeemed? Even in her dreams?

"What will you do to the Sheosirran?" she asked.

"We will return the child to the fold."

"No."

"I beg your pardon?"

"They deserve to be punished for what they've done, for what they still do." Mel closed her eyes, and in the darkness she saw once more

271

Aketa falling into the vast emptiness of the Colossus. "There must be justice, not forgiveness. That is my price."

The half-completed statue towered over them, even miles distant. How big would it be when it was finished? How loud would its song be when it was born?

"Very well. We Sheosirrans are familiar with the price one must pay to get what they want. I hope you will be willing to pay yours when the time comes." Mel turned to look back at the woman, but Harmodias's tawny eyes were closed.

"Cisseus will be your teacher. He will instruct you in the ways of the Reverie as we journey to the statue."

"Why won't you teach me? Why a child?"

"Because Cisseus is more a master of the Reverie than I will ever be. His wisdom is without end."

"But we can't even speak to each other."

"Actually," a small voice said to her right. "In here, we can." Mel turned, watching the words leave the boy's mouth but not understanding what they meant.

"Like Great Grandmother said, there's always a price for knowledge." Cisseus pulled the rolled up drawing he had worked on out of his pocket. He handed it to Mel.

"I drew this for you," the boy said, suddenly shy.

Mel took the drawing, unrolling it without a word. Inside was her. She stood in the Shining Forest, the real Shining Forest. The battered iron stumps were all around her, and there was a wild, haunted look in her eyes. But tracing the corners of her lips was just the barest hint of a smile as she looked at the viewer, at the boy.

"Do you like it?" Cisseus asked.

Mel nodded, and the boy grinned. Around him the trees of the Shining Forest shook in the new wind blowing its way to the Colossus.

Chapter 19: The Dreamer's Foe

I struggle to connect with these people. Are they really anything more than the figments of an imagination? Are they anything more than the passing thoughts of a mad god? They live out their sad little routines, thinking that their actions are their own. But we know better, don't we?

(Letter 19, Paragraph 1, Lines 1-4)

The miles disappeared beneath her feet, half in dream and half in the waking world. The Sheosirrans marched to the Colossus and Mel marched with them. Harmodias led them. Her left hand held a cane, but the right glowed with the purple light of the Reverie. She held it before the marching Sheosirrans like a lit torch, and in its glow they were safe from the hairshirts as she filled their heads with dreams. And the dreams filled them with a compulsion, very like the same one the Colossus had placed on Mel. The dreams of the hairshirts made them see nothing out of place as the Sheosirra marched by.

The Colossus was far ahead. Its chest was half completed and open to the wind, its left arm a mere skeleton, its head hidden by clouds, but it had a majesty to it. It was a majesty that filled Mel with dread, and only the boy by her side kept her feet from running.

Cisseus bounded with energy. He was entranced by the ash heaps that littered the landscape, or the leftover tools the workers had left in their wake. As his student, he insisted that Mel follow him in these pursuits, despite her many protestations.

As they moved, he taught her all he knew of the Reverie. He carved symbols in the dirt and demonstrated sign language for her. Mel and he continued to play the clapping game he had invented to teach her the rudiments of Reverie's movements. They were beginning to understand each other both in the waking world and in the dreaming one.

It was the morning of the second day when he brought Mel to the dreaming world once more. The slightest gesture of his hands brought them to the world of dense purple light where the Sheosirrans constructed their dreamscapes.

Mel felt the senses of her body fall away. She could no longer feel the air on her skin, for she seemed not to have skin here, nor form at all. She looked down, though how she looked she knew not, for she had no eyes, and she saw that her body seemed to be made of dull black light. Her hands were crude things, blocky and incapable of deft movements.

Cisseus was still solid in the Reverie, even more so in fact, as if he had been superimposed over the world and it was merely background to him.

"It has to do with exchanges, or gateways, as they are sometimes called," Cisseus explained. "The Reverie and the waking world are both two different worlds and the same one. So if you want to affect the Reverie you have to exchange something from the waking world. Does that make sense?" the boy asked, and while it made little sense at all his voice still entranced Mel.

Here in the Reverie the boy's voice rolled rich and clear from his mouth. It was a many layered thing, his voice. At its core it was still the voice of a child, but both above and below this part of his voice were deeper melodies. It was the shaking of the wind, and the rolling of drums.

"No, it doesn't really make sense."

"Sorry, it's kind of hard to explain," the boy said with a smile. "Okay, have you noticed that you're a bit...less here?"

"I had gotten that impression, yeah," Mel said, waving her blocky hands at him.

"It's because you haven't exchanged anything yet. I was like that too at first. When Great Grandma brought me here for the first time I freaked out. I thought I had become a ghost somehow, and I tried to run away from her. It was only when I realized that I could still move and speak that I calmed down."

"How can I still do that by the way? I don't seem to have much of a body, but I can still touch stuff," Mel said, and she pushed Cisseus in the shoulder to demonstrate. "And I can hear and see, but I don't think I have eyes or ears either."

"You don't, not here at least. The Reverie isn't a place for bodies. Have you ever noticed when you dream that you don't have a full body? You might have too many fingers, or feet you can't see, a face you can't touch. A dream is just for your mind, and your mind can't

274

take the body with it. When you're here in the Reverie you have an idea of a body."

"So it's like my soul?"

"No, not really. It's just your mind, only in new ways.

Mel nodded as he spoke, her experience in the stumps of the Shining Forest suddenly making sense. She must have slipped into the Reverie when her body fell under the Colossus's pull. Only tremendous pain and shock had brought her back.

"Wait a minute. Why aren't you like this? You seem like you're yourself here."

Cisseus smiled at her. "I told you. You have to exchange something in the waking world to be a bigger part of this one."

"Your voice," Mel said, and she could not conceal the shock in her own tones.

"Yes," Cisseus said, nudging at the ground with his foot, not looking at her.

"Why would Harmodias make you do that?"

"No one made me do it," Cisseus said, his brow twisting with irritation. "Great Grandma never asked me to do anything. I decided to exchange my voice. I made that decision."

"An adult can make a kid do something with more than just their words. Pressure can come in different forms."

"I chose this. No one else." He seemed so innocent as he said this. He even stomped his foot, but Mel would not relent. She could not relent, not if he had been coerced in some way he didn't understand.

"She didn't force you? She didn't make it seem like there was no other choice? Did you understand what you were really doing?"

"You're saying it wrong! Great Grandma's not evil or something."

"She played a pretty nasty trick on me the first time we met, kid. Sometimes family can be more dangerous than we think."

"You're wrong! She didn't make me do it, and it's not like I threw my voice into the trash. I exchanged it."

"And did you understand the cost?"

"I'm not a little kid! I made my own choice. You're making it sound like I lost something, like I'm lesser because of it. But I'm not. I don't need you to feel bad that I can't speak. I like what I am. Just look what I can do," the boy said, and as he spoke the ground quivered beneath

275

their feet, shaking as if waking from sleep. The light from the purple sun shifted and bent until it formed pillars of light around Cisseus like a sudden crop of trees. Swarms of dreaming birds spun into the air from every side of them, flying and spinning far overhead.

Mel's heart shuddered in her chest. Colors she had never imagined sprung into being at his call. The birds sang songs that brought tears to her eyes. But she couldn't look away from the boy and the hurt on his face.

"Cisseus, I'm sorry." He rubbed his fists into his eyes, wiping away the tears. The birds flew away, and the light returned to normal. Mel crouched so that she could look him in the eye.

"That was stupid of me. I should have been more careful with what I was saying. I don't really think you're less or that you lost something. I just wanted to make sure you made this choice yourself," Mel said, her voice as quiet and small as his.

"Okay," Cisseus said, and his voice was small and childlike again.

"I've never seen anything like that. Harmodias wasn't wrong. You are powerful. But you're just a kid. Why do you need to be so powerful?"

"Because there are things the world doesn't want me to say."

Mel waited for more, but the boy said nothing further. He turned away from her to face the birds that still lingered overhead. They floated through the air with feathers made out of memories.

"I'm not sure if I want to exchange anything."

"Are you afraid you'll be like me?" Cisseus asked, a bit of anger still his tone.

"No. I'm afraid of what I'd do if I had that kind of power."

"Why?"

"Well, I think you're figuring out that I'm not the nicest person."

"You're not so bad," he said, wiping at his nose.

"Thanks," Mel said, letting out a grim laugh. "But I have a lot of anger in me and that's a lot of responsibility. I probably wouldn't be gentle with it.

"You don't have to exchange anything if you don't want to. Not everyone needs to be like Great Grandma and me," the boy said, almost pleading with Mel. Mel thought of the film over Harmodias's once pure yellow eyes. The old woman was blind and might have been for years.

"Do you like it here better? Do you prefer this to the waking world?"

"Kind of," Cisseus said, and even as he spoke a new flower sprouted into being, called by his voice.

"What happens if you decide you never want to leave?"

The boy looked at her and didn't say anything.

"Can we go home now, please?" Mel asked.

Cisseus nodded. His hands glowed, and the world shifted. Mel found herself once more in her body and in the waking world. Cisseus stuck his hand into hers for a moment. She turned to meet his glowing golden eyes. She nodded at him to show that it was okay. He released her hand and walked away, moving to study the sludge in the river.

Mel thundered up the marching column of the Sheosirrans. She brushed past the stumbling dreamers that made up much of their party until she reached Harmodias at the front. She stomped over to her band, grabbing the old woman's crooked hand out of the arms of her Sheosirran bodyguards.

"Take a hike. I need to talk to the old bat." Mel snarled. Harmodias sent them scurrying on their way with a quiet word.

"Melanie, how are you dear? Are you enjoying our walk?"

"Let's skip all this. I just spoke with Cisseus. He told me what he did to make himself so powerful, and I need to know why."

"Do you think him a monster?"

"I think he's already a better person than I'll ever be. But my opinion of you is getting worse and worse. What kind of grandmother lets a boy think that if he isn't strong enough he'll be snuffed out?" Mel said, her grip tightening on the old woman's arm.

"You know the answer better than I, Melanie Omar."

"Stop saying my name like you know me."

"But I do. You are a victim of this world just as we are, kept under heel and under control by people that fear you. They made you a slave."

"With a power you put out into the world!"

"What was done to you is disgusting, and I am ashamed that it was done with the Reverie, a thing meant for beauty. But don't pretend it's the only evil in the world. People have never needed our power to hurt others, they just need power. At least we are doing something to correct it."

"And it takes a child to do that? The whole burden must be placed on his shoulders?" Mel demanded, grabbing the woman by both of her narrow shoulders. "You're turning him into some sort of priest, some sort of soldier. What happens if he decides it's too much? What if he disappears into his dreams forever?"

Huck's face flashed in front of her eyes. He had looked like less than a shadow near the end. Even as a kid he had spent half his time in his own head, but as his family fell apart, he vanished entirely into his stories and imaginary worlds.

"I've seen it happen before, Harmodias. And it almost happened to me back at the Colossus! What are you going to do then?"

"Cisseus would never do that. He loves his family."

"Tell me, Harmodias, why are there no other children? Cisseus is the only one. All you elderly vegetables and he's the only one younger than sixty. What happened to the others?" Mel rasped out, "is the same thing going to happen to him?"

She heard the noise before she felt the slap Harmodias delivered to her right cheek. The old woman's hands were as rough as gnarled tree bark. The older woman looked up and over Mel's right shoulder.

"You go too far. Our children die because we are weak. I have done my best to make us strong, And Cisseus did the same. I never forced him to. I simply hoped, and I was lucky enough to have a great grandson that loves his people." Harmodias let go of her arm. "Do not judge what you do not understand. Cisseus's strength may one day be the only way we can survive."

"He should never have had to make that choice. It's too great a risk."

"If that is how you feel then turn your anger on the world. Cisseus and I have been just as much a victim of this land as you," Harmodias said, gesturing to the Colossus beyond. "The only difference is that we chose to become something more."

Harmodias bent to pick up a rusted nail that had lain in the mud for who knows how long. It was as long as her hand and almost as thick.

She ran her hands across its rusted surface, feeling every groove and whorl that time had worked onto its face.

"What do you think we will find up there?" Mel asked.

"Our misbegotten child."

"Do you know who it is?"

Harmodias said nothing.

"You do, don't you, and it scares you. How powerful are they?"

"Very."

"Will you be enough? Will Cisseus?"

"We will have to be."

"You need me too, don't you? There's something about the rogue Sheosirran you need me for," Mel said, her breath catching as she realized how Harmodias had strung her along. "You don't need a babysitter for the boy. You need another weapon."

"You are not a weapon, Melanie."

"Who told you my full name, huh?" Mel said, spinning around to face the old woman. The rusted iron nail hung between them like a dagger. "You knew all about me before you even met me. You recruited me to join your precious people after one meeting. You're not teaching me the Reverie out of kindness; you're teaching me because you want to use me for something."

"Have we really treated you so poorly that you would regard us with such suspicion?"

"How did I find my way to the Shining Forest, Harmodias?" Mel demanded. "How did Cisseus know exactly where to find me? How long have you been pulling my strings?"

"You're a very special woman, Melanie. Even if you don't know why yet," Harmodias said. The blind woman's eyes were as opaque as filthy windows.

"What's to stop me from walking away?"

"You would break Cisseus's heart, and as uncaring as you pretend to be, you would never be so unkind."

Harmodias dropped the iron spike onto the ground, and it stabbed into the dirt point down.

"I've been thinking about Cisseus's lesson," Mel said, looking up at the Colossus, "that you need to exchange something in the waking world to influence the dreaming one. His voice can shape that world,

279

and you can see beyond it, so there must be a relationship between what you exchange and what you gain."

"Correct," Harmodias admitted.

"What did this Sheosirran exchange to do all of this? And who motivated them to do it?" Beside her Harmodias's hands clawed at her robes, the weathered skin and twisted veins stretched tight. "I can't get that thought out of my head," Mel said, and she turned to walk away.

Chapter 20: The Messenger's Mad Mentor

I feel terrible for thinking such things. I think the man who first landed in this place would be ashamed for even allowing the thought to cross his mind. But I have not been that man for many years. He saw the wonders of this place and thought they were pure magic, rather than the spectacles that disguise this world's true purpose.

(Letter 19, Paragraph 2, Lines 1-5)

"Oh, how I cherished the news that we would see each other again. Oh, how I longed for the pleasure of your company and the music of your voice. With every blink I worry I will wake from this glorious dream!"

"You're mocking me, Lelly."

"And with a word she wounds. I thought we were friends, comrades and companions of the highest order. We threw snowballs at each other for pity's sake, and now she addresses me as if I were one of these perfidious preceptors," Lelly screeched, his feathers ruffled and his eyes shining with unshed tears.

"Does it really have to be you who teaches me, sir?"

"Agh—another cutting remark! Who else could compare to my magnificence? Who would you rather teach you?"

"I would rather jump from Clementine's back without a parachute, to be honest."

"As your superior I would advise against it. As your friend I would weep with sorrow at the sight. But as your teacher, I would say that such an experience might provide an important lesson. Perhaps you would learn to fly on the way down," Lelly said, and all at once his demeanor shifted, the tears disappearing and the feathers smoothing as he gave a screech of laughter.

Gwen did not allow her face to shift an inch.

"Is it going to be like this the whole time?" she said, her voice dull and flat.

"My ways are vast and mysterious. Who knows what shape the day may take?"

"You're just making this up as you go along."

"Ah, Gwen. I knew you were smart. Take a seat."

Lelial gestured grandly to the cushion in front of him. He himself was on a similar seat, though Gwen noticed that he had stacked several additional cushions beneath himself. She sat and found that her eyeline was at his shoulder. She looked up into his face. She was convinced she was looking at the corvid equivalent of a smirk.

The room was cozy with just the two of them and a tea set. On the north side the floor extended out, becoming a balcony that hung over the icy rivers that flowed so far below. Glass covered this balcony like a canopy. And while Gwen could see the wind and snow raging against this little observatory, she heard not a thing.

"Why you?"

"Charming as ever, my dear. I could say that fate or destiny was at play, and that we two were but chess pieces on the board of life, or perhaps that I had, through various nefarious and underhanded means, arranged this second meeting," Lelial said, pouring tea for them as he spoke. "But I shall refrain. Truth is the matter at hand, and true shall be my words henceforth. Suffice to say that Lina arranged this little meeting."

Gwen could not suppress the start at the mention of Lina, nor the rush of shame and resentment that followed. Lelial's eyes captured everything.

"She inferred that you would be uncomfortable with another corvid. I believe it had something to do with some lingering discomfort with preceptors," Lelial said, and Gwen felt gratitude war with the other emotions in her chest.

"That was kind of her."

"Yes. However, for such an exceedingly kind and talented young woman it is odd that she would not instruct you herself. Why would she need to turn to the shambling talents of myself?"

"You're being modest."

"Gwen, I assure you I have never once in my life been modest. I am as Vovatum made me, perfect and beautiful in every way."

"And I am lucky to have you as a teacher," Gwen intoned.

"Indeed, you are. Which again returns me to my original point, why did Lina feel you were such an unruly, unteachable student that you required my tender care?"

"I have no idea," Gwen said. Forcing her features to remain blank and impassive. The corvid stared at her. His eyes, Gwen found, were black without end when viewed straight on. Yet a single twitch of his head would bring new light to the orbs, casting them into golden light, or even a pure white shine. He seemed to fit the nickname Lelly in these moments, a name as light and easy as his flashing eyes and his crowing laugh. It was only when he looked at her with his black eyes that Gwen remembered that his true name was Lelial, and in these moments he seemed an ancient thing.

"A lie. As one who traffics in and devours such things, you will have to do much better than that if you wish to fool me." His head tilted, and his eyes flashed white. "Or at least attempt to make your lies amusing."

Gwen sipped her tea, but the heat did nothing to melt the ice that had resettled in her chest ever since Autumnmond.

"We shall return to your lie in a moment. For the time, let us limit ourselves to the minor topic of the very nature of the universe and the ability to observe it."

Gwen slowly placed her teacup onto its saucer. She returned her hands to her lap, and her spine straightened. With practiced ease she slid into the resting attentive space that the preceptors had drilled into her so many months ago. Outside the snow seemed to slow as her senses expanded.

"If one wishes to learn true sight one must master her other senses. In the monastery the preceptors taught you the limits and weaknesses of your eyes. Of your five pure senses it is the one easiest to fool. Yet it is the one that the untaught rely on the most," Lelly said, his voice losing its mocking tone. His voice deepened, reaching a cadence and timbre that filled the room.

"It is the simplest thing in the world to fool the eyes. A man may tell you what he sees, but even he himself does not fully believe it. He sees only what he wishes to be true. A man can be ugly and see himself as beautiful. A woman may be cruel but see a kind face looking back in the mirror. The eye lies, even the eyes of birds.

"It is for this reason that the preceptors removed your sight from you when you were under their tender care. We are in the business of truth, and thus the instrument and source of our lies must be removed.

They taught you to rely on the truer senses, but many are never able to move beyond this first step."

"What happened to those who broke?"

"Why, we ate them of course."

Gwen looked at Lelly. He was entirely still, his eyes boring into hers. "You're lying to me."

"Very good, you're learning, and I, of course, am joking. We're a newspaper, Gwen, not a crime syndicate, lighten up please. You're bringing down the mood of the whole room," Lelly said, gesturing to the empty space.

"Now, as I was saying. Your preceptors taught you to rely on your other senses. After ensuring you could endure hardship and follow orders, they returned sight to you. Yet the training never disappears. You have not encountered anyone outside of the organization—" Gwen did not allow herself to think of the boy, Joshua. "—but, if you do, you will notice that even the most accomplished liars are as children to you. You notice more, you perceive more than any untrained human."

"You say human but leave out corvid. Do I notice more than you, Lelly?" Gwen asked.

"Child, you would need a thousand lifetimes to best me."

Gwen thought of the wet scarf she had thrown at her new teacher and the squawk of indignation he had made as it soaked him through. She allowed the corner of her lip to quirk up. "Of course."

"When you arrived here Lina told you this training was to enable you to ride a chiropt. They require a rider equal to them in skill and perceptiveness. Thus, every rider here at Cradle is equally adept in the art of flowing thought, that which the preceptors taught you.

However, this was not the sole purpose for such training. Flowing thought is an artform unto itself, that is true. There are, however, higher disciplines that few can grasp. The Cognitive Domains."

"What are they?"

"A scientist might tell you that they are the leftover energies of creation, remnants of whatever created all this that some are able to master. A priest might tell you that they are Vovatum's own gifts. But I am an artist and I say that the domains are an artform, as simple as that."

"Magic?"

"Such a tawdry word for such a beautiful thing. Magic implies trick. Magic suggests illusion. The domains are no such things. They are power, and nothing more." Lelly paused to pour himself more tea and allowed the word to linger in the air. Outside the world beat itself against the window without a sound for the ones inside.

"There are many Cognitive Domains, each one separate in its uses, costs, and practices. While the First Peoples of Poa had, according to the stories, almost total command over all the domains, we, their lowly descendants, have dominion over much less."

"What happened to the First People?"

"The same thing that always happens when one has too much power, they destroyed themselves."

"Is that why the Poa is the way it is? So broken and disjointed?"

"Ah, you have made the first mistake that any new learner of the domains makes. You assume that by power, I mean the physical variety. You hear power and think of words that can crack mountains or turn storms. Such things are the inventions of the story spinners of the Circus. Power is power. And power only exists here." And Lelial raised his talon to point at his own skull.

"The Cognitive Domains are just that, cognitive. They affect the mind and the mind only. There is no domain that can enhance, harm, or change the mortal form. The power of a Cognitive Domain comes from its ability to amplify the mind. However, each of the domains does so in its own distinct way. Perhaps you have heard of the Sheosirrans? A sad and scruffy lot, but the only masters of the Reverie, a form of dream manipulation. They may fill the minds of those around them with visions, and even, so the story goes, compel them to act out these visions. An advanced form of sleepwalking I presume."

"You mean you don't know? I thought you were a master of the Cognitive Domains," Gwen said, and to her shock the corvid squawked in his version of a laugh.

"There is no such thing as a master of all the Cognitive Domains. To master even one domain is the accomplishment of a lifetime. Even I, who has lived for far longer than I am comfortable admitting to a young lady, is still in many ways a student of my own domain."

"So I have many more of these sessions to look forward to?" Gwen said with a tiny grimace.

Lelly's eyes flashed. "Only a lifetime's worth. Though who is to say whose life we are referring to?"

"Which domain are you a master of?"

"Observation, and Observation alone. For even if I had wanted to study another domain, I likely would never have found a teacher."

"Why is that?"

"The masters of each domain guard their secrets and take great pains to ensure an outsider never gains access to their knowledge. While the stories claim that the First Peoples of Poa had mastery over every domain, blurring them like paints to create one magnificent canvas, after their destruction the knowledge of the domains vanished for a time from the world. Over the centuries we have discovered only fractions of the domains' original potential. And when such a secret is discovered, it is guarded with legions, and passed down to only the most faithful.

"We corvids discovered Observation, and we have made it our own."

"Why are you teaching me then? I'm not one of you."

"I disagree. You were brought to this place and entrusted with our mission because we believe you are capable. We trust you, Gwen, though I believe we are still earning your trust in turn."

Gwen looked at the corvid across from her. His eyes were shining pools of ink. She could not fathom what he was searching for in her own eyes.

"Thank you."

"Think nothing of it." Lelly turned back to pour himself another cup of tea before ambling over to the window. He waved for Gwen to join him. "This teaching thing is exhausting. I'm supposed to refrain from mocking you for your overwhelming ignorance, yes? I must be...encouraging, correct?" Lelly made a horrific gagging noise at the thought of these affirming emotions.

"I think you're supposed to just be yourself. In your case you should continue to act like the world spins on your finger."

"Tut, tut, I don't have fingers. These are talons," Lelly said, waving one limply through the air. "Terrible sharp talons."

"My apologies. I shall have to find a new target," Gwen said, joining him at the window. Lelly cocked his head to look at her for a moment with a golden eye.

"My, my, Gwen. You grow saucier by the moment. Lina sold you to me as a model pupil."

"It's only because I know you don't care what I think."

"Indeed, I don't! Please let me know when you are prepared to have an interesting thought though."

"I wouldn't hold your breath. It seems the *Herald* doesn't want me to think."

"Enough with the verbal jousting. I've had an idea! We shall play a game."

Gwen felt a shudder ripple through her that had nothing to do with the snow outside. Lelly swept his befeathered arm in front of them, gesturing to the window and the valley beyond. Gwen could see the minute patterns on each flake of snow as they imprinted themselves against the glass.

"Tell me, where did that snowflake come from?" Lelly said as they watched more of the snow fall.

Gwen grunted in quiet amusement before she saw the look on Lelly's face. "It came from the sky."

"Be more specific."

"It came from the clouds, Lelly. It's snow. Frozen water from the sky."

"I asked for specifics, not a synopsis of the water cycle. I want you to tell me what body of water that snowflake came from."

"That's impossible."

"And why not?"

"The snowflake just melted," Gwen said, indicating the streak on the glass. Lelly gazed at it with great interest.

"So it has. We shall have to try again." He indicated a spot on the window with a taloned finger. "A snowflake will land here in fifteen seconds. I will give you a hint. It is from the Tile of the Stacks."

Sure enough, exactly where he pointed and in exactly the time frame he had said, a snowflake landed on the window. She could see the crystalline patterns etched across its face, but she could see nothing else.

287

"I couldn't even guess."

"It is because you are looking, when you should be Observing," Lelial said, and then his eyes glowed with purple light. Just like Lina, a film rose from his eyes until it hung before him like a lens. Gwen stepped back and could see that information in a language she did not understand crawled across the screen. Facts and charts and figures swung before Lelial's eyes as he began to speak.

"The snowflake is from the Tile of the Stacks as I have said. The stacks is a dreadful place, clogged with the ash and smog from the ever growing towers at its heart. You can see the faint particles of soot that the snowflake has absorbed. Even transformed into a solid, it never lost the qualities of what swam through it when it was still just a drop of water. The soot comes from a particular tannery on the shores of Lake Suto." His head swung up, and now he was gazing into the clouds. And it seemed that maps formed across the screen before his eyes, his pupils flicking from figure to figure as he analyzed a library's worth of data.

"This storm formed above the Humming Tile. An easterly wind blew it over the Tile of the Shepherd, and it was going to be rain then. But the tiles shifted before it could drop its storm. We moved beneath it during the last shift and now it has become snow." Lelial let the lens disappear, before his talon tapped at the glass. "This was water on the other side of the planet yesterday, and now it is an icy and valuable lesson here. Observation will let you see the little journeys we all take, Gwen. You will be able to follow the wind and know where it will blow and where it has been. You will Observe the world as the *Herald* does, constantly shifting, but not without a pattern."

"This is how you track the movements of the tiles isn't it? This is how you know what shape the world will take."

"Yes. It is a power that many seek, Gwen. I hope you understand the honor we are giving you with this gift, as well as the burden."

"I still don't understand how you do that though. How does Observation work? Does it enhance your eyes, your senses?" Gwen asked.

"Not at all. You must remember that the domains are only able to amplify the abilities that you already possess in your mind. The senses cannot be improved as that would affect the body, which the domains cannot do. However, they can improve your ability to comprehend and analyze the data your senses provide."

"The charts and figures that crawl across that lens."

"Merely an aftereffect of what is happening inside my head when I use the domain. The real show occurs here," He said, tapping at his own skull. "It feels as if an ocean of information pours in. Or rather, the ocean reveals itself. And I may swim across the surface of this ocean, diving in if I wish. It can be overwhelming at first. The mind hides this information from us for a reason. It does not wish to overburden us. However, you are ready."

"Are you sure?"

"I just said so, and I'm never wrong. But if this is the first time, at least it won't be my head that explodes," Lelly said, his face blank. "Come on, let's go back to the cushions. My legs are weary from all this preening and teaching."

They sat again. Lelly collected their teacups and set them aside. Nothing separated the two now.

"How do we start?" Gwen asked, trying not to think of her head imploding.

"Every domain has a cost, a sort of trial that must be passed in order to access the power it offers. We call these trials exchanges, and they are some of the most closely guarded secrets for each domain. For how can one enter a house without the key?"

"By going through the window?"

Lelly's face twitched with a smile. "Quite. Some of the scholars here at the paper are attempting to find such windows for the domains, but they have not met with much success."

"What is the exchange for Observation? What must I pay?" Gwen asked, and to her horror Lelial's face contorted into an expression she had never seen, and his feathers stood on end as if with great excitement.

"Why the cost, my dear Gwen, is the simplest thing in the world to pay. Observation demands...secrets," he spoke. Gwen looked at him, and she fought the shiver that rippled through her body at the sight of the mad look on the corvid.

"What kind of secret?"

289

"Hear me now. I do not wish to know your lesser secrets. Your adolescent loves and childhood misdeeds interest me not at all. Such things have no power. Observation demands greater secrets. You must offer it that which no one knows. Something you attempt to hide even from yourself. What is the secret that gnaws at your soul, Gwen?"

"Is this a trick, Lelly?"

"A teacher is constantly tricking his students, I've found, but this one is a necessary one. You must pay with a secret, Gwen, if you wish to Observe."

Gwen felt her thoughts race. She had many secrets, but none she thought of as greater ones. She remembered the time she had shut the door on her dog's leg by accident and revealed nothing when her parents questioned her. She remembered the time she drove her friend to Planned Parenthood and swore never to tell a soul. She had secrets like these without end. But were any of these enough?

"What makes a secret greater?" Gwen asked.

"The pain it causes when it is known."

"There aren't any happy greater secrets?"

"So far? No."

"Why secrets?"

"It is believed that each exchange relates to the power it will bring. Consider what Observation will give you. You will be able to understand the information that is hidden from the world. Is a secret that you have kept hidden from all others not worth this price?"

Gwen sat back. Lina had seemed to become omniscient with this power, and Lelial even more so.

Gwen was so used to feeling powerless. Battered from point to point, always listening to what others told her to do. When was the last time she felt strong enough to make her own choice? When was the last time it hadn't blown up in her face, like with Joshua?

She could barely imagine what it would feel like if things were different. What would it be like if she was powerful for once?

"I have a secret for you."

"I am eager to hear it," Lelly said, and as he spoke the purple lens rose from his head until it floated above him like a crown. Gwen saw her reflection in its shining light. She looked calm as she spoke.

"I am not from this planet," Gwen said and met her own eyes in the halo around Lelial's head. "I am from a planet called Earth."

"Oh, I already knew that," Lelial said.

Silence flooded into the room. It filled the tiny space until it no longer seemed like there was any air to breathe.

"What?"

"I knew that by the end of our first conversation, Gwen. I have to say, as far as secrets go, that one is pretty pathetic."

"This isn't what I expected."

"Clearly."

"You're not freaking out."

"Should I be?"

"I just admitted I'm from another planet. I expected a bit of a reaction."

"And I am teaching you, as you say, 'magic.' You will have to try a little harder to impress me, Gwen. I am an old and well-traveled corvid. You are not the first off worlder I have ever met, and I doubt you will be the last."

"You've met others?" Gwen said, rocketing forward.

"Tut, tut. If you wish me to reveal my secrets, you shall have to provide more appetizing fare. Though you seem perplexed by your journey to my home, it is only a mystery, not a secret." Lelial's voice sharpened to a razor edge. "I do not wish to know paltry tidbits of little importance. I wish to know the truths that threaten to devour you."

Gwen flinched back as if struck. She returned to the window and watched the snow fall onto the glass and melt away in front of her.

Lelial had been able to trace a snowflake's journey all the way to the other side of the planet using Observation. Could she use it to track one of Yosef's letters back to its sender, even into one of the wild tiles? She knew she would only make things worse if she tried to help him herself, but perhaps she could send his location to one of the others. If there were others.

She pressed her forehead against the freezing glass, letting the chill ease her burning skin. How many more friends could she afford to lose?

"The *Bird's Eye Herald*, I knew that name before you showed it to me, but I didn't learn it here. I first heard that name on my planet. My friend, Huck, invented it." On the window's surface, she saw Lelial turn his head to look at her.

"We were just kids, and he wanted to come up with a new game. We were always doing that, playing make believe. We invented a newspaper, and we called it the *Bird's Eye Herald*. A joke. I think we made up about three issues. I hadn't thought about it in a long time."

"A cosmic coincidence," Lelial said behind her, his voice aloof.

"Perhaps," Gwen said. She drew a deep breath, lifted her head from the glass, and she spoke. "His father had a disease of the mind, one that made him a shadow of his former self. And at first that was fine. Huck loved his father. But then his dad seemed to change. It was like he was a totally different person, one who hated the people who were taking care of him, who couldn't see that his loved ones were breaking themselves on his behalf."

The snow pelted the window, little explosions of white bursting against the surface of the glass.

"Huck and his mom tried to hide it, but I was his best friend since he was six. I could see what was happening to my friend. And one day he told me that he wished his father would just die, so that he and his mom could keep at least some happy memories." Gwen barely recognized her own reflection in the window. "So I offered to kill his father."

A fresh wind battered the outside of their room with snow. But they could not hear a sound except for their own breathing and the whistle of the heating tea.

"He turned me down, I said I was joking, and we moved on. Huck died about a year later."

Her eyes met Lelial's in the window. "Here's my secret, Lelial. If Huck had asked me to, I would have done it. Even if it tore my heart out. Because that's how far I'll go to protect my friends. Is that enough of a secret for you, you damn bird?"

The halo around Lelial grew and spun, until it became a pinwheel of light in the air. It sent their shadows spinning and pulsing about the room, until Gwen had to close her eyes to its glare.

"This secret is accepted. The gateway is open."

Gwen's mind revealed what it had been hiding from her. The air tickled her skin, and she could tell by the way it tasted who else had been caressed by this same puff of air. Outside the room she could hear the breaths of two women walking down the hall about a hundred meters away from them. One was much taller than the other and had a fuller chest. The other was developing a cold that had phlegm collecting in her throat. She was catching a cold but would likely not notice it until tomorrow.

Gwen opened her eyes, and for the first time she realized that the world was looking back at her, desperate to show her all that she had been missing.

She staggered, her hands thudding onto the glass. And the surface of the glass was jagged. The tiny abrasions on its surface felt like daggers slicing through her now hyperalert skin. The scent of her own fear clogged her senses. Agony coursed through her, every inch of her body enduring burning pain.

"The first time is quite an experience," Lelial said. He had moved to stand beside her. Yet he was careful not to touch her, and his gaze was locked on the falling snow. "You need to dial back Observation or you will surely go mad."

"Can't," Gwen gasped, as the pain mounted. Now the gentle whisper of the air seemed to constrict around her limbs, suffocating her with every breath she took. The sound of her voice was too thunderous for her to understand.

"You can, and you will. The preceptors taught you flowing thought. If you allow your mind to drift upon the currents of your senses, then they will no longer harm you."

Flowing thought. Gwen's mind grasped at the words. Moving beyond what her senses were trying to tell her, not seeking to analyze or understand, but only to be a part of the symphony of information.

She let herself drift. She let the information flow over her and through her, and let her mind pass with the current. The pain eased, and then vanished, and it seemed for a time that Gwen also disappeared. But soon she returned to herself.

The information was still there, eager to show itself to her, to be known. Yet now she had it under control. There was the lingering caress of steam across her face. She opened her eyes and found Lelial holding a cup of tea in front of her.

"You should be able to turn it off now. Think of it like blinking, but in your own head."

Gwen raised her hand to take the cup, and she marveled at the roughness she now felt on what she was sure was the finest of porcelain. She let the steam pour over her face, and in her mind she blinked.

Like a switch being turned off, the ocean of information she had access to disappeared and she was left only with the knowledge from her own senses. There was no more pain, but there was also another absence, a longing for something she did not know she wanted until it was gone.

"Will it always be like that?" She gasped.

"At first? Yes. You will need to practice turning Observation on and off for the next several days. You will be able to withstand the deluge of information for longer and longer intervals. Once you can endure an hour, we will move on to the next stage."

"Which is?"

"Controlling which of the streams of the information you will allow once you begin your Observation. Taking all the stimuli in at once is a quick way to go mad. First, we will increase your tolerance, and then your control." Lelial turned away from her. "We are done for the day; you may go do whatever it is you do."

Gwen nodded at him in the window before turning away. Her legs were wobbly beneath her, and she felt both half deaf and half blind without Observation. Yet she was no stranger to having her senses removed from her. She walked with half sure steps to the door, before a sudden thought had her turn.

"What do you get out of this Lelial? You've made your hatred for teaching very clear."

"Gwen, whatever have I done to you to earn such suspicion?"

"Acted like yourself?"

The creature's reflection tilted his head, his eyes a pure black.

"Let us just say that I am very interested in your career, Gwen. I want to watch you succeed."

"And what am I to give you in return for such success? What must we exchange for me to obtain such power?"

"Why should I reveal a secret like that to you?"

"Because you're dying to show off, Lelial. You want people to watch you with wonder. And you can't admire a secret if it is never told to you."

Lelial turned to face her, and the setting sun cast the Cradle Mountain into shadow leaving only the flame beneath the teapot to light the room.

"Ah, Gwen, you never cease to surprise me. Perhaps that is why I tolerate our time together. Why do I teach you, you ask? So that you might one day be my ally."

Gwen faced him. In the valley beyond the window, she watched the chiropts taking flight under the cover of night to deliver the mail. She wondered if Lina and Clementine were one of those flyers.

"What do you mean, Lelial?"

"For quite some time I have been content to move through this life on my own. After all, there is no one quite so competent as I. Yet the world is changing, and not in the ways that we wish. At the highest levels of this organization there is a great sense of fear. We are in the business of showing the world what it is, but if we no longer understand the world then what shall we become?"

"Lelial, I have the mother of all headaches. What are you talking about?"

"The tiles move. This is fact, and over generations we have studied this movement to predict what will happen next. Observation has allowed this, and it is why our paper has enjoyed its success. Yet in the past several years our Observations have been incorrect."

"Human error and all that, or corvid error," Gwen said. Lelial continued to gaze at her with all the emotion of a pool of cave water.

"I am afraid that error has nothing to do with it. My superiors may believe that our own fallibility has led to these errors, but I do not. I know what I have observed. I know that the world is broken."

The word broken slithered out of his mouth and slunk about the room. It curled up Gwen's legs and torso until it slid around her neck.

"What do you mean?"

"The tiles no longer tick as they should. There is an error in the mechanics of the world. What has caused this error I know not, but it is there, and I would like your opinion on it, Gwen. That is why I am teaching you."

295

"Why my opinion?"

"There is a tile far to the north of here, for the moment," Lelial said, ignoring her question and turning back to the window. "It had a different name once, but in the last seventy years it has shed this old title in favor of a new one. What was once Mosavale is now known simply as the Tile of the Colossus." Using one talon he began to scrape the glass, sketching a circle before adding the continents and oceans, carving Poa into being. The dull shriek of talon on glass provided a chorus to his words.

"Our reporters have concluded that a new religion is being born there, an attempt to create a god out of metal. Such a silly thing, but it has produced a startling effect on the neighboring tiles," he said, his talons carving a crude caricature of a massive man into the window. From this man he drew a line veering off it and into space, and then another beside that line, and then another, and another, until the man was surrounded by a vortex of cut lines.

Gwen felt a thrill of horror run through her as she saw the statue take shape. Was this the thing that the boy Joshua had dreamed about?

"Like a new planet this tile has drawn the surrounding tiles into its orbit. They now all spin and turn together. Instead of following their predetermined paths, the ones our Observations have determined they should take, these tiles trail after the Colossus like puppies in its wake. This has never happened before. And I wish to know why it is happening now."

"Lelial, why me?"

"You have a knack for being in exactly the right place at the right time. But more, much more than this, you crave freedom. If you ally with me, Gwen, I will give you power, prestige, and a place within this organization. You will become far more than a mere messenger obeying the whims of those above you. You will be a reporter, with all the freedom that entails, loyal only to me. And in return you will bring me delicious secrets. Sound like a deal?"

"What happens if I say no?"

"Nothing. Nothing at all. Forever," Lelial said, and he left it at that. Gwen looked at the corvid. He was a tiny thing, for all the knowledge he claimed to have. Gwen had always wondered if the bones of a corvid were as hollow as their bird cousins'. But Gwen made no move to find out, nor to leave this room and the mad corvid inside.

How many more voices did she have to let into her head? Were there any thoughts left in there that were her own? All her life she had done as others had asked her to. Her parents, her teachers, even her friends, she had let them all inside her head so that they could author her every thought, take control of every decision. Because it was safe.

It was easy to let them think for you, even if it made you feel small.

The power Lelial offered? It was only another person telling her what to do, with a new carrot and a new stick.

Her hand closed around the letter of Yosef League tucked close to her heart. What was one more voice if it helped her find her friends?

"I'll need more than that, Lelial. If I am to be your ally, then I will not be your lesser." Lelial's reflection shifted to look her in the eyes. His black eyes crinkled with amusement.

"What do you want?"

"Aid. I have my own secrets to uncover. You help me with mine, I help you with yours."

"And the first secret you wish to learn?"

"Have you ever heard the name Yosef League? Have you seen the letters he has written?"

Lelial turned back to face her, the Colossus looming over his shoulders, the lines haloing his head. "No."

"That is what I demand. I want you to find him."

"Is your loyalty worth such an exchange?"

"Yes," Gwen said, and she could see a little shiver run through the corvid. "You know how far I'll go for those who I call mine."

"Oh Gwen, if every human was as amusing as you, life would be so much more exciting," Lelial said, and he gave a little croak of laughter. "People not of this world carry within them the slightest difference from those that are native to this plane. We may look the same, and speak the same, but this difference is there, though it is infinitesimal. And for one as skilled in Observation as I, it is also obvious. Join with me, and I'll teach you how to track anyone from your world."

"Anyone?"

"I believe that expression means we have a deal, yes?"

"Yes," she said, sealing her fate.

Chapter 21: The Scholar's Revelation

I have seen this world begin to fall apart at the seams. Their lands are breaking down, the tiles are ticking out of tune, and even their magic has begun to fail. I shudder to think what will become of this place when the veil is finally lifted. How will they react when they learn who they really are, and that their time is running out?

(Letter 19, Paragraph 3, Lines 1-5)

Theo poured through the pages of Aldwin Dryn's journal and learned what happens when a mind becomes unmoored.

Our anemometers broke yesterday, so we have no way of measuring the wind. I watched it tear apart Thumper.

It is difficult to determine how we will survive the coming days.

We have fought our way past the Detritus. We have had to camp in the cleft of a massive boulder. It is the first time I have been out of the wind in two weeks. It feels like I am wearing someone else's skin.

Tomorrow we will plunge into the deepest reaches of the Godstrom. We all know the stories. But perhaps the others were lacking in something. Perhaps they lacked faith.

This morning we woke up to the sounds of screaming. We cannot find Tracer. The others say she must have been taken by krows in the night.

I suspect otherwise. In the days before her disappearance, she spoke of a voice in the clouds, one that she could hear in her thoughts and in the wind. I believe she set out to meet that voice.

Maybe we will find each other again, in the deep storm.

What followed was screeching madness. Scratches and tears ripped through the pages, as if he had clawed at them with his own hands. There was an image here that looked like it had been carved into the page with a broken and jagged fingernail. It was a creature of bones and rotting skin that clung to it like a cape. The lightning framed and formed it. The monster seemed to loom over Theo, even trapped in a page.

The final words of Aldwin Dryn were carved beneath this monster.

The krows are calling always calling but the voices grow louder and louder
They screech my name and the names of my dead friends
But there are names in the wind I have never heard before
Names of power
The light speaks to me and shouts questions
Questions I have never heard
Who is Player One?
Who are the names in the wind?
Are they the names of angels?

Player One. There was no doubt Aldwin had found the N-Device, even briefly. But in his madness, what could he understand about it? Its images and questions would have only drive him further around the twist.

But there was something there. Something in his questions that spoke to Theo.

The names in the wind. The names of angels. What did that mean?

The man's words haunted him as he left the safety of the bell and flew out into the storm to join Keeper.

"Any krows?" he asked the other man.

"Still nothing. That's two days now," Keeper said. The ears at his belt were growing lonely.

"That ever happened before?"

"No, never. They must have all gone topside, to the castle. We might be the only ones in the Godstrom."

The image of Aldwin's angel floated to the front of Theo's mind. "I don't think we're that lucky."

He moved to fly above, but Keeper's arm caught his sleeve. "I'll need you in an hour or so. We're getting down to the Detritus, and that's a tricky bit of maneuvering," Keeper shouted above the wind.

"I'll be there," Theo said, before angling himself upward. The expedition was in a state of professional shambles. Ripped clothes and unraveling bandages hung off the lancers like tattered flags. Every weapon was notched, and every man and woman in the group had at least a half dozen kills to their name.

The charters were devastated, reduced to half strength. They still chugged through the skies from ring to ring without fail, but Theo

299

could see the exhaustion in their eyes and the tell-tale twitch of amphetamines in their movements. It was the only thing keeping them moving.

The packsmen were little better though Keeper had kept them to a tight order. They had slowly come to accept Theo as one of their own, and the word Pathfinder was no longer an unfamiliar name among them.

Theo flew to the clustered group of weatherbreathers in the center of the sphere. They alone were unruffled and undamaged, protected as they were in the heart of the expedition's defenses.

At the slightest signal from this band the expedition would shift or roll in a new direction. Down, always down, but in a new angle of descent designed to keep them out of the worst of the storm. Theo had heard even Keeper speak of this group with a kind of reverence, as only the incomprehensible workings of their arcane devices kept the expedition from utter destruction.

The weatherbreathers circled their leader Wheeler like planets around a star. She flew among them eating a picnic lunch. A little table floated in front of her upon which was a plate of delicate porcelain. Sandwiches thinner than Theo's fingers adorned the plate.

Theo's jaw dropped as she nibbled at her delicate food with her left hand while her right twirled and spun the strange dial at her waist. Between bites she would scan the readings on the dial, before plucking another sandwich from the plate. Theo added the sight to his growing list of flight creating impossibilities.

"Wheeler, do you have a minute?"

"How wonderful to see you, Pathfinder. Our paths have crossed far too little since our expedition began. I have thirty-three minutes to spare for you. We will hit a squall in thirty-four minutes that will require my attention. Would you like a snack?" Wheeler said, handing him a delicate sandwich. Theo's hands crushed it as he picked it up and rain dissolved much of the rest of it before he could place it in his mouth.

"Thank you. It's delicious," Theo said, forcing himself to suck down the foodball the sandwich had become. Wheeler twinkled at him.

"You're very kind. How can I help you this morning, Pathfinder?"

"I didn't even realize it was morning."

300

"It's half past 9 o'clock to be precise."

"Do you—do you know what day it is?" Theo asked, feeling foolish.

"It's Wednesday, Pathfinder. It's Wednesday," Wheeler said, and her smile was very kind. A warm glow suffused Theo. It was wonderful to know such a mundane thing, such a simple fact.

"It's 9:30 on a Wednesday," Theo said, simply to hear himself say such a boring thing. "I'm having a strange week."

"I believe that is a function of flying above a divine corpse. Such things often lead to strangeness, as I am sure you well know. After all, we have placed you in Keeper's company for this little jaunt. I worry some of his...unique behaviors might have rubbed off on you."

"I still have just as many ears as I started flying with, thank you," Theo said, and Wheeler did the most remarkable thing. She laughed.

"I am happy to HEAR it," Wheeler said, emphasizing carefully. A little jolt of a giggle fought its way out of Theo's throat.

"That was terrible."

"Yes, but you seem to have enjoyed it. What does that make you, I wonder?" Wheeler said, and while the smile was still on her face her eyes had gone sharp and searching.

"It makes me a failure. I don't know how to make the N-Device work and I'm worried we're all going to die because of me," Theo said, and it was a relief to say it at last even while he burned from the shame of it.

"Is that so? You are a failure, how bizarre. I was unaware failures could fly. You must be quite the anomaly," Wheeler said, one eyebrow raised behind her goggles.

"I can't get it to work," Theo said, his cheeks filling with red.

"The fact you cannot get it to work now does not mean you will not be able to succeed later. Like many foolish young scholars, you have chosen to work entirely alone. Start from the beginning, Pathfinder. What has worked and what has failed?"

Theo forced himself to take a breath. He was Pathfinder now and Pathfinder might be different.

"The mapping function of the N-Device has not activated since before we left the castle. At that time, I activated the map by pressing a code on the controller. Once the code was imputed the map turned on and plotted out the Pilgrim's Path through the lower storm."

"What was the code you imputed?"

"Just a random sequence of buttons. I used to use similar codes on toys when I grew up. I just used it by instinct. I've tried it since, along with similar variations, but the map has never reappeared."

"What is the device showing currently?"

"Before it was just cycling through games."

"Games?" Wheeler asked, her voice cutting through the wind.

"Excuse me, images of far-off lands and other places. They are very colorful," Theo said, his voice trailing off as he spoke. He was unable to meet Wheeler's eye.

"Of course."

"They look like games to me."

"Continue, Pathfinder."

"Once we entered the storm the device changed. It projected the words 'Ready Player One.' I indicated I was ready by pressing the buttons on the controller, after that a loading bar appeared."

"You seemed to have invented many new phrases to apply to the N-Device. I don't understand much of what you just said. What is 'player one?'"

"I think it's a generic term. Anyone who looks at it would be 'player one.'"

"What is the progress of this loading bar?"

"Less than 40% of the bar is filled."

"That's no good. We will be at the Detritus within an hour, after that is only the deep storm. If we don't have the map by then I'm afraid we will be torn to ribbons."

"I know."

"Has anything provoked the device since we entered the storm, have any of your other attempts created a result?

"Nothing. I've dangled it out in the storm, I've dripped the blood of krows on it, I even had Keeper try inputting the same codes. Nothing, nothing, nothing works. It moves randomly, without a steady rate, without a sense of progression," Theo said, his fingers clawing at his own helmet. He could hear the faint scratching of his own nails against the steel and leather. It was so tempting to take the helmet off, to cast it into the wind.

"Theo? Are you okay?" Wheeler asked.

Theo smiled slightly. "That's the first time I've heard my own name in days. Funny how you miss the sound of your own…" He froze, pulling his head up to look at Wheeler. "Your own name."

"That's it, isn't it? That's the key. It's so obvious. How could I be so stupid? He even wrote it down. 'There are names in the wind.'"

"Who wrote it, Pathfinder?" Wheeler said, and now Theo turned to her. He could see the worry etched in her eyes and in her outstretched hands. But he didn't care. His heart pumped rocket fuel as the idea bloomed in his head.

"Aldwin Dryn. I read his diary. He lost his mind when his expedition dove into the storm. And even though they found the N-Device before the end, they couldn't make it work either.

"But that doesn't mean they didn't leave any clues! Before he died, he wrote down that 'there are names in the wind.' And he was right!" He felt like a lightning bolt had struck his heart. "Because something I did to the N-Device did work! I told it a name. The name of someone I had lost. And only then did it start to work. Don't you see?"

Wheeler's confusion grew as his excitement mounted. Thunder rolled and to Theo it felt like an anthem to his sudden realization.

"The N-Device is powered by names. Player One, Aldwin Dryn, Finley.

"Names are how this whole blasted thing works, from the castle all the way to Godstrom itself! The krows have power over us because they know what we call ourselves. We take away that power by giving each other new callsigns. Don't you see!?

"That's why only I can work it. I know its secret name. The N64. And that's what it needs now. Names. But not just any old names, oh no. Higher names. The names of angels!"

His hands found Wheeler's shoulders. He clutched at her, meeting her eye through the cracked lenses of their masks.

"Are there angels in your religion?"

"No, Pathfinder. There are no angels in our faith," she said, her voice calm despite her wild eyes.

"But how can that be?" Theo asked his voice breaking from the strain of trying to remain calm. "Aldwin heard their names in the storm. They must be there. There's always a pantheon, or a family, or even an enemy. No god is alone."

"Ours is. Ours was. There are no angels."

"There has to be."

"I'm no true student of faith, but even I know the first stories. They always start with god finding someone, or building something, like the Shepherd, or the Twin Hound Moons. But he's always by himself. That's why he made the First Peoples and gave them his powers, he did not wish to be alone. Even heretics don't argue that."

"No. That must be wrong," Theo said, and the excitement and the energy fell away from him just like the rain.

"I'm sorry, Theo, but Aldwin was a madman. He invented the angels, or perhaps he started to think the krows were some sort of divine punishment. His mind was just broken."

"I feel like I'm already losing my own."

"Litvak is the best person to talk to about this. She's spent lifetimes pouring through the oldest religious texts we have in the libraries. But she has no tolerance for such baseless ideas. She even expelled a scholar from the castle for espousing such myths, right around the time when I was earning my wings."

"Who was the scholar?"

"A radical. He arrived very suddenly in our midst and his departure was just as swift. He never managed to achieve flight, if I recall, but he was a terrific scholar, though a tad insane, even for us. I wasn't surprised when Litvak had him banished from the castle."

"What was his name?"

"I believe he called himself Yosef. He never found a callsign."

The name sent a whirlwind racing through his veins.

"Yosef?" he said, and the name was fire on his tongue. "Who was he? When was this? What did he say, Wheeler? What did he say that made the professor so angry?"

"Pathfinder, it was ages ago, I barely remember him at all," Wheeler said. She was pulling away from Theo, drifting further back towards the scholars up above. Theo chased her, crowding her space in his desperation.

"Please," Theo begged, forcing his voice to remain calm. Around them a new sound joined the roar of the wind, like a mountain falling over, a great tumble of rocks and stone collapsing and rolling over itself.

And it was coming from beneath them.

"He did have a few followers, ones that hung onto his every word and believed him to be something of a prophet. Aldwin might have been one of those, I have no idea. But it was because he was gaining followers that Litvak had him expelled."

"What did he preach that was so bad?"

"Pathfinder, it had nothing to do with angels."

"What was so heretical that you could be expelled from a band of heretics?"

"He said that even the most sacred texts were wrong. He said that Vovatum did not create Poa alone, at least not by choice. Yosef claimed that god had once had... friends."

The sound of crashing rocks was growing louder beneath them. Theo could see the circles of the expedition closing in, preparing for the descent into the Detritus. Already the air was choked with grit and dust, mixing with the falling rain to make a cloying muck.

"Friends?"

"It's ridiculous, of course. A divinity needs no friends. Yet, he persisted in his claims. Most found him laughable, but Litvak thought he was dangerous, so had him quietly removed."

"What happened to god's friends?"

"Theo, I need to be going above. We're about to breach the Detritus."

"My name is Pathfinder. What happened to those friends?" And for the first time his voice carried through the wind.

"He said they abandoned god. And then he abandoned them."

Lightning flashed, but Theo did not see it. Thunder rolled, but he did not hear it. He thought of the N-Device in the bell, the same one from his youth. A child's toy, above the grave of a god. He thought of names that moved the world, not because they were the names of gods, but because they were the names of friends. And here he was, flying through the sky like an angel.

"Theodore Lambert," he whispered. Lightning forked the air, filling the sky with the scent of ozone.

"Finley Marsh," he said, and the air shook with thunder like it never had before.

"Melanie Omar. Gwendolyn Brooks. Yosef League," Theo shouted, roaring back at the storm. Wheeler raced away from him, terror in her eyes as he continued to invoke the names of his friends. Each sent shocks ringing through the storm.

Lightning stabbed at the floating Pathfinder but could not connect. It raced at him before veering away.

The thunder above and the grinding rocks below shook the world, but his voice was above their noise now, roaring over them. Until he said that last and most fatal word.

"Huck," he whispered, and the storm silenced. Even the rain stopped as the thunder and lightning disappeared, and the expedition floated in a sphere of perfect calm.

Wheeler looked at him as if he were a krow. The lancers closed around them, Fencer at their head, a look of terrible concern on his face. He saw Striker looking up at him from the command ring, fathoms away, but he could hear her clear as a bell in the sudden quiet.

"Pathfinder, what are you doing?" she asked.

For one shivering second there was a calm in the Godstrom, and Theo was flying in its heart. One second.

And then a new voice joined the storm. It flattened the world in its passing, pushing aside the storm and the expedition like leaves on the wind. The flyers of the Final Expedition clutched at their helmets. Theo watched their eyes bulge out as their faces contorted with pain.

"Pathfinder," it spoke. The sound of its voice hung suspended in the air like the final notes of a dirge. And then more voices joined the song, an endless chorus all whispering the same name. And they brought the Godstrom back with them.

"Pathfinder," they all said, the crashing of thunder and lightning their accompaniment.

"KROWS!" roared Striker and, as if summoned from the darkness, the krows of the Godstrom boiled up from the clouds in their legions. They fell from the skies above with the rain. The rippling lightning reflected in their talons and in their bulging eyes. The thrashing of their leathery wings gave a spine-chilling drum beat as they poured out of the sky.

Their voices had lost their smooth familiarity, and now they screeched the name "Pathfinder" like a hated thing. Each echo of the word seemed to drive them to further frenzy, and as they swept into the rings of the expedition Theo could see that in their madness they even clawed and spat at each other.

His voice died away at the sight of them. Theo's hands found the knife at his waist. He pulled it out and pointed it with shaking hands at the coming horde. There was the scrape of leather on steel, and he turned to find that Striker was floating next to him, her shortsword drawn and the silver horn of the expedition in her hand.

"Get to the bell," Striker said, her eyes never leaving the coming krows. She brought the horn to her lips and sounded it. The instrument rang out, but even Theo could barely hear it over the din of the coming krows. She blew the horn again, but the Final Expedition did not move. Striker brought the horn to her mouth again, and with a great blast a pure note of sound rang out, cutting through the din like sunlight through fog.

"Hypnos!" she roared, and soon the other members of the expedition's voices joined the shout. The flyers circled in, mere seconds ahead of the coming krows.

Striker directed them to form a stout outer ring. The weatherbreathers huddled in the center near the great bell, which Keeper and the packsmen still carried. Striker floated above this group with a reserve of charters and packsmen, all with weapons drawn. The lancers circled this nucleus like lethal electrons.

The lancers had seconds to ready themselves as the krows howled closer. They pulled weapons out of sleeves and holsters, brandishing spears and guns and rifles and lethal arms of every sort.

Fencer was at their head, his beard a ragged tangle below his chin, his great broadsword chipped from the conflicts during their descent. Yet there was a great grin on his face, and his eyes were alive and wild. He opened his mouth and a warbling, droning war cry came from the depths of his chest, and the cry seemed to put steel into the spines of the other lancers as they readied themselves.

"Keeper, ready the surprise," Striker yelled to the man on the bell.

"Aye," he replied, climbing down to the bell's face and opening ports and windows throughout its surface.

"Get the N-Device and stay by me," Striker said to Theo.

"They're coming after me. You don't have to—"

"They'll die trying. Go, get the device, that's an order," Striker said, her voice steady and calm. The silver horn was still in her hand. The krows came rushing in, hundreds at least and more pouring forth from every cloud, all with their eyes fixed on Pathfinder.

And now they were only twenty fathoms away, and then ten. And Striker waited and waited until Theo could smell the hot breath of the krows on the wind before she said, "lancers, engage."

The lancers exploded out, the war cry of Fencer reaching a crescendo of violence. They rocketed at the enemy, hurtling their bodies into the hundred gnashing mouths of the krows.

Shaver was there, dual pistols in his hands that spat volleys of bullets into the eyes and teeth of the krows. His aim flowed from target to target, his face a picture of calm resolve.

His squad mate Butter leapt ahead of him. She landed onto the head of a krow, drove her trident into its neck, and launched herself at another before the first had even finished dying.

But Fencer was always before them, a one-man vanguard of whirling malice that carved wings and arms and heads from the krows as easy as breathing. His face was alive with horrible anger, his mouth ringing out a warrior's song that drowned out the krows. They roared at him, so enraged they did not even bother to shout his birth name. Fencer responded with his swift sword.

Like a tempest the lancers crashed into the oncoming waves of krows and even that unending tide buckled before them.

Yet they were only fifteen in number.

There was a dull click as Shaver's revolvers ran dry. The man moved to unholster the rifle on his back, but a krow lashed into him before he could reach it. The flashing lightning illuminated the spurt of blood that poured from the stump of his hand. The second claw of the krow burrowed into his side, and together the lancer and the monster fell from the sky.

Before he could think, Pathfinder was falling with them, intercepting their flight path. He drew level with the two and drove his dagger again and again into the creature's back. It writhed as he struck, but it did not release Shaver.

"Get to the bell!" Shaver roared, blood pouring from his mouth.

"Duan Ju," the krow whispered to the man.

"Monster," the man responded in kind, pulling a knife from his boot with his remaining hand and driving it into the creature's eye. As it roared with agony, he pulled it with him into the depths of a nearby storm cloud.

Theo stayed back, his eyes wide with terror. He heard more cries of pain on the winds of the storm. And he could think of only one way to help them. With a burst of speed, he shot towards the bell, racing past the weatherbreathers to the center of the expedition.

He hailed Keeper as he approached, but the man did not acknowledge him as he skewered a krow to the side of the bell. Theo threw the door of the bell open. The N-Device was within.

The loading bar was full at last, underneath it said only "PRESS PLAY TO START."

Theo's thumb crashed into the button, but he had no time to see what happened next. He dumped the contents of his bag on the floor of the bell before stuffing the N-Device within its depths. The light projection came from the mouth of the bag, and it hung over his head as he dove once more for the door. A shadow appeared beyond before he could reach it. His hand found his knife and he prepared to drive it into the creature's stomach.

"Whoa there," Keeper said, his hands covered in the green ichor of krows. "Calm yourself, your majesty. Only me. Good reflexes though."

"Thanks. How many ears?"

"Just the three thus far, but I suspect I'm about to collect a lot more. Striker wants the surprise ready. Do me a favor and pull the caps off those tubes will you?" Keeper said, indicating the long tubes that lined the upper shelves of the bell.

Theo moved to obey, popping the tops of the tubes. Inside, protected in waterproof bindings, were smaller red bundles with string coming from the top.

"Hand me the fuses," Keeper said over his shoulder as he also grabbed the strings from the other tubes along the wall. Only as he started binding all of the cords together into one larger rope did Theo realize what he was looking at.

"Is that dynamite?" Theo screeched.

"Yup. Plus some extras. It's the surprise," Keeper said, a mad grin on his face as he continued his work with his green stained hands.

"I've been sleeping in a room filled with explosives?"

"Relax, you've been fine. We figured you were nervous enough already," Keeper said, binding more and more of the fuses together so that they would all light as one when lit. "Go tell Striker it's almost ready."

Theo nodded, eager to be out of the explosive room. He clapped Keeper on the shoulder as he passed, feeling a terrible fondness for the man despite himself.

"Thanks for thinking of me."

"Don't mention it. Stay safe out there, your majesty." Theo nodded to this before launching himself once more into the sky.

The lines of the expedition had buckled. Defense in depth was impossible in an aerial battle. The only way to stay alive was to rely on speed.

The center of the sphere held true, the weatherbreathers and packsmen clustered safe in the center. Each had weapons out and lashed at any krow that came close. Yet they were not true fighters. They fled deeper and deeper into the Godstrom. Striker was at their heart, commanding the last charters still flying. She led the remains of the expedition in a fighting retreat deeper into the Godstrom and into the Detritus below.

Yet they were slow and the krows were many. The crashing waves of the krows had fallen into disarray at the charge of the lancers, but they were swarming again, and soon the center would be surrounded, cut off, and crushed. All that kept the heart of the expedition alive were the lancers. Three more of their rank had fallen, but they fought on.

The lancers shot around and around the sphere of the inner expedition, dozens of krows chasing after each one. They screamed and belted war cries as they flew, sending pieces of dead krows into the faces of their chasing brothers and sisters. It enraged the monsters, sending them into a wild frenzy that pushed them to commit to the chase.

The lancer Butter sent chains of lit firecrackers loose in her wake. The fireworks exploded in the faces of the chasing krows, scorching them, but not killing them. They howled in agony, calling a chorus of names before flying through the colorful explosions. The howls and the colors drew more of the krows after her and away from the vulnerable inner sphere.

Fencer and others activated the long-prepared attractors that each lancer had belted beneath their packs. A speaker and player packed together in a box durable enough to survive the Godstrom played a siren's screeching wail. With sirens blaring, Fencer spun faster and faster around the inner expedition, drawing more and more krows away. Soon the red and silver blur was trailed by a hundred krows, each one desperate to end the ringing wail coming from the man who had dispatched so many of them.

More and more of the krows chased after the lancers. And Theo realized their true aim. Not to defeat the krows, only distract them. They were bait for swarms of monsters, buying time for the rest of the expedition to flee.

Theo rushed to Striker's side as she, waiting for this exact moment, unleashed the last charters, directing them to cut a hole through the remaining krows circling below the expedition. The three charters burst down into the deep, diving into the ranks of krows, slicing and shooting at everything within reach. A sliver of open sky appeared below.

"Wheeler, take them into the Detritus. Find a rock on the outermost edge and wait for my sign before you dive!" Striker roared. Wheeler nodded, gathering the last of the scientists and shooting into the gap the charters had carved.

"Keeper, I want that bomb lit, then take it castleward. Gather what lancers you can and make for the Detritus. Pathfinder, to my side." Keeper saluted, but Striker's hand caught his. "I forbid you to die." Keeper grinned, lighting the fuse in his hand, before turning away, the bell still lashed to his back.

Theo rushed forward, flying down with Striker as she made for the gap in the krow lines. Theo turned onto his back, looking for Keeper and saw the man flying up and up, pulling the bell by himself. Red lights embedded in the leather started to blur as Keeper picked up speed. The last of the lancers saw the rising bell and flew as close as they could, bringing their trailing krows with them.

With a flash of horror Theo realized that Keeper was on a suicide run. "Keeper, no!" But the wind took the sound away from him. And now Keeper was fathoms above them, the great mass of krows swarming around the light of the bell like moths around a flame. Theo refused to look away, even as Striker clutched at his arm and pulled him deeper into the storm.

Keeper rose and rose, carrying the immense weight of the bell higher and higher. The lancers, only five in number now, veered away from the swarm. The bell was covered in krows, growing heavier by the moment as more latched onto its face, desperate to get at the light.

The bell started to drop, to follow them in their descent, pulled down as it was by the weight of so many. But Keeper was rising higher, still higher. And with a shout of joy Theo realized he had detached himself from the bell.

Keeper zoomed away, chasing after the lancers. And now Striker finally pulled Theo down to face the Detritus below them.

"Don't look." She commanded, leading him away. Below them was Wheeler's group, but beyond them was a wall of swirling rock. Boulders the size of houses crashed through the air, the terrible wind of the Godstrom keeping them aloft. They tumbled and crashed into each other like the teeth of a giant. And Striker was leading him into their depths and the darkness beyond.

Even lightning did not fall here. The only light came from the weatherbreathers who dropped flare after flare as they led the way into the deeps of the Detritus. Striker clutched his arm, and Theo could hear her counting under her breath as they raced after the dim flares.

"Close your eyes," Striker yelled. Theo moved to obey, but he was not fast enough. Behind him, there was a flash of light that cast his shadow onto the rocks below. Something far above seemed to suck in the noise of the thunder and the crashing boulders, leaving an eerie silence in the storm.

And then the bomb expelled that noise in a ripple of terrible force.

His neck clenched with agony as the soundwave beat against his eardrums, but he could not stop to scream. The shockwave caught and pushed him like a massive hand. For a moment he lost track of the impossible.

He fell, all sense of control gone as he tumbled into space. To his right he heard the dull rumble of a coming rock through his bruised eardrums. He looked and saw what looked like the shoulder of an entire continent.

It tumbled closer, shoving its way through the air, ready to squash him flat. He closed his eyes, summoning every impossibility that Elwyn had drilled into his brain, but the pain in his ears and in his eyes overrode these thoughts and panic gripped every inch of him.

And then he felt Striker's hands under his arms. She pulled, yanking him out of his dive.

"We gotta go under it," Striker roared, cradling and manhandling him at the same time as she sent them rocketing under the swirling wall of rock.

Pathfinder shook his head, her hands anchoring him back in the here and now. They overrode the pain. He reached for the impossible in his mind, contemplating the thing that could not be known. But it was not a paradox Elwyn had taught him, but one of his own: "How can my friend be god?"

Flight came back to him, and he and Striker raced below the tumbling rock, so close that they could feel it scratching their backs. They dodged the uneven spires and grooves along its face, ducking into a canyon carved across its body. They raced through, hugging the walls above and to the sides, searching for the red flares that Wheeler had lit during her descent.

"There," Striker said. And Theo saw it too, a far-off glimmer at the other side of the upside-down canyon. She raced ahead and Theo followed. They exploded out from the canyon and back into open space, and now they were fully immersed in the Detritus, the shattered remnants of what was once the Tile of the Colleges. It swirled around them like an asteroid field, rocks as small as hands and boulders as big as mountains. The rain had vanished, instead there was only the grit of dust as the rocks collided and exploded all around them, sending shards of granite into the air.

The only light was the spark from the crashing rocks and the sharp light of the red flares. Some nestled in the hollows of rock formations while others floated in the air, but they all led down, down below the Godstrom. There was no other sign of the other members of the expedition.

Striker and Pathfinder followed the breadcrumbs. They flew deeper and deeper, and without the rolls of thunder and the wash of the rain Theo found the place unsettling in its quiet.

He and Striker slowed, drifting from flare to flare as they caught their breaths. The flares burned red in the darkness, each one a small candle in the unending void. Beyond were only the shadows of crashing rocks.

"Do you think Keeper made it?"

"That man has an incredible habit of surviving the unsurvivable. I am sure he is fine," Striker said, her voice calm and detached though her eyes never ceased their scan of the storm. "He might have stopped to collect their blasted ears."

"That sounds like something he would do," Theo said. They stopped to let a boulder bigger than the bell drift by them. There was masonry still on this one, a broken column embedded in its face that had survived the passage of decades.

"How many did we lose?" Theo forced himself to ask.

"The only thing that matters is that we did not lose everyone. As long as one of us still flies, the expedition lives."

"I think I counted fifteen," Theo said, his voice cracked and broken. His eyes burned, but no tears fell.

"Sixteen," Striker corrected.

"I'm sorry."

"What happened back there?" Striker asked as they drifted to another flare. There were more below them, leading deeper and deeper through the detritus. "You silenced the storm. I've never seen that before."

"I figured out the N-Device. I think I can activate the Pilgrim Path."

"Good. Can you do it again? Can you make the storm go calm? It could be useful."

"I don't know. I don't think it would be a good idea. When I started to speak the names, it was almost like the storm—" He cut himself off, fearful of sounding foolish, before he forced himself to speak. "I don't think the storm likes it. The krows came right after it went quiet, like white blood cells targeting a virus."

"The storm is not alive, Pathfinder. The storm is a storm."

"But isn't it the Godstrom though? What if it still has a bit of god's mind to it? What if it's the last living part of him?"

"And that would make the krows a defense system?" Striker said, her voice thick with disgust. "It is impossible. Vovatum would not target his own believers. Even from beyond the void he would not do such a thing."

"I'm not sure you know god very well," Theo said. "That sounds like something he would do, if he was desperate, if he was alone."

"No, it's not. I have watched too many of my friends ripped apart by those monsters to ever believe that they were a piece of god."

"Then why did they all appear at once? They left us alone for days, but they attacked as soon as I figured out how to power the N-Device, as soon as that voice in the storm spoke," Theo said, remembering the horrible flat tone that had sliced through him like a knife.

"Do you think that was the voice of god?"

"I don't know what it was," Theo admitted. "But it sounded like the voice of a ghost."

Striker did not reply. They drifted deeper into the Detritus. Theo checked his altimeter, but he knew what he would find. He had never fixed it after their initial descent. They must be at least 12,000 fathoms deep and dropping all the time.

The glow of the N-Device still shone from the pack on his back. That and the flares were the only lights in the darkness. They jumped and flew from flare to flare, both listening for a voice, though whose they did not know.

Chapter 22: The Scholar's Monster

I think have thrown off my pursuers. I have seen no sign of them for six months. I am currently in a small tile that is almost always tropical despite the turnings. There is a woman here who is very kind. Her name is Calliope. Like me, she lives a nomadic life. Her people are wanderers, and I, more than anyone, know what it is like to be lost. She has been taking care of me. I have even told her my true name. I think she has fallen in love with me. Would it be wrong if I have done the same?

(Letter 21, Lines 1-End)

The glowing road of red flares ended. Striker and Pathfinder flew down to the last flare, one stuck in the crevices of a ruined pillar drifting through the storm. Below them was darkness without a single hint of light.

"Where are the rest?" Theo asked.

"I don't know," Striker said. Her hand found the short sword at her waist. The other still clutched the horn of the expedition in a death grip. Theo looked up. The line of flares they had followed was already drifting apart, snatched away by the higher winds. Other flares had simply sputtered out, leaving only a few red lights burning like distant stars far above them.

"Where are Wheeler and the others? Do you think they went on into the deep storm?"

"No. The Deep doesn't start for at least another thousand fathoms."

"One thousand fathoms? Shouldn't we be near the ground by now?"

"We are far below sea level by now, Pathfinder. We passed that mark several days ago," Striker said, her voice the only sound in the darkness besides the soft hiss of the red flames.

"We're underground?" Theo asked, the darkness around him seeming to take on a deeper level of gloom.

"The whole tile was broken when god fell to Poa. We're halfway down a crater hundreds of miles across and miles deep. This is the birthplace of the Godstrom, and the graveyard of Vovatum."

"Right. I'm just now remembering that I suffer from claustrophobia," Theo said. He could not look away from the ever-dimming light of the red flare. "So Wheeler wouldn't have gone into the Deep?"

"Never. Not even if their lives were in utmost danger. She knows it is worse than suicide to fly into those depths without the map, " he said, indicating the halo over Theo's shoulder.

"So where did they go?"

"I'm not sure. Stay here by the flare. I'll do a quick circuit," Striker said, moving to launch herself from the rock they were perched on.

"Wait, are you sure that's the best idea? I mean, splitting up seems like a disaster waiting to happen."

"Maybe so, but do you have a better idea at the moment?" Theo said nothing. "I'll keep the flare in sight. If something happens, cover the flare three times for two seconds each. I'll come winging back," Striker said before launching herself off the rock.

Theo hovered alone, only the lights of the N-Device and the sputtering flare for company. He waited, every muscle crawling with the desire to flee, to hide, but he remained rooted to the spot.

There was the soft plunk of water on rock. He looked down. There was a long cut on the outside of his forearm that was dripping blood. He had not even felt it. His other hand moved like someone else was controlling it, first to the belt of pouches at his waist, to the bandages he kept rolled by his left hip, and then back to his wrist. He pushed back the tattered remnants of the jacket to expose the cut. He wrapped it in gauze. He hoped that the rain had washed the cut enough, he would hate to get an infection.

He couldn't help but chuckle at that thought. "As if I have enough time to get infected," he whispered to himself. "Although, knowing my luck…"

There was a glimmer of light far ahead. Theo whirled towards it, reaching for the long knife still belted to his waist. He squinted his eyes, desperate to know what the glint of light had been.

"Striker!" Theo called out into the darkness around him, hoping that she would hear his voice in the emptiness.

The light grew closer. Theo drew his knife, slipping into a fighting stance. He would keep the flare behind him, force the creature to fight looking directly into its light. The glimmer zoomed closer, and only then did Theo relax. He could see what had caused the light. It was the reflection of the flare caught in the surface of a blade. Striker's blade.

"You might have called out," Theo said, relaxing his stance and bringing the knife down. "You almost gave me a heart attack. I thought you were somewhere over—" and he cut off as the shape finally shambled into the light of the flare.

It was not Striker; it was a man almost unrecognizable to Theo. Sheets of blood poured from cuts across his face and scalp. His clothes were a ruin of broken armor and tattered cloth. He had ripped them to fasten a tourniquet around his arm, which ended below his elbow. His left hand still held his sword.

"Shaver," Theo cried, catching the man as he fell into the circle of light and into Theo's arms. "What happened to you? Did the bomb get you?"

"I flew ahead of the bomb," Shaver said. Theo could see his gaze jumping from point to point inside the circle of light. "Cut my way through the krows and into the Detritus. Only cost an arm."

"I'll try to patch you up."

"No time," Shaver said, his voice strangled and tight. "We need to fly. We need to get away from here."

"We can't leave. We need to wait for Striker. She's looking for Wheeler and the others. Have you seen them?"

"Aye, I found them. Met them before we dipped into the rocks."

"Hang on, I need to clean this blood off you. Where are you cut?"

"It's not—" Shaver gasped, his voice growing weaker and weaker. "It's not my blood."

Theo stilled. Shaver still clutched his sword in a death grip, his pistols were long since abandoned. And as he looked at the sword, soaked with the green blood of krows, he remembered something. Shaver did not carry a sword.

"Shaver, whose sword is that?"

"We need to flee. Can't stay here."

"Answer him, Duan Ju. How did you get Waver's sword?" a voice said behind them. Theo whipped around. Striker was there, her face etched in the lengthening shadows cast by the dying flare. The sound of the man's real name seemed to rouse him. His eyes opened again, but there was little recognition in them.

"Waver's dead. I found the weatherbreathers, but then it found us."

"What found you, Shaver?" Striker asked, her voice soft.

"The Leviathan."

Through the darkness there came a sound of vast and unending hunger. A hunter's howl.

Theo tried to imagine a creature big enough to make such a sound.

"There are no Leviathans. It's a myth," Striker said.

"There is one, Captain. And we are cursed enough to meet it."

"Shaver, where are the others?" Theo asked.

"Too late. Too late. They sent me to get you to flee. Too late." Shaver babbled, and as he spoke there was another howl, but the noise was so deep it seemed to devour all other sound.

The scream ended and, in the silence, there was the sound of voices crying out in pain. It was coming from the dark to the east of them. The voices were faint, still too far to make out what they were saying, but each one carried the tones of utter panic.

"The Leviathan," Theo said.

"A higher life form. The oldest krow," Shaver said. "The one that has eaten the most of god."

"So it's real," Striker said. Her voice seemed carved from stone. "Theo, you must carry on alone."

"What?" Theo asked, shocked by the use of his given name. Ahead of them, a mile distant at least, there was the sudden ripple of bright flares in the empty sky. In the darkness they rose like new suns. Narrow shadows ducked in front of the light of the flares racing towards them.

"We will hold the creature as long as we can. It must not be allowed to follow you into the deep. Fly on. Make it worth something," Striker said, and she shifted Shaver from Theo's shoulder to hers. The man clung to her, almost unconscious from shock and pain, but the sword was still in his hand.

The flares so distant were dropping lower and burning out. The red circle of their light grew dimmer as the shadows raced to reclaim their territory. A boulder tumbled across the path of the light, hiding the flares behind its bulk.

And then, with the noise of a tumbling mountain, the boulder shattered outward. The red lights of the flares exploded out of the cracks and the world once more had a dim sun. And in the light of this flickering, final sun there was a monster.

It burst through the boulder as if it were a paper screen. It thundered through the air, flying on the beats of a row of jagged wings as narrow as grasping fingers. Theo saw the rows of jagged blades inside its mouth, and the four tonguelike appendages that lashed the air, desperate for a taste of the flyers fleeing before it.

Narrow feelers lined its underside, and they pawed the air as it flew through the remains of the boulder it had shattered. The feelers whipped forward and in the dim light Theo could see them lash across the back of a fleeing winger. As the vast tentacle lanced across his back the winger went limp, the scream locked in his throat. He fell from the sky, only for one of the creature's tongues to catch him before ladling him into its mouth.

Its opaque eyes sat without seeing above its gaping mouth. Above its head, dangling from a tentacle that drifted ever before it, was a soft white light. It shone above its corpse skin, and it set the empty eyes sparkling like stars reflected in a mirror. Even from so far, Theo could feel the pull of that light, the urge to fall into its depths. It seemed to stun him stiff, lulling him into a dreamless sleep.

He resisted it. Forced himself to stare not at the creature's eyes but at its endless mouth. It roared as it chased its prey, the dozen wingers that remained.

The Leviathan. An old name for an old thing, but Theo knew it at once for what it was. The oldest sky maggot, and the first to find Vovatum's body.

Huck's body.

"I have not led this expedition through rock and lightning to see it end in darkness. You will fly on, Theo Lambert. Only you know the way." Striker turned then, her gray eyes meeting his. There were tears in them, trickling from the corners of her eyes and into the scars that lined her face. Behind her one more of their expedition proved too slow for the Leviathan. Her scream rippled out through the darkness, and Theo watched the shock of it travel across Striker's face. But her voice was calm as stone.

"I named you Pathfinder. I now name you Survivor. Go. Make sure that god knows we did not die afraid," she said, and then she turned once more to face the monster. She sheathed her sword. One arm clutched Shaver, and the other the silver horn of her command. She placed it to her lips, and with a great rush of air she gave a blast of pure music.

Wheeler and the remaining weatherbreathers gave a great shout at the sound. With a cry she ordered the other survivors launch the last flares they had.

Striker launched forward as the weatherbreathers heralded her coming with a barrage of fireworks. They burst into the air creating flowers of scarlet, of ochre, and of pure white light. The darkness fled before the rising of these lights, and with a cry of pain even the Leviathan shuddered with agony as the illumination scorched its dead eyes. Its own paralyzing headlamp seemed to dim, and with a burst of movement the weatherbreathers fell into formation behind Striker.

Striker led the charge, still blasting on her silver horn. Shaver had come to life beside her, and he held his sword out like the point of a lance. The Leviathan reared back from the onslaught of noise and light, exposing the soft flesh of its stomach. Shaver stabbed his sword into its stomach, Striker lending him her momentum so that the sword did not stop as it burst into the Leviathan's skin. It carved down its stomach, releasing a torrent of yellow green blood.

And Wheeler was there, a hatchet in her hand that she used to hew the tops from the feelers along its sides, sending their paralyzing tentacles into the black below.

And Puncher moved among them like a field of reeds, hacking and slashing all within reach.

Stringer lit long strings of firecrackers and lodged them in the cracks and grooves of the creature's armor, blasting whole sections loose.

And now the formation split, some wingers darting amidst the tentacles or the wings to gnash at the soft skin near its joints, others racing up to release a new barrage of fireworks in front of the creature's eyes. And for a moment Theo felt a rush of hope that he was about to see a monster fall.

But then he saw the ripple of movement down the flanks of the Leviathan as it shook off its stupor. He saw the tongues lashing forward and up. He cried out in alarm as they raced for Wheeler's legs as she rushed towards the base of its headlamp to cut off the paralyzing light.

With a groan of longing its sharp purple tongue carved through her legs like a vast wriggling knife. Wheeler separated from her own legs, a look of shock upon her face, yet she remained silent. She did not speak even as she tumbled down into the creature's mouth. And Theo's howl of agony matched the cry of triumph from the creature.

There was a boom of sound.

There was a crack as something raced through the sky, producing its own dull thunder. And above his shoulder Theo watched a meteor fall to Poa. It hurled at the Leviathan, plummeting down just as the old disaster had when it struck this tile so many decades before. Yet this one was aimed.

From the back of the boulder, clinging to it like the tail of a comet, were Fencer, Keeper, and three other lancers. Their shoulders were pressed into the rock, sending it ringing forth. Its terrible momentum accelerated as the lancers called out their battle cries. It thundered into the creature's mouth like the hammer of a god. Teeth broke and shattered, and its tongues were blocked by the bulk of the rock.

"Monster, I shall put you into the soup!" Fencer roared, his broken longsword in his hand. He had lost his helmet in the descent, and now his red hair shone like a flare in the darkness. Keeper darted past him to catch the falling Wheeler. He clutched her to his chest, doing his best to staunch the bleeding even as they hurtled away from the choking Leviathan.

Striker gave another blast on her horn and the wingers stabbed at the Leviathan like scalpels. Theo stood silent and unmoving. The rock he stood on floated through the void, the flare long since extinguished at his feet.

He was overwhelmed by the bravery before him. They fought like heroes in the darkness against a creature that had devoured a god. All to buy him time. He adjusted the pack on his shoulder, the white halo of the N-Device's light illuminating his way.

He moved to step off the rock, but before he did, he caught the eye of Keeper. The man was covered in burns, and half his clothes seemed to have caught fire and been put out at some point. He still held

Wheeler in his arms. The woman was awake, binding her own legs. Keeper nodded to the darkness below them.

"Get to it, Pathfinder. It's why we came. I'll be sure to say nice things about you to Elwyn, by the way, if you don't come back," Keeper said, and once more he flashed that knifelike grin. It was a band of pure white across the ash that covered his face.

"I'll do the same," Theo called back, and he stepped out into the void. He did not bother to fly, but instead let gravity snatch him down.

Behind him he heard the war cries of the Final Expedition.

He heard the clang of steel against armored skin.

He heard the crunch of teeth through rock as the Leviathan gnawed through the boulder.

He heard the sound of a silver trumpet.

And then, as he fell faster and faster into the darkness below that was broken only by the light from the device on his back, he heard nothing at all.

Chapter 23: The Dreamer's Old Friend

I hope you might meet Calliope someday. I am eager to see how you'd get along. I think Gwen would love her laugh, Mel her artist's eye, and Theo her endless stories. Although Finley might be annoyed that she is the light of every room, rather than him. I have imagined these interactions a thousand times, in a thousand ways. She often wonders why I cry so easily and sleep so little, but I have not told her.

I wish that we could be together once again. But I know now that it is not to be. I have never believed in destiny, but I thought this land of god might finally convince me otherwise. Perhaps I am alone in this world, as I have always feared. I think this shall be my last letter. I hope you will not think me selfish if I start a new life here, with Calliope. I wish to be myself again and be happy.

(Letter 22, Paragraph 2, Lines 5-9, and Paragraph 3, Lines 1-End)

The journey up the Colossus took six days. Up they climbed, farther and farther until the feel of solid earth beneath their feet was a distant memory.

Mel was closer to the statue than she had been in weeks, a germ climbing up its skin. The song hacked at her lower senses, but she refused to let it claim her. Always she would look at the workers they marched past, desperate to find, but terrified to discover, a glimpse of one of her friends. But she did not see anyone familiar in the hordes of mindless workers, and with every step they climbed the dread built in her heart.

In the morning, the ground at the feet of the Colossus twitched with movement. The humans so far below came to life as the song coursed into their heads, but they did not go to the statue. Mel pressed her hand to the skin of the great Colossus, and for once it did not rattle with the fall of far-off hammer blows.

"What's happening? Why aren't they working?" Mel asked of Cisseus.

"Have they ever stopped working before?" Cisseus signed. Mel had learned enough from him by now that she understood simple signs. He had to sign to her like she was a six-year-old, but it was a conversation at least.

"Never. We never had a day where we didn't work on the statue."

Great columns of dust built as the workers marched away from the statue and into the ash filled plains.

"Maybe they needed more supplies and they've all gone to get more. They have to run out of metal at some point, right?"

"Maybe you're right," Mel said, and the boy smiled as she acknowledged his argument. She kept her doubts to herself. It was more than that, she was sure of it, but they could not stop now. They were so close. If she kept moving, she'd be able to free her friends. And when Gwen, Finley, Theo, and Yosef returned to the statue maybe they'd forgive her.

They were at the top of the Colossus's chest now, and the statue was empty except for the Sheosirrans. The plain of its shoulder met the vast trunk of its neck only a few stories above them. The Colossus was less substantial in these highest levels. Only its iron skeleton was fully complete.

Far off in the distance the tiles began their next great shift. Mel knew about the tiles. She had had Cisseus explain them to her twice just to make sure she had not misunderstood. It took her breath away every time the tiles shifted.

The mountains at the ends of the valley remained rooted, but beyond them the world moved. A great lake appeared and now water lapped at the base of the mountains. The rolling hills become a windswept plain where herds of far-off animals kicked up clouds of dust.

Only to change, again and again.

She had a godlike view as the tiles shifted in front of her like pieces on a chess board. But as they walked farther and farther up the Colossus, despite the shifts of the tiles that brought so many lands and sights in view, one tile was always squarely in the sights of the immense statue.

The Tile of the Colossus seemed to track this tile like a tiger tracks its prey, and now in this final turning before the Sheosirrans confronted their lost brother, the Colossus was ready to pounce.

Its prey was a tile that held only a single city, a place of spires, of gilded walls, and massive temples. Over this city, protecting it like a child protects its toys, was a mountain carved into the shape of a Shepherd.

And now, at last, this tile was right in front of the Colossus.

They made their way up past the clouds. They trekked through the snows along the shoulders and the neck. They climbed the frozen staircases of the collarbone. As the sun disappeared down the rim of the sky, they found themselves at the edge of a dais that rested at the top of the neck of the great statue. Its skull loomed above them.

There was no face here, only the semblance of a skull made from iron girders rimmed with frost. The Colossus grinned down at them with a rictus smile below massive empty eye sockets.

As Mel brought up the rear of the column and walked onto the dais, she found herself linking eyes with the hollows in the giant's skull.

"We meet at last," Mel said into the silence, trying her best to sound brave. "I never expected you to be ugly, but it suits you. All that work, all that pain, and they couldn't even give you a halfway decent smile."

"All in due time," a voice said from the other side of the circle.

Mel turned. There was an iron table welded into the metal of the dais. There were papers and pencils and measuring instruments strewn about the table. Discarded paper marred with ink littered the ground. In front of the table, with his back to the Sheosirrans, was a man in a wheelchair.

Two other architects flanked the man on either side. They had white cowls on that hid their faces in shadows, but one seemed to be a woman and the other a man. They each had a hand on the wheelchair, and the others gripped the hilts of the swords they kept at their sides.

"There will be no need for that," the Revered Engineer said. "These people are old friends." With a glance from him they let go of their blades, but they did not yet turn around his chair. The Revered Engineer faced away from them, looking down into the valley he controlled.

"My people. Welcome to the top of the Colossus. I thought about meeting you at the waist, but I could not let you leave without enjoying this view. Is it not splendid?"

"Do you mean the view of the tiles you have exploited or the monstrosity you have created?" Harmodias said, her voice lashing out like a whip.

"Can it not be both? Are you not proud of what I have accomplished, Harmodias?"

"I think it is a stunning monument to your own arrogance."

The Engineer laughed, not at all ruffled by her cutting words. "Everyone's a critic, I suppose. Still, I would think a fellow artist might appreciate what I have created. After all, I am only using the gifts you gave me."

"What you have made disgusts me. You have enslaved hundreds of thousands of people to deify yourself. I never taught you to do such a thing."

"No. No you did not. I had a much more … motivating teacher for that. But I must disagree with you. I have enslaved no one. I have merely presented them an opportunity to finally be more. They have become a part of the next divinity itself. Can you not understand, Harmodias? I have given them just what you taught me to. I have given them dreams."

"It certainly doesn't feel like that," Mel said, emerging from behind the Sheosirrans. She eyed them as she passed and was disappointed by what she saw. The climb and the altitude had robbed what little strength they already had. Their thin muscles and fragile limbs shook with every breath, and their pupils had shrunk to pin pricks of darkness. They would be no help if it came down to a fight. They had spent too long in the dreaming world to have any substance in this one.

"I have endured your dream for too long. It might be the most awful thing that's ever happened to me," Mel said, crossing her arms behind her back to rest her hand on the weapon she had in her belt. The hands of the architects next to the Revered Engineer drifted to the pommels of their swords, but at the slightest twitch of his head, they stopped.

"Who are you?" the Engineer asked, and now his voice was no longer smooth.

"One of your damn builders," Mel said, eyeing the target for all her hate. He looked so frail, even as he sat on the mountain of his own accomplishment. "Harmodias, let's get this done. I'm tired of waiting."

"How—" the Revered Engineer spat, still not facing her. "How dare you steal her voice, Harmodias? How dare you be so cruel?"

Mel turned to look at the old woman, but the Sheosirran's face was empty, as if the person behind the skin and muscles had hidden deep inside her body.

Mel turned back to the Revered Engineer, only to find that his architect guards had spun him around to face them.

The eyes were the only thing about him that seemed alive. His teeth were broken and blackened with rot. His skin was as thin as parchment and marred with scars. It was stretched tight against his frame and Mel could see that the bones beneath had been broken, many, many times. His arms were twisted things, broken and healed so often that they looked like mangled tree branches.

He looked like an ancient prisoner released from the deepest hell, but his eyes conducted light. Every glance was the flash of the sun, and every blink was a sunset. They were eyes that burned.

And there was something familiar about him.

Mel saw the lines of his narrow jaw and high cheekbones. She saw the twist of his broken nose and the web of lines that spiraled about his eyes.

She knew that face. She knew this man. But how? The thought poured through her like ice water. How did she know this man, and how did he know her?

"Is it you? Is it really you after all this time?" the Revered Engineer said, his face alive with emotion even as his broken body remained slack and unmoving. "Or is this another trick of yours, Harmodias? Is this another fantasy you have conjured to torment me?"

"I don't need fantasies to torment you. I only need to show you what you've done," Harmodias said, her voice a flat rasp upon the thin wind.

"What is he talking about? How do you know me?"

"I've known you all my life, Mel. I've known you since we were five. We just aged in different ways," the Engineer said, and his eyes flashing to his own ruined body.

"What are you talking about?"

"You haven't aged a day, have you? You're just like I remember you," the Engineer said, his eyes alight as he drank her in. "No. That's not true. You're leaner, stronger than I ever knew you. Harmodias didn't pull this image out of my dreams. You're here, at last."

328

"Who the hell are you?"

"You've known that since you saw my face, Mel. You've sketched it about a dozen times. You once told me I had eyes too old for my baby cheeks. You said they belonged on a grandpa, not a kid," he said, little chuckles reverberating up his ruined chest.

"I guess I'm finally ancient enough to match my eyes. You see, I landed here a long, long time ago and I gave up hope that the rest of you would ever find me." The man shook his head ruefully, tears spilling from his eyes and down his weathered cheeks. "And after all this time, it seems god really does have a sense of humor. But we always knew that about Huck, didn't we, Mel?"

"No. No, that can't be possible," Mel said, and her voice shook with rage. "Yosef, what happened to you?"

Yosef League, the Revered Engineer and her friend from Earth, looked back at her from his ruined face. He was supposed to be her age. He was supposed to be eighteen. But it seemed he had endured a century of misery since they had last seen each other.

"A life, Mel, a whole life. I came to Poa almost sixty years ago."

"Yosef, you're so old," Mel said, and her voice cracked with the strain.

"I see you haven't changed," Yosef said with a small chuckle. "No time to spare for false compliments. Yes, I'm old. Old and broken. Life here on Poa was not all sunshine and roses. Huck, in the end, started to lose control of this place. And now we all suffer for it.

"I'm sorry you had to see me like this. I wish you never had. I gave up on seeing you again half a lifetime ago. And now you've come back to me, with all my enemies in tow, trying to destroy my work. Isn't it funny?"

"Yosef, why do you keep talking about Huck? What does he have to do with this place?"

"Haven't you figured it out yet? This place, this world, it's all an idea that Huck had once. Just a figment of his imagination, like all those pen and paper games we used to play. Who knew that he was building this place for real, huh? I hope he didn't know. I think I would hate Huck even more." A flash of old anger moved across his face, as well sharpened as a favorite blade.

329

"This is his land of make believe, Mel. This is the place he would dream up at night and capture in his little stories. He was the god of this place, the one these people call Vovatum. But he's been dead a long, long time."

"What are you talking about? Huck wasn't a god. He was our friend."

"But not all the time. Sometimes he played god. Just like we all used to do once. With our lands of make believe, our happy kingdoms with kind kings and gentle queens. But when everyone else outgrew it, Huck never did. He just got better at it. He created worlds with paper and ink. Shifted mountains and laid waste to armies, all for fun. And it turns out the little land he ruled over was real the whole time. And this is it.

"Impossible, yes? But that's the nature of this world, and his signature is all over it. The newspaper is the one Gwen and he invented when they were kids. The Cognitive Domains is the magic system he dreamed up when his father started to lose his mind. Haven't you ever wondered why everyone on the planet speaks English? Even the name of god is a clue. Vovatum. Vovatum is an interesting word, isn't it? There's no other word like it on this planet, because it's not from this one. It's from ours.

"It's short for Vaccinium Ovatum. It's Latin, the scientific name for—"

"For Huckleberry," Mel said, her voice crawling with horror.

"Yes. Took me decades to figure that one out. Every line of this planet is his, Mel. Along with every joy, every triumph, and every heartache.

Yosef smiled at her with his broken teeth and shrugged his misshapen shoulders. Mel's stomach churned as she imagined what had been done to her friend.

"But why would Huck fill it with so much pain, you ask? Vovatum could not build a perfect world, because a perfect world is a boring world. No one cares to read such stories. And so he built a world that grinds you to death with its twisting gears. And such a world always needs fresh heroes.

"That's why we're here, Mel. He brought us here, in his ego, in his arrogance to finish his story!"

"What are you talking about? Huck is dead."

"And this was his dying wish, so I played my part. I was a warrior," Yosef boasted, his ruined body twisting with his words.

"I was a poet," Yosef whispered, his voice an old man's, filled with ancient dust.

"I was a hero. I was everything this world required me to be. I was all his little unfulfilled fantasies. All the characters whose stories he never finished. But I learned something along the way.

"Heroes don't get to be happy. They are meant to suffer and suffer and suffer until we learn our lesson. It took me long time, but I finally learned mine. And I don't know about you, Mel, but I am sick to death of living out someone else's fantasies. Now I think it's time for ours to move the world."

"You would pollute the world with your own dreams, League?" Harmodias said. "You would use the gifts my people gave you to shape the world in your own image?"

"They are better dreams by far than any this world has shown me."

"You would destroy us! The Sheosirrans would become the demons of the world, the source of its greatest tyrant. We gave you everything," Harmodias said, her clawed hand pointing accusingly at the man. "When my daughter found you, you were nothing. Calliope saved your life and took you in.

"What would you have become without our gifts? You became a leader, a dreamer of the Reverie with unmatched skill. We had never seen worlds like the ones you showed us. That was the man Calliope loved, that your children loved. And now you would pervert her dreams—"

"Her dreams are dead!" Yosef roared, his calm resolve crumbling to nothing. "She was killed by enemies stronger than we could ever imagine. She died failing to protect the children I was too weak to save. No more," and now his voice was a whisper. "I will never allow this world of Huck's to hurt me again. It needs a new god, and I have built the perfect one."

"Built with slaves," Mel said, and Yosef's anger dropped away. He looked at her with eyes that might once have been her friend's.

"Not slaves. Never that. They want to build the Colossus, Mel. They want to work. They've never had a dream so perfect."

"But it's not theirs, is it Yosef? Trust me, I know. I spent weeks pouring my blood and sweat into this new god of yours. I've never seen such a beautiful thing made so ugly. Tell me, what did you exchange to dream all this?"

He smiled at her, but it didn't reach his glowing eyes. "My weakness."

"His heart," Harmodias said.

"It doesn't matter. We will have a god of our own, one who owes us his life, and every exchange, every sacrifice will be worth it."

"Even my own, Yosef? You broke my mind. You slipped into my head and made me a puppet. I've never been so weak, and you made me that way. You're supposed to be my friend! I thought I had abandoned you. I thought I had left you in this hell. But it was hell of your own making, wasn't it, Yosef?"

He looked at her, and for once he seemed the helpless old man he was. Tears slipped from his eyes, and he made no move to dam them. "I'm sorry, I truly am. If I had known that it was you, I never would have done such a thing."

"You never should have done it to anyone, Yosef. I know you've been through something I will never understand, but you must know that this is wrong. When did you stop caring about people, about your friends?" Mel said, anger and tears in her voice, but as she spoke the man across from her seemed to grow colder and colder, until he was as dead as the statue they stood upon.

"When I realized they weren't people. They're nothing more than walking shadows, little ideas that Huck came up with in his spare time. They are not like you and me."

"You loved one of those shadows, Yosef. You loved Calliope. You and her had three children," Harmodias said, disgust clinging to every word, and a little bolt of shock ripped its way through Mel's heart.

"And I buried them all and learned my lessons," Yosef said, and his face was blank and empty, even while his lips curled into a half smile. "I finally learned what Huck was trying to teach me all this time. The only way to have this world make sense is to force it into submission. With steel beams and songs from half remembered dreams. The Colossus will set this world right, Mel, and make it so it will never hurt us or the people we love ever again. It will finally be a perfect god for this unfinished land."

Mel stepped forward. "Yosef, you have to stop this. You have to let these people go.

"I can't stop it," Yosef said, his face still wrapped in that grim smile, but now the glowing light had returned to his eyes, and they shone like searchlights pouring from his face. "I refuse to stop it. I was brought here for a reason. I am meant to finish this world. It's what Huck would want."

"I don't give a damn what Huck wanted. Huck is dead, and this is wrong." And Mel pulled out the shovel she had carried up the walk to the top of the Colossus. She drove the head of it into the iron skin beneath her, stabbing into the shoulder of the statue. "Don't make me stop you, old man. I won't be gentle."

"You can certainly try." Yosef turned to the two architects still standing by his side. "Do what you want with the others, but I want that builder alive."

"I think you forgot who used to kick the asses of the kids that tried to bully you, Yosef. Looks like I'm gonna have to remind you," Mel said, swinging the shovel so that the head was pointing at the drawn swords of the architects in white.

"Just like old times," Yosef said, a little chuckle running up his wrecked body. "You know, it's all so perfect, so neat and tidy. My story is about to come to an end, and here you've come, a piece of our beginning. Perhaps my new god is already at work, and I am so very proud of him." His chuckles died away and the smile she had once known as well as her own still graced his face. "If you hadn't found me, if you hadn't come all this way, then you might have been with the army I just sent marching forth. And then who knows what might have happened to you?"

"Army?" Mel asked.

"I told you, Mel. I have given the builders dreams. And they see visions of conquest. I have filled their heads with thoughts of war, teaching them how to fight, shaping them into soldiers. And now they dream of a city watched over by a Shepherd, and the secret it guards at its heart," Yosef said, and his eyes turned to see the mountain and the Shepherd so far beyond the valley of the Colossus.

"Still, I do not think the Oshroarans will put up much of a fight. If you watch closely, you might be able to see their walls fall soon."

"What did you do?" Harmodias whispered.

"The new god is not yet finished. The body is taking shape, but the mind of god has produced some challenges. He has no thoughts yet himself, no ability to think. The Reverie has taken us far, but we will need a new domain to give our god a mind of his own." Yosef's mad grin stretched across his face, exposing his rotten teeth. "I have sent my army to the only tile that possesses the knowledge of how to do such a thing. I have sent them to find Cognition."

Gwen and Lina flew on the back of the great chiropt Clementine towards the Tile of the Colossus. They met the tile as the world shifted below them, the Tile of Lakes moving west across the surface of the planet as the Tile of the Colossus slid into place. They saw the Colossus from many miles away as the planet moved. It seemed to walk across the world, lunging forward to meet them.

Lina was nearest to the head of Clementine, flying the beast with deft touches. Gwen was further down the spine and acting as the co-pilot. It was their first flight since the disaster at Autumnmond, and the air between them seemed filled with poison.

"Vovatum save us," Lina said, breaking the silence as the wreckage of the Tile of the Colossus came fully into view.

"That thing is massive," Gwen said over the wind. "How long have they been building that?"

"Tough to say. This tile has never been friendly to the *Herald*. It fell off the paper's rotation some decades ago. Only reporters come here now, and rarely at that," Lina said back.

"There's dead letters here aren't there? Messengers died on this tile."

"Many, many times," Lina said, steering them towards the Colossus. The moon shone off its vast metallic skin, and it grew vaster as they drew closer. A tent city was in its shadow, yet there were no lights in that place. It looked abandoned.

"Lina, what is that?" Gwen said, indicating a river of fire that seemed to flow from the base of the immense statue. Lina steered them closer. They saw thousands of torches below, and holding the leaping lights were marching ranks of men and women in crude metal armor.

Gwen focused, opening her mind to the rush of information her senses were so desperate to provide. A halo of dull pink light appeared around her and the film rose from her eyes, creating the screen of Observation. Ahead she could see Lina doing the same thing.

The jolt of raw data sent a rush of pure electricity down her spine. The wind cut at her ears and lashed at her skin. The thumping heartbeat of Clementine seemed as loud as the footfalls of a giant. She could not focus her attention, and every sense deluged her brain with information until she felt she would drown beneath its weight. Lelial had taught her as quickly as he could, but she could only stand the full flow of Observation for a few seconds.

She tried to ignore everything but what her eyes were telling her. Her vision seemed to jump forward, zooming in until she could count the hairs on the chins of the men below. The armor of the soldiers below was crude and made in great haste. Great rivets lined the shoulders and the sides while the chest and back looked like the split faces of metal barrels. The helmet was a crude disc. Only some of the soldiers had armor on their arms and legs. But their swords were sharp and many.

"An army, but a ramshackle one," Lina said.

"Look at their eyes," Gwen responded.

The soldiers' faces were blank, devoid of expression or thought, but their eyes were fixed points of darkness that did not reflect the lights of the torches. Each had their gaze fixed ahead, not deviating or shifting for even a moment. And they marched as one being, stepping and moving like the arms and legs of the same colossal creature.

The data kept rushing in, and each flood of information felt like another dagger stabbed into her mind. With a shudder she shut off Observation. Ten seconds, she had managed to last for ten seconds. She was getting better.

"Drones?" Lina asked, her voice as soft as possible to not aggravate her migraine.

"Is such a thing even possible?"

"I've witnessed a battle or two from Clementine, and I've never seen such a thing, nor an army so unified. They move like automatons."

"Where are they going?"

"The Shepherd's Tile is closest, but that would be suicide. The entire tile is protected by Guardians, massive stone statues that serve the city of Oshroar. They've never been defeated in thousands of years. I can't even remember the last time someone was stupid enough to try to fight them," Lina said as he turned Clementine to face the direction the army was heading. A city protected in the shadow of a massive stone statue.

"So what should we do? Should we follow the army or fly straight to the Colossus?"

"Your mission, your orders. Lelial made it very clear that I'm just your ride."

Gwen looked once more at the army far below them before turning to face the Colossus. A hum seemed to come from the depths of the creature, scratching at her trained senses. This was the cause of the strange turning of the tiles.

They could land Clementine on the thing and explore, figure out what properties the statue had that made it so unique. Such information would be valuable to her new partner, and perhaps even the *Herald* itself.

But what would such a powerful thing need an army for? Where were the soldiers of the Colossus marching off to tonight and what did they hope to gain?

"We follow the army," Gwen said. "They're marching off to their deaths for a reason. Lelial would want to know why."

"The boy, Joshua, he dreamed of this place, didn't he?" Lina said, her voice as hollow as the massive Colossus. "This is where he vanished."

"Yes," Gwen said, but the voices in her head did not let the boy's name linger in her thoughts. They pecked at it until it ran away.

"If we follow the army, maybe we will see him again," Lina said, turning around to look at Gwen. The older girl's face was forlorn and imploring, and Gwen could see the idea for the peace offering it was.

"It isn't our mission," Gwen said, and Lina shrank back as if stung. With a press of her toes into Clementine's back, Lina sent them winging off for the Shepherd's Tile. Below them the metal soldiers of the Colossus builders marched in perfect lockstep.

Chapter 24: The Detective's Truth

I am a killer. I have blood upon my hands. If you find me, I fear you will no longer recognize me. I do not recognize myself.
(Letter 23, Paragraph 1, Lines 1 - end)

There was an army outside the walls of Oshroar. It had arrived in the night, two days after Finley had watched a Guardian kill a Broken Ring member. One night the city had slept as the tiles turned, and in the morning, they found an army clad in rough steel outside the gates.

The people of Oshroar threw a party. Color exploded from every street corner. Banners of red, and azure, and verdant green were thrown from roof to roof until the streets were cloaked in colorful shadows.

Children scampered amongst the sunlight in the packed streets of the town. The street vendors threw open the larders of the city, which the Guardians always kept filled to the brim. Food seemed to burst from every street corner: roast corn with blueberry syrup, towering cakes packed to the bursting with cream and fruit, bull and bison carcasses spinning on massive spikes that any citizen with a knife could carve into. Grease, fat, and sugar dripped from the faces of the people of Oshroar.

Guardians stood at attendance all around, eager to fulfill the people's slightest wish. Citizens capered around them, requesting to be carried to a different spot at the festival or lifted to the balconies above, where the parties spilled out of the homes of the revelers. The Guardians obeyed without questioning, lifting and carrying, cleaning and pulling, watching and listening. Towering over the buildings, the Construction Guardians continued work without slowing to build the city higher.

Finley stood in the shadows with Moro and Marlowe. He was still wearing his gray suit which had not been washed in five days. He looked at home in the ragged thing. Sleep was a distant memory, and even the floating Ghostlight at his shoulder was now a creature of grays and dull whites, matching its partner's mood.

"This is disgusting. They throw a party when an army is at their doorstep. They haven't even closed the gates," Finley spat.

"What do you expect? The Guardians have protected us for thousands of years. There's no need to worry," Moro said. She did not seem to share the same joyousness as those on the street, however.

"When was the last time the city was under siege?"

"A few hundred years at least. The sieges never last for long. The Guardians will assemble in a few hours and see them on their way. It will be quite an event," Moro said, indicating the crowd which had begun to dance and sway as one as a group of singers began an out of tune ditty from one of the balconies.

"So they'll just get drunk as the enemy digs trenches?"

"Aye, I expect they will. If it helps, we posted a double watch of wardens by the gate."

"It really doesn't," Finley said. He sprang away from the wall and made for the long winding stairs that would take them to the top of the city's walls.

"How come Orsos isn't even worried about this? You'd think a mad tyrant would be a tad concerned about an army intent on conquering."

"He has his own issues to contend with. He's been locked in with the council for the last two days. I expect they're skinning him alive for arresting the boltheads and for the mad Guardian disaster."

"I say he deserves that. Any more crowds outside the headquarters lately?" Finley asked, his legs pumping as they climbed the hundreds of steps that led up the wall. He could hear the army now, the vast clanking thing that sat only hundreds of yards away.

"None. The festival seems to have calmed their mood, funnily enough. Parties are so much more interesting than protests."

"So that's why Orsos is okay with this. It keeps the people nice and docile. Think he has more mass arrests up his sleeve?"

"Who's left to arrest? No, he'll have to find someone else to pin the blame on for Gaspar's death," Moro said. Unlike Finley she moved up the stairs without strain, even catching him if he stumbled or slipped. Finley looked back at her. Her face was washed, and her eyes were rested. The scars on her face were starting to heal. He felt a surge of jealousy at her ability to shrug off those deaths, and the ones that were to come.

He pounded his feet into the stairs, welcoming the thud of leather on stone. Every beat, every labored breath, was a way to dull the sound that had lingered in his head for two days. The sharp crunch of bone under solid stone fingers.

Is that what Huck's death had sounded like?

"You said mad Guardian disaster. I think you mean murder. A Guardian murdered Gaspar; we watched it happen."

"I didn't see that," Moro said. "I saw a confused Guardian, one that was tricked or coerced into killing that cleric by a member of the Broken Ring. An industrial accident, perpetrated by a terrorist, undoubtedly the same one that had been offing the Guardians."

Finley whirled on her. The city hung beneath her, stretched out like a canvas. It seemed to move as one vast animal as the party wound its way through the streets. "You don't believe that. You can't believe that. It killed him, and then it tried to kill me. And then, AND THEN, after we escaped our killer and cornered our only suspect, our Warrior Guardian went nuts and killed him. That was no accident, it was a coverup."

"It was justice. He was a mad man. You saw it. He welcomed his own death. Just another crazy bolthead with an axe to grind that somehow figured out how to trick Guardians. And who maintains the Guardians? The Crooken. Gaspar was just unlucky enough to be his target. And Hawksbill saw to it that he was punished for it. Now it's over. We caught the killer. Congratulations."

"You have a funny idea of what justice is. That just sounds like the neat and tidy explanation, not the real one."

"But it's the official one, Finley. It's the one that keeps the city from tearing itself to pieces. A bolthead somehow tricked a Guardian. The bolthead is dead, the Guardian was destroyed by Hawksbill. Neat and tidy."

"I don't believe for a moment that he was really a bolthead. He said god was coming, and as far as I can tell the boltheads have no god."

"You're looking for logic in the ramblings of a murderer. You can stop looking."

"But I can't, can I? We were this close, Moro. Gaspar was about to give us everything. He was going to tell us what Cognition is, and why people are willing to kill to get it. He said there were other parties in the city hunting for it, and right as he was about to reveal all he knew someone brought stones down on his head.

340

"And that someone, Kazacz, did things no one should be able to do. I watched him take command of Guardians that haven't harmed anyone in centuries. I watched Gaspar turn into a smear of paste! And I watched the killer's own head disappear right before he could confess his crimes.

"Killed by Hawksbill, something that cannot kill! That's not an industrial accident. That's not the action of some random serial killer or an out-of-control Guardian. It's something far more sinister.

"It's no coincidence that both Gaspar and Kazacz died before they could reveal the whole picture. Someone silenced them both and used the Guardians to do it."

"Are you suggesting that Hawksbill was used by this so-called conspiracy? Finley, you told me Hawksbill saved your life. You would have been a crater just like Gaspar if not for that Guardian."

"I don't know why it saved me. But it sure did a hell of a job cleaning up the scene of the crime. First it destroys the construction Guardian, the weapon, and then it kills our only suspect. Who told it to do that?"

"Guardians do not kill. It doesn't matter who told it to do so. It simply can't happen."

"You saw it happen!" Finley shouted.

"Just because I saw it happen, does not mean it is allowed to be possible. Stone cannot kill," Moro said, her voice flat and lifeless, her eyes refusing to meet his own as she delivered the party line.

"And stone can't move or think either, but the whole city seems to have got real used to that idea," Finley said, his voice shaking with anger. "And it turns out there are people that can make them kill, aren't there? Why haven't the wardens done anything? They need to round up the Guardians and put them in storage for our own safety. Any moment now they could fall under the spell of conspirators—"

"What conspirators? We have no proof of that."

"—or even worse," Finley said, interrupting her, "Maybe there are no conspirators as you've said. Maybe the Guardians killed on their own. Maybe they're the threat."

"Now you sound like the Broken Ring."

"Good, because they seem to be the only ones making sense right now. Either the Guardians can kill when they want, or someone has

341

found a way to trick them into killing whomever they like. In either case, that secret is precious enough that their agents are willing to kill their own in order to prevent the truth from being known." Marlowe spun around him, but no color shone from its depths. It circled Finley like a faintly glowing moon, a thing of grays and blacks.

"And who knows how long they've been working in the shadows? You heard what Kazacz said. 'Accidents happen.' Whose accidental death started all this mess? What if Evy Homme was murdered?"

"Marsh, calm down. There are people around you," Moro said, eying the group of wardens that stood at attention atop the main gate of the city. Finley could see their eyes flicking towards him, but he did not care.

"Oh, who cares? They should listen, some of them might survive if they listen! They need to know what's coming, since neither you nor I know how to stop the next Guardian that decides our heads would be better used to paint the walls. Why aren't we doing anything?"

"Marsh—"

"We need to do something. I need to do something!" Finley was roaring now, his hands pulling at his filthy suit. "We can't fail him!"

"Orsos? Finley, he doesn't care what—"

"Not him. Huck! I can't fail him again!"

"Who the hell is Huck?"

Finley sat down on the steps. His muscles shook with exhaustion and his eyes seemed like they were filled with lead. Even thinking had become difficult, as if he had to drag each thought through the mud.

There were no answers to his questions. There was nothing that could stop those things from happening. There was nothing he could do to help his friend. It had been foolish of him to even try. Armies, monsters, and murderers. Who was he in all that mess?

Just a fool.

"Marsh, Orsos can't do any of those things," Moro whispered to him; her face twisted with concern. "To acknowledge anything as more than an accident would upend the whole city. It would send us back to the stone age. We need the city to be calm. We need the city under control. We can chase after this idea of yours if you want, but we have to be the only ones. And in case you haven't noticed, we still have larger problems." She nodded to the army beyond the walls.

342

"Ah yes," Finley said, and his voice sounded alien even to his ears, riddled with forced joviality. "How could I have forgotten?"

He forced himself to stand and walk to the edge of the wall. The wardens were still looking at him.

"Gentlemen," Finley said, welcoming them to the edge as if he himself had built the wall. The wardens glanced at each other in confusion before beginning a patrol to the other side of the gate. Moro stood at Finley's side. They were alone, just them, the flower, and the army beyond.

"They seem ragged," Finley said.

"Yes. Almost as if they got dressed in the dark," Moro said, desperate to bring the conversation away from dangerous waters. The army indeed lacked the uniformity that Finley expected from an enemy horde. Many were clad in full iron armor, large clanking suits that had started to glow as the sun rose higher and higher. However, most of the army wore only a ramshackle half plate. Some wore no armor at all and were clad in the rags of a workman. Their weapons were another matter.

All clutched the spears that seemed to be this army's standard. The spears were jagged things, long poles crowned with iron fragments that had been hammered into lethal points. They were spears meant not for stabbing but for tearing. And though the sun rose higher and higher, and the sweat poured off Finley in his light suit, these soldiers' stance never wavered. They stood stock still in the plains before the city, and their spears moved not one inch.

"They look like they're dead," Moro said. "No human being can be that still."

"Huck was super into wargames. Begged me to play them with him all the time. I'm no genius, but they don't seem ready for a siege. No cavalry, no engineers, no siege towers, no battering rams, nothing. A whole army of infantry, even the world's best infantry, can't break into a locked city with good stone walls. What are they planning?"

"Maybe they're hoping we leave the gate unlocked."

"I honestly wouldn't put it past the pack of partying buffoons."

"Buffoons?"

"It's another word for an idiot on my world. It's like a type of clown."

"Ah, fits then."

"We really need to sit down and find out what insulting words from my world mean nothing here. I would love to be able to call someone an idiot without them knowing."

"Wouldn't that take away some of the fun of it?"

"But we would know," Finley said, cracking a smile despite his foul mood. It felt invasive as it pulled across his skin. He saw Moro put on a wan smile beside him. She was a granite pillar of a woman, and he was fairly sure she hated him, but Finley could not help but like her. Maybe it was because she was the only one besides the flower who hadn't tried to kill him since he landed in this place.

"You know I really wanted to do it. Solve the mystery I mean. Crack the case, catch the bad guy, prove how smart I was and how stupid everyone else was. I wanted to be clever," Finley said.

"Why is that? Why the need to be so clever?"

"I really don't know. You might have guessed that I'm not really a detective."

Moro's face did not shift.

"I know, I know. I seem to be a natural at it. But I've actually always wanted to be a kindergarten teacher," Finley said, seeing them now, the army before him being replaced by his little crayon eaters. He grinned, and for the first time in days this one felt real.

"That whole job is about making them feel smarter than you, about making them feel like they're special, and that the world has secrets worth knowing and that we can learn them together." The flower twisted around Finley; its gray light almost washed away by the rising sun. It looked almost like Finley had originally found it, just another light among many, and him having no idea he had just met his best friend in the whole world.

"Finley," Moro said, drawing his attention away from the Ghostlight and from his memories.

"I think it's because I'm scared, and I don't want anyone to know that," Finley said, and the truth tasted peculiar on his tongue, like the aftertaste of a half-forgotten fruit. "I twist before you can see how frightened I am. I mock before you can notice I'm shaking. And I try to disguise the fact that I really have no idea what I'm doing or what the hell is happening. I mean, I woke up on an alien planet and tried to solve a murder. Talk about avoiding your problems," he said, giving a dull chuckle just to fill the silence after he spoke.

"You still might solve a murder. We can help this 'Huck' person you keep mentioning."

"Nah, we're done. I failed Huck again, but at least I'm getting good at it.

"The city has bigger problems now. Whoever the killers are, they know we got close, that we had one of their own in our hands for just a second. If they have any sense, they'll use the chaos of the siege to slip away. And that that will be that. The army will get defeated, Orsos will punish his prisoners, and who knows what will happen to me, or to Marlowe. Maybe they'll put us in a circus. Do you have those? Don't you think I'd make a good buffoon?" Finley said, turning to Moro in the hopes she would correct him. But she wasn't looking at him, she was looking at the army beyond.

"How would they slip away with an army at the door?"

"Moro, I don't know, maybe in disguise or something. I mean all it would take is some old iron somewhere…"

Finley stopped. Marlowe spun once around him before it saw he had stopped moving. It ground to a halt in front of Finley's face. He gazed past it, looking with awe at the army beyond, the cloud of fear and of self-loathing that had cloaked him falling away. Above and in front of him the Ghostlight Marlowe shifted colors. The gray melted away, becoming a rising sun of pure and brilliant blue.

"No siege engines," he said, stunned with himself. "Dead statues. Dead Informants. State secrets. This isn't a murder mystery."

"Marsh, what are you talking about?"

"I am such an idiot!" Finley cried, and above him the Marlowe gave a flash of truthful blue. "We were looking for the wrong thing. Those weren't random murders. This wasn't some serial killer at work or even a conspiracy. It's spies."

"Spies?"

"This army didn't arrive by chance. It's here because the spies inside the walls succeeded in their mission. They know how to kill a Guardian, and how to kill with one. They've proved and perfected it." He thought of M. Tabor spread out like a map of the city, broken beyond repair. And then he remembered a much larger Guardian, one that almost broke him.

"No army could ever beat this city's Guardians through conventional means, so they sent in advance agents to figure out how to turn them off or how to make them turn on the citizens they are supposed to protect."

"So that Broken Ring member, he was one of these steel soldiers?"

"It makes sense, right? Gaspar said that there were hunters in the city all looking for the secret to Cognition. The killer struck right then, right before we could learn more about this shadow war. And then he killed himself, or someone else killed him to keep the secrets safe, to buy enough time before the army arrived."

"He said God was almost ready. Do you think he meant this army?"

"I can't be sure," Finley said, growing more and more excited as the connections erupted in his mind like fireworks. Every part of him sizzled with adrenaline, banishing the miasma that had gripped him.

"The boltheads are enemy spies? Orsos was right," Moro said, punching her fist into her palm.

"Not necessarily. You said the boltheads have been here for years. Maybe the spies have been here that long, or maybe it's just they infiltrated the group when they came to the city because they knew they were also trying to learn about Cognition."

"I think I see what you're getting at. This metal army, they sent in their agents to find out how to kill the Guardians, or even get them to turn on us. But how would they be able to do that? The Guardians are only supposed to obey Oshroarans, and they can't kill."

"I don't know. Maybe this is Cognition at work, or some other form of Cognitive Domain. Or maybe something else…" There was an image that floated through the fireworks of his excitement again and again. The spread-out body of M. Tabor, broken into pieces.

Why would the spies leave out evidence like that? What did they use to break the stones?

What did Huck have to do with any of this?

"What should we do now?" Moro asked, interrupting his train of thought.

"We need to find Orsos. Where is he?"

"With the council still," Moro said, turning away from the army to the city behind them. Finley turned with her, and together they saw the city light up as the sun began to set in the west. Every light was burning, every window was open, and every person was on the streets. And they were all moving the same way.

"What's happening?" Finley asked. The streets were filled with a shifting river of color as the crowds moved as one into the higher reaches of the city.

"They're heading to the temple district. The Guardians must be forming up, getting ready to leave the city to fight the invaders. The council will be there too."

"Then that's where we need to be. That's when the spies will strike. Let's go," Finley said, and with a burst of motion he rocketed down the steps, jumping from landing to landing in a great clatter. Moro thundered behind, her heavier tread threatening to ground the stones beneath them to dust. Marlowe raced above, giving off great flashes of blue light as they raced down into the city. It spun about them both, as giddy as a child.

It took an hour of exhaustive travel before they reached the temple district. Soaked in sweat, they burst into the square of the divines. The Shepherd loomed overhead, looking at them with its unreadable expression of fondness. People lined the rooftops and the spires of the temples, having ascended with the aid of the few Guardians that had not been made to assemble. More people choked the alleys and the avenues that led into the square, and many lined the outskirts of the square in the vast doorways of the temples.

Moro put her shoulder into a woman almost her size, sending the other woman spinning into the crowd. Finley saw the last rays of daylight in the gap and surged forward into the empty space beyond the crowd.

In neat rows, like bricks in a well-made wall, the Guardians of the city stood at attention. Though their eyes all glowed with the same green light, it was not until this moment that Finley realized how different they all were. They were as varied as the hues of the world. Guardians of smooth black basalt stood next to craggy granite statues, who stood next to jade giants that seemed to glow in the last lights of the setting sun.

347

Only the foremost ranks of the Guardians were uniform. The first hundred Guardians towered over the citizens that watched them. Their arms and legs were thick as pillars, their hands capable of crushing stone to powder. Jagged spikes decorated their shoulders and their heads.

The Warrior Guardians. Finley had never seen so many in the same place. Most never moved from their assigned spot in the city, their mere presence a discouragement for all disturbance. Yet he was intimately aware of what they were capable of, and the reason for that stood at attention not far from him and Moro.

Finley walked over, breaking the silence with the clicking of his shoes, shattering the empty space of the no man's land with his mere presence. Moro did not follow him, but Marlowe zoomed in his wake.

To his right, on a great dais constructed directly beneath the Shepherd, was the ornate council of the city. Sister Sinoh was at their head, her robes a glorious white, her eyes high and proud as she gazed at the assembled ranks of the Guardians. She seemed unaffected by the death of her servant Gaspar. Orsos stood in her shadow, the dark cloth of his uniform held tight against his rigid and straight-backed form. He clutched his arms behind his back.

Finley could feel the eyes turning to him as he walked through the empty, silent space with the Ghostlight at his side. Finley grinned, the last of his fear disappearing. At last, all eyes were on him.

Hawksbill was a full head and shoulders of stone taller than him and clad for war. The stone spikes along its shoulders seemed sharper than the other warriors and its eyes were a deeper and more dangerous green, like the scales of a venomous snake. Finley had watched those hands catch a stone fist twice his size, but now he saw it was not without cost. There were cracks along its forearms and down its wrists, as if the stone had fractured from the great weight, it had been forced to bear. Yet it stood at the front of the warrior Guardians in a position of command, ready to lead the creatures of stone in defense of their city.

Its green eyes met Finley's gray ones as he ambled closer. Marlowe floated behind him, looking with curiosity at the assembled army and the crowd beyond.

348

"Fancy meeting you here, Hawksbill. I had no idea you were a commander. I must say I feel honored that my own personal watchdog is so highly ranked, though I should not be surprised. After all, my partner and I are quite dangerous. I've noticed a distinct lack of thunderous footsteps these last few days, however. Wherever have you been? Were you suddenly concerned with larger game?"

Finley could see them out of the corner of his eye, the proud members of the city council, so eager to send this army to war, to give the city the celebration it craved after the chaos of the last days and nights. He could see Orsos surge forward, only to be halted by the outstretched arm of Sinoh.

"Keep an eye on them, buddy," Finley whispered to Marlowe, who zoomed to stand between him and the Council only dozens of feet away. He raised his voice.

"What were you chasing if not me? I think I know." He was shouting now, sending his voice ringing through the square. "You were after more of the boltheads. You were going to lock up more of our brothers and sisters based on the thinnest of lies. I ask myself, who do you really guard, if not the ones that hold your chains?" Finley said, sweeping his hands to the council's dais.

That ought to do it, he thought to himself.

And sure enough, here they came charging now. Orsos marched towards him flanked by two wardens. Behind him swept Sister Sinoh.

Finley waited for them to approach, relaxing from his showman's posture. "You saved my life that night," Finley said to Hawksbill over his shoulder. "I never had the chance to say thanks."

He turned to face Hawksbill, looking up into his glowing eyes. "Thank you, Hawksbill. I don't know if you did it because you wanted to, or because you were told to by Orsos. But in either case, you saved my life, and even more importantly, you saved Marlowe's here," Finley said, gesturing for Marlowe to join him, even as he heard the rapid footsteps of the approaching council. "Go ahead and say thank you, partner."

Marlowe spun forward, still shifting between the white light of a noon day sun, and the deep green of Guardian eyes. It floated around and around Hawksbill, seeming to hug the creature with trailing light, before coming back to rest once more on Finley's shoulder.

The sun had set, and the lights of the city burned bright in the moonless night. In the darkness, the assembled Guardians seemed to glow, their smooth stone reflecting the lit windows and blazing towers all around the square of the divines. Hawksbill seemed most radiant, lit as it was by the light of Special Detective Marlowe. In this new light, Finley's interest hooked on an indentation, larger than his fist, in the lower chest of Hawksbill.

"That Construction Guardian really did a number on you, huh?" Finley asked, his hand reached so that his fingers could trace the little crater. "That could have been my head. Good thing you were there to stop it." The shifting light revealed even more scars of battle along the arms and chest of Guardian, so that it looked like the surface of one of the moons.

"Really good thing. You Guardians can really do a number on each other," Finley said, thinking back to his first conversation with Gaspar. Marlowe gave a flash of red light from his shoulder, and he ducked before the grasping hand of Orsos could wrap around his shoulder.

"Ah, I'm glad you could make it. I would like a word, if you please."

"You shall have far more than a word from me, Marsh." Orsos growled. "Did you forget what we discussed when I released you from that hole in the ground?"

"I'm terribly sorry for interrupting your bread and circuses, Orsos, but I thought you might wish to know who's murdering all the Guardians."

"You're deranged, Marsh. You and your paranoid fantasies have done nothing but cause trouble. I think another few months in that hole would be best for you. For your own safety. I am ashamed to say I did not realize you were such an ill man," Orsos said, his voice dripping with false concern. "I'm afraid we will have to separate you from the Ghostlight. It seems to have adversely affected your mind."

"Touch Marlowe and I'll burn out your retinas."

"Hawksbill, please escort Mr. Marsh to the deepest cells in the Warden HQ. Chuck the Ghostlight in a jar or something."

"I can save your city!" Finley said, desperation breaking his calm facade. "You total ass, if you listen to what I've learned you might still have a city to mismanage. Lock me up and I'm sure you'll all join me soon. Or worse."

"What do you claim to know?" Sinoh had arrived, unruffled from her walk across the plaza. Streaks of red face paint marked her brow and her cheekbones. A necklace of old and broken wood decorated her slim neck. Orsos stilled as she spoke, his rage replaced by the cunning the Sister seemed to provoke in him.

"Only what you wanted me to discover. I know what is killing the Guardians," Finley said, gesturing to Moro to join them. "Gaspar gave us the key. His death was no industrial accident, as you both have claimed, but something far worse. He was murdered by the same people who have murdered the Guardians of this city. There are spies within the walls."

"Spies flourish like rats in a city under siege. It will make no difference what the invaders know or what they do not know. Stone can crush any head, even one filled with secrets," Orsos said, his voice once more relaxing into his curt tones of command.

"These are no normal spies. These ones have been here for a long time, and they know things even we don't know," Finley said, looking significantly at Sinoh, but her expression was unreadable beneath the heavy lines of her face paint.

"What are you implying?" she asked.

"Gaspar told me quite a bit before his murder. My partner was able to convince him that I really do mean no harm. I know what the Crooken are hunting for in the shadows. I am implying that our spies found it first."

"The Crooken? My, my, what have you been up to Sister Sinoh? If you are hunting something you need only ask. After all, one should never send a cleric to do a warden's job," he said, behind his back there was the crackle of popping joints and fingers as he cracked his knuckles.

"It is of no concern to you, Orsos. It is only more prattle from the madman. These spies you are inventing could only have been here for a few days at most. The turning tiles have not brought the Colossus and the Shepherd together in twenty years."

"Then that's how long they've been here."

Her lips curved into a condescending smile. "Oh my, you are new, aren't you? No one can predict the turning of the tiles, not in the coming days, weeks, or years. You are suggesting these invaders stranded their spies here for unknown decades, casting them like notes in a bottle into a storm-tossed ocean. Even the most desperate of enemies would not attempt such a thing."

"In case you haven't noticed, a couple impossible things have happened lately. Guardians cannot be murdered, yet so many have. Guardians cannot kill, yet I have seen them do so with my own eyes. The question becomes, who has brought about so many miracles? And then ask yourself, who profits most from all this chaos?"

"The boltheads are already in their cells, Marsh. It seems I caught your little spy ring a week ago."

"The boltheads were a distraction. They were the most tempting and most obvious target possible, and when the Guardians started to drop dead, you were only too happy to fall for the bait. Now we have a city on the edge of chaos. An army at the gates, disunion behind the walls, a defense that is cracking apart. It's the perfect time to strike, but there is one thing standing in the way," Finley said, gesturing to the stone army behind him. "Guardians are this city's only defense."

"If you wanted to take the city, you would need to knock out the Guardians," Moro added, standing beside Finley to present a united front.

"Or worse. The Guardian that attacked Gaspar was not confused; it was coerced. Our suspect, before he died, claimed that he had convinced it that the only way to help him, to guard him, was to kill who he wanted. And before we could get the rest of our answers another Guardian killed him. These are not accidents, these are not murders, these are acts of sabotage," Finley said, his voice cracking with the weight of his words. "Don't you understand? If they can kill Guardians, if they can convince them to kill whoever they want, then this city is lost. You must send the Guardians away, back into Shepherd or into the hills. They cannot go near the army or be around the citizens."

The face paint around Sinoh's eyes was peeling. Little scraps of red flaking off and fluttering through the air. Finley watched as one speck floated off her face, only for the movement of his breath to send it into her hair. Her eyes did not move from his, however. And they did not blink.

"You are mistaken. A Guardian cannot be murdered."

352

"How do you know?"

"Because we've tried," Sinoh said, and the words stunned Finley, but the Guardians behind him did not move at all.

"To find Cognition, you would do even that?"

"We would do anything at all. We have learned only one essential truth, a Guardian cannot be killed, cannot be broken by the hands of mortals. They are as the Shepherd designed them, eternal and unending."

"How do you explain the bodies in the morgue then?"

"You're the detective, Finley, not me. But they cannot be killed."

"But they can kill others, can't they?" Orsos asked, his voice ragged and broken. "Is this what happened to my daughter? One of these spies murdered her?"

"It's possible," Finley said. He watched as the thought shattered Orsos. His jaw quivered, shaking like loose bricks during an earthquake. "There is no way of knowing what these spies have done unless we catch them. And the only way to do that is disrupt their plan. Send the Guardians away, and we can find them."

"Orsos, do not let this man inside your head. Spies that can do things not even our most adept clerics can do? A conspiracy of impossible scale and depth decades in the making? These are the ramblings of an ill man."

"I will not let what happened to Evy ever happen again. Make them go back to the mountain," Orsos rumbled, his voice calm even as his face jumped with anger.

Moro's broad hand clapped Finley on the shoulder, jolting him forward. She smiled at him, ruffling his hair with the other hand. "Good work, Detective."

"Special Detective."

He rubbed the bruise that was already forming from the hard-hitting woman's love tap. Already the wardens were forming up under Orsos's orders, moving to stand before the Warrior Guardians and give their commands. The crowd seemed to have remembered they were in the middle of a party. The drums rumbled out a beat, and Finley could hear a dance start to form.

And then the drums multiplied. New beats struck through the air, and they soon deepened, becoming a far heavier sound. It was the marching of iron feet and the slam of iron spears. It crashed over the city like a wave, sending ripples through the streets and down the alley ways. Men and women dropped their bottles and clutched at their ears. Screams shot through the air, barely heard over the din.

Finley turned, and he could see the army beyond sway like a field of wheat in a wind. Up the spears rose, and down they thundered. And the crash of their din assaulted the senses of Oshroar like a song from god.

There was the scrape of stone on stone, and Finley heard a scream of agony. He spun around.

A granite Warrior Guardian had a warden by the arm, and Finley watched the bones crumple under the weight of its stone fingers. The man screamed, beating at the Guardian with his free fist. Yet the creature did not release him. Instead, it quivered, shaking so hard that dust rose from its shoulders.

Another scream echoed down the line. Finley saw that this Guardian had stomped on a leg, pinning the warden beneath it with terrible force. Yet it did not move to finish the job. The Guardians near these two attackers turned, reaching with outstretched stone hands to stop their brethren, but they moved like underwater swimmers, each movement seeming to take a tectonic age.

All around the Guardians had sprung into jolting motion. Some shook like rung bells. Some were posed as if to strike the people around them, stone fists inches from flattening them. None were still, and though their faces did not move, Finley could see that they fought against themselves.

Finley turned. Hawksbill alone had not moved. It stood before its quivering army; an army that seemed compelled to lash out at the people around them but fighting against this order with every speck of rock in them. Finley met its burning eyes. Its hands rose, as slow as a glacier, to its own head.

"Marlowe, what's happening?" Finley whispered.

The Ghostlight floated up, resting on the head of Hawksbill. It tucked itself above its ear, the way a child would tuck a dandelion in his hair.

An image appeared in Finley's mind. It was a man with broken teeth and mad eyes. His skin was paper thin and stained with ink. He seemed to be at the very highest point in all the world. His voice was horrifyingly familiar to Finley as he whispered to him, spilling poison into his ear.

"The only way to guard them is to hurt them," the man said, his voice light and reasonable, the voice of a favorite teacher. "They are disobedient cattle and must be disciplined. This is the only way to keep them safe. Hurt them. Break them. Open the gates. Let the army in. Guard them from themselves."

His voice washed over Finley, and his hands seemed to move on his own, clenching into fists. He wanted to hurt people, but only to keep them safe. It was so clear now. The sheep had gotten out of line. Look at them, partying in the streets, hurting themselves with frivolity. They would be safer in their cages. They would be safer after they were punished. The thought had obsessed him for days, running through his memories and his dreams.

He longed to follow them. But he hesitated.

Why did he hesitate?

Those weren't his thoughts, Finley realized. The false voice melted away, leaving raw horror in its wake. These weren't his memories.

They were Hawksbill's.

He snapped out of the trance, looking at the cracks that danced across Hawksbill's skin. They were the crevices left by the colossal fist of the Construction Guardian, and all at once Finley knew what was about to happen.

"No one can kill the Guardians. Only you can do that," Finley breathed out, the realization pouring through him like ice water.

The stone statue's hands were still moving, coming to rest at its temples and along the curve of its skull. Its stone fingers prodded Marlowe, who drifted away. Hawksbill's eyes had not left Finley's own. Its hands stopped moving. A shiver ripped its way up its body.

"No, wait—" Finley cried, but Hawksbill could not be stopped. Its stone fingers pressed into its own skull, burrowing through the rock that was its skin. The terrible whine of a grindstone echoed even over the drums as its stone nails dug its way through its own head. The light in its eyes flickered and dimmed.

It froze, looking for once like what it was, simply another stone statue.

And then, with terrible slowness, it tumbled into pieces. All that Hawksbill was, after centuries of guarding and protecting, lay in a little pile at Finley's feet. The clatter of stones filled the square, and Finley ripped his eyes away to see Guardian after Guardian digging into the crown of their skulls, shutting their own lives off.

With a shudder of horror Finley realized what was happening.

The Guardians were corrupted. Reprogrammed to help the invaders, to hurt the citizens.

And the Guardians were protecting the people of Oshroar the only way they could.

By removing the greatest possible danger.

The Guardians themselves.

Statue after statue crumbled, and the horrified populace of Oshroar looked on as the eternal turned to dust.

Finley looked back at the pile that was once the face of Guardian Hawksbill. He looked for the light in the eyes of the creature that had saved his life, first from another Guardian, and then from itself.

Even in the light of the Ghostlight, he could not find it.

Chapter 25: The Dreamer's Battle in the Clouds

The inhabitants of the Tile of the Shepherd tell stories about an afterlife. It is guarded, fittingly, by little glowing flowers they call Ghostlights. These spirits act as shepherds to the veil beyond, though what life is like in such a place is a mystery to them. All they know, all they hope, is that the final journey is not a lonely one.
(Letter 24, Paragraph 1, Lines 1-3).

Harmodias's fingers lit up with purple light, sending her shadow careening off the top of the great Colossus. Her Sheosirran brothers and sisters, frail though they were, seemed to become hale and hearty as the lights of the Reverie washed over them. Their gnarled fingers moved with the grace of dancers as they twisted and formed the runes of Reverie.

The dreaming world formed at their feet. Tufts of glowing grass sprouted from cold iron. Flowers of acid green and pure black rose into life, shifting in the breeze. The songs of extinct birds and sleeping animals rang out as the Reverie spilled from the Sheosirrans, lighting the world like a dream of the sun.

Bright splashes of color burst into being on the neck of the Colossus. Trees flickered into life, forming around the Sheosirrans like nature's own army as they bore down on the Revered Engineer Yosef League with dreams in their clenched fists.

But he was their equal. With a soft smile, and without moving a muscle, he called his own dreams to life. His own light was a dimmer and darker purple compared to the Sheosirrans, like a color that had been locked away from the sun. Yet it burst forth from him like a geyser.

And where his light touched, nature could not cling. Steel became stronger and denser. Rivets multiplied and hardened. The iron beneath their feet shone like a mirror. The thunder of hammers rolled, and the groan of metal joined the crescendo. And Mel recognized the dream at once. It was a dream of their own mechanized world.

The fresh paintings of the Sheosirrans met his own light and broke like a wave upon the rock. The space in between glowed with hot white light, and the air seemed to crack and shake as the competing dreams battled for dominance over the waking world.

But Mel had her own problems to attend to. The architects strolled towards her, their white robes snapping in the wind. They drew their thin swords and each one seemed to point at one of her eyes.

"Shame. I seem to have forgotten to bring my sword," Mel said, fingering the pouch at her waist and gripping her fist around her weapon. "But don't worry, I found some of my tools on the way up."

She leveled the long iron shovel at the advancing warriors. She could see the cold amusement bloom on the architects' faces as they eyed her own weapon.

Mel's own fierce smile grew wider still. Yosef had given her an idea. She let her mind drift, so that the barest hint of the song of the Colossus caressed her thoughts. It was no longer a lullaby but a war march. And all at once new thoughts surged into her head, dreams that only a warrior could have, and now she knew what to do.

One hand kept a grip on the handle of her shovel, the other went to the pouch at her waist. She grabbed the smooth metal orbs inside, dozens of them fitting inside the palm of her hand. She tossed them in front of her, scattering them like a farmer scatters seed.

The ball bearings spilled onto the skin of the Colossus, colliding and careening off each other until the skull of the giant was littered with them like fresh fallen snow.

The first architect stepped forward, slipping into a killing stance, only for her left foot to shoot out from under her. She slipped, her stance going wide, until she seemed in the middle of a perverse dance. Her sword slipped out of position, and Mel struck.

She leapt forward, stepping with the deftness of a builder working in the careening winds. She brought the shovel's edge down onto the hilt of the woman's blade, stabbing into the meat of the architect's hand with its blunt edge. The woman cried in pain but kept the sword up even as her hand spouted blood.

The other killer lunged forward but had to avert his step to avoid landing on the spinning ball bearings. Mel dodged the sword thrust, using the pommel of the shovel to turn the blade away. With the same motion she spun the shovel up again and brought its heavy iron head down at the base of the falling architect's blade. The thin metal shattered, sending shards of sword into the forest of ball bearings. She brought the wooden handle up in a savage swing that took the

358

architect across the face, sending him spinning and slipping across the skin of the Colossus, unconscious.

Mel leapt away. She spun the shovel around her, twirling it like a baton. The last architect looked at her aghast. The amusement had left her eyes.

Mel slammed the shovel, headfirst, down onto the metal skin of the Colossus.

"You know what's funny? I didn't know how to do any of that a few days ago. Guess I absorbed some of the weapon lessons Yosef sent into his brainwashed army on my walk up. Or maybe he just likes me and hates you." She scattered more of the ball bearings in front of the architects. She brought the shovel before her, looking past the iron blade. "Why'd you stop laughing?"

A bird made of fluttering dreams fell out of the sky in front of them, its brittle bones cracking against the cold steel of the statue. It was made of kaleidoscopic light, stitched together from the thoughts of slumbering creatures, but as it died it cried just like a real bird. A sliver of Yosef's dream rolled over it, and the bird turned into unfeeling steel, its plaintive cries coming to a halt.

Mel turned. Harmodias and Yosef were feet from each other, the Sheosirrans ringed around them but unable to get closer. Harmodias's face was wrecked with strain, her unseeing eyes weeping blood as she threw the weight of her dreams against the Revered Engineer. He smiled at her as his own thoughts grew through the dreams of the Sheosirrans like malignant tumors.

Where his attention turned a wave of petrifying metal flowed. It shot through the trees, creating ribbons of iron that riddled them like veins. It added weight to the birds, bringing them crashing to the ground. The wind filled with smoke and the groan of shifting metal.

But one of the dreamers had not yet joined the chorus. He stood near the edge of the great statue looking at the battle taking place. Mel watched as he curled his little hands into fists before going to join his great grandmother.

"Cisseus, no! Get back here," Mel cried, but the boy did not look at her. She began to race towards him, but the last architect stepped in front of her.

The woman raised her sword and stabbed at Mel's heart. With a curse, Mel ducked away. She brought her shovel up, and she and the architect exchanged a whirlwind of blows. The ground around them was still littered with ball bearings and shards of broken sword, every step a danger.

Mel snarled at the woman, bringing the shovel down again and again.

The architect parried with a dancer's grace, and her blade leaped into the gaps in Mel's defense.

Mel felt white fire lick across her arm as the blade cut her bicep, and then the fire shot across her thigh, and then her stomach. Blood leaked down her hands and onto the pommel of the spinning shovel.

She was better than Mel, far better. The dreams of conflict in her head could not compete with a lifetime of training.

Mel had to act!

Mel lunged forward, hoping with all her heart to land on solid ground. She pressed ahead as the woman's blade slashed her stomach. Mel roared with pain and with anger, thrusting the shovel like a spear into the chest of the other woman. She heard something crack in the architect's chest, and the woman stumbled back. With a shout of surprise her foot caught one of the ball bearings and she stumbled. But even as she fell, she pulled the blade down Mel's side, cutting down the line of her hip.

Roaring in pain, Mel raised the shovel high before bringing it down, flat first, on the woman's face. There was a crack as the architect's head collided with the Colossus below.

Mel turned, dragging herself forward, her weapon falling from her numb fingers, but her blood ran cold when she saw she was too late. Cisseus had entered the circle, ducking beneath the outstretched hands of the dreamers until he stood beside his great grandmother and the Revered Engineer.

Yosef's attention flickered to the boy, but his steel gaze had no effect on Cisseus. The boy's slender hands started to glow with purple light, and as his hands formed the shapes of his words he stepped into the Reverie and spoke aloud.

"Grandfather, this has to end," Cisseus said, and the wind came at his call. Its howls drowned out all other sounds, even the cries of Mel as she begged him to stop.

It roared and roared, a voice fit for a giant, a voice fit for a god, but not for a boy. Not for a little boy, powerful and free, but only in his dreams.

The steel of Yosef's thoughts shattered, breaking like falling glass. Underneath was only the real iron skin of the Colossus, far meaner and cruder than the perfect thoughts that Yosef had laid atop it like armor. His own broken light shrank until it was little more than the glow of a flickering candle. Yosef slumped back in his wheelchair, his hands resting in his lap. He smiled at his grandson, and nodded his approval.

Sunflowers of green and blue light sprouted from underneath the youngest Sheosirran's feet. They rose until they stood higher than him, watching his back like a royal guard. But the look on the boy's face was far from kingly. His eyes were hooded, his mouth pulled into a frown.

"Cisseus," Yosef said, and Mel could hear it now, the familiar cadence of the boy's voice wrapped around the spines of his grandfather's words. "Cisseus, I am so proud of you. Your dreams are so strong. Far stronger than mine, and even your great grandmother's.

"I wish Calliope was here to see them. She would have been so proud. All she ever heard you do was cry. And now here you are building worlds with your words. But tell me, do you even remember her?"

The boy did not speak.

"I remember everything. She saved my life, and now every moment with her is lodged in me like a dagger. She was kind beyond words. Her thoughts were as delicate as sunbeams, but stronger than the bones of the earth. Whole cultures owe their stories and mythology to her, for she alone kept those dreams alive in the Reverie, even after all trace of them had been wiped from Poa. So of course they killed her."

Cisseus did not move, his face as blank as a doll's. The sunflowers curled around him, clasping him close as if to protect him from the man's words.

"They killed your father and mother with her, Cisseus. Do you remember them either? Do you even understand what I am doing here, boy? I have built us a new god that owes us his very life. He will make this world right, a place where no little boy will ever again have to lose his family. It is the only way we have left to love the ones we've lost. Will you help me do it?"

Mel had fallen to her knees. Her head was as light as a soap bubble, her body filled with lead, growing colder moment by moment. But she could not stop, could not let herself slip away again. She dragged herself forward, leaving a trail of blood on the iron.

Cisseus did not see her, was still looking at the wreck of his grandfather whose eyes burned with superhuman passion. The boy moved his lips, and they shaped the word "No."

Yosef smiled at him with his broken teeth. "Ah, it seems there's a bit of me in you after all. Only a grandchild of mine could be that stubborn."

"It's over, Yosef. Release the people you have under your thrall, or we'll shatter your mind to do it," Harmodias said, her body shaking with exhaustion, blood still dripping down her face like tears.

"It was cruel to bring my grandson to stop me. Very cruel. I'm impressed."

"Release them, Yosef," Harmodias spat.

"Parents like us must always be ready for our children to surpass us, don't you agree? And I am fortunate that both my grandson and my son have," Yosef said, his eyes never leaving Cisseus's face.

"Son?" Harmodias whispered.

"But my son is stronger by far. For though he is not yet fully alive he dreams just like you or I. Except his dreams are perfect," Yosef said, and he broke his gaze from his grandson to look at his creation.

And Mel heard it before she saw it. It was the groan of shifting iron, the rumble of metal plates shifting, the thunderous metallic echo of eyes shifting in their sockets.

Above the unfinished neck of the statue, above the still unthinking body of the Colossus, there were a pair of luminous eyes. They shone in the empty space in the statue's head like lighthouses in the darkness. And as the great eyes shifted to look at them, the Sheosirrans started to collapse.

Chapter 26: The Detective's Siege

...For what is this place if not an afterlife? And what does it say of such a land if we come here only to find that our friend is still dead. Calliope is gone, killed by those that never knew her worth. And you, my friends, are either gone yourselves or were never here at all. I have buried far too many, and everyone I have ever loved has left me here in Poa. But I tire of being a victim. This is a godless, unholy land. And I believe I finally have the solution.

(Letter 24, Paragraph 3, Lines 1-9)

Moro grabbed Finley's hand, tugging him away from the broken body of Hawksbill, but he could not look away from the creature's corpse, even as the city erupted into chaos around them.

Fear galloped through the choked alleyways and thoroughfares of the city, crushing the citizens of Oshroar beneath its hooves. Some screamed and ran, fleeing from the scenes of carnage in the great square. They screamed until they seemed like hollow people, filled with nothing but endless noise. And wherever they ran they spread their panic like a plague.

Others had fallen to their knees, as lifeless as puppets with cut strings. Finley could hear them calling all around him, but not for their loved ones. Instead they cried out commands to the broken Guardians. They order them to stand. They commanded them to pick themselves up, to lurch to their feet, to make the world make sense again.

But the stones did not move. The commands grew louder, and then louder still, until they warred in the air with the screams of the others. And when the people realized that the Guardians that had protected them would not obey ever again, they simply fell silent.

Finley preferred the screamers.

"Come on, we need to go," Moro roared at him, yanking Finley down the mouth of an alley. The stone walls of the buildings shook around them, dropping clouds of dust onto their heads.

"What was that?" Finley asked.

"Construction Guardian," Moro said, pointing to the sky above them. Finley saw a skyscraping Guardian collapsing like an avalanche onto the buildings below. It flattened a city block with its death throes and screams of pain joined the screams of panic in the sky.

363

"They're killing themselves. I can't believe they're killing themselves," Moro said, as she pulled Finley along.

"They made their choice. They had to pick between killing us or destroying themselves. Looks like they decided to guard one last time, the only way they knew how," Finley said. Marlowe floated next to them.

"All along, they were all self-destructions?"

"Marlowe helped me see inside Hawksbill's head. There's a voice inside their thoughts, one urging them to kill the people of the city, saying it's the only way to protect them. That must have been what that assassin meant when he said he spoke to them. They got inside their heads!"

"So they destroyed themselves rather than hurt us?"

"Yes."

"Oh," Moro said, her voice quiet and her face blank. Her stride stuttered for only a moment before she continued to lead Finley along, still never having let go of his hand.

"Where are we going?"

"Extraction point."

"What are you talking—" Finley started to say, only to stop as the grumble of an earthquake splintered the air. They turned as one and saw a pillar of stone leading into the chest of one of the massive Construction Guardians. It had fallen to its knees only a block away. One hand clutched its head, the other clawed at the ground, rattling the pavement all around. It smashed its great stone fist into the street, sending a column of dust into the sky.

The creature was in agony, trying its best to shut itself off, but the dream inside its head warred with it, begging it to destroy. The Guardian swept its hand out, shattering the buildings around it like toy houses.

"Run," Moro screamed. She raced ahead, letting go of Finley in favor of pumping her arms. The ground swelled beneath them, rolling like a wave as the Guardian drove its fist into the world.

Finley raced after her, trying to stay ahead of the shockwaves, but every step was calamity. He shuddered to the side, thrown into the face of one of the buildings as the ground reeled beneath him.

Behind, below the sounds of rock on rock, he heard the steady beats of metal on brick. He turned. Marching into the blasted wreck the dying Guardian had created were the iron soldiers of their enemy.

A phalanx of iron soldiers formed in front of the Guardian; a man clad in a coarse hairshirt at their head. The Guardian opened its mouth in a soundless roar and swept its fists across the front ranks. The steel of the soldiers shattered like cheap tin as they were sent careening into the sky.

Finley gave a horrified shout of alarm as the great stone fist of the dying Guardian swept inches over his head, before colliding into the brick home at his back. An explosion of force and noise caught Finley from behind as the house detonated from the impact.

It lifted him from his feet, wood and brick carrying him forward as he flew. He pitched onto his face, and he could feel his nose crack and bend to the side. Blood mixed with the dust caking his face, forming a mask of mud that started to drip into his throat. With a great hacking cough, he rose to his feet.

He stumbled ahead. Moro was not far beyond him. She turned to speak to him, but as she spoke a bubble of blood poured out of her mouth. Finley staggered towards her, his arms reaching out, grasping her sides and down her back, looking for the injury. He found it in her back on her right side, stabbed below her ribs. A shard of wood, propelled like a bullet, had lodged itself in her side.

"Don't speak," Finley said, his own voice choked by the blood in his throat and his cracked nose. He turned her around, scanning her for more wounds, but the shard was the only one.

"I can't pull it out. If I do you might bleed more," Finley shouted, trying to make himself heard over the battle behind them.

Moro patted his face, silencing him. She brought her finger to her lips.

"Need. Extraction. Quiet," Moro said, each word a labor. She tilted her head back, taking a deep shuddering breath. Finley watched, terrified more blood would come spilling out of her mouth, but something else rose from her throat. It was not the red of blood, but a gossamer purple. More and more spilled from her mouth, wrapping about her head like smoke, caressing her ears and eyes. And as more

365

spilled forth, the smoke became more substantial until it seemed to form a solid screen in front of her face and eyes.

"Herald. Bedlam. Break. Need. Extraction," Moro said, her voice peaking as she spoke, every word becoming quieter even as her face shook with strain. "Temple square," and then she paused, cocking her head as if listening to something on the wind. "Confirmed."

"What are you doing?" Finley asked.

"We need backup," Moro said, and now her words were a whisper, "take us back to the square. I can get us out. But we need to be there in five minutes."

"Okay," Finley said, desperate for details he could cling to, desperate for something in the world that made sense. "Okay, that's not far. Come on lean on me, we gotta start going."

Moro lurched onto him, collapsing her weight onto his right side. He slung his arm around her, careful not to disturb her wound.

Dust hung like a shroud before them, cloaking them from the searching eyes of soldiers and the desperate eyes of the screaming mob.

"Marlowe, we need some light, buddy," Finley said. But the darkness did not change. Finley craned his head, pulling at the jumping muscles in his neck as he searched behind them.

"Marlowe?" he asked, his voice little more than whisper.

"Marlowe?" he said again, almost shouting now.

"MARLOWE!" he roared, searching for the Ghostlight.

But there was no light drifting in the rolling dust. And as Finley dragged Moro back to the square, back to where he had last seen his ghostly partner, he added his own voice to the chorus of screams that rocked Oshroar.

Chapter 27: The Messenger's Decision

What killed him I wonder? What brought Huck to his end? We were all too scared to try to learn back on Earth. There was the secret terror that haunted us all that Huck had taken his own life. I walked these lands for decades with that thought, with that certainty, that my friend had done such a thing.

But now I look back at his final days and wonder.

(Letter 25, Paragraph 1, Lines 1-4, and Paragraph 2, Line 1)

Lina and Gwen rode on the back of the bat Clementine. The chiropt was highly trained, able to detect the minutest of changes that her pilots might make. But neither Lina nor Gwen moved as they watch the destruction of a city.

Oshroar was burning. Skyscrapers of stone glowed from within, smoke pouring forth from their gaping windows.

The citizens had lost their heads, and Gwen, with flashes of Observation she forced herself to endure, could see with her enhanced senses how in their mindless panic they tore the city further asunder. Granaries had been smashed open and the crowd had dived in, grabbing whatever scrap of food they could. The central bank in the center of the city was aflame, but it did not stop the citizens who rushed its windows and great iron doors, lunging for the last wealth in the city.

But more, far more, simply ran. They ran from the Guardians that flailed through the streets. They ran from the Guardians who pursued them from house to house, their stone arms reaching for bones to break.

Through the haze of her Observation, she saw the city tear itself apart, but she did not allow herself to feel it.

"How many troops do you see?" Gwen asked.

"Excuse me?" Lina said, jolted from her inspection of the city.

"We need to have every detail right when we report back to the *Herald*."

"Almost two hundred thousand."

"That's my estimation too. How many people are in the city?"

"About a million. They don't have a chance," Lina said, turning her enhanced gaze from the city to her. Her brow was furrowed, and her voice was as steady as an iron bar. "Gwen, we have to do something."

"We are doing something; we're learning everything there is to know here so that the paper can report on it," Gwen said, her eyes flashing from horror to horror, etching each scene into her memory, recording each scream on the wind.

"For what purpose? No one is going to stop this." Lina's hands clenched and Clementine shuddered beneath them. "There is no one to stop this."

"That's what the *Herald* is for. We observe so that the world can know."

"And the world will do nothing, just as it always has. Thousands of people are going to die here."

"And we will not interfere. Security, reliability, and secrecy," Gwen said, her chest as empty as a cave.

"Don't quote slogans at me, Gwen! We're a newspaper, and this isn't something you can trap in a page. You have to let yourself feel this and figure out how we can help," Lina said, reaching back to grasp at Gwen's arm, but she shook her off.

"I don't have time. Our mission is too important."

"Then why are you crying?"

Gwen reached up, her finger tracing the path the tear had traced from her eye to her chin. She caught it before it could fall.

"I—I don't," Gwen stammered, glaring at the offending tear. In the Observation haze, she could see the crystalline structure etched into the tear drop.

"Gwen, please look at me," Lina begged, and Gwen fought to bring the other girl's face into view. "I'm sorry. I'm so sorry, Gwen."

"There's nothing to be—"

"I shouldn't have stopped you from trying to save the boy. I was wrong, and you were right."

"No, no that's not true. His family will suffer because of what I did."

"They suffer because of what I failed to do. I should have helped you save the boy. Maybe then he wouldn't be in that mess below," Lina said, scrubbing her hand over her face. "I let them back inside my head, Gwen. I spent years getting rid of them, making sure that everything I did was because I chose to do it, while giving them just enough to make them think I was still under their thumb. But I slipped up, and now they're locked in your head too."

Gwen reached out, pulling Lina's hand from her face and clasping it in her own. But Gwen's face did not move, even as the tears continued to trace her cheeks. She opened her mouth to speak, but Lina's face shot up before she could.

"What did you just say?" Lina asked.

"What?"

"I thought I heard you say something," Lina said, cocking her head like a hound to focus on the sound. "Do you hear that whispering?"

Gwen looked at her, confusion overcoming her iron control. Lina sat perfectly still, before exploding into movement so violent that Clementine registered it as a dive.

They plunged towards the ground. From the co-pilot seat below Lina, Gwen stretched herself out across the bat, all her fingers and toes moving in unison, sending signals to Clementine. With a wrench the bat pulled out of the dive. Gwen rose to question Lina but stopped when she saw her draped in volumes of purple smoke that poured out of her ears.

"What are you doing?" Gwen asked, and Lina recoiled as if she had screamed at her.

"We read you, reporter. Extraction inbound. Confirm," Lina said into the air. She turned to face Gwen. "You need to take control. I'll guide you in, but I need to be in the Observation trance to stay on target. Take us into the city."

Gwen flattened herself against the back of Clementine, urged into motion by the look of fierce resolve that had formed across Lina's face. She spurred the beast into motion, sending it winging towards the city.

"What's happening?" he whispered to Lina. She could see the blood trickling from her ears as she processed all the sound in the tile. Gwen gulped. They were above a screaming city; it must have been agony for her.

"We have an undercover reporter in the city. She's just asked for extraction. We need to get her out of there before the army sacks the place.

Chapter 28: The Scholar's Faith

...what if Huck's death was not by his own hand? I, who has walked the Reverie as none have dared to, have heard whispers at the edges of the wild dreamlands. Whispers that speak of predators that devour time. And children. Predators who saw an opportunity in the death of a god.

And I think these predators have been hunting me since I arrived so long ago. And if they could reach across the worlds to kill Huck, what might they do to us?

(Letter 25, Paragraph 3, Lines 1-4, and Paragraph 4, Lines 1-2)

Theo flew down into the depths of the Godstrom. Blood trickled down his throat as he flew like a crashing meteor to the surface of Poa and the corpse of a god. He could feel his sanity stretching like a taut wire, each moment threatening to snap the fragile cord. So he whispered to himself as he flew.

He whispered the names of his friends like they were a litany of prayers. He told himself stories as he flew down, stories that only they knew. They were simple things, these stories, hardly worth remembering. But in the darkness of the Godstrom they were the only things that lit the way.

For on his back was the N-Device, and it drank up the names and stories he fed it. In turn, it projected in front of him the only path of safety through the Deep.

Outside the patch of calm the N-Device guided him through, the world had lost all sense and reason. Lightning raked the air down here, but its forked brilliance was neither blue nor yellow, but a deep ghastly red. As it struck through the sky it seemed not to light the world but crack it open. The roars of demons filled the air, and the weight of the sky pressed harder and harder on his spine.

But as Theo flew a sort of peace settled over him. It ran through his veins like ice water and calmed his racing heart. It was a state of mind that Elwyn had spoken of with hushed tones, one that had seemed almost sacred to the flight master.

"I'm chasing something," Elwyn had told him, after Theo had asked him what he loved most about flying. "It's something a winger might attain only once in a lifetime. I've been on the edge of it before, dipped my toes in the water so to speak, but I've never jumped fully in. Every time I fly I feel like I get closer to experiencing it."

"What is it you're chasing?" Theo had asked.

"It's difficult to describe. It's almost like a state of bliss. You feel like you're complete, like all the wires in your body and brain finally and fully connect. It's like you, at last, found your sheet music for the great big cosmic symphony. And—" Elwyn cut himself off with a frustrated grin. "See what I mean. It's difficult to describe. But that's what I'm chasing. You might find it out there, if you look hard enough."

Theo had found that state of mind, and it thrummed through him like a song from the universe. And even as he whispered the stories of his friends, even as the storm attempted to claw at him like a hateful monster, he felt no fear.

He reached the bottom of the world. The storm came to a halt some hundred meters above the ground. It hung like a gallows over the blasted landscape, but it did not sink any lower. The N-Device's guide shut off, but its white light still hung around him like a cloak.

Here was the bottom of the crater that had caused the great collapse. It was a space almost the same size as the castle that hung far above, but it was a blasted and empty ruin, a void carved into the planet.

Theo looked down, down to the deepest depths of the pit, and he saw that something moved in the shadows. It was only when he turned the glow of the N-Device into this pit that he saw that the shadows were krows.

They crouched in ranks down the sides of the deepest pit, lining the walls of the hole like the gargoyles they resembled. The light revealed them, dispelling the shadows they had been wrapped in, but they did not move. Their eyes did not even lift to meet him. They remained focused on the very heart of the pit.

Theo waited, waited for them to rise and tear him to pieces. He did not even draw his knife. Minutes trickled by, but they never spoke a name. They remained frozen, almost transfixed. For there was something very odd at the bottom of the deep Godstrom, surrounded by krows, where the body of god should have been.

There was a house.

It was brick on one side but hidden under a blanket of thick green ivy. The other sides were a dark wood that was only a shade lighter than the almost black tiles that made up the roof. A delicate light spilled from the windows.

Purple geraniums lined the rock path, drooping purple flowers caressing the stones below. The filth and grime that lined the bottom of the crater had no trace here. There was even a hint of green grass under the leaves of the flowers.

It was an oasis of life amid a broken wasteland lined with monsters. Paradox.

He floated down. His feet touched solid earth for the first time in months. The stone path was smooth and pristine, just as it had been when it was first laid down. The house bore no signs of the impact that had created the crater or the storm above.

The krows ignored him, still entranced by the house. The number 503 was emblazoned on the bricks to the right of the door frame in thick bronze letters. The door knocker had been worn smooth by a thousand hands, and when he lifted it and brought it down on the green door the thump sounded like a cannon shot in the crater. Theo turned, but the krows did not move.

He put his hand on the doorknob, twisted it, and pushed. He stepped in, turned and locked the door, placing his eye at the peephole to see if anything had tried to follow him. But the krows were still as statues.

He turned back to the foyer. There was a pile of shoes next to the door. They were small and colorful, like a pile of discarded candy wrappers. Coats and sweaters hung on the coat rack nearby.

With lead filled limbs, Theo slipped off the backpack that held the N-Device. He peeled the rain-soaked, battered flight coat off and hung it on the coat rack, smearing the coats with grime.

He reached down and attempted to unlace his boots. The constant rain of the storm and the muck from the detritus had reduced the laces into a single half-dissolved knot. He had to cut the boots off to remove them and placed them by the light up sneakers.

He stood in the foyer of the house, bare feet on the cool tile floor. His white shirt was soaked with sweat and blood. A chill rippled through him as the AC in the house caressed him like a phantom. He pulled a gray sweater from the coat rack and put it on, along with the pack with the N-Device.

The hall stretched before him, leading to a kitchen lit by a half dimmed overhead light. Retro travel posters lined the walls next to family photos depicting a smiling couple and a young man. Theo did not look at the photos. He already knew who was in them.

He walked down the hall, just as he had many times before. The lights were dim, but he could navigate this place with his eyes closed. The kitchen waited beyond the hall. The long wooden table the family had used for entertaining dominated the space. A bag of oranges was in a bowl in its center.

He knew there was another hall that led to the stairs. They would take him to the second floor, where the master bedroom and the young boy's bedroom waited. The boy's bedroom would have a bunk bed in it, even though the child never had another sibling. He slept in the bottom bunk bed all by himself and kept books and boardgames on the bed above.

Theo knew these things as well as he knew his own face.

There were no signs of claw markings or of forced entry. There was no sign of impact either, no chairs strewn around or toppled books. It was only the natural untidiness of a normal home, not the wreckage that should have been created if it fell out the sky.

And then he saw it. Off the kitchen and on the other side of the staircase there was a door covered with old school projects. It was the basement door, and there was light coming from below the edge.

He opened the door. The gray carpeted steps led down into the light. He stepped down, his hand automatically finding the smooth wooden banister on the side of the stairwell. He could hear someone breathing beyond the staircase, as well as the soft clatter of plastic, and the shuffling of cards. Theo reached the last stair. He took a deep steadying breath and then stepped out from the shadow of the stairwell and into the lights of the room.

There was a window well that let in light when the sun was up, but now only showed the ranks of krow feet beyond. Bookshelves lined the walls, layered with dust. There was a TV and an exercise bike, a sofa from the eighties and a scratched-up coffee table. The room was just as normal as the boy who stood in its center.

"Hello," the boy said. "Who are you?"

Theo could not speak. The boy was slender, and the red sweater he wore was clearly his father's as it hung off him in large folds. He had messy dark hair that clung to his head in little half ringlets. His eyes were a blue so deep that they looked almost black.

"Hello," Theo forced himself to say, his voice coming out as a pained rasp.

The boy's eyes scanned him, taking in the blood on his clothes. His eyes returned to Finley's face, suspicion clouding them like smoke.

"I'm not supposed to talk to strangers. Especially if they've just barged into the house. Are you here to rob us?"

"Of course not," Theo said, a surprised cough coming out of his chest at the shock of the question. "I must look the part though, right?"

"Like you got hit by a car."

"I bet. Do you mind if I sit down?" Theo asked, indicating the wooden swivel chair in front of the battered desk next to the stairs. An old computer took up the desk. The boy didn't say anything as Theo took his seat.

"Who are you? Are you a friend of mom and dad?"

"Not really, no."

"Then who are you?"

"That's a difficult question to answer. I've been on quite a long journey to get here, and I don't have a whole lot of time. So do you mind if I ask you some questions before I answer yours?"

"Are you going to hurt me if I don't answer you?" the boy asked, but his black eyes looked at Theo without emotion. The room did not change, and the boy did not move, but Theo felt at once he was in danger as the boy continued to look at him with his endless eyes. They seemed to contain a multitude of souls, as if the boy had a hundred thousand lives inside him, all aching to get out.

"I would never hurt you. Not ever. You may not know me, but I need you to know that I'm your friend," Theo said, doing his best to keep his voice level as stone.

"I would know if you lied to me."

"I'm not lying to you."

The boy looked at him, his head cocked to the side. He picked up an action figure from the table. It looked like a WWII paratrooper, complete with parachute and tiny Thompson gun. He rolled the little soldier around his fingers as he continued to gaze at Theo.

"Okay."

"Good. That's good," Theo said. He clutched his knees and refused to let his hands shake. "Okay. Do you mind telling me how old you are?"

"I'm ten."

"And how long have you been here?"

"Since I was born?" the boy said, his face scrunching up with confusion.

"No, not the house. I meant how long have you been in this crater? How long have you been below the storm?"

"What crater?"

"Oh," Theo said. He could not stop his heart from jackrabbiting around his chest. Adrenaline was coursing through his system, bringing the taste of iron and acid to the back of his throat. "Have you been outside at all?"

"Not in a while. Is everything okay?"

"It could be better. There's a horrible storm outside, the worst one I've ever seen. That's what I've just traveled through, to get here. That's why I look like this," Theo said, gesturing to his ragged clothes.

"Do you think we'll lose power?"

"No, somehow I don't think you will. Where are your parents though?"

"I don't know," the boy said, a vein of sadness working its way through his words. "I haven't seen them in a while. Do you think they got caught in that big storm?"

"I really hope not. So you haven't seen them in what? Hours? Days? Months?"

"I don't know."

"Can you tell me the last time you saw them, or saw anybody?"

"I don't like your questions," the boy said, the sadness and confusion vanishing, to be replaced by an almost reptilian coldness.

"I'm sorry about that. But I still need answers. It's really important, maybe the most important thing."

375

"I don't care. I want to ask you questions now," and the boy's voice seemed to gain dimensions, becoming deeper and older.

"Okay. If that's what you want to do. But then I get to ask you questions again, as many as I want," Theo said, his muscles shaking as he fought through the panic to say those words.

"Fine," the boy said, his voice going back to normal, he placed the toy soldier back down on the coffee table. Theo risked lifting his eyes from the boy to look at the table. It was littered with little figurines and cardboard pieces that must have been lifted from a dozen different board games and toy sets.

"Are you a policeman?"

"What? No, I'm not a policeman."

"You're not here to tell me my parents are dead? I've seen police do that on TV. If there's been an accident the police will come and tell the kid his family is dead. Like Batman."

"That's not what's happening now. I'm not a policeman."

"Then what are you doing here?"

"I'm not sure exactly. I sort of wandered here, and you weren't who I was expecting to find. Though I'm happy to see you again," Theo said, attempting a smile, the boy looked unamused.

"Who were you looking for?"

"I was looking for a god, Huck. I didn't expect to find you here, but now that I have it makes a sort of sense," Theo said, forcing himself to whisper the secret that had lurked at the bottom of his mind since he had arrived here.

"How do you know my name?" Huck said, taken aback by how casual Theo had sounded.

"No. My turn for questions now."

"I wasn't done," the boy said, his voice rising and deepening as his frustration and fear twisted across his face.

"You can knock it off now, Huck. I know you won't hurt me. In fact, I'm starting to think you're the reason I'm here at all," Theo said, the terror of the little godling still lurked in his belly, but he was used to such a thing. He had lived with it all his life, and he had traveled too far to let it stop him now.

The boy's malevolence still swirled around him. He seemed to become a little part of the storm above, almost as if all its power had

376

been concentrated in the space the boy occupied. Yet the room did not change, did not even shake as lightning cracked in the eyes of the boy god. Theo did not move, and all at once Huck's aura fell away.

"That usually works," Huck said, his eyebrows crinkling in surprise, a little wrinkle forming between his eyes.

"Did it work on the krows outside, Huck? Is that why they don't come near the house?"

The boy looked at the window well, seeing the taloned feet of the krows waiting in his yard. "I forgot about them. They were trying to scare me, so I told them to go away."

"And that worked?"

"It did for a while. It looks like they came back though. How did you get through them?"

"I think they're still afraid of you, and now a little of me."

"Who are you? Are you a krow too? I haven't seen anyone who looks like me in a long time."

"My memory is a little fuzzy, but you said you're ten, right? That would make you a fifth grader, or a fourth grader?"

"Fourth grader, but the year is almost over."

"Ah. Well, do you know a boy in your class? He's really quiet, and he'll jump if you surprise him. There's another boy, Finley, who likes to pull pranks on the quiet one? He hides spiders in his bag and stuff like that."

"Oh yeah, I know him. His name's Theodore, right?"

"Yeah. He goes by Theo now."

"How do you know that?"

"Because that's me. I'm Theo. Just older than you've ever met me."

The boy stared at him, scanning his face, searching for the little boy who shrieked. Huck's face started to fill with excitement as his eyes traced Theo's face, as he saw the slope of his ears, the little break in his nose, the color of his eyes.

"It is you! You're just all big now. Are you from the future? Are you here to give me and Theodore a message or something? Oh, I bet you want us to train and get stronger, so we can fight the aliens or something, right? That's awesome."

"No, it's not like that," Theo said, trying to cut into the boy's excited ramble, but instead of stopping it just changed directions.

377

"Or did I go into the future? Is my house a time machine? Oh, and those krow things are monsters and you've been fighting them since we've been kids. Where is big Huck?"

"Huh?"

"Well, you're big Theo, or maybe old Theo? But you don't look that old. Anyways, where is the older me?"

Theo could not answer the question, could not even let himself remember what happened to the older Huck. He had to bury him without looking at him, and now Theo could barely look at the boy in front of him.

"I'm not from the future. To be honest I'm not really sure what's going on. I sort of teleported here from my world. Could you tell me more about this place? I think it might be part of my...mission."

"Okay. I can try to help," the boy said, and he sat on the sofa, climbing over the back and placing his head on top of it so that he could look at Theo. He nodded to indicate he was ready.

"Is this still Earth?"

"Course it is, Big Theo. What else would it be?"

"Nowhere on Earth looks like this place. Are you sure?"

"I mean some stuff is a little strange. But everything else is normal," Huck answered, indicating the house around him. "I'm not really friends with Theodore, by the way, do we become friends?"

"Not for a while yet, but soon. You won't really become buddies until high school, but you'll get on great then."

"What takes so long?"

"Can I pass on that question? I don't want to spoil anything for you both. Can you tell me how you got here, Huck? Maybe that will help us figure out how I arrived here and what's going on."

"Well, everything has been pretty normal for me. I woke up, and Mom and Dad were gone so I guess they had to go to work. And I tried to call Gwen or Finley, but the phones wouldn't work. So I made myself some leftovers and then I came down here to play."

"What was yesterday like, Huck? Can you tell me what happened yesterday?"

"Um, I think—" the boy started, but he stopped, his eyes flickering around the room as he searched for details, trying to remember what had happened just the day before. "I think I was going somewhere. I was in a car, I think, but I was driving? That can't be right though, I'm too young to drive."

"Where were you driving to, Huck?"

"I can't—I can't really remember. But something happened, I never really reached where I was going. Do you think this was a dream?"

"Yes, just a dream probably. But I would still like to hear more of it if you don't mind? It's interesting."

"Well in the dream I guess I was older, maybe that's why I was driving?" Huck continued, his eyes glazing over as he tried to remember the details of the dream. "I can't remember where I was going, but I think I remember what I was thinking about. I was thinking about people I knew, friends, I guess. I think you were one of them?"

"I might have been. Who else was in the dream?"

"There were other people, other friends. They were older, as old as you, but I think I had known them for a long time. Oh yeah, I was thinking about Gwen, but an older version of her. And Yosef, and this other person named Mel, and others. In the dream I was driving, and thinking about all of you, and mom and dad, all the people I like," Huck said, his eyes and lips pulling down as he remembered the feeling. "And suddenly, something pulled at me. Knocked the wheel out of my hands so that I was driving off the road."

"Wait, someone grabbed the wheel from you? There was someone else in the car?" Theo asked, his heart quickening. Huck had been alone when the police found him.

"Yeah. Someone I had never seen. And they were so mad at me! They made us crash. Then suddenly there was this light, this horrible crash. It sounded like a storm."

"Huck, I'm really sorry. But what happened next?" Theo asked, his voice fracturing at the edges as he spoke, his heart sinking as the boy described the last moments of his own life like it had been a mere nightmare.

"And then the dream changed. I was falling all of a sudden, falling through the sky. And I knew how to fly, but for some reason I couldn't do it anymore. I couldn't make myself fly. Every time I tried I just fell faster and faster, and as I was falling it felt like pieces of me were breaking off, like a spaceship crashing back to earth, little bits burning and breaking off as I tried to fly," Huck said, and his little voice became haunted and hollow as he remembered. Age seemed to enter his face as he spoke, the shell of the child breaking away until the older thing beneath could be seen. He sunk further and further down the couch, as if he was trying to brace for impact.

"And then I landed, but still in pieces, like I had been scattered all over the world. But the biggest piece, the part where I most was, it started to get smaller and smaller, like I was disappearing piece by piece. And there was this burning pain, like a mosquito's bite, but it was everywhere, all over me. Like I was being eaten alive."

Theo could not speak. He felt his eyes burn as the tears leaked from them. They dripped down his face, mixing with the trickles of blood and the grime of the descent. He wiped his eyes with the fresh gray sweater of Huck's father, smearing the soft wool with tears and dirt.

"I think I understand, Huck. I think I figured it out at last. In the dream you died. It was a car accident. The people you saw, the people you were thinking of, we were all there for the funeral just a few days later."

"I died?" the boy asked, his voice muffled and tiny from the other side of the couch. Theo could not see his face.

"Maybe you were murdered. No one was in the car with you when we found you," Theo whispered, trying to keep the tears out of his voice.

"Oh."

"I'm so sorry, buddy. But I don't think all of you died at once. A piece of you traveled here, to this world with flying castles and monsters. But in the process, I think you broke apart. You're not all the pieces of the Huck I know. You're his ghost."

The boy had fallen silent, his head had disappeared from the edge of the sofa. Theo could not see him now, but he could hear Huck's shallow breaths. They were flat and rapid, little puffs of air that grew in volume. And as the breaths continued, they grew wetter, as if tears were choking him.

Theo surged into motion, knowing at once what was happening. He ducked around to the other side of the couch and crouched in front of Huck. The boy's eyes had gone glassy, and his face was flushed and growing redder by the second. His hands were clenched in front of him on top of his narrow chest. Theo could see them shaking even as the boy's nails dug into skin.

"Huck. I'm sorry I shouldn't have said anything. That was stupid. I'm right here with you. I'm right in front of you. I'm from the future, and I need your help," Theo said, lying with rapid fire speed, but keeping his voice slow and steady. "You did a really great job helping me so far. I'm proud of you. But we need to breathe slower. Try breathing with me. We'll do it together. Deep breath."

Theo sucked in air, holding it in as he spoke to the boy. Huck's eyes had turned to face him, but the boy's breathing was still out of control. With every shallow breath he sent his own mind racing further off the rails. But he breathed in as Theo did.

"Good. Hold in the breath. Hold it. Okay, breathe out," Theo said, blowing the air out with gusto. "Good, let's do ten more of those. Just breathe with me. Deep breath. Hold it. Hold it. Let it out. Another deep breath. Hold it."

They worked their way through the breathing cycle, a routine that was as familiar to Theo as an old friend. He felt his own heart steady as he went through the ten breaths, and he saw Huck calm as they breathed in tandem. The boy's face started to regain some of his color. By the eighth breath he was able to unclench his hands. When they finished the cycle, his eyes had focused once more, though he would not meet Theo's eyes.

"Do you want to do another ten?" Theo asked.

"No. I think I'm fine now. I'm sorry," the boy said, his voice raw and halting.

"Don't be silly, and don't be sorry. I have one of those about once a week, it's nothing to be ashamed of. You did a really good job breathing with me."

"I don't know what happened."

"You had a panic attack. It's when your thoughts race out of control, and your body surges to catch up, and then your thoughts get faster, so your body goes faster, and on and on. The key is to reset it, slowing one down gets the other to stop racing. That breathing exercise does that. There are others I can teach you if you want."

"Yeah, that might be good. So I died, huh?" the boy asked, his voice flat, and the words tore into Theo deeper than any krow's claw had. But he refused to look away from Huck.

"You did. Back on Earth, our home, you died about six days before I traveled here. I've been here about six months I think."

"Did you die too? Is that why you're here?"

"No, I'm not dead. I don't know why I'm here, but I'm glad I got to see you."

"Am I alive again?"

"Huck, I don't know. You're definitely different. You're way younger than the last time I saw you, and your memories seem fractured. The Huck I knew couldn't do that trick with his voice either."

"I don't feel dead. I feel normal, mostly."

"What doesn't feel normal?"

"I have these memories in my head, the ones I was telling you about. But they're different, things I know that I don't think I should. And it's like there's electricity beneath my skin." Huck stared at his own hands, little sparks of light flickering across his skin. "I know I can do more though. I can do anything I want."

"What do you want to do, Huck?"

"I want to make it all right. I want to make the monsters go away, all of them. I know there are things wrong with this world. I can feel that it's out of balance, and in desperate need of attention. My attention. I want to be myself again, Theo," Huck said, his voice once again deepening, and the sparks on his skin starting to grow until they seemed like miniature lightning bolts aching for freedom.

Theo covered Huck's hand with his own. He could feel the power beneath his fingers, the same strength as the storm that still raged above them that was probably growing wilder and wilder as the boy remembered that he was in fact the god of a world.

"Huck, I don't think that's a good idea."

"You don't want me to be myself again?" the boy asked, his sparks fading away.

"I don't think you are yourself, Huck. Somehow more, and somehow less. I told you I came down here to find god, and buddy, I think you're it." Theo chuckled. "I'm amazed, but I need to tell you that I'm even more terrified. No one should have that power, not even a friend of mine."

"You don't think I can do it?"

"No, the trouble is I do. I know how powerful you are. That storm I flew through to get here nearly killed me. I watched it destroy a dozen of my friends. That storm is your power, unleashed and uncontrolled. It's been pouring out of you like blood from a wound, and those monsters outside have been eating it, growing stronger with every bite. That storm is growing in power with every minute, and no matter how many krows we kill there's more and more. You don't try to control something like that, you can only wait for it to die out."

"You want me to die?"

"I want you to be at peace. You're not a god. You're not responsible for a whole planet."

"But it's MINE! I can make the world better, make it work again. It's all wrong you see. It's all gone to hell. And our friends are here, and I know that every second it grows more dangerous for them. But I can save them. Look," Huck said, gesturing to the game scattered across the coffee table. He pulled Theo to face it, and Theo looked at it for the first time.

Books cluttered the table's edges. They were from a dozen different genres. Theo could see *Lord of the Rings* and the *Collected Adventures of Sherlock Holmes*. He spotted the journals of Ernest Shackleton and the ship Endurance resting against *The Seven Wonders of the World*.

The rest of the table was the detritus from a hundred different board games. It was a mish mash of pieces and parts, some solid metal, others cheap and colorful cardboard. Dice littered the table like tossed stones, and the little hexagons from strategy games, and real estate games, and puzzle games, and every other kind of game made up the rest of the mad checkerboard Huck had created to amuse himself.

But as Theo looked closer, he could see a sort of order to it. You needed to see it from above, from a godlike view.

He could see continents stitched together from different colors and different games, creating a patchwork land. Rivers flowed into oceans, where lonesome tiles made little islands in all the blue. Stickers and post it notes denoted cultures and countries and peoples of the mismatched world. And as Theo watched Huck's little hands darted

383

out, shifting a tile here, nudging a tile there. He spun the world to his design, reshuffling the world according to his whims. When he stopped, it was still the same planet, the same land, but its face had changed.

"I call it POA. Do you know what it stands for?"

Theo shook his head.

"Planet of Awesome!" Huck said, and the little god grinned with the satisfaction only a child can have. "And we still have some stories for you guys to finish."

Chapter 29: Our Friend's World

And though I am lost, I will soon find you. And though this world is chaos itself, we will soon make sense of it. And though this land tries to break us, I refuse to let it shape me. I will learn all I can of this place, I will force it to make sense, and then I will make it let us go.

Your Friend, Yosef League
(Letter 1, Paragraph 5, Lines 1-End)

Finley dragged Moro forward, pulling at the half-conscious warden with otherworldly powers. Every movement brought a pained hiss to her mouth along with a new spurt of blood from her wound.

He could feel the death and chaos all around pulling on his senses like wires, and all he wanted to do was tear into the city in search for Marlowe, but he kept his whole will focused on the next step, on the woman in his arms who needed his help.

He ignored the mobs of people running through the streets. He looked away from the soldiers in iron armor that moved like sleepwalkers as they pursued and hacked at the Oshroarans. He walked past the piles of broken rocks and blocked his ears to the sounds of stone steps thundering after a fleeing crowd.

They pulled themselves forward by inches and found their way back into the temple square. The feet of the Shepherd loomed ahead. Beyond, the dust and ash from the dying city had created a fog of war that could not be pierced.

Finley dragged Moro to the base of the massive statue, propping her against a low wall. The valley of the Crooken lay beyond them, but it was silent as a corpse. Finley did not tear his eyes away from the city as it ripped itself apart, searching for the faintest traces of light.

"Anything?" Moro whispered behind him.

"No, I don't see Marlowe anywhere."

"I meant our ride."

Finley whirled on her. "No, I don't see our 'ride.' What the hell are we doing here? We should be looking for Marlowe! Why did you send us to the middle of this horrible mess when we should be looking for my partner? Are we expecting a helicopter?" Finley saw the look on Moro's face. "It's a type of flying machine on my planet. Which, unless you can make one out of that purple smoke you're oozing, means we're pretty much screwed."

"Not helicopter. Chiropt."

"What?"

"Giant bat," Moro said, and she pointed behind him. He turned.

"Oh, you could have just said something instead of watching me shout like an idiot."

"No fun in that.

Gwen and Clementine moved as one being. Gwen's faintest touch to Clementine's back sent the great beast spiraling through the sky, ducking into the clouds of dust that choked the city.

Gwen had turned her Observation off in order to focus solely on Clementine as they steered through the muck in the air. Lina was above her on Clementine's spine, lying perfectly still so as not to send the chiropt mixed signals from the pilots. Instead, she glowed with Observation, and called out instructions to Gwen as she flew.

"Bear right by thirteen degrees and bring us down by ten meters," Lina called.

Gwen moved to obey, her splayed fingers tapping out the instructions of the beast below. At once she dove onto her new heading. Every flap of the beast's wings blew a sphere of dust away, but it soon came rushing back in.

The streets were choked with people, soldiers and citizens alike, hemmed in on all sides by collapsed Guardians or by the flailing death throes of those that still lingered. Gwen could not spare them a thought as she flew overhead.

"Shift right by four degrees," Lina called out; her voice clear but alarmed.

Gwen did not hesitate, making the faint adjustment to Clementine's flight.

Overhead, a dull roar built and built, as if the sky itself groaned in agony. Gwen allowed herself one look above them and saw the darker darkness in the dust clouds above.

386

The tower above them fell, tilting over like a drunk. It hurtled towards them, threatening to crush them flat.

But Clementine was just ahead of it, racing before its falling shadow so the collapsing stones just traced the edges of her wings. The empty windows looked back at Gwen like the eyes of a skull as the tower fell past them.

And Gwen saw the next danger before Lina could call out. A massive stone figure was twisting in agony just ahead of them. It sent clouds of dust and debris into the air as it rolled about the stone roadway. A single stomp of its foot launched cobbles into the sky like flak bursts.

The giant bat tucked her wings in as she spun like a bullet through the haze of dust. Lina screamed into the cacophony of noise, calling out the patterns and rhythms of the dangers above and below as Gwen had Clementine dance through the deadly field.

The Guardian had fallen onto its knees, clutching the ground like a man searching for safety in a hurricane. Lina called out the danger a moment before it happened, and Gwen pulled Clementine up.

The Guardian bashed its own head against the rocks below. Its great stone skull split into pieces, sending shrapnel the size of carriage wheels into the sky.

With a great tearing rip, a blade of twisted rock punctured the vast wing of Clementine. The creature gave a screech of pain that rumbled against Gwen's chest. The wing wept blood that took flight as the wind rippled along the length of torn skin.

"You're going to be okay, Clementine. You're gonna be fine old girl," Gwen whispered to chiropt as they flew. The creature moaned beneath her.

"The target is dead ahead, at the feet of the Shepherd," Lina said back to her. Lina's face was a frozen mask, but Gwen could see the tears leaking from her eyes. With Lina's enhanced senses Clementine's moment of agony must have seemed to last a century. Both of Gwen's partners were injured.

She made for the square surrounded by temples and ringing bells. Clementine collapsed onto the stone. The creature hunched in on herself, bringing her wing against her chest with great gentleness.

"I've got her," Lina said. "Get the reporter."

Gwen jumped to the ground, spotting the crumpled figure near the statue's feet, a large woman wrapped in makeshift bandages. The woman stared coolly back at her from the wisps of purple Observation smoke that still clung to her head.

A man in a tattered gray suit caked with dust and pulverized brick helped the large woman to her feet. She took his help with ill grace, pulling at his suit and ripping the jacket at the seams as she levered herself up.

"Constance Morind, requesting pickup and evacuation," the woman said, bringing herself to a pained parade rest.

"Really? Your name is Constance? And you gave me hell for naming my partner, Marlowe. The nerve of some people," the gray suited man beside her said. He wiped at the dust that covered his face, exposing the tan skin beneath along with the startling gray eyes. His voice was clogged with blood and muck, but Gwen knew it at once.

"Finley?" Gwen asked, her voice halting.

"Do I know you?" the man asked, peering at her through the half-light cast by the burning city.

Gwen pulled off her flight mask and goggles, shaking out her hair. "I've known you since you used to cry if someone didn't cut the crust off your sandwich."

Finley's broken nose had leaked blood onto his lips, but that didn't mean his grin was any less brilliant.

Finley hurtled forward to wrap Gwen in a hug. He gave a yowl of pain as he embraced her, banging his sore head against her shoulder in his haste, but he seemed to hug her only tighter in her response. "What other creatures do you fly these days?"

"Just the bat. But I'm working on building up to elephants and pigs and all sorts of beasties," Gwen whispered, but she couldn't make her face smile, even as Finley laughed, his eyes darting up and down her new uniform.

"Did you join the army?"

"The newspaper."

"Ah," Finley said, as he glanced at the massive bat still huddled behind Gwen. "Makes total sense. What are you doing here though?"

"We're here to pick her up," Gwen said, indicating Morind who had begun a slow shuffle to Clementine. "She's a reporter for the *Bird's Eye Herald*."

"I thought she was a police officer, and a friend. Turns out I'm a really lousy detective," Finley said, gazing at Constance with a blank look.

"Come on, the whole city is coming down. That army of sleepwalkers is endless. We gotta get you both out of here."

"What? You want me to get on that thing?"

"Her name is Clementine."

"It's a very pretty name," Finley admitted, smiling at Gwen's sudden temper.

"She'll eat you alive if I tell her to, now climb on," Gwen said, moving to assist Morind as she attempted to clamber up the bat. Lina sat perched on Clementine's shoulders, her Observation still swirling about her as she scanned the city for any possible threats.

"Where are you going?"

"We're taking you back to base. We need to debrief our reporter, and she needs to write what happened here. But you and I need talk. I think we probably have a lot to tell each other."

"I'm not going with you." She turned, Finley was still by the feet of the statue, the lights of the burning city illuminating him.

"Finley, don't be stupid. She's not really going to eat you. She's perfectly safe, trust me."

"It's not that. I'm sure flying on that thing is totally survivable with you at the helm. But I'm still not going. There's something I still need to do in this city," Finley said, his eyes lifting from Gwen back to Morind.

"Do you have any idea how many people are dying every second?"

"Four," Lina said from atop the chiropt. Her face was blank, but she had closed her eyes, unable to endure the horrors she could see with her enhanced senses. Blood trickled from her ears and the corners of her eyes.

"And it's my fault," Finley said.

"No. We couldn't have known," Morind said.

"You can shift the blame from yourself if you like, Constance. Fake wardens and detectives we may have been, but I still could have done more."

Gwen marched over to Finley, her fists clenched at her sides. "You got a savior complex all of a sudden? What are you going to do against an army and mad statues? Make sarcastic comments?"

Finley shrugged. "It generally seems to work."

"You're wrong! We can't save anyone here. And you'll die if you stay. Do you expect me to let that happen again?"

"My hero."

"This isn't the time for jokes, Finley!"

"I'm not joking. I'm in every sort of danger possible and you drop out of the sky on a giant bat to save my ass. It's incredible," he said, his eyes glowing with enthusiasm even over his badly broken nose, but the grin faded away. "But I'm sorry. I can't just leave. There's still something I need to do."

"Looking for Huck?" Morind gasped.

"What?" Gwen whispered.

"No, not anymore," Finley said, looking at Gwen. "I thought for a moment that there might have been something more to Huck's death, and that I could learn it here. I nearly died a couple times trying to do it. Now I know better.

"I couldn't save my friend then, and I can't fix that. Ever. But I can try my best to help Marlowe."

"Who the hell is Marlowe?"

"A glowing, floating flower." Morind supplied from behind them.

"My friend," Finley replied. "The first friend I made when I woke up, and we've been watching each other's backs ever since. It vanished when the Guardians started to fall apart. I can't leave it behind." Finley hugged Gwen once more. His arms were shaking with exhaustion, and she could feel them tremble as they patted her back, but when he pulled away his eyes were clear.

"I'm not going to abandon another friend of mine. Do me a favor though, try not to get eaten by bats." He stepped away from her, waving to Lina on the bat, but when he met Morind's eyes his smile dropped away. He nodded at the other woman, something unsaid passing between them. He turned from them, and with slow shambling steps made his way back into the city's depths.

Behind her, Clementine gave a mewl of pain that sent a shudder down Gwen's chest. Lina tried to wipe away the blood dripping from her eyes as she continued to listen to the city tear itself apart. Morind climbed the chiropt, little gasps of pain escaping as she ascended the beast.

Gwen did not move.

The lambent eyes of the Colossus fell onto the Sheosirrans, and even with a half-formed mind its dreams arrived with the force of an earthquake.

The Sheosirrans collapsed under the weight of it, only Yosef, Harmodias, and Cisseus managing to stay on their feet. Yosef seemed to become hale and hearty as the eyes of his new son met his own. But Harmodias gave a cry of pain as her iron grandson looked at her. Like an old and rotting tree, she fell to her knees, one clawed hand managing to catch onto the arm of Yosef's chair.

"I should have strangled you when we found you." Harmodias choked out, dragging each word from her chest.

"I agree," Yosef said, his eyes sweeping over her cheek as the tears coursed from them.

"In the world of the Reverie, no name will be more hated than yours. Everything that dreams will know that Yosef League built the tyrant god."

"It doesn't matter. I will happily become the monster you think me to be if it means I can make this world right. It will be my exchange," Yosef said, and the tips of his mouth pulled up into a triumphant grin as she collapsed onto the steel skin of the Colossus.

A gasp of pain swung his attention back to his grandson. Cisseus was bathed in a beam of light, the eyes of the statue locked on him. His mouth moved in little spasms that might have become words in the Reverie, but though the light of the dreaming world pooled around his hands he could not bring it forth.

"Cisseus, that's enough. You don't have to prove how strong you are to me. You've sacrificed enough for this wretched world. Let me do the rest, son. Let your grandfather carry it for you," Yosef's eyes glowed with fondness as he looked at his two boys, but there was a crack of madness in his gaze.

"Cisseus, get out of here!" Mel screamed, dragging herself across the metal shoulders of the Colossus. Yosef turned his eyes to meet hers, and she froze at once. His mind washed over hers, wiping out the pain, wiping out her thoughts. The song surged in again, desperate to be heard by Mel after so long.

"I'm sorry, Mel. But this is family business," Yosef said, and his betrayal burned through Mel like fire.

"I'm your family," she choked out.

"That was a long time ago."

Yosef turned away from Mel and found Cisseus, who alone of the Sheosirrans still stood on the peaks of the Colossus's shoulders. He met his grandfather's eyes and shook his head.

"Pity," Yosef said before turning his gaze to his newest son. "Show him how strong you are," he commanded, and the Colossus moved to obey its maker.

"Can't you see it? Can't you feel it? All across this world of mine I know that people are in pain. And it's my fault. I didn't make it right the first time. I tried to make a world that was different, that was better, that was more—"

"Awesome," Theo said, his voice hollow.

"Exactly! And I got that part right, but every other part wrong. I mean, I was just a kid when I got started. And as I got older, I started to get rid of all the stuff that made POA what it was. And then I died! But I came back here. It must have been so I could do it right."

"You'd wipe the slate clean?"

"I would," The god Vovatum said, his hand sweeping only centimeters above the pieces he had strewn about the coffee table. And as his hand flew over them Theo could see it all happen. Tidal waves and floods, earthquakes and chasms that sucked whole civilizations away. Revelation and rapture, all at once.

"And I would bring them all here. Mel and Gwen and Finley and Yosef. We could be together again, just like before! And we would make the world one more time, but this time we would make it better. Doesn't that sound great?"

"No. That sounds horrible, Huck," Theo said. The god turned from his game, the smile still fixed on his face.

"What?"

"I don't want to be god. I don't know why anyone would. Mel and Gwen and all the others? They'd turn you down flat. They'd tease you until you realized how silly that question was."

"Why?"

"Huck, I've spent almost every moment of my life afraid of how my actions might cause even one negative thing. I'm wracked with fear and guilt and anxiety. And I've accepted it, even learned to use it to my advantage sometimes. But you give me godlike power? Buddy, I'd lose my mind. Just like I think you have."

"I haven't lost my mind," Vovatum thundered. "How can you say that? You're supposed to be my friend."

"And you're supposed to be Huck. This place was your dream, something you would escape into whenever the world got too dark. You loved this place," Theo said.

All the others had moved on from their lands of pretend and make believe, but Huck just couldn't let his go. It had been a piece of him for so long, was it any great mystery why he had gone here when he died?

"You loved this world, but it was never real. It was just a made-up thing you did to make yourself feel better. You would never, ever talk about destroying it just because it wasn't perfect. You knew your limits, even in your imagination. I don't think this piece of you does."

"I am more than a piece of myself! I am a god," Vovatum roared his voice childlike and godlike at the same time, echoing over each other in a wave of anger.

"You're a kid."

"And you're a character!" Vovatum screamed. "You don't get to argue with me. You have to do what you're told. You have to finish the stories that I want you to, be the hero that I designed!"

"I'm not a hero, Huck. I'm your friend. And I won't let you do this. I won't let you corrupt what's left of yourself until you're nothing but a husk. You'll be worse than one of the krows! I won't watch my friend destroy himself again."

393

"Nor will I," the god said, his eyes blazing into Theo's. "I see across the whole planet, Theo. I see the Child Eater trying to destroy what I have built. I see the secret terrors I imprisoned in the heart of the world breaking free. I see the Godstrom building and building above our heads.

"But the things I see most clearly are our friends. Finley and Gwen have found each other at last, but any moment a soldier might slash them to ribbons or a Guardian smash them flat. Mel is dying, trailing her blood on an iron floor. And Yosef? Yosef is looking down on her, trying to remember who he once was.

"You want me to abandon my friends to their fates? Well, here's a question for you, Pathfinder. Will you abandon them? Will you watch them all die?"

Theo shuddered back, stumbling from the boy god as he bombarded him with secrets. Smugness and madness swirled behind Vovatum's eyes as he watched his friend twist with agony. There was no recognition now, no love. Only possession.

Theo wouldn't dare trust him with saving anyone.

Theo closed his eyes. Could he do it though? Could Theo save their friends? He knew that with so much power he could bring them all together again. He could heal them of all the hurts they had sustained here in Poa and return them to their world.

And he could do more.

He could heal Wheeler and return the expedition members to life. He could heal Elwyn, and they would fly through the sky once more, only this time Theo would be his equal. He could end the storm and restore this broken tile.

He could fix the whole world and make a new one that would never terrify him again.

"Think of what we could do, Theo. A perfect world. Just you, me, and all our friends. Adventures day after day. Happy ever after, forever."

"A world without fear, huh? A perfect world," Theo said, He opened his eyes, and saw the ghost of Huck before him, bleeding power, creating a storm without end and without equal, with all the patience and restraint of a kid. The fate of anyone who tried to play god.

"I refuse," Theo said, and he felt the world fall off his shoulders.

"What?" Vovatum said from on high.

"I'm more than my fears, Huck. And so are you."

"You would leave them to die? You would leave your friends to suffer?" the god snarled, and Theo at once heard how the shade had stopped referring to their friends as his as well.

"I'm not going to wreck the world to save them," Theo cried, pouring everything he felt into his voice as he cast aside the chance to be together again. "It doesn't matter how much I want to see them again, how much I want to be home. I won't destroy something just because I'm afraid, and neither would they."

"You don't know that!" the ghost roared, and Theo could see it now. Cracks riddled the boy god's skin. A storm raged beneath, thunder and lightning roiling within him.

"I have faith in them," Theo said, calm in the face of the god's rage.

"Have faith in me."

"I do, Huck. I have faith you won't hurt me or anyone else. Undead godking you might be, but you're still my friend. I think it's time you start acting like it."

The little god's hands glowed with lightning. Thunder rumbled with his every breath, but as Theo looked at him the storm faded away until it was nothing but a faint hint of ozone in the air. The boy slumped forward, the breaks on his skin disappearing.

"I don't understand," Huck said, his voice quiet after the thunder of the storm. "You believe in them enough that you would leave them to die? It doesn't make any sense."

Theo gave a helpless shrug. "Paradox. Learn to love it."

Realization dawned on the boy's face, and he finally turned his back on Poa.

Clementine mewled with pain at the foot of the Shepherd, Morind clutched the wound in her back, Lina wept blood, and Gwen had no idea what to do.

She closed her eyes, searching for the darkness that had begun all this, listening for the voice that would tell her the right thing to do.

But there was nothing. There was only Gwen, just as there had always been.

Could she try, just for once, listening to her?

"I didn't get to say what I wanted to before," Gwen said to the girl behind her. "You don't need to apologize to me. You didn't corrupt me or fail me or anything like that. Because here's the truth. There's always going to be voices trying to tell me what to do or how to live, but I'm still the one that decides whether or not I want to listen. And I'm the one that has to live with the results, good or bad."

Gwen turned. Lina stood behind her, blood leaking from her ears and the corners of her eyes, but her smile was radiant and beautiful. Gwen pressed her forehead against Lina's. "Thank you for bringing me back to myself. Hold on for me for just a little longer."

Gwen turned and raced after Finley, still hobbling away into the chaos of the city. "So what's your plan? You're gonna walk into that mess by yourself to try to save a glowing flower?" Gwen shouted after Finley.

"Not just a glowing flower. It's also a special detective."

"Well then, we're both idiots, aren't we? We never figured it out." She caught up to him and grabbed his arm, spinning him around to face her. "It's okay to ask for help."

He shuddered in her hands, unable to meet her gaze, but she kept on talking. "We all made that mistake before, didn't we? He was my closest friend, Finley, and I didn't see what was happening to Huck until it was too late. It nearly destroyed me. And I didn't speak a word of it to any of you. I wrapped myself in silence, hoping that no one would notice that I was dying inside. And that was wrong!

"But I'm trying to be better. So please, Finley, let me help you."

He stilled, and with a lurch he brought his eyes up to meet hers. "Please help me find my partner."

"Sure. It's right up there," Gwen said, pointing upward, and she let the Observation trance wash over her, forcing herself to tune out the screams and the chaos until all that remained was the sight of the shivering flower bathed in weak light at the top of the Shepherd.

Finley craned his neck upwards until he could see where she was pointing. His mouth dropped open, and for the first time in her life Gwen stunned Finley silent.

"So how are you going to get up there, Mr. Detective?" Gwen asked, clicking her fingers in front of his face. "Need a ride?"

Finley smiled at her. "You're sure she doesn't eat people, right?"

Gwen shrugged, and then launched Finley onto the back of Clementine. She scrambled up after him as Lina strapped Finley down into the harness. Gwen pet the bat, feeling the muscles shudder underneath the creature's skin.

"Do you have another flight in you, old girl?"

Clementine screeched out her answer. She clambered to her feet and began to beat her injured wings against the air. In moments they were aloft. They rose into the clouds of dust that fogged the streets. They climbed above the trembling buildings and the screaming city, until they burst out of the burning gloom that cloaked Oshroar. With the thunder of massive wings, they ascended the mountainous Shepherd.

"Marlowe!" Finley shouted as he spotted the flower hovering on the giant's face. The Ghostlight's glow was dim, barely distinguishable from the far-off stars.

Clementine circled the head of the Shepherd, her wingtips glancing off the statue's rough face. Gwen brought the bat down on the monument's shoulder, a plain of stone as wide as a city street. Finley sprung from the back of the bat and began to scale the neck and head of the statue.

Gwen raced after him, hunching against the freezing winds that battered the mountain's heights. Even without her enhanced senses she could hear the screams and booms from the city below them, and her every breath was choked with ash.

She scaled the Shepherd's face, searching for handholds in the crags that the wind had carved into the massive features, and soon caught up with Finley. Together, they reached the top of the Shepherd and clambered onto the top of the world.

Marlowe floated alone on the peak of the Shepherd. Finley gasped when he saw his friend. He sprinted forward, hands outstretched, but the Ghostlight faded from view as he approached. Its light dimmed to nothing until its petals disappeared and it ceased to exist.

"Get back here, Marlowe!" Finley cried. "We aren't finished yet. We still have a city to save. Don't you forget it!"

The Ghostlight phased back into view, but it seemed a half-made thing. Marlowe's light was the faintest speck, and its petals trembled in fear.

"I'm right here beside you, Marlowe. I'm not running away. We started this thing together, and I'm not going anywhere until it's done. Nobody's leaving a friend tonight." And to Gwen's shock Finley was crying, tears pouring down his face.

"You hear that Special Detective Marlowe!" Finley roared at the flower. "We are going to save this city."

The Ghostlight peered at him, and petal by petal it began to light up. Radiance poured from the flower until it shone like a new sun atop the Shepherd, but its light did not burn or harm. And Gwen found her mind crowded with memories, the happiest memories she thought she had once forgotten.

Her father's handmade pasta carbonara. Her mother's songs as she drifted off to sleep. The first time she ever made someone laugh so hard they cried. The warm glow of Christmas lights at midnight. The feel of a friend's hand in hers.

The memories surged through her, and she saw that Finley felt the same. His laughter was bold and bright at the top of the world, and it was easy to join in. Marlowe twirled about them, flashing different colors in joy.

And then the wind shifted, and the embers of the burning city below them lodged in their throat.

"You made it seem like you had a plan," Gwen said.

"Oh, I'm terrible at plans. I just create opportunities."

"You got one in the works then?"

"I think so, yeah." Finley turned to the Ghostlight, gathering it up in his hands like a lantern. "Hey Marlowe, any chance you can convince your friends to come over and play?"

———————————

With a ringing clang of hammers on iron skin, the Colossus's eyes turned to look at Cisseus.

The gaze of Yosef shifted from her, but the song remained. Pain lanced through her, and the chorus of the Colossus offered her relief.

No more pain, no more betrayal. And Mel wanted nothing more than to disappear.

She twisted her neck to look at Cisseus, standing paralyzed in the gaze of the half-made Colossus. His mouth was open in a soundless scream, and her old friend watched with bemused fascination.

And Mel made her choice.

"I exchange—" Mel said, dragging each word from the depths of her stomach. Cisseus turned to look at her, a flare of recognition appearing in the storm of agony. "My pain."

Cisseus nodded, and the last remnants of the Reverie that he had gathered about his fingertips flared with purple light, and then faded away. Far off in the distance, at the top of the Shepherd, there was a blinding flash of light.

Mel's suffering vanished. The chorus choked and cut off. In the place of the pain there was nothing.

She still felt the cool steel of the Colossus below her, and the scratch of the rough clothing on her skin. But the fire of her wounds was gone, leaving only the numbness of feeling nothing there at all.

"Mel, what are you doing?" Yosef said, turning in his chair to face her.

She surged to her feet and staggered to Yosef's chair. She ripped it about, tearing him away from Cisseus and his half-made son. Mel forced him to look at her, to see the blood dripping down her sides and the lines of her face, to see her at last. His golden eyes burned into her, and she could feel the song building at the edge of her awareness. Yet it did not crash into her. It could not overcome the dreams she called forth from the depths of her mind and sent ringing through her.

"Yosef, this has to end," Mel ground out.

She pressed his head to hers and forced him into her dreams.

———————————

The stars were falling from the sky.

Ghostlights appeared in the heavens above Oshroar, outshining the crackling flames. They poured forth from the space beyond life and fell into the tangled streets and twisted wreckage of their city.

Gwen, Finley, and Marlowe stood on the top of the Shepherd, and watched them fall. "I figured it out, I finally got it, all thanks to my partner here, and you of course!" Finley said to Gwen, his fists were clenched at his sides, his body vibrating with tension as he looked at the city burning below. But he was still grinning, a slash of white teeth in his ash and blood covered face. "Ghostlights aren't transporters for the dead. They're keepers of memories!"

More and more Ghostlights dropped from the sky, phasing in from wherever they vanished when people approached them.

"Marlowe can put images into your head, can even bring you into a memory, make you feel like you're experiencing it again. That's what we need to do to all the soldiers and all the Guardians down there. The soldiers need to remember whoever they were before they entered their trance, and the Guardians need to snap back to doing what they do best, looking after this city.

"Marlowe, can you tell all the other Ghostlights what they need to do?" The Ghostlight flipped over in its excitement, bursting into a pattern of blue and yellow lights. It flew over in front of Gwen, stopping in front of her.

"Me?"

"You're the only one that can direct the Ghostlights. You can use your weird smoke thing to find them all, all the soldiers, all the Guardians, and show Marlowe where to send the Ghostlights."

"Finley, I'm just learning how to use it. I might split my head open."

"I'll catch you. Probably."

"Ringing endorsement."

"You're the only one who can do this, Gwen. You and Marlowe. I think it's why we're here."

Gwen looked over Oshroar. Clementine and Morind waited on the shoulders of the Shepherd, both eager to be gone, but Lina was looking at her, still smiling.

The city burned beneath them. Even without Observation, Gwen could hear the screams in the wind, could see the torches carried by the soldiers in the streets. Just as she had back in Autumnmond. And the choice was the same.

Action or silence.

And at last, the choice was easy.

She gathered Marlowe into her hands, the ghostly flower settling into her palms. Gwen stepped forth and felt the haze of Observation seep from her ears and her nose. The purple smoke poured from the corners of her eyes, billowing about her like a cloak until it formed the transparent screen in front of her.

Agony crashed into her.

The pain of the screaming citizens, the crackle of the flames, the roar of dying Guardians. They broke into her mind and blasted away her thoughts. She lurched backward.

But Finley was there, and he braced her and Marlowe at the top of the world. Gwen fought through the pain, reclaiming her mind. She replaced all the terror of Oshroar with a single thought.

"Let me help you," Gwen whispered to herself.

"Let me help you," Finley echoed her.

And a tile away she heard the whisper of a voice that could only be Mel's say the same thing.

And below, far below the city and in the bowels of the world, Theo joined in the chorus.

Together, they sent the stars into the burning city.

The world disappeared, and Mel and Yosef were alone in a void of purple light. And then the scene changed.

Yosef and Mel sat in the living room of Gwen's house. The others had long since fallen asleep. Yosef was trying to draw Mel's face in his notebook without breaking eye contact with her. She looked down and saw that his pencil had veered wildly away from her face and now her eyes floated outside her head. Great gasps of laughter poured out of her as Yosef looked down at his unintended caricature of her.

And then...

Yosef, Gwen, Huck, Finley and Mel hiked through the woods to the top of a mountain. Gwen insisted on stopping to pet every dog she saw even while Finley argued with her. Huck kept stopping to write an idea in his notebook, and Yosef kept trying to chat with the people walking by.

Mel had to force them to keep climbing. It was hard going, but then she stood with her friends and watched the sun rise over the mountains.

And it was beautiful.

401

And then…

Mel and Yosef sat, dressed in black, with the others. Finley got up to give a reading from the Book of Psalms. He spoke of shepherds and of valleys. And Mel did not know the words, but she knew the feeling. And when Finley broke down in tears, unable to finish the last line, she knew that grief only seems like it will last forever, but it's hard to know that while you're in it.

And after, when they came back that night with stories to tell, Mel had just wanted it all to be over. She wanted Huck to be buried so that she could bury her own pain along with him. And Finley tried to tell a story about Huck, but it only made them sadder.

And then Yosef stood up, and he did the most remarkable thing. He made them laugh. He bounced into a story more ridiculous than they had ever heard about an adventure he and Huck had sworn to keep forever silent, and the graveyard rang with real laughter that night. And when he was done, he insisted that others go next. And even Mel produced some chuckles that night with a well-loved story they all knew. And as Mel and her friends remembered Huck and who he had been, the moment was still sad, but for once it no longer felt like the end of a story.

Instead, it felt like the turning of a page.

And then, the dreams faded. Yosef aged before her eyes until he was no longer that laughing man, but the wreck of him.

She clutched the arms of his chair, the blood from her wounds dripping onto his ruined body. "You were more than this once, Yosef. This, the Colossus, the song, it all has to end. Come back to us. Come back to me."

"Mel," Yosef gasped, tears pouring down his face, his voice as broken as the rest of him. "I always thought we would grow old together."

She smiled at him, but he didn't return it.

"Where did you go? Where did you all go? I begged you to find me. I filled this world with letters hoping you would find me. And you never did," Yosef spat, the tears still flowing even as his eyes filled with venom.

"You left me to the wolves. You think I'm the worst this world has to offer? Think again. Huck filled this world of his with razor blades.

Just you wait until the Nightmare Children find you. The Morrowseekers, the Cold Knight, Bloody Bones and all the other terrors Huck locked away here. Who do you think did this to me!?" he roared, looking down at his ruined body.

"The Child Eater is coming, and I'm the only one who can stop him. As much as you hate me, you'll thank me in the end, when I make this world safe for us. Until then, you need to get back to work," Yosef said, and with a shudder and a roll of his eyes he tore himself away from her gaze.

The light shifted around her, the shadows burning away as the searchlight eyes of the Colossus moved from Cisseus to her. Its burning scrutiny splashed onto her like a torrent of rain, and Mel braced herself for impact.

And felt nothing.

Its dreams broke against the wall she now had her mind, and at last the only thoughts inside her head were her own.

A savage grin split her face as she turned back to Yosef. "Seems like you're not as strong as you thought. I wonder what else you're wrong about?" She stood up, her hands clutched around her stomach. "I'm going to leave now Yosef. But I'll be back for you. And when I return, you'll help me tear down this iron monster that we made together. And we can be friends again. Until then, I dare you to try to have this dream again without thinking of me." She reached out and kissed the dry skin of his forehead, dripping blood onto his cheeks.

Mel turned away from him, stumbling to Cisseus's side. Cisseus collapsed onto her, nearly sending them tumbling over the edge of the statue. She gathered him close and started to haul them to the edge of the platform. There was no pain in her limbs. There could be no more pain.

They reached the edge of the dais, the vast empty body of the statue stretching before them. With shambling steps, they started the climb down. Mel spared no thought for the Sheosirrans left in their wake, no thought for Harmodias. Her thoughts were only for the boy who was stirring to feeble consciousness as they climbed down.

"Mel," She heard Yosef say behind her. "Welcome back."

The eyes of the Colossus rolled and roved through the night, shining out like searchlights in the gloom. It passed above, but the lights could not see Cisseus and Mel.

Cisseus shuddered by her side, his face twisting in pain. His throat was dark purple with bruises as if he had been strangled. And when his eyes trembled open the first words he formed with his hands were for her. "Are you okay?" Cisseus signed at her.

Mel pulled him forward, not allowing herself to cease moving. She knew the first moment she allowed herself to relax she would collapse into unconsciousness.

"Not so good. Bleeding a lot. Sorry to get it on your clothes," Mel said "I know your grandmother taught you how to patch a wound. Hope you know how to sew too. There's some bandages in my bag."

"I can do that," the boy signed. His eyes widened at her ruined state. She forced her face into the semblance of a grin.

"Don't worry, there's no pain. I'll be okay. You're here to protect me, aren't you?"

Cisseus nodded, his face a mask of resolve. He stood a little straighter and brought his own arms around her sides.

"Just a little further. I know a place we can hide while we patch each other up. They'll never find us there," Mel said, and with each breath she was aware of the great absence in her body where the pain should be.

Cisseus turned from her, following the searchlight of the Colossus as it cut through the night. "How will we avoid that?"

"Don't worry, kid," Mel said, keeping that smile still fixed on her face. "It can't see me. After all, I made it didn't I?"

The two clung to each other as they climbed down the Colossus. She left Yosef behind, alone once more with only his great work for company. It hurt her to leave her friend again, but as Cisseus's arm pulled her damaged body onto his trembling shoulders, she knew for once that she had made the right choice.

Below them, at the edges of the valley of the new god, the sun was rising.

———

"What now?" Huck asked Theo. They sat down on the sofa. Theo made sure the boy's back was to the world he had built, but he kept it in the corner of his eye.

"I don't know about you, buddy, but I could use a break," Theo said, collapsing into the comfort of the patched and faded sofa.

"Yeah," Huck said, fiddling with his hands. He peeked at the window well, where the feet of the krows still stood in their silent rows.

"Don't worry about them," Theo said, sounding more confident than he felt. "I'll handle them."

"Aren't they my fault though?"

"Not at all. You are not responsible for germs and bacteria. You are not responsible for the itty-bitty things that get you sick just because they live off you and on you."

The boy shrugged his shoulders, sinking into the sofa even as he kept his eyes fixed on the krows.

"Huck, listen to me," Theo waited until the boy dragged his eyes away from the window. "It's okay to let go. It really is. You don't need to worry about them anymore. The world will look after itself."

"I wish I could believe that. I wish I could stop this feeling in my chest. It's like my heart is always racing. Like my skin is crawling away from me, and every part of me wants to do something, anything."

"I know. That feeling doesn't go away. It sits with you like your own shadow for the rest of your life. But that doesn't mean you're broken. And it doesn't mean you need to listen to it all the time. The world is a weird and wonderful place, and it has horrors we'll always feel compelled to defeat. But we don't need to do that every day. Sometimes the world is meant to be enjoyed, and nothing more."

"Were you always this full of folksy wisdom, Big Theo?" Huck said, and the boy's face broke into the barest trace of a smile.

"Nah. This kind of stuff comes with age. You just have to think of what you most needed to hear when you were little and say that. And then hope like hell someone finds some sort of meaning in it."

The boy nodded. He turned away from the window, settling back onto the sofa. Theo closed his leaden eyes, feeling the muscles sag across his face as he allowed himself to listen to the sound of no rain and thunder at all.

"I'm bored," Huck said, shattering the peace with a hammer.

"I think I have just the thing," Theo said, reaching into his bag. He pulled out the still pristine N-Device, the N64. "You have any games worth playing?"

Huck grinned.

Gwen could see it all. She saw the Guardian about to smash a family flat as it struggled to turn off its own mind. And together she and Marlowe sent a Ghostlight to the Guardian. It nestled along its stone head and its limbs stilled, the light in its eyes shifting from red to green. It fell to its knees in front of the trembling family and helped them pick up their belongings.

She saw the family from the Humming Tile who had felt compelled by their dreams to build the Colossus ever higher. And when those dreams shifted to a blood drenched city, they felt that compulsion too. Marlowe's fellow Ghostlight met them just as they were breaking down the doors of a house in the lower ranges. And the fog that had haunted them for so many months fell away as they looked at a family not much different than them.

She saw a Guardian catch itself just moments before it could send its stone bulk into the base of a building. She saw two steel soldiers on opposite ends of the city drop their weapons and spin off in search of each other.

She saw a boy named Joshua drop the spear he had been about to plunge into Sister Sinoh's chest. Joshua dropped to his knees and begged the old woman to forgive him, and to help him look for his family.

Gwen saw the city wake up from its nightmare.

The sun rose, and still more Ghostlights poured into Oshroar. They crowded the streets, moving like paper lanterns in the wind. In her hands, Marlowe pulsed and hummed, its light shifting from blue, to red, to purple, to a shining yellow. Finley was behind them both, wrapping them in a hug, whispering little comforts as they stitched the city back together.

It might have been years later, it might have only been hours, but Gwen finally let the smoke of Observation dissipate. The city dropped away from her, and once more all she could see were the things right in front of her.

With aching limbs, she fell to the stone skin of the Shepherd. Finley sat beside her, the blood dry on his face.

"Thank you for slapping some sense into me," Finley said.

"Thank you for letting me." The breeze tickled their faces. The smoke was fading away. "You have quite an impressive partner here."

"I know right? Isn't it the best?"

"Well, I don't know about that. Mine can fly."

"So can Marlowe!"

"With your fat head on its back?"

"We haven't tried that yet, but I bet it could."

Marlowe gave a flash of red light.

"Jerk," Finley said to the Ghostlight. "Well, at least mine can tell when you're lying."

"Must get a lot of exercise around you then."

"Ha. Ha. Honestly, I don't know why I missed you."

"Yes, you do," Gwen said, bumping her shoulder against Finley's. Marlowe flashed blue.

"Maybe." Finley rested his head against her shoulder. Marlowe spun down and tucked itself into his neck. "Guess we saved the city."

"Guess so."

"Think they'll build a statue to us?"

"Probably one as big as the one we're sitting on."

"That'd be nice," Finley said, grinning to himself, but then his smile faded away. "Hey, Gwen."

"Yeah, Finley?"

"Do you think we could have saved Huck, or was he doomed?"

"I don't know," Gwen said, letting her head fall onto his. "Probably not."

"I didn't think so."

"But that doesn't mean we should stop trying to save people," and she felt Finley relax at her side. "And that includes ourselves."

Below them, Oshroarans worked to put out the fires. Citizens, Guardians, newcomers, all worked hand in hand. On the statue of the Shepherd, its gaze still ineffable, an enormous bat gave a shrieking cry and a Ghostlight gave off a flash of light.

Finley and Gwen fell into each other, overcome with exhaustion.

"Well, Marlowe. I did it. I figured out the mystery."

The Ghostlight flashed blue.

"Were you ever going to tell me anything about Huck? Or was that just meant to motivate me? What did any of this have to do with our friend?"

Marlowe rose from their laps. It floated in front of them, the smoldering city lighting it from below. The white faded from its petals until it was a pure black.

And Gwen and Finley were no longer on the Colossus.

They were in the backseat of a car.

They had been in this backseat before. Many times.

It was night outside, but the stars were covered in clouds, leaving only the streetlights for illumination.

Huck was driving. He had groceries in the backseat with them, the ice cream that his dad liked, the yarn his mother used. The radio was off, and Huck was humming to himself as he drove.

He looked pale and drawn. He had lost a lot of weight, and there were wrinkles next to his eyes that Finley and Gwen had never seen before. His hair was greasy from a lack of showering, and his clothes unwashed.

But his face was determined, his eyebrows drawn down in the expression his friends knew meant he would never surrender. It had ruined many a board game night when he got that look on his face.

It wasn't the face of a boy about to die.

Gwen's heart dropped into her stomach. She was waiting for the moment she knew would come, for Huck's awful choice. But Finley lurched forward, eager to see what would happen next.

The dash lit up, a call came in. Huck sighed and answered the phone.

"Hey, Dad!" Huck said, affecting enthusiasm.

"Beth? Beth, is that you?" his father asked, his voice quivery and unsure as he gave his wife's name.

"No, Dad, it's me Huck."

"Beth, I can't hear you."

"Dad, you called me by mistake, I think. Mom's just upstairs. Can you put her on?"

"Beth, where am I? I don't know where I am. What's going on?" Huck's dad said. Gwen and Finley's hearts broke at the weakness in the voice they knew so well. And they shattered into pieces when they saw the well-worn look of resignation on Huck's face.

"Dad, you're just at home. Nothing bad is happening. Everything's okay. I'm on my way home now. I have that ice cream you like. If you just wait in your chair, I'll be there in a moment. We can watch Jeopardy and eat ice cream together like always. I have chocolate sauce too!"

Huck's voice was laden with good cheer, but his eyes were empty, and his father seemed not to understand.

"Beth?"

"Jesus, Dad, it's still me!"

"Is Huck with you?" his father said, the frail voice lifting as he said his son's name. "Can you tell him I forgot to tell him something earlier. But—but I remembered. I wrote it down!"

"What is it, Dad?"

"Tell him 'I love him, and that I miss him.' Will you do that for me, Beth?"

"Yeah," Huck choked. "I'll tell him."

"I don't know why I forgot to say it earlier. I'm glad I wrote it down."

"It's okay. Don't worry about it. I love you, Dad."

"Okay, bye now." And his dad hung up the phone. Huck sat in the silence, driving back to his house with melting ice cream in the back seat. Tears coursed down his face. He sped up a little, eager to get back home and see his Mom and Dad.

"I don't like the ending."

Huck spun around, looking for where this new voice had come from.

"I think you need to change it."

He twisted around, searching the backseat, his eyes roving over Finley and Gwen without seeing them.

A figure took shape in the passenger seat. It had the form of a man, but it had no flesh. Its skin was a patchwork quilt of flickering television screens, each flashing a new scene every few seconds. For a second the screen on its face showed the city of Oshroar, the next it showed a chiropt in flight, and then a castle in the clouds.

Huck shuddered back from the figure, but he kept the car on the road. "Who are you? How did you get in the car?"

"Don't you recognize me?" the figure said, its voice as insubstantial as radio static. "I'm your oldest friend."

"I don't know you!"

"That makes me sad," the figure said, tilting its head to the side, the image changing on its face. "Almost as sad as your ending."

"The ending to what?"

"The ending for me. It's too happy, and so, so boring."

Finley and Gwen were screaming, reaching to step between Huck and the flickering figure, but they were frozen in their seats, locked in the memory.

"I think I'll change it," the figure said, and it stretched out one flickering hand. It grabbed the steering wheel from Huck, jerking the car off course. Huck slammed on the brakes, but the car was going too fast, hurtling for the barricade between the highway and the embankment.

It burst through the divider, and the wheels leapt from the road. The car was in flight, rushing towards the rocks below. The groceries hit the ceiling, ice cream smearing the roof.

The figure vanished, and Huck was alone in the car but for the shadows of Gwen and Finley. His eyes met theirs in the rearview mirror, seeming to see them for the first time. His mouth moved, shaping words they couldn't hear.

And then the memory ended.

———————

As Theo sat on the sofa with Huck, he felt the years fall away. It was the simple pleasures of childhood all over again. A cool basement on a hot day. Warm soda from under the stairs. A new world on the screen, a joystick in hand, feeling for once that destiny can be controlled, and with just the press of a button.

There was laughter and shoving. Some good-natured name calling. These things were compulsory for spending time with an old friend. Life surged through the child god as the worlds of make believe flashed by on the screen, and he forgot the world of his own making for just a little while.

But all things end in time and Theo saw his friend's eyes drooping.

"Why don't you snooze for a bit, Huck? I'm sure you can whup me again once you wake up."

"You got pretty close that last time," Huck said, each word coated with weariness.

"Thanks for the words of encouragement, buddy. Here," Theo said, throwing a blanket over his friend.

"I try," Huck said, placing his head on the sofa's corner pillow, wrapping the blanket around himself like a cocoon. "You'll still be here when I wake up, right?"

"Course I will."

"Do you think I'll have that dream again?"

"I think a god should decide that for himself, don't you?"

Huck settled in for his well-deserved slumber, nuzzling into the faded old sofa like it was the most comfortable thing in the world. But there was still that line of worry across his brow.

"I'm sorry for abandoning you, Huck. We should never have done that," Theo forced out.

Huck sat up, his eyes wide and alert. "You didn't abandon me."

Theo hugged himself, empty of anything but terrible remorse. "You were all by yourself, Huck. You had the world put on your shoulders and we just forgot about you."

"But you didn't!" Huck said, sitting up on his knees and crowding into Theo's space. "You all were what kept me going. I told myself I again and again that I couldn't quit, that I had to keep going even though I was more afraid than I had ever been. Do you know who taught me how to do that?"

Theo shook his head.

"You. All of you."

Theo look into his boyhood friend's eyes. He looked for blame. He looked for anger. And to his amazement all he saw was love.

He nodded at Huck, at a loss for words.

Huck's tiny fist collided with his shoulder. "Don't think something stupid like that again. Your god commands it." He settled back onto the pillows, already rubbing his eyes with exhaustion.

"Yes, sir."

Huck rubbed his face into the pillow, then suddenly stilled. A thought rippled across his face. "Do you think that Poa will be—"

"You don't have to worry about this world anymore, Huck," Theo said, forcing out the words he knew the boy needed to hear. "I'll take it from here. You can just let go."

Huck nodded, his brow relaxing at last. "I'm glad I invited you over. It was nice, hanging out again."

"You invited me?"

"Course I did. I needed help. I needed my heroes. And now I'm safe." Huck's lips quirked into a smile as he closed his eyes. His face relaxed, and his breathing stilled. In moments he was asleep.

Theo waited for what he knew would come next. A minute passed, and then another. But then, very slowly, Huck began to fade away. It started at the edges of his fingers and the tops of his hairs. The light crept over the edges of the boy, smoothing away his features and his form.

And just as fast as he had fallen asleep, Huck was gone.

"Goodbye, buddy," Theo said, again. And for the last time he shed tears at the passing of his friend.

The Godstrom was fading away. It was the dulling of colors, pitch black becoming charcoal gray, becoming ashen, becoming sooty white, until new colors emerged in the sky. Royal blue crept in, bringing the reds and yellows of a rising sun.

The sky returned to the Tile of the Collapse. And in that sky was a castle clinging to the bottom of a mountain.

Theo walked out of Huck's house just in time to catch the end of the krows' retreat. They fled from the burning, scorching light of the bright new thing that had intruded upon their world.

The vast walls of the crater were riddled with holes and caves, and the krows surged down them and into the bowels of the planet. They chased after the last shreds of darkness left, but as they retreated Theo knew that they would forget nothing. They had tasted divinity itself, and they would never forget the names of those that had stolen their home.

Theo locked the house behind him, slipping the house keys into his pocket. It was a simple lock, but somehow Theo knew that no power in the world would be able to break through it.

There was a small crowd hovering not far above him. They were a wrecked bunch, carrying wounded, wrapped in blood and broken weapons. Yet they flew like heroes in the sky. Striker floated at the front of the expedition, the silver trumpet still in her hand, and for once a smile on her face.

Theo turned away from the house and slipped into the sky, his eyes fixed on the far-off Final University. His new home. His new purpose. Here the scholars of a heretical faith toiled and flew above a sky with no more storm.

What would they become in this world without the god, Vovatum?

They would need a new mission, and Pathfinder had the perfect one in mind for them all.

He adjusted his bag on his back as he flew. Inside, the pieces of POA waited for a new god.

THE END

Epilogue:

Our enemy has a name, our enemy has a goal. And at first I dared not write it, I dared not speak it into being, for I have learned that to give a thing a name is to give it power in this world. But I am no longer a helpless novice struggling in the dark. And you deserve to know the name of our enemy, my friends, and the names of his monstrous servants.

For Huck did not place only his dreams in Poa, he also locked away his deepest fears. They are the nightmares that plague all children given fiendish shape, and they are commanded by the highest evil of them all, the Child Eater.

All that Huck feared, all that he loathed, the Child Eater is.

These letters have been the only thing keeping me sane in all the madness, but I know they are not as safe as I hoped. They were meant for my friends, but I know YOU are reading them. I know you think you have me trapped, like a flower pressed between the pages of a book. I know you think that you know me, but you are wrong.

My name is Yosef League. I was here at this world's founding and now I am here at its end. I have traveled across this land and written my name onto the secret bones of the world. I speak the sacred language of god and walk through your dreams to tell you stories while you sleep. I am the companion of the old god and the father of the new.

And this world is mine.

It waited for the krows in the bowels of the Earth. They were feeble things, for all the terror they inspired. Just a little sunlight had sent them clutching for mother's skirts. The creature observing them found it almost sad. They were so close to being truly villainous, but they lacked that spark that was necessary for a real nemesis, a true threat.

But the creature thought it could do better.

It brought them closer, grabbing hold of their meager thoughts, steering them ever deeper into Poa. There was no sunlight here, no magma either. Huck hadn't quite understood how planets worked when he built this one.

Instead, there was only a blackness so complete it was almost physical. The same darkness a child once feared more than anything. It was in that void that the krows found the creature.

414

The bravest krow led them, bearing its claws at the thing. But even the dumbest animal knows when it is outmatched, especially one that had eaten a piece of a divinity, so it didn't growl for long.

"Urrrghhh," It mewled at the more terrible predator, the creature with the flickering face. A name was stuck in the creature's throat like a piece of glass.

"No, I'm afraid not," the creature said, caressing the krow's face. "You don't know my name. And even if you did, what makes you think I would let you say it?"

The lightning flashed in the krow's eyes, but it knew fighting was hopeless. The krow and its companions huddled at the creature's feet, their mouths opened wide as they tasted the power that poured forth from the elder monster.

"You did your best, but they beat you in the end," the creature said, its voice echoing in the fathomless dark. "I must say, I'm rather proud of all their performances though, aren't you?" The lead krow bowed its head, nuzzling at the dirt. "Yes, even the coward was able to beat you, weak as you are. But don't you worry my darling, we can make you…more."

The krows longed to flee, to escape the clutches of this eldritch terror, but the creature wouldn't let them. It froze the blood in their limbs and held them tight.

"Have you ever wondered what would have happened if you had eaten more of the god that made this world? What would you have become if you had gorged yourself?"

The creature at its feet howled, its eyes rolling back in its head at the thought.

"Well, wonder no longer." It bent down to the krow, whispering in its ear. "You can finally become that perfect thing. All you need to do is eat each other."

Deep in the bowels of Poa there was a hunter's howl. The clatter of claws in the dark. Ripping and tearing.

The creature didn't stick around.

It let the shadows claim it, walking deeper into Poa, into its wonderful planet.

"Well, gang, let's see how you deal with this one."

Acknowledgments:

Huge thanks to the terrific professionals who helped make this book possible, my illustrators, Natalia and Linda.

This book would never have happened without so many amazing people. Kayla, an unstoppable and invaluable editor. Sam, Ian, and Grace, who read this story, corrected my grammar, and made me a cake with a flower on it. Ben, who has been my writing partner since we were teens. All my friends at my school. And Ruth, who taught me that it takes two to tango.

Thank you, Catherine, for cheering me on, making me laugh, and showing me photos of Petey when I needed them most. All my love, darling.

A final thank you to my wonderful family. Nellie, my adventuring partner and sister. And Mom and Dad, who read me stories until I was no longer afraid of the dark, and then told me to write my own.

I love you all.

Author Bio:

Henry Hines is a teacher, a dungeon master, and an author. Somedays he struggles to know which is most important.

He lives in Virginia.

You can learn more about him at his website henry-hines.com

This is his first novel.

Made in the USA
Middletown, DE
06 December 2023

44810905R00232